AF425315

THE LUSITANIA CODE

THE LUSITANIA CODE

A LADY BUTTERSCHLOSS MYSTERY

LINDA ROBERTSON

First published by Level Best Books/Historia 2026

Copyright © 2026 by Linda Robertson

All rights reserved. No part of this publication may be reproduced, stored, or transmitted in any form or by any means, electronic, mechanical, photocopying, recording, scanning, or otherwise without written permission from the publisher. It is illegal to copy this book, post it to a website, or distribute it by any other means without permission.

Linda Robertson asserts the moral right to be identified as the author of this work.

The Lusitania Code is a work of fiction. The historical characters who were public figures at the time, and the events associated with them, are matters of public record. All other characters are products of the author's imagination. In all other respects, any resemblance to actual persons, living or dead, events, or locales is entirely coincidental.

Author Photo Credit: Linda Robertson

First edition

ISBN: 979-8-89820-133-3

Cover art by Level Best Designs

This book was professionally typeset on Reedsy.
Find out more at reedsy.com

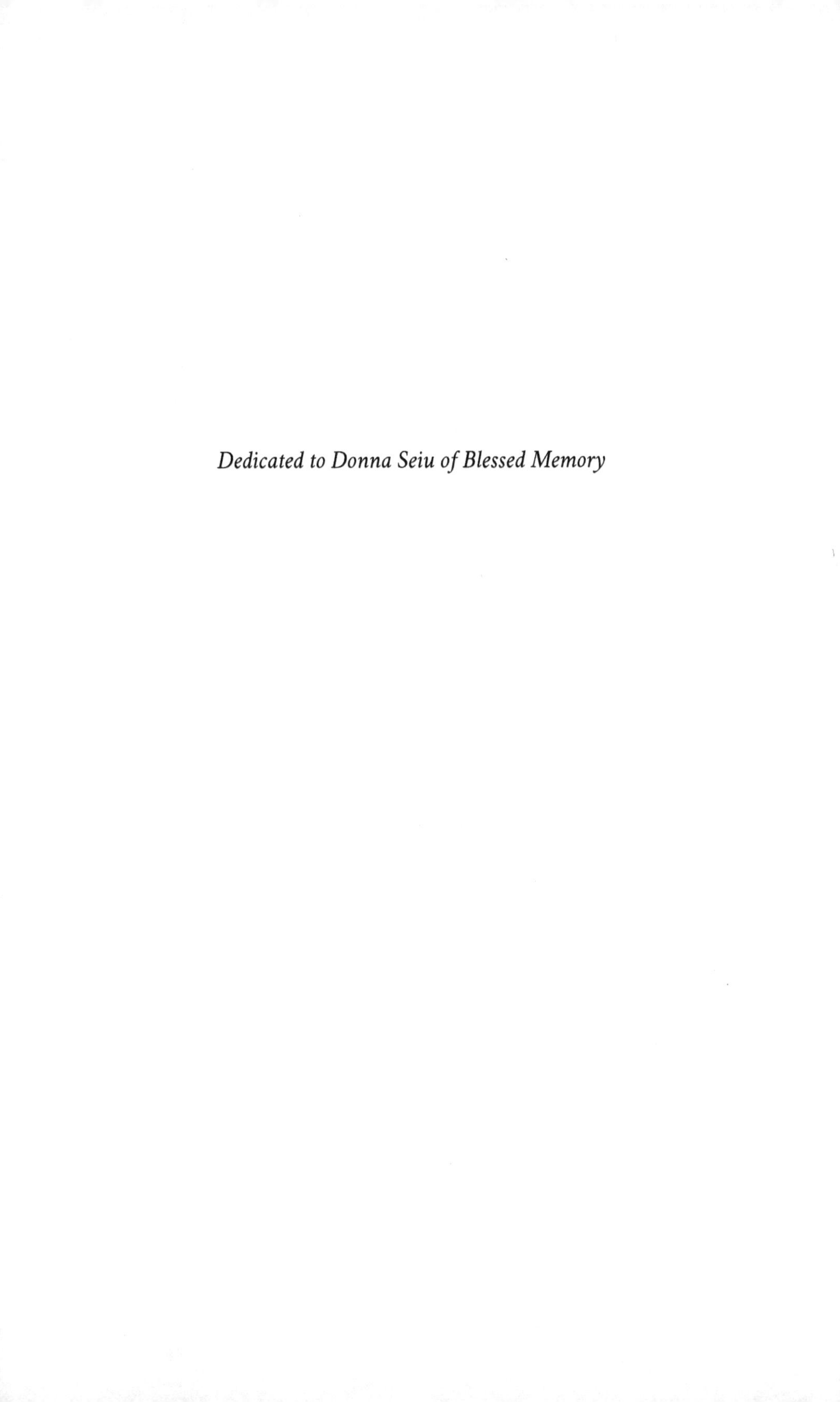

Dedicated to Donna Seiu of Blessed Memory

Preface

May 1, 1915

As for submarines, I have no fear of them whatever

When Mr. Sumner was asked about
the precautions which are being taken
with regard to the Cunard vessels he
said that he had absolutely no fear
with regard to them.

"No passenger is permitted aboard
them unless he can identify himself.
No express matter of any sort is taken.
Every passenger must identify his bag-
gage before it is placed aboard. There
are now no German cruisers in the Atlantic, and the 'danger zone' does not
begin until we reach the British Channel and the Irish Sea. Then one may
say there is a general system of con-
voying British ships. The British Navy
is responsible for all British ships, and
especially for Cunarders."

"Your speed, too, is a safeguard, is
it not?" it was suggested.

"Yes; as for submarines, I have no
fear of them whatever."

Interview with Charles Sumner, Press Secretary for Cunard Line, New York Times, *May 1, 1915.*

Chapter One

They that go down to the sea in ships, that do business in great waters;
These see the work of the Lord, and his wonders in the deep.
For he commandeth and raiseth the stormy wind, which lifteth up the
waves thereof.
They mount up to the heaven, they go down again to the depths: their soul
is melted because of trouble.
They reel to and fro, and stagger like a drunken man, and are at their wits'
end.

—from Psalm 107, KJV

The Lusitania

Comfortably plump, with grey hair, a cheerful round face, and a brisk step, Mabel Every came into the duplex townhouse of Commodore William Turner, OBE, carrying the morning mail and the newspaper. She shook her umbrella and closed it. She was ostensibly his housekeeper, but everyone knew they were common-law man and wife and had been since not long after she came to work for him in 1906, when he separated from his wife, eighteen years ago. She was twenty-six then; he was fifty.

"It's blowing and raining out there again," said Mabel. She glanced at the headline. "There's flooding everywhere upriver. Terrible wet summer, and it won't let up now that fall has come."

"Yes, I know," said Turner, stocky of build, with close-cropped iron-grey hair, and a square face with a slightly flattened nose that made him look pugnacious. "It won't flood here in Liverpool, though," he said to reassure her. "Hasn't in centuries." He reached a hand from his comfortable sitting chair and smiled with love and affection as he took the newspaper, a few pieces of mail, and a package wrapped in brown paper. "Come and sit by the fire and warm yourself," he said.

"I'll fix tea and a few biscuits. Then we can see what else is in the news." She went humming into the small but efficient kitchen, boiled the water, made the tea, arranged the tray, and carried it back into the sitting room. She froze when she saw him bent over, his head in his hands, rocking back and forth, as if in physical pain, but silent. Utterly silent. The only sound was the downpour flailing against the windows.

"*Not again,*" she said to herself, feeling a mourning agony for him. She set the tray down quietly and sat by him, rubbing her hand on his back, saying to him in a kind of chant, "It's all right. It's all right. You're here now."

He did not hear her. He continued rocking back and forth, silently, his head buried in his hands, bent over as if he wanted to curl himself into a cocoon. Beside him, on the floor, was the brown paper wrapping. On it lay a book. She bent over and picked it up. *Oh damn!* she said between gritted teeth as she read the author and title: Winston Churchill, *The World Crisis,* Volume 2, 1915. It had just been published, a brand-new copy. *Who would be cruel enough to send this to Bill? And why does Churchill rake this all up again now?* She asked herself. *Hasn't he caused Bill enough pain?*

Captain Bill Turner was not in the warm sitting room at Number 40 De Villiers Avenue in a suburb of Liverpool on a cold, wet day in the fall of 1924. For him, it was May 7, 1915, at 2:12 p.m. He saw his weathered hand reach for the latch to his day cabin on Deck A of the Cunard liner *HMS Lusitania.*

He heard the lookout call, "Torpedo!"

He looked over the starboard rail and saw the white, foaming trail of the torpedo as it passed under the hull. Time stopped. It seemed an eternity, the agony of waiting, waiting. Then, the explosion, so loud it stunned the senses. The deck quaked. A column of water, coal dust, steam, and debris shot high in the air, above the wireless lines, and hung there for a second before crashing down.

The spray came down on him like a blow. He ran up the stairs to the bridge. The deck shook from the second explosion.

"Full astern! We can't lower the lifeboats until she stops moving." His voice did not quaver. Outwardly, he was in calm command.

The helm did not respond.

"Set a fifteen-degree turn toward land. If we can't stop her, we may be able to ground her. I reckon we are twelve miles offshore." The helm responded.

"Correct course. Bring her back fifteen degrees."

This time, the helm did not respond. The ship continued on a slow arc out to sea.

"What does the spirit level show?"

"Fifteen-degree tilt to starboard."

"We won't be able to lower the port lifeboats. Lower the starboard lifeboats to the rail in preparation for loading passengers once we slow. Have the stewards make sure the passengers are assembled on deck. We will have to wait until the sea itself stops us."

"Aye, sir."

"Tell Leith to send S.O.S. Tell him to keep transmitting continuously, giving our position."

> *"S.O.S. From Lusitania. We think we are off Kinsale. Last position ten miles off Kinsale. Big list. Please come with all haste."*

"Sir, the electricals have failed. The elevators are not working. It is complete darkness below decks."

Turner put on his life jacket.

"Johnson, what is our list now?"

"Twenty-five degrees to starboard."

"My God." He saw water flooding over the forecastle. "Johnson, save yourself," he shouted into the wheel room. Johnson emerged from the wheelhouse. Before he could ask for confirmation of the order, he slid off the bridge and into the cold sea.

We're lost.

He saw passengers lowered in lifeboats. Some spilled the terrified passengers, some broke apart in the sea. Some passengers leaped into the water. Some were swept overboard. The screams filled his ears. He felt the cold seawater swirling around his ankles. He grabbed a halyard, struggling to stay on the bridge. The deck fell away. The ship was plucked from below his feet as if by a giant hand.

They mount up to the heaven, they go down again to the depths: their soul is melted because of trouble.

He surfaced in a calm sea and bright blue sky. He inhaled deeply, gratefully, and shook the seawater from his face. The dying ship loomed above him, blotting out the sky. He saw the rows of portholes climbing up her dark hull; some, he knew, were already below the sea. Hundreds of bodies whirled slowly about him. Men, women, children, babies tied in baskets, their faces grey, their lips blue, drifted along with planks, empty lifeboats, and detritus. Some of the drowned bumped gently against him, staring at him with lifeless eyes. *My passengers. My responsibility. They were in my care.*

The water was cold. He started to swim. He saw a passenger he knew, William Pierpoint, a police detective from Turner's hometown of Liverpool. Just as he started to hail him, he saw Pierpoint's horrified face as he was sucked into one of the funnels as it filled with water. It sank beneath the waves. Turner was frozen in disbelief, his mind repudiating his senses. Pierpoint was dead. Then he saw the resurrection. Pierpoint shot from beneath the sea in a burst of steam and air, covered with a wet, black, sticky soot, momentarily stunned. Then he swam away as fast as he could without a backward glance.

Turner saw the ship's descent halt as the bow struck the bottom. It stood with its stern in the air. The entire eight hundred feet quivered like a wounded animal. The ship sank below the waves with a long groan. Turner looked at the calm sea, the blue sky, and the nothingness where his ship, the *Lusitania*, was no longer. *How could it be? His ship. The pride of the Cunard fleet. One of the fastest ships on the sea. Gone.*

He swam, following Pierpoint. He saw 40 of the ship's firemen, dead, upside down, with their lifejackets on.

He fought off a swirling mass of seagulls, batted at them with his arms, shouted at them, cursed them, tried and failed to grab one and break its neck. All of his shock, fury, sorrow, shame, and grief focused on the screeching mass that swirled above him. Hundreds of them swooped in a crazed frenzy from the sky and pecked out the eyes of the dead.

"They reel to and fro, and stagger like a drunken man, and are at their wits' end."

He was three hours in the watery Inferno. He saw sights he would never forget and never be able to describe to anyone. One of his crew in a lifeboat, who had been rescuing survivors from the sea, grabbed him and pulled him aboard. Turner realized his savior said something to him, but he was dazed, past understanding. He was taken to the fishing trawler, the *Bluebell.*

He heard others in the trawler's cabin. They were giddy at having survived. They were no longer numb, wrapped in the warmth of the cabin. They held mugs of hot tea in hands that finally stopped shaking. They wore a motley assortment of dry clothes given to them by the fishermen who had raided their personal stores. They were animated, talking to and over each other, excitedly. They were alive and surprised at their own intoxication with the joy of it. They were unable yet to confront the harrowing questions that lurked beneath their delight at being plucked from certain death. What about husbands, wives, and children?

He sat apart, silent and alone in his soaked uniform, staring straight ahead, neither living nor dead. *Where were the Royal Navy escorts? Where the hell were they? The Admiralty had promised protection, promised it to Cunard, to the passengers, to him. They would protect the Lusitania once it entered the Irish Sea. Nothing to fear, nothing to worry about.*

He became vaguely aware of a woman, haggard, dressed in the oversized clothes of a fisherman. She spoke to him in a low monotone. She put her little son on a life raft. It capsized. Her boy was gone. His death should not have happened. Her boy was dead because of the crew, their lack of discipline, trying to launch the lifeboats and rafts.

"No, no, no more!" he screamed. "Full astern! Save yourself! Where were the escorts? Where were the escorts?"

From a far distance, he felt arms surround him. "Come back, Bill. You're safe." It was Mabel.

She held him tightly, kissing his forehead, feeling his body tremble. "You are here, with me. It isn't 1915. It is 1924." She felt his hot tears on her face. He hugged her as if clinging to a life raft.

"Damn that Churchill," she hissed through clenched teeth. "Damn him to hell!"

Chapter Two

Lusitania Lost Again

Dinwiddie Marcos Custus stood in front of the large mirror in the entryway of the London townhouse on Grosvenor Square. He put on his peaked cap, checked his dark blue Royal Naval Volunteer Reserve uniform with polished brass buttons, and straightened his tie. Dinny's American father, Beriah Custus, had lumbered his son with the risible name in honor of a distant, long-dead forebearer who had emigrated from Scotland to America and made the Custus family fortune in the cotton trade.

"Shove over and give another fellow a chance." He was jostled by his best friend and housemate, Tristan Earnest Dashwood. He also wore the uniform of the RNVR. Standing side by side in front of the mirror, one looked like the Yin to the other's Yang. Tristan was tall and muscular. He looked like an Adonis and knew it. His blonde hair was combed back, setting off the healthy glow of a golden tan. He was just returned from two weeks escorting his two aged aunts on a tour of the Nile. Dinny was tall, slim, not weedy exactly, but certainly neither muscular nor athletic. His dark hair fell over his forehead, and his round-framed glasses gave him an owlish look. Tris looked out upon the world from clear, blue eyes that told of inner confidence, if not vanity. Dinny had a quiet, inward expression. He had the habit of hanging his head slightly, which gave him a diffident air. They were both glad to be back in each other's company.

"Before you came down for breakfast," Dinny said, "Nora reminded me it is her half-day off. So it's our night to make dinner."

"So, whose turn is it to make soup?" asked Tris a little slyly.

"Yours, of course," said Dinny, laughing. "You've been gone, remember?"

"Oh, yes," said Tris, feigning that he had just remembered. "So, which do you want? Split pea with ham or ham and split pea?"

"We really ought to learn to make some other kind," said Dinny. "I'm getting rather tired of split pea and ham."

"But it makes it so easy on Nora," said Tris. "She makes us ham the night before, and we use the leftovers."

"Yes, yes, I've known her since I was ten, remember? She is a creature of habit and wonderful. I just thought maybe the two of us could learn to concoct something different, that's all."

As it was a fine October day, they agreed to walk the thirty minutes to Whitehall.

"Are you able to face the daily grind after sailing the Nile on a *dahabiya*?" Dinny asked.

"Actually, I am. I enjoy the challenge," said Tris eagerly and instantly self-absorbed. "I think it will make a great difference if we can find the exact effects of vibration and pressure on the steel plates of submarines. I've thought about spending some time studying whales because the design, for submarines, I mean, was originally based on whales. How do they dive so deep without being crushed? That's what I want to know. Of course, my superiors are not interested, but still, I can't help but wonder. To answer your question, I go back to work on the hydrostatic pressure on the outer hull at a maximum operable depth." He said the latter in the officious, self-important tone of a scientist trying to impress a journalist.

Dinny smiled at his friend's usual garrulous enthusiasm. They both graduated a year earlier from Cambridge, where they studied physics and engineering.

"Want to meet for lunch?" Tris asked. "I think I might be able to get away around 13:00."

"I can't. I will be going over archives from the Admiralty Records Office today." Dinny was part of a division of scientists and engineers experimenting with underwater wireless transmission to and from submarines. "I've been asked to review the wireless communications with submarines during the war. I've asked to see the files on the *Lusitania* to find out how far signal intelligence traced the wireless transmissions of the submarine that sank her."

Tris stopped walking and turned to Dinny. "The *Lusitania*?" He paused for a moment, then broke into a bemused grin. "I cannot believe this. What a coincidence." Tris started walking again, talking quickly. "I can't tell you everything right now. But I learned something about the sinking of the *Lusitania* while I was in Egypt, from my aging aunts. You know, I was chaperoning them. On the *dahabiya*. But you know that. Obviously. What you don't know about my dear relatives is that they are on that side of the family related to the Churchills. Distantly, I admit, but still, there is a rather direct line between the Spencer-Churchills and the Dashwoods. You see, it goes back to Elizabeth Spencer…"

"I take it as said," said Dinny, interrupting because he knew Tris would recite his entire family tree.

"Yes, well, one of them, my aunt, you see, heard something from her husband during the war about the *Lusitania* and Churchill. You know, he was First Lord of the Admiralty when it sank. Churchill, I mean, not my aunt's husband."

Dinny was, as always, patient, listening to Tris's slow windup to the punch line. "I do know that. Obviously," he said. "I am not actually investigating that, but still, I'd have to be really obtuse not to be curious about Churchill and the *Lusitania*."

"I think you might be interested in what I heard. It has to do with Naval intelligence during the war. It might help you with your investigation. Listen, if you can't meet me for lunch, let's meet at the Above Board after we finish for the day?"

"Great. Can I bring Addie along?"

Tris felt the pang of an old wound. "Of course. Why, do you two have a date?" He knew he was trying too hard to sound offhand.

Dinny gave a shy, self-deprecating smile. "No, actually. She offered to help me out today."

"Help you out how?" asked Tris, suspecting this was a mere ruse for the two of them to have an excuse to meet.

Dinny laughed at the suspicion in Tris's sly tone of voice. He was too deferential to comment on it. "I have asked for all the files on the sinking of the *Lusitania,* especially the orders sent by Admiralty to the *Lusitania.* Addie agreed to ask for the records of the wireless decrypts of the German submarine. We both have top security clearance, and the files might help her with her assignment, too.

"Why?" asked Tris too quickly. "She is working at the Government Code and Cypher School. How can she 'help' with your project?"

"She has been assigned to find out all she can about the use of some sort of decoding machine by Naval signal intelligence during the war. She needs to understand the history of decryption, especially submarine decrypts." Dinny glanced at his friend. "Come off it, Tris. Addie and I wouldn't cook up a project to see one another during work hours when we can see each other every day of the week if we want to."

They arrived at Whitehall. "All right, all right, I believe you. I was just having you on." They both knew this was a half-truth. Dinny and Tris had fallen for the brilliant, witty, and spirited Addie when the three of them met at Cambridge, where she studied Maths. "I'll meet both of you at the Above Board."

Such is the optimism of youth.

Tris went to the Admiralty Extension, Dinny, to the original entrance to the Admiralty Building. As he passed through the arched gate, he looked up and smiled at the two hippocampi facing each other, mounted on the tops of the supporting columns. The ferocious heads of winged horses with coiling, flirtatious fishtails always amused him.

As soon as he settled in his office, he reached for the interdepartmental phone to call the Admiralty Records Office. Before he could dial the extension, a courier knocked on the door. Dinny called out for him to enter. He placed the file Dinny had ordered on the desk. "From the ARO,

Sir, as requested." Dinny opened the red archival box stamped Top Secret. The first item was a picture of the *Lusitania* under full steam. The pages behind it showed the plans of each deck. He was just beginning to examine the next document when the phone rang. It was Addie, calling from the archive, which was in the basement, two floors down. He smiled at the sound of her voice, then realized she sounded annoyed.

"Listen, Dinny. I requested the *Lusitania* wireless decrypts. But they are nowhere to be found. The librarian is as confused as I am."

"I'll be right down," said Dinny.

He was greeted by Addie and the ARO librarian, who introduced himself as Jan Gruter. He was in his mid-fifties with a long face, high forehead, thinning hair, and a mouth that drooped slightly. His clear, blue eyes showed a shrewd intelligence and a hint of acerbity. His bearing was dignified, certainly reserved, and slightly world-weary. He spoke to Dinny with regret and confused agitation. His accent was British and not Dutch, as Dinny had assumed it would be from the name.

"I simply cannot understand," Gruter said, wringing his hands. "The folders are clearly listed in the catalog. No one has ever requested them, so they should be on the shelf in an archival box."

Addie said, "Yesterday afternoon, I left a request for decrypts of any intercepted wireless communications from the German submarine that attacked the *Lusitania*. When I arrived this morning, Mr. Gruter said he had been unable to find them."

Gruter nodded. "Yes, Miss Gold. You left the order just as you should. Under the marlin spike on my desk. I found your request, too," he said, turning to Dinny.

"Yes," said Dinny. I was just starting to read when Addie called." He saw the consternation on her face. He felt it, too. "What do you suggest?" he asked Gruter.

"No one would have been allowed to take them from the archives. So, even if the record is wrong, and someone, some time since 1915, requested them, they would remain here." He paused and added with professional pride. "I am not suggesting the record is incorrect," he said. "But perhaps during the war, things were a bit more lax than they are now. I suggest Miss Gold and I walk the stacks to see if the files have been misshelved."

Addie readily agreed. Dinny and Addie exchanged smiles to reassure each other that the wayward decrypts would be found and that this was nothing more than a shelving error. Dinny said, "I'll go to my office and look through the file. Maybe there is a note cross-referencing information with the decrypts. It might give us a clue about where they were filed if it differs from the catalog."

Gruter gave a 'tsk-tsk' in unspoken condemnation of his predecessor if such an error had occurred.

When Dinny returned to his office, he blinked in confusion. The red box file was not there. At first, he could only gape at the place on his desk where he had left it. Dinny never let paperwork pile up. His desk was clear of any clutter. There were the requisite letter trays, the Naval issue lamp, and pen stand. He left the red file in the center of the desk. Irrationally, he explored under his desk and the desk chair, and in a desperate last resort, his desk drawers. Finally, he gave up. He sat down and slumped in his chair. He ran his hands through his hair and sighed deeply. He knew what he had to do.

First, he called the ARO. Gruter answered and put Addie on the phone.

"Have you found something in the file?" she asked eagerly.

"Um, no, no, I haven't." He paused. "The file is gone."

Addie waited. "What do you mean?" she asked slowly when Dinny did not elaborate.

"I mean, I left it on my desk, and when I came back, it was not there," Dinny said with a heavy voice. "I have looked everywhere. It is just not here."

"So, it's been stolen? When you were down here?"

"That's what it looks like," said Dinny. "There is a remote possibility that a Messenger retrieved it thinking I was done with it."

He heard Addie's muffled voice as she put her hand over the receiver and asked Gruter if the file had by any chance been returned. "Dinny, Mr. Gruter says the file has not come back. He wants to know why I've asked."

"Can you tell him, please? I have to report this," Dinny said, his voice now matter-of-fact. "Any luck finding the decrypts?"

"No, we've walked quite a few shelves, and there is no sign of them," said Addie, aware of the implications.

"Then I will report both as missing," he said.

Chapter Three

A Drowsy Numbness

Lady Butterschloss, Emmeline to her friends, and Foxy to her intimates, was in the Morning Room where she always had her coffee precisely at 10:00 am and always *"mit Schlag,"* or whipped cream as Cook called it. In 1915, she declared no German word would ever cross her lips again, no matter what fancy Hun word Lady Butterschloss wanted to call her cream. Lady Butterschloss was slumped in her yellow silk, winged armchair. Her cup rested on an imposing Anglo-Indian hardwood table. The base was a realistic sculpture of a camel, its proud head borne aloft by a curved neck. The hump, at twenty-eight inches, was surmounted by an ornately carved flat octagon. The Morning Room was flooded with light pouring through the Palladian windows overlooking the Italian Garden. The early October sunlight glinted off Chinese porcelain vases filled with bright flowers. None of this cheered Foxy as she sipped her coffee. She was deeply depressed, overwhelmed by bitter, wretched memories. Unbidden, the words of Keats came into her mind:

> *My heart aches, and a drowsy numbness pains*
> *My sense, as though of hemlock I had drunk,*
> *Or emptied some dull opiate to the drains*
> *One minute past, and Lethe-wards had sunk.*

A complete lassitude overtook her. She felt too tired to even imagine getting up and walking the few steps to her writing desk to decline several invitations to dinner parties. She had stopped all her considerable number of charitable and political activities. These spells of inertia crippled her for days every few months on top of a habitual state of depression. She wanted to understand what was wrong with her, but couldn't think clearly, as if her brain were stuffed with cotton wool. Part of it was profound mourning. The terrible losses of the war, millions dead, and for what? Surely there would be another war within a few decades. She also felt the sting suffered by all "surplus women," women who had no place in society because they had lost their husbands or lovers, lost the meaningful jobs they held supporting the war effort, and had no prospects for remarrying in a society where so many men had died. Not that she had any desire to marry again, to risk suffering again. *It isn't just the mourning, the loss, the futility, the intentional isolation. It is the sense of complete uselessness.*

She looked at the familiar photographs in their silver frames arranged on the camel's back. One was of the day she married her dear Robby, Sir Robert Grayson Pagenel-Butterschloss. He was tall and handsome in his Naval uniform. She scarcely recognized herself in her long white dress, smiling into the camera. *So young. So happy. So untouched by sorrow.* There was the picture taken in his dress uniform when he became Admiral. She looked tenderly at the snapshot of them at the seashore, she holding their dear little Timmy up to the camera in his shorts and floppy hat, Robby with his arm around her, smiling his warm, loving smile. *Gone. Both gone. Both taken from her.* Her coffee cup held only dregs, the cream a flat brown at the bottom. Out the window, she saw the trees in a blaze of autumn color, stained glass shimmering in a light breeze. She felt nothing except the foreboding of death and loss that autumn portended.

Then she looked at another snapshot, this one of Dinny, standing next to her when he was about eleven. Her spirits rose. She smiled. *I still have him in my life.* Dinny was Foxy's grand-nephew by marriage. His mother, Adeline, was Robby's niece, the daughter of his younger brother. Adeline married the wealthy American, Beriah Custus. Dinny was their only child.

When Beriah and Adeline died in an avalanche while skiing at St. Moritz, Foxy and Robby had taken the ten-year-old Dinwiddie under their wings. That had been in 1909. He had lost his adolescent gawkiness but was still the shy boy she remembered. He still hung his head slightly to one side most of the time and constantly pushed his glasses up the bridge of his nose. *He doesn't really need me anymore. He has his job at Admiralty and seems very happy. He's grown into a fine, independent man. He hasn't really depended on me since he went to Cambridge.* Her spirits sank again.

Dinny returned to the townhouse. He called Tris and left a message that he wouldn't be meeting him at the Above Board, nor would Addie. Something had come up. He would brief Tris later. He put down the receiver. He stared at the phone. He was irresolute, indecisive. He wanted to call Auntie Em, but should he drag her into the mess he was in? Dinny's nickname for his Great Aunt was one way this usually diffident young man showed his deep affection for Foxy, a reminder of how many times, reading to him, he in her lap in the big rocking chair, she whisked him off to Oz. He could not have been closer to his Great Aunt and Uncle had they been his real parents, but his bond with Foxy was especially strong. Uncle Robert had often been away at sea for long periods. Left on their own at the Butterschloss seaside estate, the two had grown very close. Foxy was as enthusiastic about exploring the estate as Dinny was. She was equally indulgent in receiving everything he found and made sure there were plenty of display cabinets for his collections of fossils, rocks, insects, and bird feathers, as well as the skeletons of fish and the shells he found washed up by the ocean. Even more important to Dinny, she had given him the emotional shelter and support he needed after the sudden loss of his parents. At twenty-one, Dinny recognized Foxy was his anchor in every storm, and even more, the gentle but insistent force that pulled him out of the shell he built around himself after the shock of becoming an orphan.

After reporting the loss of the files, he said goodbye to Addie under the archway of the Admiralty Building. She had given him good advice. "You should call her now. What will she say when she finds out how much trouble we are in if you wait? She's bound to find out."

Now, he took a deep breath, summoning his courage, and dialed her number on the wall phone in the townhouse.

Foxy's thoughts about Dinny were interrupted when she heard the phone ring in the hallway. *God, I don't want to talk to anyone.* The butler entered and said, "It's Master Custus on the phone."

Foxy's torpor lifted. She went quickly to the phone. "Dinny, how are you?" she said with a cheerful voice she hadn't used in weeks. There was a pause. "Dinny? Dinny, are you still there?"

"Yes, Auntie Em. Sorry. It's just that…I have a problem, and I don't know if I should drag you into it," said Dinny.

"What is it? Please tell me," She said calmly. "Whatever it is, we will sort it out together."

"It started this morning," Dinny said. He told the story of why he and Addie were interested in the *Lusitania* files and decrypts, of the apparent theft of the file, of the mysterious missing decrypts. Foxy listened without interrupting.

"I knew I needed to report this immediately. It was just too great a coincidence for the file to be stolen off my desk and the decrypts gone as well."

"Quite right," said Foxy, not certain how this led to Dinny being in some kind of a mess.

"The Officer of the Day has relieved me of duty pending a court-martial," said Dinny, the words spilling out, "And he relieved Addie of her clearance to use the records in the ARO. We're being accused of theft and espionage."

Chapter Four

Bring the Eternal Note of Sadness In

Sir William John Ainsworth bore much of the grace and ease of his youth. He was tall, slender, and while there was just a hint of jowl, his face was even featured, his eyes keen and dark, and his hair—which was still thick—was silver. He stood in his study looking out the French windows across the green lawn sloping to the sea. He was as much at peace as he could be, given that he felt generally at odds with himself. No, that wasn't it. He felt at odds with this moment in history, his era. He was a man who knew too much and could do too little about it. He carried with him a habitual tension, and sometimes, an anger at a low boil, like a storm on the horizon at sea that pushes before it changing winds and troubled cresting waves.

He was an officer in the Royal Navy during the war. For most of it, he was a liaison officer assigned to the Naval Intelligence Division. Before that, he was aboard ship at the Dardanelles. The memory of that disaster surfaced from time to time, only it wasn't a memory. He was there again. The war was supposed to end all wars, and the deaths he saw, the screams of the wounded, the secrets he learned, the betrayal and subterfuge that were inherent to wartime intelligence were supposedly justified by that one dream: peace, no more wars. He scoffed to himself as he saw the calm sea under the clear October sky. He recited to himself:

Listen! You hear the grating roar
Of pebbles which the waves draw back, and fling,
At their return, up the high strand,
Begin, and cease, and then again begin,
With tremulous cadence slow, and bring
The eternal note of sadness in.

The uprisings in India and Egypt, the descent into a failed state in Germany, the rise of Mussolini and Stalin, the struggle between the socialists and capitalism, and now fascism, all came in the wake of the war and portended the coming of yet another. *Millions dead. Cities in ruins. Unemployment. What had it all been for?*

A servant knocked once on the door and entered. "There's a phone call for you, Sir. It's Lady Butterschloss."

William smiled ruefully. Another secret he must keep—his deep love for Foxy. His estate shared a boundary with the Butterschloss Estate, and he grew up with Robby Paganel. The two had gone up to Cambridge together and shared everything as if they were brothers. When Paganel introduced him to Foxy after meeting her while on a climbing trip to the Matterhorn, William had fallen in love with her as had Paganel. She had come up to Cambridge the following year to study Maths, and the three had become nearly inseparable. She chose Paganel, and William, whose rivalry remained his secret, never married.

He picked up the phone in the hallway. "Hello, Foxy, this is a pleasant..."

"Yes," said Foxy briskly. William heard strain in her voice. "Listen, I've called you because Dinny is in trouble. He was in charge of some top-secret documents from the war, and someone stole them. He is being blamed for negligence or worse and threatened with court-martial."

William watched Dinny grow up ever since he arrived at Butterschloss, when he was an introverted, sad little ten-year-old. "But that's absurd," he said. "What do you mean by 'or worse'?"

"Dinny was working with Adelaide Gold. You remember her from last summer when Dinny invited his friends from Cambridge to stay. She is working on something for the GCCS about intelligence during the war. Her assignment overlapped with Dinny's work. She was in the ARO looking for files for him, but those boxes have gone missing, too. It's too complicated to explain it all now, but they are threatened with a charge of espionage." Foxy's voice shook with a combination of anger and fear.

William glanced at his watch. "Don't say another word." His voice was even, calm, the result of years of what he liked to call self-discipline, or grace under pressure, but which was a product of the habitual suppression of his emotions. "The next train to London is at 1:00. I'll call ahead and have the Chelsea house made ready. You'll stay there, of course." He had extended his hospitality to Foxy whenever she came to London ever since she had generously given her townhouse to Dinny and Tris to use when they landed jobs with the RNVR. "You give Dinny a call and tell him to meet us for dinner. I'll pick you up at 12:30."

While waiting for the train, the two talked quietly about plans for meeting Dinny that evening, but fell silent upon entering the first-class carriage. That is a curious thing about train rides. The closed carriage, the anticipation, and the slow beginning as the car rolls forward often cause travelers, no matter how well-known to each other, to fall into silence and gaze out the window until the train is moving along. Perhaps it is because the journey is fixed, determined by the train track, removing all sense of individual choice in the matter, placing one mentally in the hands of Destiny. Perhaps it is because the movement itself, as the landscape slips away at ever increasing speed, signals to the unconscious an awareness of plunging irresistibly toward an unknown future. These were Foxy's thoughts as she saw the autumnal countryside roll past slowly, then quicken as the train picked up speed. *How would she help Dinny? How would she help Addie? What if I can't? What if I can't?* Her questions kept time with the clackety-clack of the wheels on the tracks.

It was William who broke the silence. "Do you mind if I smoke, Foxy?" he said, smiling his deferential smile as he pulled his pipe from his pocket.

"You know I don't," she replied, "as long as you open the window a bit."

Some time was taken up as he opened the window, and then fussed a bit with his pipe, tobacco pouch, and matches. "So," he began, taking several quick puffs, "what do you know about Dinny's problem?"

She explained as well as she could.

"But you don't know what the files or decrypts were about?" asked William. He saw the worry and self-doubt in Foxy's expression, heard them in her voice. William would very much have liked to lean forward and take Foxy's hand to comfort her. He knew she had not let go of Paganel, still held him close to her heart, used her grief as a shield against loving again. Foxy was unaware, or refused to be aware, that he loved her "in that way." William had to accept that she thought of him simply as an old friend and companion—rather like his Gordon Setter looked upon him.

Foxy sighed. "All I know is that he was working on whether undersea wireless transmission is possible and was assigned to study the intercepts from German submarines during the war to understand the range of transmissions when the submarines sent messages while on the surface."

William was silent as he puffed his pipe. "Yes," he said at last, "I can see where losing that kind of file would be quite serious. Although it is difficult to grasp why that would lead to Dinny's court-martial."

"I agree," said Foxy, emphatically. "Sounds ridiculous to me, too." She paused. "But even if he is exonerated, it will be a blot on his record." She paused again. "It will ruin his career. And if they convene a court-martial, you know the odds will be stacked against him." Her voice shook.

"I know," said William, calmly. I don't see how it can come to that, or even why the threat of a court-martial was made. And as for Adelaide Gold, it is impossible to see why she has been implicated. Her career is every bit as much at stake. This whole thing stinks to high heaven."

They sat in silence. William watched the world go by as he thought about what he wanted to say to Foxy.

"You don't sound like yourself," he said quietly, even gently.

Foxy looked at him with surprise and self-recognition. "What do you mean?" she asked, knowing much of the answer because she had said it to herself.

"I miss Spunky Foxy," he said, smiling. "I miss the spirited Foxy who persisted at Cambridge and faced down any professor or undergraduate who thought women didn't have the brains for it. I miss the feisty Foxy who was smart as hell working in Room 229 on the decoding machines while the male cryptographers called you "typists." And you led the fight to get a women's WC installed for all of you working in signal intelligence. I also miss the mettlesome Foxy, who went to endless meetings to get women the vote, who marched and demonstrated, and whacked a policeman with a protest sign.

Foxy smiled, "That was an accident."

"He didn't think so. You were hauled off to jail," said William. They both laughed. "The point is you didn't care. You never flinched." He took a drag on his pipe. "I remember when you told Paganel you volunteered as an ambulance driver at the front. He was beside himself. But of course, he didn't try to stop you."

"Until he pulled me out of that nightmare," she said. One dark, rainy night, a transport truck slid in the mud and hit the ambulance Foxy was driving. She escaped with minor injuries. "The next thing I knew, I was 'magically' recruited into Naval intelligence." She paused. "Robby's doing," she said quietly.

William nodded and let another silence settle between them. He cleared his throat. "What I meant to say," he hesitated, "is you haven't been yourself for the past year or so. You have hidden away at Butterschloss. And now you are afraid you cannot face this."

Foxy nodded. "The same might be said of you."

William took a deep breath. "As usual, you got it in one. With me, it is anger at the waste of the war. The dead. The wounded, maimed. The unending crises and chaos because of the idiotic terms of the Versailles treaty." He looked out the window and saw the countryside, England, slipping away. He looked at Foxy. "I watch it happening but cannot change it." He was surprised at his confession.

"We have both run to ground, and for the same reasons. I feel as if stones are piled on my heart. Suffocated with grief. I have felt useless since the war. Helpless. There is nothing that can be done to repair the world now.

Nothing. Greed, vengeance, politics. They didn't stop when the war ended. Wilson and his Fourteen Points meant nothing to men used to carving up Europe and the world into empires. I wonder what it was that Robby died for." Her voice trembled, "And another war coming, and what will happen to Dinny? He wasn't old enough for the last war, but…" Her voice broke. If she went on, she would weep, and she refused that.

They rode on in silence.

As they were pulling into the station, Foxy took a deep breath. "Let's make a deal. Let's get on with what we must do, the way we did during the war. We never doubted we would win."

"Deal," he said.

Chapter Five

Much Ado About Nothing

There was an inviting simplicity about William's Edwardian townhouse on Carlyle Square, with its flat, corbelled roof atop yellow brick walls. Wisteria softened and outlined the curves on the arched windows on the second and third stories. Spiral topiary trees in pots flanked second-story balconies extending over the ground-floor bay windows.

William's father, Admiral Ainsworth, built the house to his specifications. He fitted it out like the efficient interior of a ship of the line. Along the walls of the sitting room were built-in cabinets and drawers of mahogany, with brass fittings that folded flush to the doors. The wooden floors gleamed in the light that flooded the room. The leather tufted Chesterfield, and matching wing chairs left no doubt that the old Admiral had been the Master of his domain, at least in the last decade of his life, when he was a widower.

Foxy went straight up to her usual guest room. She would not have time to change for dinner, but wanted to get out of her shoes. Her feet had swollen, naturally, and the straps on the Mary Janes were digging into her. She took them off with something between a sigh and a groan and put on her Persian slippers with curled toes and embroidered silk. She took off her cloche in front of the mirror. She saw a short, slightly overweight woman and surveyed her hair, which was auburn with hints of grey. She still had only one chin, but it drooped and threatened to spawn a second. *Who the hell is that?* She asked herself, not for the first time. Her hat pushed her hair flat against her head, but it would soon spring to unruly curly life. She really could do nothing with it, so she shrugged, adjusted her dress, and her toilet complete, decided she had let herself go, become too careless of her appearance since retiring with her grief and ennui to the country. She went downstairs and sat in a leather armchair near the fireplace where a fire burned brightly.

She looked around the room with her usual admiration at the harmony of design. Her eclectic style was what she called Late Attic, with no reference to the Greeks, but to the furniture in the large attics at Butterschloss, which she brought down as her needs required. Her favorite was the camel table. Anyone who looked upon it with anything short of admiration was sure to take a step down in Foxy's estimation.

William entered the room just as there was a knock at the door. Dinny and Addie arrived. Foxy gave Dinny a long, strong hug, which naturally embarrassed him while he found it reassuring. Foxy was also generous in her affectionate greetings to Addie. She had large, intelligent dark eyes with dark, rather elfish eyebrows, high cheekbones, and full lips. Her beauty was Classical rather than pretty; her open, intelligent face was framed by dark hair, parted in the middle, and held back from her face by two lapis lazuli barrettes. Foxy liked Addie when she met her the previous summer, and was determined to know her better.

Dinner was no time for serious conversation. They had all been brought up with the "not in front of the servants" creed and the etiquette that food was prepared to be enjoyed, not ruined by discussing disagreeable subjects. Dinny especially did all he could to show the stiff upper lip and engage in the light banter expected of a well-bred gentleman, but Foxy could see he was wound up and very worried. Addie wasn't much better off.

"You were at Newnham, if I recall," Foxy said to Addie. "I was at Girton." These were two residential colleges for women at Cambridge. Girton, the oldest in the country, was founded in 1869, Newnham in 1880. While women could attend, they could not be granted degrees. "You must have been terrified when those asinine undergraduates stormed your gates."

In 1921, the University Senate voted to deny women a degree but award them a certificate that had none of the rights associated with a degree, including membership in the Senate. Although this was a loss for the women, over a thousand male undergraduates had literally stormed the gates of Newnham College and caused havoc and damage for an hour and a half.

"I don't know that I would call it fear, exactly, not in the sense of 'paralyzed with'" replied Addie. "Of course, we were scared, but many of us were very, very angry. They pushed a coal truck through the gates to try and get in. They certainly had blood in their eyes, and who knows what they would have done if the Proctors hadn't stopped them. But I am not alone in thinking that if they had gotten into our rooms, they would have left bloodied. Our preferred weapons were fireplace pokers. We were not about to be cowed by a bunch of over-privileged, public school boys."

Addie looked fondly at Dinny. "Dinny and our friend Tris—you met him last summer—came over to Newnham early next morning after they heard what had happened to make sure I was all right." She gave a sardonic laugh. "It was just another day at Cambridge for women. Our revenge was to do very well on the Tripos exams. Our scores are not recognized because, after all, we are female and couldn't possibly be as intelligent as the men. These entitled-by-birth dinosaurs will have to give way to a superior life form eventually."

"I'll toast to that," said Dinny, smiling for the first time as he looked with undisguised admiration at Addie.

When they gathered in the sitting room over coffee, their conversation turned serious.

"All right, Dinny," said Foxy, trying to lighten the mood. "You better spill it."

Dinny glanced at Addie, who gave a slight smile and a nod to encourage him.

He cleared his throat. "Perhaps I should explain what I've been doing for the Admiralty. My assignment is to see what can be done to improve submarine wireless communications. Not that there is a big effort to build up our submarine force." He turned to William. "You know how submarine warfare is thought of by the old Naval officers."

William replied, mimicking the voice of a gruff Admiral schooled aboard wind-powered ships. 'Submarine warfare is despicable, cowardly, underhanded, and un-British.' I know my father shared the view." He said this lightly. He admired his father and even thought he had a point about submarine warfare, but William also recognized that the war had ended whatever remnants of chivalry there were.

Dinny nodded. "There still is a small group devoted to developing submarines. I was brought in to assist."

"They recognized your talent," said Foxy, smugly. "And quite right, too."

"Things were going along well enough," said Dinny, blushing slightly. "I became interested in improving wireless submarine communications." He became boyishly enthusiastic. "I think it might be possible to develop wireless underwater communication. I know it sounds slightly mad, but…"

He became acutely aware that he was losing his audience. "Yes, well, anyway, I was given free rein to pursue my idea. I wanted to learn about submarine wireless transmissions during the war and decided to look into the sinking of the *Lusitania*. To be precise, I wanted to look into German submarine wireless intercepts to find what exactly was our capability at the time, what distances we could track and how accurately, that sort of thing."

"Loathsome," said William, stirring cream into his coffee. "Twelve hundred passengers drowned in the twenty minutes it took the *Lusitania* to sink. Two torpedoes fired into a passenger liner. Absolutely reprehensible. Of no military use whatsoever."

Dinny nodded. "The Germans torpedoed it without giving the passengers time to get into the lifeboats. And without any other warning. That is what made me wonder when, exactly, we developed the ability to intercept and decode German wireless submarine transmissions as we did the German warships. If we couldn't, what was the obstacle, and how was it overcome?"

"I was in the Dardanelles when we received word the *Lusitania* was sunk," said William quietly. He cleared his throat. *The Dardanelles. Another disaster, another disgraceful, wretched waste of life, only this time, it wasn't the Germans.*

It was us." Foxy saw what was for her the familiar, haunted look on William's face. It came over him whenever he was drawn back into the vortex of his service in the war.

William regained his self-control. "They hung Captain Turner out to dry," said William, sourly. "Or tried. Tried to make out that the whole thing was down to his negligence. Complete nonsense, of course. The review board exonerated him." He paused. "My father, the Admiral, knew him." This was an understatement. Turner saved the life of his father's best friend. But William was not one to elaborate. He was too used to keeping information close to his chest, even when he didn't need to.

Dinny knew that William had been assigned in some capacity to the upper echelons of Naval Intelligence and was vaguely aware that Foxy had been some kind of assistant in cryptography, probably a typist.

He said thoughtfully, thinking he might probe a bit deeper for information. "I asked my superiors for permission to look into when exactly we were able to intercept German U-boat signals and what the early technology was." He noticed the exchange of glances between Foxy and William. So did Addie.

Dinny paused long enough to pour himself another cup of coffee. "So, I requested the file box on the *Lusitania* be sent up from the archives in the ARO and asked Addie to find out if there were any decrypts from German submarines either before or after the sinking."

"And that's where I come in," said Addie brightly. "I landed a position in the GCCS at first because they thought with my not-quite-a-degree in mathematics from Cambridge, I would be a wiz at accounting." She scoffed bitterly. "One day, I was in the cafeteria and couldn't help but see a fellow nearby shaking his head over long lists of numbers and complaining to his pal that he could not crack it. I just got up, walked over to the table, and asked if I could have a go. They both looked at me as if I were a talking seal or simply mad, and smirked. I knew they would, of course. They said I could try, knowing I would fail. It was just a test code, not a real encrypt. They were both in training. There were ten sets of numbers, arranged in five-digit groups. Below that row of fifty numbers was another set of fifty. The problem that had to be solved was subtracting the entire bottom row from the top row, in sequence. I looked at it for about five minutes. It made no sense because the numbers on the second row were larger than the first. Then it hit me. I was looking at four minus nine and figured that if I just invented a phantom number ten, the solution would be five—fourteen minus nine, you see. That was the solution, so the rest was a snap. I added the phantom ten to each set of five numbers on the top row." She smiled gleefully. "After those two smug gentlemen took the solution back to their boss, and confessed I had cracked it, I found myself called into the cryptography section the next day and have been working there ever since."

She broke it using non-carrying addition and subtraction, thought Foxy. *She's very, very clever.* She noticed that Dinny was looking at Addie with rapt admiration.

"My assignment is to dig into the cryptography during the war, especially any machines that were developed to speed up the process." Foxy did not betray her surprise and interest. She was bound by the Defense of the Realm oath, which swore her to secrecy about her work for Naval Intelligence forever. "Since Dinny and I were working on the same kind of thing, we decided to work together. I had requested any decrypts of German submarine transmissions for 1915. Only there weren't any. I mean, there were decrypts listed in the catalog, but they were missing from the shelves. The archivist, Jan Gruter, helped me look, but we found nothing."

"And," said Dinny, "when Addie called me to say the decrypts couldn't be found, I went down to the ARO to see if I could help. While I was away, someone took the *Lusitania* files off my desk. They have vanished, with the result that I have been suspended pending investigation, and Addie has been denied clearance to work in the Admiralty Record Office."

"Why both of you?" asked Foxy. "Surely, the supposed blame falls just on you, Dinny."

"Everyone knew we were working together," Dinny sighed. "When the *Lusitania* files went missing, and there were no decrypts for 1915, the higher-ups decided we must be in some kind of conspiracy. That's why I have been threatened with a court-martial."

"What nonsense," said William irritably.

"Bullocks," exploded Foxy. "Who threatened you?"

"Captain Howell McCreedy," said Dinny. He sighed. "I was told to report to him while I was working in the ARO."

Foxy and William exchanged glances again. "Time for the brandy, I think," said William. "And I'd better throw another log on the fire. I think it is going to be a long night."

After distributing drinks and stirring the fire, William settled again into the armchair. "You know, this sounds to me like some kind of prank that has misfired. Are you sure this isn't something cooked up by your friends?"

Addie shook her head. "You met my flatmate Josie Fairbairn last summer. She and I were at Newnham together. She knows how very hard it is for women to get into jobs like mine, and we would never do anything to undermine each other like that. And Josie has her head buried in tomes at the LSE library most of the time. She's doing graduate work in history and economics."

Dinny agreed. "And I cannot imagine Tris mucking about with war records just for a joke. It would jeopardize his own career if he were ever found out. He is engrossed in the problems of stress and tension on metal." He paused for a moment and looked at Addie. "I called and left a message earlier, by the way, to say we couldn't meet him at the Above Board after work today. I didn't want him to worry when we didn't show up."

Foxy looked thoughtfully at Addie. "If I understand rightly, then, there has never been any kind of friction among the three of you?"

Addie thought, *I might have known that Foxy would follow that trail, which was just a bit obvious when we visited this summer."*

"As a matter of fact," she said, warming the brandy glass between her palms, "In July, he asked me to marry him—well, suggested is the better word, to save face in case I turned him down. I did. Turn him down, that is. It was all so casual and kind of a joke. That ended it, and all of us, including Josie, still see a lot of each other.

"Yes, we are all very close friends," said Dinny. "Well, to be honest, he sometimes needles me a bit about Addie. He did it this morning while we walked to work. But he doesn't really mean anything by it. He wanted to put the awkwardness of his proposal behind us as much as we did."

"And you can't think of anyone else or any other reason why someone might have it in for either of you, maybe jealousy or envy because you landed your positions so soon after graduating?" asked William. "Times are difficult."

They both shook their heads. Dinny said, "Tris never had to worry about a posting because his father is so well-connected. He is distantly related to Churchill, a second or third cousin or something. Not that Tris needed any extra pull. He is as good as anyone when it comes to engineering."

They talked until close to midnight as Foxy and William prodded and probed to find out more about the people they worked with, their other friends, or anything that might explain why anyone would have it in for either of them.

At last, having exhausted every avenue, William said, "It is getting quite late. Let me put both of you in a cab. You had best leave it to us for the time being. We'll see what we can do to sort this out."

"But what can you do?" asked Dinny with a hint of panic in his voice.

Foxy said, decisively, "William and I can have a Council of War tomorrow morning and come up with a plan of action. Then, we will be in touch. Where will you be, if neither of you is going to work?"

"I've convinced Dinny we should not mope around. We're driving up to Stratford. They're doing *Much Ado*. That should cheer us up," said Addie, with a grin at her own irony. "We will be back the day after tomorrow."

"I've agreed because I think I will go mad if I have to sit around doing nothing but worry," said Dinny. "Maybe this is much ado about nothing, although I doubt it."

As they rose to get their coats and say goodbye, Foxy went up to Dinny and took his face gently in both her hands. "Listen to me. You are going to come out of this. We are here to help you and Addie."

"I know, I know, "said Dinny softly. "I will leave it for the moment in your hands and try not to brood on it. But, as soon as we get back, I want to be part of the plan." He paused. "And thank you, Auntie Em." He managed a brave grin at their private joke and hugged her.

After seeing Dinny and Addie into a cab, William and Foxy consulted their watches.

"Right," she said. "No sense talking about this anymore tonight. We meet right after breakfast in the morning. Nine o'clock all right?"

"Certainly," said William. "I'll order coffee in the Conservatory. *Mit Schlag, natürlich.*"

"*Natürlich,*" beamed Foxy.

Chapter Six

In Sure and Certain Hope

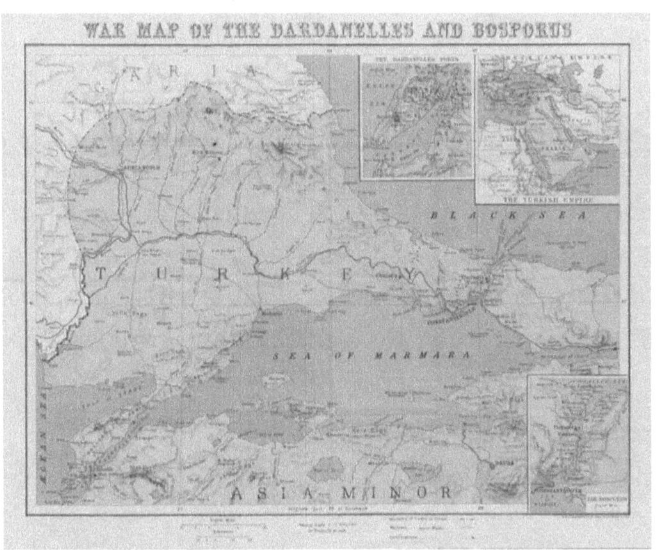

William brooded in his bedroom. He emptied a snifter of brandy and poured himself another. He removed a green, clothbound diary for the year 1915 from the top drawer of a small writing desk. Several maps slipped out.

A colored map showed the Dardanelles Straits, the Sea of Marmara, and the Bosporus Straits leading to the Black Sea. Without that route,

Russia, which was part of the Triple Entente, could be neither supplied nor supported in fighting the Turks, who were in alliance with Germany. The British planned to send warships up the Dardanelles into the Sea of Marmara to seize Constantinople at the mouth of the Bosporus. That had been the goal: Constantinople, the shining prize, the capital of Turkey. With that bold stroke, the war would soon end.

How could the War Council have allowed itself to be seduced by Churchill, the First Lord of the Admiralty and self-appointed God Almighty? They foolishly thought the Turks could be no match for the British and French combined navies. Especially the British fleet, the largest in the world. Just bring the big guns to bear on the Turkish forts, blasting the way to Constantinople. The Turks will capitulate. No need for any amphibious troop landings. The Navy would carry the day. They knew better. All of them knew better, even Churchill if he were honest with himself. But he persuaded them, badgered them, relentlessly pushing his plan through. To say it was a catastrophe showed the limitations of language and imagination.

The memories crowded in—the chaos William suppressed—but they were always there, locked in a dark cabinet of his mind until something turned the key. That was why he never mentioned the Dardanelles, avoided anything that might remind him. Tonight, Dinny mentioned the *Lusitania.* William heard about it while serving as a signal officer aboard *HMS Agamemnon.* The key turned, and William was aboard ship.

The salty tang of the brisk air, a blue sky, the clear, calm water. The deck shuddered beneath his feet. The starboard heavy guns fired one shell per minute, regular, deafening eruptions of smoke and fire. The shells screamed toward Fort No. 1 on the tip of the Gallipoli peninsula. The rugged, rocky hills spewed columns of earth and smoke. He felt a thrill at the sight. The *Agamemnon* was at anchor ten thousand feet offshore. The dreadnaught *Queen Elizabeth* fired on Fort No. 3, the French *Gaulois* at No. 6. The air vibrated and filled with black smoke from the funnels and guns. Above their noise, William heard the regular, orderly commands to the gunners, who functioned as well-oiled machines. Shells from the Turkish forts fell short of the ships, making great plumes of water rise like some angry, giant sea gods before returning hissing to the deep. One of the commanding officers chose this moment to order a detail of men to paint the port side. William stared at him. The man had either lost his reason or was moronically complacent, assuming that since all the "action" was on the starboard side, why not take the opportunity to freshen the hull up on the quiet side? As soon as the officer left, William quickly reassured the men that the order could be ignored. They would have anyway, judging by the looks on their faces.

The words were scarcely out of his mouth when the deck rose and fell beneath his feet. A shell hit amidships. William was thrown backward. For a few seconds, he saw red and could not hear. Then came the screams of the wounded men, the shouted orders for stretchers. Three men lay dead, their bodies twisted and covered with blood. Yeoman Bishop had a large, metal splinter in his leg, which was connected to him only by exposed tendons. He had been reading a flag signal from another ship when he was hit. He continued shouting the message to the captain, as if his leg did not belong to him, or was expendable, like the tail of a salamander, which regenerates if pulled off. Next to him, Petty Officer Worthington screamed and clutched the metal splinter that pierced his stomach, his eyes wide with terror. When the stretcher party came up, Bishop would not allow them to touch him until Worthington was taken below.

William could make no sense of what he saw and succumbed to a chaos of feelings for which there were no words, no precedent. The big guns on the starboard side continued to fire. The wounded were screaming; officers shouted orders. The world, the universe froze when he saw the ship's Boy, Walter Mockett, bleeding from his mouth, a metal splinter stuck in his abdomen. He was screaming. He was fifteen years old. Slight, still growing. Fifteen. Always cheerful, always looking underfed.

William had no time to comfort the Boy. He wanted to vomit but couldn't. A shell crashed through the upper deck with a deep roll of thunder, sending hot splinters flying, hitting the marines' barracks. Then a shell exploded on the foremost funnel and drove a hole into the deck. Another shot hit the topgallant mast. An armor-piercing shell smashed through the aft deck, then drove through William's office and two cabins. It landed with a resounding thump between two ammunition storage rooms and started a fire. William's consciousness compressed into one thought: put out the damned fire before the ship was blown apart. He shouted, hurried, insistent, orders: "Pump the fire extinguishers! Man, the hoses! Keep the flames away from the walls! Cool the walls with water from the hoses!" Then, after what seemed an eternity but was no more than ten minutes, "Well done, men. You saved us all today."

William, shaking, wet, and covered in soot, returned to the signal room. His throat was raw. He needed water. He didn't have time. Orders came to weigh anchor and get out of the line of fire. While trying to get the winches to work—they had been hit—the ship moved forward, then astern, then repeated the maneuver to make it harder for the Turkish guns to fire accurately. Once out of range, the ship's guns opened fire again. The ship was in action for six hours, under attack for about twenty minutes. There was no sense of time for William. Everything became one moment, a series of flashing images, like a film being run in an endless loop on a defective projector.

Once *Agamemnon* returned to base, William visited the wounded in the ship's infirmary before they were evacuated to the hospital ship, *Soudan*. He sat next to Walter, not knowing what to say. He was bandaged, and the blood was cleaned away. His round black eyes stared from his tiny, pale face. William had been one of the officers who joined the crew to celebrate Walter's fifteenth birthday party four days ago. He had given Walter his penknife.

"Are you in a great deal of pain?" asked William.

"No, not at all, really, 'cos they gave me a dose of painkiller. I can't remember the name, though."

"Heroin," suggested William.

"Yeah, that's it. I'm awful thirsty," said Walter. His voice cracked. It had just broken a few days earlier. *What the hell is this child doing aboard this ship in a battle zone?* "They gave me some sweet tea, but the doctor said no more. They are going to operate. So I can't have nothing to eat, neither. What does that mean, Sir, operate?"

"It means they are going to make you better. They will put you to sleep so you will not feel anything while they stitch you back together," said William quietly and gently.

"Stitch me back together? What, like me Mum did to me sister's doll when the dog chewed off its arm?" He paused, his lower lip trembling. "I miss me Mum," said Walter, as tears welled up.

"Yes, and I am sure she misses you," replied William. "They will stitch you up, and when you wake up, you will be fine, fit as new for when you see your Mum again." Walter looked frightened. "And anyway, the grub aboard the *Soudan* is much better than ours."

Walter's eyes brightened. He wiped away the tears with the back of his hand. "And can I have as much as I want?"

"Yes, I expect so," said William. "Nothing's too good for our heroes."

"I ain't no hero," said Walter. "I were just in the wrong place at the wrong time."

"No," said Walter, "anyone wounded in a battle is a hero."

Walter was silent for a moment as he thought that over, uncertain whether it was true. The orderly came with the stretcher to take him to be transferred. Walter panicked. "Will you come to visit me, Sir?" His voice trembled.

"Of course, I will. Don't you worry about that. I will see you when you are all fixed up and eating heaps and heaps of sausages."

William's heart sank as he saw the orderly lift the tiny, underweight boy onto a stretcher, cover him with a blanket, and signal to the other stretcher-bearer to carry him away.

The next day, they buried the dead. Three men sewn into the canvas hammocks they slept in lay out in a row on the deck. "We therefore commit William James Mason, George Small, and Bertie Worthington to the deep… in sure and certain hope of the resurrection of the body, when the sea shall give up her dead." The three wrapped bodies slipped into the sea. The bugler played Last Post.

The following day, William and some others from the ship took the lighter to the *Soudan*. He found Bishop sitting up in bed, smoking a cigarette. "I brought you some fags," said William. "How are they treating you?" He saw the bandaged stump where Bishop's leg had been.

"Oh, I'm fine," said Bishop, cheerily, and sounded as if he meant it. "First, I am alive, and second, I get to leave this hellhole. Sorry, Sir."

"You almost make me envy you," said William with a smile.

He sat beside Walter. The color had returned to his face.

"How are you?" he asked.

"Just like you said," replied Walter, pulling up the bottom of the hospital gown. "See? Just like Mum's." He showed off his dark stitches running up and down his small abdomen. He was proud of them and accepted the idea that he was a hero. "Wounded in action, ain't that right?"

"Yes, it certainly is," said William, relieved Walter survived the surgery and seemed to be recovering well. "Is there anything I can bring you?"

"Well, you was wrong about one thing. They won't give me real food. Not for a while yet, anyway. You couldn't smuggle me in somethin' could you?"

A week later, William stood on the deck of the *Soudan* and saw the tiny, canvas-wrapped body of Walter Richard Mockett slip into the sea. "...in sure and certain hope of the resurrection of the body, when the Sea shall give up her dead." It was William who wrote the letter to Walter's mother and father. Seated in his bedroom, William wept again as he had the day Walter's body slipped beneath the sea nine years earlier. Only it wasn't nine years earlier. He wasn't looking back on it. He was there again, as he was so often, haunted by the moment the shroud slipped below the surface, reliving it. He didn't know whom to hate more, God or Winston Churchill.

The next two weeks were a time of frenetic activity. The entire armada of British and French battleships was to sail up the Dardanelles to the minefields, firing on the Turkish positions to protect the trawlers charged with clearing the mines. William poured himself another brandy. He studied the chart showing the plans just as he had on the morning of March 18. The *Agamemnon* was flanked on the starboard side by *Lord Nelson*. On the port side sailed the impressive might of the *Queen Elizabeth,* the lead ship in the most formidable class of battleships in the Royal Navy. Behind them sailed another two lines of British and French ships in formation. As they made way up the bay toward the Narrows, the hinges of hell swung open. Shells fell all around the fleet in a vicious rain. Savage, untamed plumes of water rose and fell, churning the ocean. The ships returned fire. The hillsides exploded, an inferno of dust, earth, smoke, misery, and death.

William felt the ship reverberate like a coiled beast awakening as the shells screamed from its guns. For a short time, he could hear nothing, was cocooned in silence except for the sound of his own heart pounding, pounding, pounding with excitement, fear, panic, exhilaration. He experienced a dreadful glory, sailing in the vanguard of the finest fleet on earth, black smoke roiling from the funnels, white bow waves cutting the way to the Narrows.

In the wireless room, as their line of ships came up to the minefields, he received the order to make way for the ships behind to continue the bombardment. The ships in his line turned to starboard to come about. William received the frantic message from the French ship *Bouvet*. It had been damaged by the shelling and was listing badly. By the time William looked out the window of the wireless room, the *Bouvet* was slipping beneath the waves. William stared with confounded disbelief. In two minutes, the *Bouvet* was gone in a shroud of red-gray smoke, with all hands on board, over six hundred men. Destroyers and small picket boats rushed to the sinking hulk.

The Turks fired on the rescue boats. The *Irresistible* opened fire to protect the rescuers and survivors. *Irresistible* sent an S.O.S. The ship had been hit and drifted helplessly into the range of the Turkish guns. The destroyer *Wear* answered the distress call, and under punishing fire from the shore, came alongside and rescued almost all of the over six hundred men aboard the *Irresistible*. The destroyer *Ocean* attempted to tow the *Irresistible*. This proved impossible. The *Ocean* took on the remaining crew from the *Irresistible* and left under heavy fire. Severely damaged by shellfire, *Ocean* hit a mine, could no longer be steered, and listed heavily. The *Ocean* drifted for a time, still under fire, and sank. The *Irresistible* was sinking. Through his telescope, William saw the destroyers come to the rescue. Shells hit the sailors lowering the rescue boats, throwing them into the sea.

William heard a shout from a picket boat. "Mine right ahead of you." He shouted to the conning tower. The order came for "full astern." He could make no sense of why the men in the conning tower joked and laughed at the brush with death.

William looked again through his glass. Destroyers rescued the crew of the *Ocean*. The *Ocean* drifted away with the tide.

That night, at anchor on the island of Tenedos, the fleet licked its wounds, but without any strong resolve to return to the fray. William and the other officers were ordered to assemble a detail to bring aboard hundreds of men rescued from the sunken destroyers *Ocean, Irresistible,* and *Bouvet*. The seamen were in shock, shaking with cold, their eyes dull, staring at nothing. William handed a cup of hot tea to a shivering French seaman, one of the few rescued from the *Bouvet.* He was eager to tell the story of his miraculous survival to anyone who would listen. William was fluent in French and sat down beside him. The seaman was sucked under by the pull of the ship as it sank. "Then, when the ship touched the bottom of the sea, I came straight up, either because of the impact or because the boiler exploded. I couldn't breathe. Blood came out of my mouth, my ears, my eyes. If I had not found a piece of wood, I should have been a goner. When I came to the surface, I could see again and saw one or two of the men who had been machine-gunned from the shore." William was mesmerized by the story of the ship dragging the seaman to his death and then saving him when it struck bottom. He was at a loss for words. He managed to stammer, "A miracle, truly."

The reports of the damage to the *Agamemnon* further depressed the mood. Eleven howitzer shells smashed the decks, guns, and funnels. There were fragments of burst shells all over the ship.

The next day, William handed the Captain a signal from the Admiral to the Fleet: "Admiral regrets to announce unfortunate loss by mines of three ships, which he feels was due to no lack of vigilance or forethought on the part of those concerned. We have to report a very serious loss of life in *Bouvet*, but in cases of other ships, it is very small…I know that everyone will be ready to make further efforts and sacrifices when necessary. A method of overcoming mines will be found."

William, reading the message which he kept pressed in the pages of his diary, poured himself another brandy. *And then the slaughter began.* He held his glass up in a sardonic toast to the hellish plans of men. *"As flies to wanton boys are we to the gods. They kill us for their sport." Only Shakespeare got it wrong. It wasn't the gods; it was men in high places studying war from half a world away.*

To clear the mines, a total of four hundred and eighty-nine thousand ground soldiers landed on the west side of the Gallipoli Peninsula in the largest amphibious landing in military history. The goal was to seize the high ground and take out the Turkish guns protecting the Dardanelles on the east side of the peninsula and those across the strait. The troops faced rough ground, mountainous terrain, deep gullies, and entrenched Turkish positions. They were doomed before the battle started.

Agamemnon was ordered to shell Turkish strongholds before the army landings. Three days after the abortive effort to clear the minefields in the Dardanelles straits, William stood on the deck watching shells fired from *Agamemnon* fall on a barn and farmhouse. He saw the farmer run away. As the guns belched fire and smoke, shells landed on the farmer's barn, setting it on fire. The bombardment continued day after day. Sometimes the shells fell on trenches and earthworks. He saw a shell explode in a Turkish trench, sending a tangle of arms, legs, and other body parts into the air. Just as often, the shells fell on a village. Within a week, all the villages around Bulair were burnt out and destroyed. William watched four horsemen ride away at a gallop when they saw his ship approaching. Cattle were just as likely to be hit as sheds and farmhouses. William saw camels sitting unperturbed by the shells hitting Turkish trenches. The Captain ordered that the camels should not be fired upon. Another absurdity. William no longer paused to consider it. There were too many. The destruction became routine. Midshipmen complained of finding it boring, a boring round of horror. William was rendered emotionally numb to these operations, the time of the baby killings. Bulair was shelled again, killing more women and children who had not evacuated. Shells hit a mosque. The Captain was very pleased. During the daily shelling, William was plagued by a line from Blake playing in his mind over and over again: *"Rintrah roars and shakes his fires in the burdened air."* Rintrah, the angry prophet invented by Blake. The line related to the barrage on Gallipoli only as a coincidentally apt description of the big guns firing. *"Rintrah roars and shakes his fires in the burdened air. Rintrah roars and shakes his fires in the burdened air."* It was meaningless, as meaningless as setting barns on fire, or leveling mosques, or terrorizing and killing civilians.

On April 25, the fleet landed the first wave of thirty-three thousand British soldiers at six beachheads. The troops came from the UK, New Zealand, Australia, and India. The French landed three thousand. They were met with ferocious resistance from the Turks. At one beachhead, the troops were machine-gunned as they set foot on the beach, or sitting upright in the landing barge. The ocean turned red.

Agamemnon provided covering fire. The Turks returned fire. Three seamen were killed. William felt a hot, searing pain in his right leg. He saw, as if from a great distance, the blood flow freely as he lay on the deck, screaming. For him, the fighting was over. *But not for the poor bastards trapped on the beaches.* As he recovered from his wounds first aboard a hospital ship and then in a Naval hospital in Alexandria, William heard stories from wounded and sick soldiers. Pinned down on the beaches, the forces had dug in, enduring sniper and machine gun fire in a prolonged stalemate. The men suffered from a lack of water, insufficient food, terrible heat, typhoid, and dysentery.

The only success in the whole campaign was the evacuation of more than thirty-six thousand men in December without a single loss of life. The final absurdity. For the first time, there had been careful planning, coordination between the navy and army, and military discipline. It was a highly successful defeat. One hundred and forty-one thousand men were wounded or killed at Gallipoli. Typhoid and dysentery swept through the men trapped on the beaches and eventually spread to the seamen, affecting a total of over ninety thousand men. William sighed. More men on *Agamemnon* died of disease than were killed by enemy fire, most of them from dysentery.

William put the diary away. *At least, Churchill was forced to resign as First Lord of the Admiralty.* As he changed into his pajamas, the light from the lamp struck the long scar down his leg, turning it silver. The brandy bottle was empty. He wasn't drunk. Alcohol rarely made him drunk anymore. It numbed his senses, made him drowsy, insulated him from the mortal horror of reliving the past.

Asleep, his dreams were troubled. Bishop, sitting up in bed smoking a cigarette with his leg bandaged, commenting on William's wound. "I see you took my advice, got your leg tore up and got out of that hell hole." Men in the conning tower laughed and laughed as shells fell all around, raising great spumes of water, until one hit the deck. Flames rose higher and higher. The men kept laughing until their skin fell away in the heat, laughing skeletons until their bones fell into a charred heap on the deck. As shells fell all around, an officer stood screaming himself purple. "Why the hell won't you paint the port side!" He kept screaming and swelling until he exploded in a great puff of fire and smoke. A French seaman sank beneath the waves as the *Bouvet* rolled over. Then, he shot high into the sky, glittering, a human Roman candle. He fizzled and fell into the water next to a convenient floating piece of wood. Sailors on the decks of destroyers clapped and whistled and called, *"Encore!"* Women holding children stood along a high ridge, silent, unmoving, staring unblinkingly straight at William, standing on the deck of the *Agamemnon* as the guns roared, accusing him. Little Walter bobbed to the surface of a calm, clear ocean. It wasn't Walter. It was a floppy rag doll with shiny black button eyes. "Show Mum me stitches," the Walter-doll said solemnly, then sank out of sight. The Four Horsemen leapt from the hills and rode across the sky. The horses were white, red, black, and pale. The riders were hooded. He could not see their faces but knew their names: Conquest, War, Famine, and Death. The galloping horses came closer and closer, their nostrils flaring, flecks of foam around their mouths, their giant hooves larger than a man's head. The cloaks of the riders trailed in the wind, twisted and folded like living things pursuing prey. The horses thundered forward, implacable. As they passed over William's head, he cringed, looked up, saw the face of Death, and recognized himself staring back at him. He screamed the silent scream of dreams. A small herd of cheerful camels in a line began an awkward but energetic dance toward him, a camel Lindy Hop. They licked his face, his hair.

William's eyes popped open with a start. He was soaked in a cold sweat. His room was lit by the half-light of early dawn. Murky, his cat, was licking him, his rough tongue on his forehead. William raised his hand to scratch the cat behind its ears absently. His mind was still on his nightmare visions. "Damn Churchill," he said angrily aloud. "Damn him to hell." Murky, startled, leapt from the bed and cast William a reproving look. *I only wanted you to get up and get me some milk."*

Chapter Seven

Up Periscope

Foxy waited for William in the Conservatory. She had spent many enjoyable hours listening to the Admiral, Sir Gideon Ainsworth, tell the story behind each specimen. With him, it was a lifelong passion. Near where she was seated, the fragrant, delicate, white, star-shaped flowers of the Evergreen Clematis were supported on a rattan arch. They were a gift from the botanist E.H. Wilson—or Ernie as the Admiral called him. Wilson had discovered the plant when he was sent by a leading British nurseryman on his first expedition to China with a commission to bring back a specimen of the handkerchief tree. Wilson had the misfortune to arrive in China at the time of the Boxer Rebellion. That is when the two met. Gillian Ainsworth was a Commander aboard one of the ships sent to relieve the siege of the Legation Quarter in Peking. Initially, he had found Wilson's passion for horticulture odd but soon found himself attracted by Wilson's knowledge of plants, their origins, and his keen sense of adventure at the prospect of finding new species. His pure, harmless enthusiasm was a profound relief from the accounts Gillian heard from his fellow officers of the brutal assault by the allied American, Austro-Hungarian, British, French, German, Italian, Japanese, and Russian forces. He was nauseated and outraged by the stories of plunder and atrocities against civilians.

Commander Ainsworth had given Wilson what advice and assistance he could. Wilson had impressed him with his resolve not to be deterred. He had headed up the Yangzi River to Yichang. A little over two years later, he returned, looked up Ainsworth, and presented him with a cutting of one of the many plants he had discovered: the Evergreen Clematis.

Foxy sighed. The Admiral was a genial, outgoing man and an engaging storyteller. He had died of heart failure in 1919. Foxy missed him. The Conservatory and grounds were maintained to the Admiral's standards by the gardener, George Wilkinson, who had learned about plants and their needs from his father, the Admiral's gardener, from the time George was a boy.

William arrived at the same time as Maisy, the kitchen maid, brought in the coffee tray.

"Where shall we start?" he asked. He was dressed in his Navy uniform, looking impeccable as always. Except for a hint of bags under his eyes, there was no indication of the tormented night he had spent.

Foxy knew him too well to ignore the signs of a sleepless night. "Did you have any trouble sleeping?"

William glanced at her and smiled. *Of course, she would notice.* "I sat up late, thinking, and had trouble sleeping." He paused, hoping he could get away with a small lie. "I am worried about Dinny and Addie." He poured them each a cup of coffee. "Particularly since our old friend McCreedy is behind all their troubles."

"Yes," said Foxy, not entirely convinced that thoughts of McCreedy had kept Ainsworth up all night. She had seen the haunted look that came over him when he mentioned the Dardanelles the night before. There was no point, however, in raising any questions about those memories. She knew he never talked about them.

I think we should start with McCreedy, don't you?" said Foxy.

"Yes," said William irritably. "But I certainly can't be the one to talk to him."

Early in the war, McCreedy had played some role in blocking the promotion of William's father. Later, after the Battle of Jutland, Gideon was promoted to Vice-Admiral and by the end of the war to Admiral. Although both Foxy and William had worked at the Old Admiralty during the war and knew and disliked McCreedy, they never heard even a whisper about what had caused the hostility. Nor had Gideon ever spoken of it.

"I'll go see him," said Foxy. "I'll spike his cannons or know the reason why. What a load of hogwash to accuse Dinny of the equivalent of treason."

"Yes, an overreaction even for that martinet," said William. "He's never been much more than a clerk with gold braid. The closest he's ever gotten to a wooden deck is that giant desk of his." He lit his pipe. "I'll go see my old contact Clive Edgerton at Military Intelligence. Maybe he can give me a line on McCreedy or put me in the way of anyone who knows something about the *Lusitania*."

Foxy nodded. "Do you think it likely that the thefts are aimed at Dinny and Addie personally by someone they know who has played a trick on them? Couldn't it be that somebody does not want anyone poking around in the records of the *Lusitania*? But why, I wonder. It's been almost a decade now." She paused. "I think I will unleash my considerable charm on the archival librarian as well. He might remember someone who was also asking about the files."

William nodded in agreement. "Good idea. But I don't think we can rule out that this might have been someone who had it in for Dinny or Addie."

Foxy considered for a moment. "Maybe we should arrange a little dinner party for their friends, a reunion from the summer. We can judge for ourselves if there is any friction. They won't know that Dinny and Addie are in hot water because McCreedy made it very clear they were to keep their mouths shut. We'll see if any of them let something slip."

They agreed to meet at The Above Board for a late lunch. Foxy was "dressed for business," as she called it. She kept in the wardrobe a dark-blue, wool dress with pintuck pleats at the shoulders, and long sleeves ending in crisp, ecru linen cuffs. The dropped waistline fell in soft folds. The deep V-neck had an ecru linen bodice panel that was attached with snaps. It was an entirely feminine dress that hinted at a matronly "no nonsense" attitude. She had brought with her a gold pin of her own design. It was in the shape of a bowler hat, the rim turned up. The crown was set with rows of dark pink rhinestones and a rhinestone hat band. This, she pinned to her left shoulder. Tucking her unruly hair under her cloche, buttoning her coat, grabbing her handbag, and pulling on her gloves, she went out the door to the waiting cab.

She had despised McCreedy ever since she worked as a "hat girl" for signal intelligence during the war. They were called the "hat girls" because they were the first line in deciphering a particular kind of code hidden in another code, called a "hatted code." She recalled one day in particular when she was overwhelmed with disgust and outrage by McCreedy's attitude toward not only the hat girls, but any woman working in the Naval Intelligence Department.

It started out as a typical day working in Room 229 of the old Admiralty building. Foxy sat at what looked like a small pianola with typewriter keys. On her desk was a stack of papers with groups of five apparently random numbers or letters, with six groups to a row. These groups formed long columns extending down the page. She entered each group carefully, working her way across the rows. She had been entering letters steadily since 8:00 am. Her keyboard clicked, turning a rotor inside with a complex set of letters. Each turn of the rotor punched a card that appeared in the "pianola" window. A machine sorted the cards with identical punches into separate slots lined up along a long tray sitting on a tall table. These batches were studied by the male cryptographers, who used the repetitions to discover the key to the code. After three hours of steady work, her neck ached; the letters swam in front of her eyes. She was thirsty. The room was hot. A single sunbeam lit her curly, auburn hair. But her concentration did not break. Around her, other women typed with equal concentration. They did not speak to one another.

The only sound was the clicking of the keys.

Every day, the male cryptographers working on German diplomatic messages sent about seventy hypotheticals—or their guesses—to the women in 229. These "Hat Girls" entered the data. Their work sped up the deciphering and led to the unlocking of the top-secret German diplomatic messages. Every now and then, one of the women would raise her hand, and Miss Robertson, who had trained all the coders, would get up from her desk at the head of the room and go to the woman. Foxy did this just before the morning tea break. The two whispered so as not to disturb the others.

"I'm seeing the letter 'V,'" she told Margaret. "It's never appeared before."

"It's good you spotted it. I'll pass it along. I think it is probably quite important."

Miss Margaret Robertson said, "Tea break, ladies." Her voice had the crisp, no-nonsense command of a Headmistress, which she had been at Christ's Hospital School for Girls. A distinguished student at Cambridge, where she weathered the resistance from male undergraduates, she was a passionate advocate for female education. She transformed the curriculum at Christ's Hospital School for Girls from sewing and home management to one that prepared women for advanced education. A number of Christ's Hospital graduates followed the way she had prepared for them and attended university.

Everyone in the room groaned with relief, rose from the chairs, and headed for the Common Room. Several, including Foxy, took their cups and saucers onto the fire escape landing that overlooked the back parking lot. Strictly speaking, this was forbidden because of the tight security imposed by the Naval Intelligence Division when it formed the cryptography group, known as Room 40. What if a German spy took a picture and identified someone? But the warm spring sunshine was too tempting for the women of 229. Room 40 deciphered military messages, while Room 229 specialized in diplomatic codes. The women had been cooped up, bent over their keyboards, for over three hours. Besides, it was the gated back parking lot. No one could see them, and no unauthorized individual could wander into the lot, much less drive into it. The two youngest women, Violet, who was eighteen, and Joan, nineteen, dangled their legs over the edge of the landing and raised their skirts over their knees, sighing at the welcome warmth of the sun. The others arranged themselves comfortably on the pillows they borrowed from the chairs and sofas in the Commons room. Some closed their eyes, leaned back, and raised their faces to the sun.

At thirty-three, Foxy was one of the older of a group of six hat girls who were by now close friends. Margaret Robertson was fifty-five. She rarely joined the group at breaks or meals, preferring to keep aloof. Sybil was forty-three and married. The others ranged in age from nineteen to thirty-two. Some were married, some single. But none of these differences mattered. They were like-minded and used to defying conventions, part of a small cohort of highly educated women; they came from privileged families who moved in the same circles; they knew they were engaged in vital war work; and they were grateful they were not serving as skivvies in the VAD.

At about 1:00, just before lunch break, Margaret called Foxy to her desk and handed her a messenger pouch.

"These are reports of any anomalies in the hypotheticals we worked on this morning," she said. "Please take them to Lieutenant-Commander McCreedy. And I've included a note about your discovery of the letter 'V.' You can answer any questions he may have."

There was a universal groan. The Hat Girls despised the condescending, obtuse McCreedy, who thought he covered his incompetence with demands that everything be "done by the book" or be "shipshape and Bristol fashion." Margaret looked at her team sharply. "Is there a problem?" she asked.

"No, not at all," said Foxy, hesitating. "Except, I wonder if I might do this after lunch. McCreedy always eats in his room instead of going to the mess."

"What's wrong with that?" asked Margaret,

"Nothing, except he always eats a can of sardines with bread and stinky cheese," said Foxy.

Sybil spoke up. "The smell really is enough to gag one, especially since he has such a broom closet for an office."

"It's why we call him 'Cold Fishy' McCreedy," said Joan, making the rest laugh.

Margaret looked Foxy straight in the eye and, in her headmistress's voice, said, "May I remind you there is a war on?"

Foxy tapped on McCreedy's door, thinking not for the first time how irritated he must be at not having a secretary-receptionist. *Serves him right for his outrage that women work in the NID.* When she heard his high-pitched voice say "Come!" she opened the door and was smacked in the face by the smell of sardines in oil and blue Stilton. She took in his weasel-like face—his beady eyes, thin lips, and pointy nose.

"Yes," he said, eyeing her coldly.

"I've brought you the work on this morning's hypotheticals and a memo from Miss Robertson," said Foxy equally coldly.

McCreedy held a piece of bread upon which he had perched a sardine and a slice of Stilton. The bread dripped with the oil of the sardines. He leaned over to avoid getting any on his uniform and popped it in his mouth. He extended his other hand and snapped his fingers to indicate Foxy should hand him the pouch. This she did while wrinkling her nose at both the smell and his atrocious manners.

"By the way," said McCreedy, leaning back in his chair and wiping his fingertips and mouth on a serviette. "You should tell Miss Margaret to keep you girls in hand. I saw a group of you sitting out on the fire escape this morning. Some of you," he paused to emphasize his disgust at the break of discipline, "had your bare legs dangling over the landing."

McCreedy's office was on a floor below Room 229. He would have needed to open his window, lean out, and twist his head like a barn owl to see them. Foxy mentally ran through all the obscene comments she wanted to make. She restrained herself. "I trust you have called the military doctor?" she said coolly.

McCreedy cast her a cold glance but took the bait. "What do you mean? I'm not ill."

"Oh, sorry," said Foxy. "I was sure you needed a doctor to treat the crick in your neck and screw your eyeballs back in." She didn't wait for him to "dismiss" her. She turned on her heel and left. She showed considerable restraint and the results of generations of breeding when she did not slam the door.

She smiled happily as she remembered the incident and how Robby had laughed until tears came to his eyes when she told him about it. She felt the sting of his loss, of not having him there to remember the laughter.

She had the cab driver stop at Waite, Rose, and Parker while she went in to purchase one can of Skipper's sardines. She told the Porter at the door of the Admiralty that she wanted to see Captain McCreedy in the Royal

Navy Communications Office. The Porter remembered her from the war, exchanged a few pleasantries, had her sign the logbook, and sent her on her way with a smile. She climbed the stairs to McCreedy's office and handed his secretary, Able Seaman Rigley, the sardines along with a folded note written on her small, silver-covered pad with her propelling pencil: "With my compliments to Fishy McCreedy. Lady Butterschloss."

The clerk dutifully took the note and the canned sardines into McCreedy's office. He opened the note, read it, and went a bit pale. Most Naval officers were given nicknames, some demeaning, but in a joking kind of way. Admiral Oliver, who had been the titular commander of Room 40 early in the war, was called "Dummy" Oliver because he was so uptight, secretive, and uncommunicative. The head of Naval Intelligence, Reginald Hall, had the nickname "Blinker" because he had a chronic eye disorder. It made him blink rapidly.

McCreedy hated the nickname Fishy. He thought it was inspired by contempt, if not outright dislike, for him by the undisciplined, eccentric, and brilliant codebreakers, who could not understand the need to follow the rules or why a Lieutenant-Commander needed to remain aloof from those "under" him. *Civilians,* he thought with a mental aspersion, and not for the first time.

"Send her in," he said in his usual crisp, cold tone. When she entered, he registered the severity of her dress. His eyes were drawn to the brooch.

"Hello, Fishy," said Foxy, taking a seat, "It's been a long time." Foxy knew he had seen the brooch, and she knew he understood it. She wanted to make sure he remembered that she had been a Hat Girl, to dispel any tendency to dismiss her as just some titled Auntie, come down from the country to demand leniency for a wayward relative.

"Yes, it has," he said, eyeing her, and resenting her use of his nickname, which he thought he had heard for the last time when the civilian gang of codebreakers were sent away after the war. "What brings you here today after such a long time?"

She took in his angular face, his thin, tight lips, the receding hairline, and the dark, weasel-like eyes. His desk was clear of any paperwork and polished to a deep mahogany glow. He hadn't changed. "It's about my great-nephew, Dinny," she said and paused. "Lt. Custus, I mean. I understand you have suspended him." She aimed to catch him off guard, putting him on the back foot immediately.

If McCreedy had eyebrows, they would have shot up. "You know Lt. Custus?" he asked, trying to keep the surprise from his voice.

"Didn't you know?" she asked disingenuously, well aware he had been ignorant of it. "He is the grandnephew of my late husband, Admiral Sir Robert Paganel Butterschloss. He's been our ward since he was ten."

McCreedy took time to recover himself. His eyes fell on the can of Skipper's sardines. It rankled him. "I see," he said. "You know as well as I do that Naval discipline must be followed. I cannot show any favoritism or take his connections into account." He said this brusquely. He resented the reference to the titled aristocracy with their networks of relatives and loyalties. He had always thought that his lack of title and connections was why he was passed over for promotion.

"Yes, of course, I understand perfectly. I am not here to ask you to pull strings," said Foxy. To herself, she thought, *Up periscope.* "What is it exactly he is supposed to have done?"

"He must have told you," said McCreedy, with a hint of impatience. "Some important papers have gone missing, papers he had, and files, too, that his girlfriend may have taken." He said "girlfriend" as if he were describing something distasteful that had landed in his soup.

"You say they have 'gone missing.' That doesn't explain why you have suspended both of them," said Foxy, removing her gloves one finger at a time to indicate both calmness and calculation.

"I see he's told you about her, too. Came sniveling to you with his tail between his legs, has he?" said McCreedy, his voice rising. "Well, it won't do either of them any good. Yes, I have suspended them. For all I know, they may have stolen those documents."

"Pish-tosh," said Foxy, laying her gloves across her lap. "You know that's nonsense because Dinny reported it to you. He wouldn't have done that if he wanted to steal the documents." She was careful not to reveal that she knew they were about the *Lusitania*. She did not want McCreedy to have any more reasons to charge either Dinny or Addie with a breach in their oaths of secrecy.

"That doesn't matter one jot," said McCreedy, his voice tight with anger. "They were damned careless at a bare minimum. Unforgivable. There has to be an investigation. Rules are rules."

"Have you actually ordered that investigation?" asked Foxy cooly.

McCreedy suddenly seemed less sure of himself. "No, not yet. I've been busy."

"Of course," said Foxy. "Then, have you put forward the orders for their suspensions?"

"No. Meaning to do that today, as a matter of fact," he said in clipped tones.

Foxy clasped her hands together, leaned forward, and put one elbow on the shiny, massive desk. *Fire torpedo one!* she thought. She said in a voice that was almost a purr, "Let me tell you why you are not going to order that investigation."

"Are you threatening me?" McCreedy scoffed.

"Not at all. I am trying to protect you," she said, still purring

"Protect me? Protect me?" he said with an angry and incredulous tone. "What the hell do you think I need you to protect me from?"

"From yourself, of course," said Foxy. "If you start an investigation, you will have to tell your commanding officer. Who is it now? Chetwode? He will be quite angry at you for letting the papers disappear in the first place. Worse, he will be quite irritated that he will have to report it to his commander. Fitzy, is it? And *his* commanding officer will be quite angry at him for letting you, McCreedy, make such a mess of things. Not to mention that this will be put in the report for The First Sea Lord, Beatty, to contemplate over his morning tea and hardtack. No, McCreedy, I don't think you want that many people up the chain of command all coming down on your head for making them look so bad."

McCreedy had gone white, his jaw clenched.

"What you want to do is conduct your own investigation. Keep it within the department," said Foxy smoothly.

"Go on," said McCreedy, in a low voice that was close to a growl.

Fire torpedo two! "What is more, you want to ask Dinny and Addie for their assistance."

McCreedy looked apoplectic.

Foxy said, "If you suspend them, questions will be asked, which is exactly what you do not want. You can cut orders to give them a few days of leave. They will be back on Monday, and both of them will be very serious about finding out how those files disappeared because their reputations are at stake no less than yours." She looked at him steadily.

McCreedy took a few moments to calculate his position. He had to agree that Lady Butterschloss was offering him a way to avoid scrutiny by the command chain. He also knew that she could stir things up. She knew his superior officers personally, through her late husband and because of her own work during the war.

"I can agree to that," he said curtly. "Anything else?" he said, allowing himself a hint of sarcasm.

Fire torpedo three! Foxy said, "Yes, as a matter of fact, there is. Consider this a job interview. I want to be hired so I can assist with this investigation." She was unabashed.

"You are kidding," said McCreedy, staring at her.

He looks exactly like one of those sardines, thought Foxy. *Glassy-eyed.*

"I have never been more serious. You know I am highly skilled in intelligence matters and that I have a wide network of connections. I will be absolutely discreet to protect Dinny and Addie." She paused, "And you, of course," she added as an afterthought. "I think an assignment to the Archives would be most suitable, don't you?"

McCreedy wanted nothing more than for this irritating woman to vanish. "All right," he said. "But everything stays in-house, in this division, and comes directly to me and me alone. And," he said crossly, "you will never call me Fishy again."

Direct hits. Periscope down, thought Foxy as she gathered herself to depart. "Fishy?" she said. "I've never heard that name." And with that, she left his office, closing the door behind her.

Foxy felt so elated that she thought she might possibly be able to fly like Peter Pan. She strode easily down the street, swinging her purse by the purse strings. She was tempted to whistle. Then it struck her. She had not gotten from McCreedy what she most wanted, which was to find out what had touched him off in the first place. What had made the *Lusitania* files so important? Or was it simply that he was nothing more than a martinet who took sadistic pleasure in punishing or humiliating his subordinates by "enforcing the rules"? She was more inclined to believe the worst of him and conclude he was simply a petty tyrant. Still, she had to keep an open mind.

She wished she could tell Dinny and Addie the good news. It made her grin from ear to ear to think how overjoyed they would be. She knew they would probably still be on the road, driving to Stratford. She would call Dinny later at the White Swan.

Chapter Eight

Jealousy and Unemployment

Tris was in his office working out some figures from a test conducted on hull stresses when his C.O. called him into his office. He was introduced to a towering, stern-faced, hard-boiled MI5 agent with drooping jowls and rimless glasses. Tris never learned his name. His C.O. ordered him to go with the agent and answer all his questions. The agent took Tris to an empty room and closed the door.

"I'm here to find out what you know about why your friend Lt. Custus is so interested in the *Lusitania*." The agent had a deep, whiskey-throated voice. He sounded as if he were asking Tris to tell him why Dinny wanted to assassinate the King.

This made Tris wary and irritated. "Why would MI5 want to know about that?"

"Never mind why," said the agent. "You are under orders to answer my questions."

Tris saw no harm in answering honestly. "Lt. Custus was assigned to work out how to improve wireless communications on submarines. He was interested in knowing more about wireless transmission distances early in the war. It was only natural that he would look into the records of the *Lusitania* sinking."

The agent asked, "How much, exactly, do you know about the *Lusitania?*"

"Only what I read in the newspapers in 1915. What is this all...?"

Before he finished the sentence, the agent slammed his fist hard on the table between them. Tris flinched. "Now listen, you little pipsqueak, I know you are lying." The agent leaned over so his red face was inches from Tris's. "You are just back from Egypt on a trip with your two aunts. Why did they take you there?"

Tris felt the hot breath of this madman on his face. *Well, Agent Knuckle Dragger, you may want to eat me alive, but I don't think I'll give you the satisfaction.* He looked him straight in the eyes and said levelly, "Because they are old, love the sun that heats their bones, and are entranced with the discovery of King Tut's tomb, as is everyone else in Britain. They did not want to travel up the Nile without an escort, for obvious reasons."

Agent KD, as Tris nicknamed him, asked the same questions over and over. "What did Tris know about Dinny's work? What had his aunts told him about the Admiralty and the *Lusitania?*" Agent KD became more and more intimidating, yelling at Tris and showing crooked, yellow teeth. He did everything but slaver. As was conventional with his class and breeding, Tris had been raised to maintain a *sangfroid* no matter how great the temptation to show strong emotion. He did not so much as blink when Agent KD threatened him with a court-martial. *You are from MI5. You have no authority to order a court-martial. Go back to your rock, or wherever you came from.* Finally, frustrated by Tris's bovine calmness, Agent KD warned grimly, "It will be better for you if no one ever knows about this meeting. You are dismissed, you little toe rag."

Tris was anything but calm. He was badly shaken and confused. His first thought was of Dinny. He wanted to tell him, to warn him, although about what exactly Tris did not know. He had read the message from Dinny canceling the meeting at the Above Board. He went to the Mayfair house, but Dinny wasn't there. Tris was too restless and unnerved to sit around waiting. The interrogation got his wind up. He felt scared, but of what? *Dinny couldn't be a threat to domestic security, and neither could his aunts.* Angry at being threatened, Tris decided to go out drinking to settle himself.

Several hours later, dressed in evening wear and very drunk, Tris pushed the button for the flat where Addie and Josie lived. Addie, who had arrived home at eleven and was still awake, buzzed him up, wondering what would bring him to see her at such a late hour. When she opened the door to his knock, he nearly fell into the room. She had never seen him so drunk, or so angry.

"So, you and Dinny couldn't stay around long enough to meet me, huh? Just sent me a message and went off together. What kind of friends are you, any, any, anyhow?" His words were slurred, his eyes bloodshot, and he was unsteady on his feet.

Shocked by his anger, Addie said, "Something important came up and…"

Tris went on as if she hadn't said a word. "Yer always doin' that. I was quite put out by how you brushed me off this summer."

Addie was taken aback. She thought they had put that awkwardness aside months ago. She said, "I didn't think you were being serious."

Tris leaned close to her. "Of course, I was. Can't you tell how much I love you? How could you treat me so crool, so crool, so croo-elly?"

Addie's anger flared. "It isn't my fault, Tris. I didn't make you love me. I have never been a flirt or a tease, and you know it!"

Tris mocked Addie's voice: "'I didn't make you love me. I didn't make you love me.' W'as that got to do wis anything? The fact is, I asked you to marry me, and you brushed me off."

Addie said, " I didn't think you meant it. And even if I had, I would still have said no."

She regretted having said it as soon as she did. She was feeling put upon and defensive and quite annoyed that Tris was too drunk to reason with. She had never seen him like that. She opened the door and asked him to leave. On his way out, he put his face so close to hers, she could smell his boozy breath.

"If you choose Dinny over me, you'll be sorry," he said. "You just wait and see."

Tris would have ample time in the days ahead to contemplate with deep shame what he had said and why.

The next morning, Addie woke up early, eager to be ready for Dinny when he arrived for the drive to Stratford. She looked at herself in the mirror, determined that the day would banish care and cheer them both up. She would forget about Tris and his drunken anger. She and Dinny would forget about McCreedy until he could be dealt with properly. She declaimed to her reflection:

Think not on him till to-morrow:

I'll devise thee brave punishments for him.

Strike up, pipers.

She raised her arm with a flourish. She saw her flatmate, Josie, reflected in the mirror, leaning against the door frame to the bathroom.

Josie smiled a knowing grin. "What are you on about? It couldn't be your weekend with Dinny, could it?"

Addie blushed but only slightly. Josie did not know about the lost papers, the threatened court-martial, or that Addie was barred from the ARO. "I was quoting from the very last lines of *Much Ado*." She grinned. "The marriage scene." She wanted to divert Josie from asking any more questions about this sudden trip.

"Oh, I see," said Josie slyly. Addie and Josie met at Cambridge and became close friends as they endured the sneers, jibes, and storming of their college by undergraduates. Addie thought Josie, who studied History and Economics, was the most brilliant person she had ever met. She looked in the mirror and laughed at the skeptical expression, Josie's long, dark hair framing her face, her dark eyes sparkling, and a smile playing across her thin lips.

Josie peered closely at Addie's expression in the mirror. "Is this an Addie I see before me? The one who swore she never would marry? The one who declared solemnly that marriage is nothing but a birdcage for women?"

Addie put away her toiletry articles in a small bag and turned to leave the bathroom. She spoke in a little-girl voice, pouted, and shook her locks in imitation of a spoiled flapper with less sense than a tiny kitten climbing up a tall tree. "This is just a date to see a Shakespeare play, that's all."

Josie laughed as she always did at Addie's play-acting. "Okay, Mary Pickford. See you at the movies." She became serious, "Addie, you should know I woke up when Tris came over. I don't think I've ever known him to be that drunk. I didn't want to interrupt, but I was worried he might not go when you asked him to. I would have come out if he refused to leave."

Addie turned from the mirror and looked at her friend. "It was absolutely horrible. I've never seen him like that, either. I feel terribly guilty that I seem to have humiliated him when I turned him down. I should have known he was only pretending to be half serious about the proposal."

Josie nodded. "I thought we had all put that behind us, too, and we were friends again. But I was wrong, too. Did I not hear right, or did he threaten Dinny?" She had been struck with a pang of cold fear when she heard Tris say Addie would "be sorry" if she chose Dinny.

Addie was also unnerved by that implied threat. She tried to shake off the feeling. She said slowly, "I think it sounded worse than he meant it because he was so drunk and angry. I think all he meant was that Dinny would disappoint me, that Tris would make me happier than Dinny ever could. Or something like that."

Josie looked at her steadily. "You are probably right. Tris is so impetuous, and then he regrets what he has done. I think he will wake up this morning with a terrible headache and if he remembers what he said, feel like a damned fool." She paused. "At least, I hope so. But don't you think last night proves he's been carrying a torch for you, and it might flare again?"

Addie agreed with Josie's description of Tris's character. He was lovable because he was impetuous, wayward, and quick to apologize for any hurt he caused. "So, you think I should expect two dozen red roses, chocolate, and an abject apology?"

Josie smiled and said, "Yes, and if they come while you are gone, I get the chocolates."

"Deal," said Addie. "Do you think I should tell Dinny?"

Josie thought this over, taking into account that Tris would feel asinine when he sobered up. "I wouldn't. At least, not until you see how Tris deals with you after his behavior last night. If it is roses and chocolates, and you two patch things up, I don't see any reason to humiliate Tris again by getting Dinny upset with him. If Tris ever bullies you again, you will definitely have to tell Dinny."

Addie thought this was wise advice, not the least because she did not want to add to Dinny's worries on top of a threatened court-martial. She would wait and see how Tris behaved, but as she packed her bag, she couldn't help remembering how Foxy had pressed home questions about whether Tris could have acted on his jealousy by playing a mean trick on Dinny. Tris was impulsive. Maybe when he learned that Dinny and Addie would be working together, his jealousy flared. He knew where Dinny's office was. He might have come by to see him, found the door open, and seen the file folder on his desk. In a moment of spite, he took it, meaning to give it back to Dinny later that day when they were supposed to meet at the Above Board. He would have had to smuggle the files past the Porter, but Tris was clever enough to manage that. Addie tried to imagine Tris playing such a low prank. She couldn't see the Tris she knew being so underhanded. But honestly, the Tris who came to see her so drunk and filled with resentment was not the Tris she knew.

After Addie dressed and closed her suitcase, she joined Josie for tea and toast in the kitchen. "I've packed some sandwiches and filled the Thermos with tea," she said.

"Oh, Josie, you didn't need to do that. But thanks," said Addie.

"I know, but I wanted you to have a good time. Don't worry about me," she said, sighing as if she meant sorrowful self-pity. "I'll be all right. After all, I have a 'date' too."

Addie looked at her in disbelief. "Seriously?"

"Sure," said Josie. "With old Professor Arensdorf this morning to discuss my dissertation on unemployment and monetary policy."

Addie smiled. "Fascinating," she said with dry amusement. With a jarring self-reflection, she realized she might soon join the already swollen ranks of the unemployed. She looked at Josie, "In all seriousness, I admire your efforts to end this plague of unemployment. This is not the 'land fit for heroes' the veterans were promised."

Professor Josef Arensdorf was in his sixties, with a high-domed, bald head and pale skin. He wore wire-rimmed glasses perched on his long nose. When the war broke out, he was a professor of economics at the University of Utrecht. He accepted a position at the London School of Economics to get his family away. In the end, he couldn't protect them. He lost them to influenza at the end of the war. He was quite alone, now. His colleagues said he was married to his work. He encouraged that.

Books were shelved two deep and lined all the walls of his office. He was wearing his waistcoat. His jacket hung on a wooden coat rack. He was concentrating on what he was writing on a sheet of white paper. He took his watch from his waistcoat pocket. It was attached to the middle buttonhole of his waistcoat by a gold fob or chain, a gift from his wife when they married. He flipped open the watch cover and saw the time. His student Josie would be arriving soon. He carefully slid the paper under the desk pad, stood, put on his jacket, and glanced quickly in the small mirror that hung on the coat rack to make sure his collar and tie were properly arranged. He would have enough time for their meeting, a trip to the florist, and then on to the Admiralty Record Office.

"Come in, come in," he said genially to Josie, helping her off with her coat. "I have prepared our tea."

The two of them got along famously ever since Josie first met him when she started her advanced degree. She had been immediately impressed by Arensdorf when he said not only "I know your father," but also, "and I very much admire your mother's work as well." Josie's father, Jonathan Farnsworth, was a Liberal member of parliament who helped formulate significant welfare reforms passed in 1906. Her mother, Octavia, had been an activist in Emmeline Pankhurst's branch of the suffrage movement. She ran a foundation for the educational support of the children of veterans who died in the war. In a very real sense, Josie's interest in politics and the economy was inevitable.

After he poured the tea, he settled back in his chair. "I think you are making excellent progress on your thesis. You have a quick mind, and your writing is exemplary. I am sure your committee will agree." He spoke in a warm accent, with rolling "r"s, flat vowels, and hard consonants.

Josie smiled, "You have been such a wonderful mentor, Professor Arensdorf. I cannot thank you enough."

Thank me after you receive honours," said Arensdorf, smiling broadly. He set down his cup and saucer, signaling it was time to work. "I would like you now," said Professor Arensdorf, "to consider two competing theories of unemployment. You are well aware that since 1920, it has fluctuated between nineteen percent and nine percent." He was lapsing into the voice he used in the large lecture hall. Josie dutifully took notes. "On the one hand, you have the view of my colleague, Professor Edwin Cannan, who thinks unemployment and rising prices are necessary at the moment to ensure a sound currency."

Josie smiled inwardly. *Should I tell Arensdorf that the graduate students call him 'Loose' Cannan for his willingness to completely ignore the damage to the working class his policies would cause?*

"John Maynard Keynes, who, as you know, is perhaps the most influential economic theorist of this decade, assailed Cannon and others like him in *A Tract on Monetary Reform.* I would like your views on which of the two—Cannon or Keynes—makes the soundest arguments for a stable currency and addressing unemployment."

Josie looked up from her notebook. "Would you agree that I ought to compare their ideas about the causes of the current high unemployment? Cannon thinks it is just part of a normal business cycle. Keynes sees it as deriving from the effects of the war on the stability of currency. I'd like to include his prediction that the terms of the Treaty of Versailles created the conditions for the next war.

Arensdorf nodded his approval. "Yes, of course. And by the way, this is just a thought, I wonder if you could include Keynes's speech to the Liberal Party last December." He paused again, choosing his words carefully. "I would like to know your father's views on that speech. Not," he said in a rush, "that his thoughts should outweigh your own

Josie tried not to show her surprise and pique. She always felt overshadowed by her father and dreaded the thought that his position and influence would affect her professors in any way. She looked up from her notebook. "I can ask him," she replied evenly, "but I don't know that he would be very interested in taking the time. If he is, I assume I can determine what, if anything, I think is important in terms of supporting my thesis." She paused. "I don't want anyone on the committee to think I use him as a crutch."

"No, no, not at all," said Arensdorf hurriedly. "In fact, leave it out entirely, and we can simply have a nice discussion about it at our next conference. Over our usual tea. Just as a matter of interest."

Josie was relieved. "Of course," she said. "I am sure he will be flattered by your interest," she said, wholly unconvinced that her father would care one bit.

Arensdorf took out his watch and flipped open the cover. "I am afraid I must cut our meeting a bit short today. I am going to the Admiralty Records Office, where I have been working for the past several weeks."

"Oh," said Josie, starting to pack away her notebook, "you must have seen my flatmate. She's been working on a research assignment there for several weeks. Her name is Addie Gold."

"I have seen a young researcher there, yes. And she is your friend?"

"Yes. I cannot tell you what she is researching. That's very hush, hush. I know she would be pleased to meet you. She has heard me talk about you."

"Well, perhaps I shall introduce myself today." Arensdorf knew perfectly well she would not be there. He had been there yesterday when the discovery that certain papers were missing suddenly exploded into a crisis of confidence in Addie's reliability.

"Oh, no. She won't be there today. She's taken the day off to drive to Stratford with a friend to see *Much Ado About Nothing*," said Josie, who was busy gathering her things and did not notice Arensdorf's bemused expression.

To himself, he thought, *Addie seems to have an ironic sense of humor—going off to see 'Much Ado About Nothing' when she is in—what's the expression?—hot water. And she doesn't seem to have told her friend, Josie, about being suspended. Either that, or Josie is an accomplished liar, which I wouldn't have thought to be the case.*

After Josie left, he took the paper from under his desk pad, folded it, put it in an envelope, addressed it to a post office box, put on a stamp, and licked the envelope. He put on his overcoat and Homburg hat, slipped the envelope into his inside breast pocket, left his office—carefully locking his door—and went down the staircase.

I must be careful about asking Josie what her father thinks of the Liberal Party's economic plans. She was irritated with me today. She had a right to be. I shall be much more nuanced in the future.

Arensdorf dropped the envelope in a postal collection box and looked forward to the fifteen-minute walk to his usual florist, Roses' of Bloomsbury. Its owner, Betty Rose, was an apple dumpling of a woman, in her sixties, and a widow. He knew her and her husband from 1904, when they emigrated from Riga to Utrecht, then to London in 1908. When the Arensdorfs arrived in 1914, they renewed their friendship. Sadly, Betty—her Anglicized name—lost her husband to influenza about the same time as Arensdorf lost his family. They remained close, bonded by their shared history.

"Good afternoon," said Arensdorf, opening the door to the small shop and tipping his hat to Betty. He breathed in deeply the airy, fresh, delightful scents.

Betty was short and plump, her white hair like a corona around her face, a twinkle always in her eyes. She smiled broadly and replied in Yiddish, "*A gutn tog. Vi geyt es?*"

"*Gutn tog,*" replied Arensdorf. "I am very well, thank you. And you? All is well with you?"

"Yes, I am doing quite well." She spoke in a lilting, Yiddish accent. "There is a big wedding coming up, and I am kept very busy getting the flowers ready. I am swimming in flowers, drowning in them." She laughed at her own complaint.

"I hope you can make me a small bouquet. Just a few Canterbury bells and bluebells," said Arensdorf.

"Yes, of course, for you, always," said Betty. "A little thank you bouquet, is it?" Betty had taught Arensdorf the code of flowers.

"As you say," said Arensdorf. "Bluebells for 'thank you' and Canterbury bells for 'a constant friend.' Do I have that right?"

"Yes, perfect. Any card?"

"Of course, of course." He took a pen from his pocket and wrote, "With deep respect, Iona Mink." He handed the card to Betty.

She read it and smiled. "One of your better ones," she said. "Your friends must think you are quite the jokester."

He nodded in acknowledgment. "Yes," he said. "They have gotten used to my puns by now. So used to them, as a matter of fact, they complain if I don't sign my card with one."

He gave her the address, paid for the flowers, and promised to return soon. Wishing Betty a good day, he took a short walk to the Russell Square underground station for his trip to the ARO.

Chapter Nine

An Officer, A Gentleman, and a Spy

William wore his uniform because it was required at the Naval and Military Club. He arranged to meet Clive Edgerton there with the hope Edgerton would use his contacts to find out what was behind the theft of the files from the ARO. They had been close friends since 1916, when they both worked in Naval Intelligence. After William's injury, his father urged him to put his considerable talents to work in the Naval Intelligence Division as the best use of his studies in International Law, French, and German. Accordingly, when his wound healed, William became a liaison officer between the head of Military Intelligence MI1b, Major Hay, and the head of Naval Intelligence, "Blinker" Hall. Clive was a Naval attaché in Berlin when the war broke out. When he returned to the UK, he kept much of what he did to himself, but William knew that Clive worked for both Naval intelligence and the Foreign Service. As Clive often joked, "I was an officer, a gentleman, and a spy." He was now working for MI5, which meant he put his considerable charm and geniality to work ferreting out internal threats to the UK.

William entered the capacious Gallery room and seated himself in a comfortable armchair facing the six Palladian windows overlooking the lush back garden. An ornate, gleaming crystal chandelier hung from the domed ceiling. His feet rested on an Aubusson rug, which protected the polished parquet floor. He never tired of the Naval and Military Club, but he always felt a bit out of place in the luxury evocative of a past era.

Clive entered the room, six feet tall, the epitome of aristocratic bearing. His uniform was tailored to fit his trim build like a warm embrace. His brass buttons were so polished a dragonfly would be startled to see its reflection in them; his tie was perfectly knotted, his shoes were so well polished they shone with the light of the chandeliers. He moved with the relaxed, unassuming grace of a cat. His sharp jaw, handsome, regular features, and dark eyes made him a magnet for women, especially when he was in uniform. William knew that behind the façade of charm and wit, there was a highly intelligent mind.

He smiled with real affection when he saw William. "Hello, Crumpet, how are you?" They shook hands energetically. William had earned the name Crumpet one morning after a night on the tiles when Clive challenged him to a crumpet-eating contest in the wee hours of the morning at a tiny bakery and tea shop. William stuffed himself with so many that he both won the bet and paid for it. He felt like a sack of wet cement with a headache the rest of the day. It was the first of many misadventures in eating he had with Clive.

When the waiter served them the coffee they ordered, Clive asked, "To what do I owe this pleasure?"

"I've a problem you might be able to help me solve. It has to do with Foxy's nephew, well, grandnephew, Dinny. You remember him?"

Clive had been part of the circle of friends that included Foxy and her husband. "Yes, of course. What's he doing now?"

He's a design engineer working on improving submarine wireless transmissions," said William, knowing he could speak freely to Clive.

Clive looked interested. "That's very specialized. Lots of Navy brass are opposed to developing submarines. With all the budget cuts, they must have to beg for every scrap of funding thrown their way."

William nodded. "That's my impression. At any rate, they are lucky to have Dinny. He's very good and quite keen. He was sent over to the ARO to research the wireless intercepts from German submarines during the war, and he decided to find out about the signal intelligence when the *Lusitania* was sunk. The reports were stolen from his desk."

Clive's eyebrows shot up. "You interest me mightily, Crumpet."

William replied, "At the same time, all the files of the wireless transmissions related to the sinking went missing. Dinny worked with a friend of his named Addie, who also has clearance. She works at GCCS on a project requiring her to research at the ARO. She agreed to take a look at the transcripts. When she requested them, they were nowhere to be found."

"And these two disappearances happened the same day?" asked Clive.

"Presumably, although according to the librarian, no one had ever requested the transcripts, so it isn't possible to know when they disappeared," replied William.

Clive took out a gold, engraved cigarette case and matching lighter. He offered a cigarette to William, who declined and reached for his pipe. Clive lit a cigarette, took a long draw, and said, "So, a coincidence? Or a conspiracy? Or some kind of prank?"

William lit his pipe. "I thought it might be a prank, too, but Dinny and Addie are both adamant that their friends would not do anything so serious just to play a practical joke."

"Let's say for the moment that is the case. I wouldn't rule it out entirely. It depends on whether someone turns up and says, 'Oh, by the way, I slipped into your office and took this file. So sorry.' Highly unlikely, but still a possibility."

"It has gone well beyond an incident awaiting a simple solution. Dinny is threatened with court-martial, and Addie has been barred from the ARO on suspicion of some kind of espionage," said William.

"Well, well," said Clive. "That sounds like the kind of overreaction that earned us an empire. Suspicious in and of itself, I would say. Who cooked that one up?"

"McCreedy," said William dryly, anticipating Clive's reaction.

"That dolt," scoffed Clive. "He couldn't tell espionage from a blancmange."

"Precisely. Foxy will be discussing the matter with him today."

Clive grinned his dazzling grin. "She'll make mincemeat out of him. How is she doing, by the way?"

"She's kept herself to herself at Butterschloss. To tell the truth, she's been in the doldrums. Too many sad memories to brood on, and a feeling that she is useless now that the war is over, and women are surplus to need. As a matter of fact, I've been holed up at Penningborne. Too many memories of the war, and wondering what it was all for. But I must say, Foxy is charged up over this. She lost Timmy and Robby. She is determined that no harm will come to Dinny. She is like a she-bear when it comes to protecting him. She is also very fond of Addie and thinks it is ridiculous she has been implicated in any of this."

"And you? Is that why you've come from your lair at Penningborne?" While he had never said a word to William about it, Clive was well aware of William's affection for Foxy. He wouldn't be much of a spy if he weren't.

"Yes," said William. "She asked for my help. She is staying at the Chelsea house while we plan our campaign." He saw Clive's expression of curiosity. "As a guest, of course. Nothing more. Put your antennae down, Spymaster."

As if. Then he turned serious. "It seems to me, Crumpet, that we need to find out who doesn't want anyone poking about in the scorched remains of the *Lusitania*. And that means someone or other is afraid those ashes might not be well and truly out, that there may be a dangerous spark or two that could ignite and burn someone badly."

"Not your best extended metaphor, but it will do," said William. "Foxy and I thought the same thing. We tend to dismiss the idea. Who is there to care? The inquiry found the Germans guilty and cleared Captain Turner of any charges of incompetence. The American civil inquiry for damages against Cunard came to the same conclusion. It happened almost a decade ago. What is there that would lead anyone to steal the records and frame Dinny and Addie into the bargain?

Clive signaled the waiter for two more cups of coffee. "I think I have the glimmer of an idea. I happen to be invited to a dinner party tonight. Blinker will be there. I'll sound him out with my usual deft touch."

William was taken aback momentarily, although on reflection, he realized he shouldn't have been. Clive had worked closely with Admiral Sir William Reginald Hall, the shrewd director of the Naval Intelligence Division. "Is a dinner party the best time and place to approach him?"

Clive took a sip of his coffee and airily brushed aside this concern. "It's one of those dinner parties where guests play bridge after dinner. Ethel—his wife, if you recall—is an avid player, but Blinker despises the game as do I. I am fairly confident I can find some time alone with him for smokes and a brandy."

"But he hasn't had anything to do with the Navy since the end of the war. He's been a member of Parliament and a big noise in the Conservative party, hasn't he?"

"Yes, indeed. But he could be a valuable source of information about the sinking of the *Lusitania* and what about it is still hush, hush."

"I still don't see why he would open up to you. Were you two that intimate?" asked William, who had never been received by Hall with anything other than formality and crisply issued orders.

Clive leaned into the deep back of the armchair. "I did quite a few off-the-record favors for him during the war."

William sat back in his armchair, knowing he was about to hear one of Clive's stories. Clive was a born storyteller, especially gifted at imitating voices and intonation.

"In the winter of 1915, Hall called me into his office. I don't know about you, but his face reminded me of a Peregrine falcon. Those keen, piercing eyes would have troubled my soul, I can tell you, except for the chronic medical condition that made him constantly blink. And then there was his beak-like nose. You know, he could sit very still, contemplating a visitor as if waiting to pounce on quivering prey. Most unnerving. He was the shrewdest and most cunning individual I've ever known, and a man of fiercely held beliefs. If he wanted something done, he would justify any means to obtain it.

'What do you know about the Young Turks?' Hall asked me. I recognized this as a way to get the conversation started. We both knew the answer perfectly well. They were the revolutionary constitutionalists in Turkey who forced the restoration of the constitution in '08. Their party splintered, and the right wing-nationalists took over absolute control and forged an alliance with Germany.

Clive tapped out an ash in the brass standing ashtray. "Blinker asked me, 'What if I were to tell you we had a chance to bring Turkey over to our side and gain control of the Dardanelles?' Of course, I told him it could change the course of the war. Certainly, shorten it if not end it."

Clive leaned forward and said to William, looking him in the eyes. "Blinker said the damnedest thing. He said, 'I agree. I have personally guaranteed millions of pounds for the surrender of the Dardanelles and the German destroyer, *Goeben.*"

Startled, William asked, "What did you say to that?"

"I took a moment to consider. I asked him, 'What does it mean that *you* have personally guaranteed it?' Blinker was blunt and unhesitating. 'I mean that no one higher than me knows about this. I am sure the Government will be quite pleased if we bring it off. By 'we' I mean our operatives in conversation with members of the Turkish government."

"Naturally, I was taken aback by the audacity of Hall in negotiating with an enemy power without authorization. I thought it was a devilishly delightful operation. Blinker asked me to liaise with his operatives in Turkey."

"And you said yes, if I know you," said William.

"You know me only too well. As you can imagine, Crumpet, there was much to-ing and fro-ing. The plans for the Naval attack on the Dardanelles were being drawn up by The First Lord of the Admiralty and the First Sea Lord." William's face turned pale, and he clenched his jaw. "In March, we put the pressure on. We let the Turks know we would be lowering our price. We should have been *raising* the offer, but we wanted them to know they needed to act. We offered half-a-million pounds for the Dardanelles and the same for the *Goeben.* The next day, we lowered the offer on the destroyer to one hundred thousand. It looked promising, I must say. A meeting was set for March 15 in the neutral port of Dedeagach. But then everything went bust.

"I guessed that," said William, dryly.

"Yes, well, you would. I know you went through Hell out there," said Clive. "Blinker called me in and said he had just received an intercept from the Kaiser that he had to show First Sea Lord Fisher immediately, and he wanted me to come along. We found "Jackie" Fisher in Churchill's room. There they were, the two misguided sods who planned the attack on the Dardanelles, standing in front of the fireplace.

"'First Sea Lord,' said Blinker to Fisher, 'we have just received this.' It was a message from the Kaiser to a German officer in Turkey, indicating the Germans were short of ammunition in Turkey, but the Turks were not to know. Fisher waved it over his head. If he hadn't been seventy-four, I think he would have danced the Sailors' Hornpipe. 'I'll go through tomorrow.' Churchill was equally thrilled. He snatched the telegram from Fisher, read it again, and said, 'That means they've come to the end of their ammunition!' 'Tomorrow,' said Fisher again. 'We shall probably lose six ships, but I'm going through.'"

William felt his stomach lurch. He took a deep breath and exhaled slowly. Clive was so caught up in his story, he didn't notice. William was on the deck of the *Soudan,* watching Walter's body slide into the sea in its little canvas shroud.

Clive continued to recreate the scene. "Churchill said, 'Then get the orders out.' He invited Fisher to sit down at his long table. Fisher put pen to paper and began writing. Blinker cast me a glance, acknowledging defeat, and we turned to leave the room. Churchill turned to Blinker and asked for an update on our operations in Turkey. To his credit, Blinker did the honorable thing. 'Sir, I've personally guaranteed the Turks a considerable amount of money for the surrender of the Dardanelles and the *Goeben.*' A dead silence fell in the room. It was pin-drop time. Churchill stared at Blinker. 'How much?' he asked.

'Three million pounds with authorization to go to four million,' replied Blinker, suddenly realizing how ridiculously high the figures sounded.

Churchill frowned. 'Who authorized this?'

'I did,' replied Blinker.

'But the Cabinet surely knows about it,' said Churchill, becoming querulous, touchy at the idea that the Cabinet would know about it before he did.

'No, it does not,' said Hall with remarkable composure. 'But if we were to get peace, or if we were to get a peaceful passage for that amount, I imagine they would be glad enough to pay.' Of course, he was pushing the bounds of insubordination, but he was always a high-flyer.

Churchill stared at Hall. Then he turned and expostulated to Fisher. 'Do you hear what this man has done? He's told his people they can go up to four million to buy a peaceful passage! On his own!'

'What!' cried Fisher, leaping from his chair. 'Four million? No, no, I tell you I'm going through tomorrow, or as soon as the preparations can be completed.' He gave Hall a direct order. 'Cable at once to stop all negotiations. All. No. Let the offer for the *Goeben* remain. But nothing else. We're going through."

Clive sighed and shook his head in resignation. "With that, Blinker and I left the room. I drafted the cable, and Blinker signed it. The thing is that the meeting at Dedeagach was already over by the time it arrived. It killed any chances of further negotiation and made the Turks deeply distrustful of us."

Clive looked at his friend. "Here, let me order you a brandy. You look as if you need it."

William sat rigid and pale. *What is this? Nightmares of the Dardanelles Week?* He took the proffered brandy and sipped it slowly. He struggled for composure. He smiled at his friend, "I am fine, or will be. Sometimes it comes over me like this. It soon passes," he lied. He dreaded what dreams would trouble his sleep that night. He took another sip of his brandy and forced himself to return from the past to the problem at hand. "I can see why you think it would be useful to approach Blinker. He must have relied on you for more than one wily operation he cooked up." He held up his glass in a toast. He willed his hand not to shake. "Here's to you calling in a few debts tonight that will help us find out why the Hell anyone cares about the *Lusitania*." Clive clinked his glass with William's and said, "I can make an educated guess."

"Go on," said William, "don't keep me in suspense."

"Let's have lunch," said Clive.

"Ah, yes," replied William, "Clive Edgerton, the one and only, known as a gentleman, an officer, a spy with a mind like a steel trap and an appetite like a man with a hollow leg."

Clive ordered his driver to take them to *Vilner's* on Brick Lane, where Yiddish was spoken more often than English. William looked with eager eyes at the large, steaming bowl of chicken soup with *lockshen*—an egg noodle—bits of chicken, and carrots. With it came his salted beef sandwich, stacked about three inches high with beef, and a pot of kosher mustard. His appetite by that time was keen. He took a spoonful of the soup and couldn't help rolling his eyes with pleasure. It was hearty, rich, and flavorful.

Clive smiled, "I take it you are glad I suggested we meet here."

"Indeed," said William. "But you didn't bring me here for the food."

Clive hesitated a moment. "No, I knew there would be so much noise here we wouldn't be overheard." He paused. "There is a great deal of talk just now about Winnie running for office again.

Now it was William's turn to be surprised. "So soon?" Churchill had been defeated in the 1922 election and again in 1923, both times as a member of minority parties.

"Yes, and the word is that he will cross the aisle and rejoin the Conservatives."

William raised his eyebrows. Churchill had been elected as a Conservative in 1900, but crossed the aisle to the Liberals in 1904. "Do the Conservatives want him back?"

Clive smiled a sardonic smile. "Any number of Conservatives would prefer not to have him. But he has made a deal they can't refuse. He is putting together a block of Liberal anti-socialist MPs who will vote with the Conservatives in Parliament until the next General Election. In exchange, he has a guarantee that no Conservative candidates will stand against them. Churchill is furious that the Liberals support the Labour Party."

"He has made no secret of that," said William, chuckling. "I've read his attacks against socialism and the Labour Party in the *Sunday Chronicle.*

Clive nodded agreement. "You should have heard Winnie in May at the Conservative Party meeting in Liverpool. It was the first time he addressed a Conservative audience in twenty years, mind you. He called the PM a "'political cuckoo…strutting about in borrowed plumes.'" He was in his usual form, and the crowd ate it up."

"How many were there?" asked William.

"About five thousand," replied Clive. William was impressed.

Finished with his soup, William tackled the sandwich. This required concentration to get one's mouth open wide enough to take a bite, and chewing the stack of beef demanded his full attention. At last, he said, "But what makes you think this has anything to do with the *Lusitania* files?"

"There were rumors circulating in MI1b during the war that there was more to the sinking of the *Lusitania* than the public was told and that it would blacken Winnie's name were it to become known."

"But surely," said William after washing down the salted beef with a swig of ale, "if anything were to be a dark cloud hanging over him from that time, it would be the disaster at the Dardanelles."

Clive smiled urbanely, pushed his plate away, and leaned back in his chair, cocking his elbow against the back. Blue smoke curled from his cigarette. "He seems to have made every effort to make that problem go away. Have you read his history, *The World Crisis*? No? It was published last year. The timing seems significant if he is determined to get back into Parliament. He puts the failure to press the attack at the Dardanelles onto Admiral Fisher. Claims Jackie was out of his wits at the time."

William said, "But from what you said to me at the Club, Fisher was determined to see the plan through."

Clive nodded. "Jackie blew hot and cold, to be honest, but he certainly supported the plan when I was in the room. Anyway, Winnie has written extensively about the Dardanelles and Gallipoli Campaigns—he blames that failure on Kitchener—so it is now a matter of controversy. I mean, the history is out in the open. It is history as told by Winnie, of course, and it will be the subject of debate from now until the crack of doom, but it *is* a matter of debate."

"But?" said William, anticipating there was more.

Clive leaned forward to make sure William could hear him. "The same cannot be said of the *Lusitania*. The case, if there is one that looks bad for

Winnie, has never been put before the public. There were some suspicions at the time. He skips over it in his history. He strongly implies that the fault was with Captain Turner, just as he did then."

"Turner was exonerated, but Winnie persists in placing the blame on his shoulders. Is that what you are saying?" said William, who also leaned forward to be sure he caught Clive's words over the loud hubbub.

"I am saying," said Clive, "that if there were more to it than an error in judgment on the part of the Captain, it wouldn't do Winnie any good to have it come out just before he is trying to regain his seat in Parliament and change his party again. He might be accused of gross negligence if the Admiralty could have done more to protect the *Lusitania*, and of being a downright, self-serving scoundrel if he were exposed for trying to cover up what really happened."

"I see," said William, soberly.

"I am not sure you have the big picture, old chum," said Clive, trying and failing to sound unassuming. "This outrage over the Campbell prosecution is just the tip of the iceberg. There are wheels within wheels to get Labour out and the Conservatives back into power by calling for a General Election very soon."

"The Campbell prosecution was quite a cock up by the Labour Party," said William. He had followed the story of a letter printed in the Communist paper *Worker's Weekly*, a paper with a very small circulation, edited by John Ross Campbell. The anonymous letter called upon soldiers to vow not to fire upon workers, whether in war or during civil unrest. The letter was seen as incitement to mutiny, and Campbell was arrested under the orders of the Attorney General Patrick Hastings.

"Hastings was certainly too hasty," said William, smiling ironically at his own pun. "From what I heard at the Club, Hastings had second thoughts when he learned that Campbell had not written the letter, was only the temporary editor, was a highly decorated war hero, and that his arrest had caused a loud outcry from Labour supporters. When Hastings told this to the PM, he very reluctantly agreed to withdraw the prosecution of Campbell."

Clive tapped his ash into the ashtray on the table. "Yes, and as you know, that blunder set off a firestorm in the Conservative press. The Conservative MPs saw their chance, and over the past several weeks have accused MacDonald of being soft on communism."

William shook his head. "Yes, I know, even though MacDonald has always been a strenuous anti-communist. The Communist Party assails him for being nothing more than a Capitalist."

"Don't think the matter is over," said Clive quietly.

"What are you saying? The Campbell Affair will be used as a pretext to call for a General Election?" asked William.

Clive nodded ever so slightly. "You have to understand that there are powerful forces gathering. So be careful." He took a slow drag on his cigarette, blew out the smoke, and stubbed the cigarette in the ashtray. "That is all I can tell you."

William realized it wasn't any easier to digest what Clive was telling him than it was his heavy lunch. He looked upon the remaining half of his sandwich. It stared back in silent challenge. *"Eat me if you dare, human!"*

The waiter appeared with the check. He stared disapprovingly at the uneaten half of the sandwich. "You're going to let that go to waste?" he said disparagingly, as if admonishing a little boy who would not clean his plate. "You do realize there are people starving in the Volga region?"

"Then, wrap it up and send it to them," thought William. He recognized the sudden flare of anger that plagued him since the war. He allowed himself just enough condescension to match the waiter's rudeness. "Perhaps you will enjoy eating it," he said mildly.

The waiter stared at him coldly. Then he shouted over his shoulder, *"Bloom, dem mentsh vil mir tsu esn zayn skraps."* ["Bloom, this guy wants me to eat his scraps."]

Bloom shouted back, *"Punkt vi ale kapitalists. Zey esn vi kings aun varfn us di skraps vi hint."* ["Just like all capitalists. They eat like kings and throw us the scraps like dogs."]

The waiter stared at William with glittering eyes. William's German fluency meant he understood the Yiddish. Feeling foolish for creating a scene, William said he would take it with him. The waiter returned with the change and some waxed paper.

William looked at Clive ruefully. "Sorry about that," he said.

"Think nothing of it, old boy," said Clive. "He had it coming."

Clive and William parted at the door to the deli. William felt bloated, uncomfortable, and dyspeptic. He was concerned about his sudden irritability and worried about what dark place in his unconscious had given rise to his spiteful indifference to the famine in the Volga, never mind his snide suggestion to the waiter. William typically hid his gloom and the dark anger that sat like a desiccated seed inside his soul.

He decided to walk off his mood and his indigestion. He ambled the short distance to St. Matthew's Church gardens, where he sat down on a bench. He knew this area had once been a refuge for Huguenots fleeing persecution in France, just as now it was a refuge for Eastern European Jews.

William was unaware of being followed by the ugliest bulldog he had ever seen. He became aware of it now. It was reddish brown and white. It stood solidly on its four feet, mouth hanging open, tongue lolling, and drooling. It had an impressive barrel chest and protruding lower teeth. Its squashed, wrinkled face looked as if it had run full speed into a brick wall. Two heavily lidded amber eyes stared intently at William. About the time William began to fear an attack by a rabid and powerful beast, it began to whimper and whine, and move restlessly from one foot to another.

"What is it?" asked William, cautiously. Then he remembered the sandwich he had wrapped and tucked in his trouser pocket. He reached for it, pulled it out, and saw the dog was agitated in anticipation, with great streams of drool coming from its mouth. The dog must have followed the scent. He placed the sandwich on the ground. The dog eagerly devoured it.

William smiled. No salt beef for the starving in the Volga. None for the surly Communist waiter. But at least it would satisfy a hungry dog. He was wondering if he should take the dog home with him, knowing that Murky would be deeply offended. Then, he heard a little boy's voice, "*Ez er is! Ez er is!*" The boy came running up to the dog. It jumped up on the boy and gave him a very wet lick. The boy was accompanied by a young, dark-haired girl of about fourteen. "Excuse me, Mister," she said in accented English. "We don't mean to bother you, but that is my brother's dog. He has been very sad because it ran away from us and got lost."

"Not at all," said William, standing and smiling. "I just gave him some of my beef sandwich. I am glad you have found him."

"Say thank you to the kind man," said the girl.

The boy held the squirming dog and looked at William with intense, dark eyes. "Thank you very much, Mister," he said solemnly.

"You take good care of him now," said William. He left the two, playing with the dog. He noticed he felt better, less heavy and bloated, less troubled by thoughts of a world filled with nothing but past and pending horrors.

Chapter Ten

Addie Was a Careful Girl

Dinny and Addie cruised along the country roads in his burgundy Morris Oxford two-seater. They were nearing Stratford. The sky was clear, bright blue, and the sun was shining. They were singing "Carrie," from Noel Coward's hit musical *London Calling*, changing "Carrie" to "Addie":

> Addie was a careful girl,
> Quite a little cultured pearl,
> The teachers all adored her, and the pupils did the same,
> At every sort of girlish sport, she quickly made a name,
> And nobody suspected that she played a double game,
> Addie was a careful girl.

They had just started raucously on the refrain when Dinny became aware that the car behind them was honking its horn, blinking its lights, and the driver was waving at them.

"What's all this about?" he said.

"Maybe he wants to overtake us," said Addie, and was about to start singing again, when she noticed something she could not comprehend. A car wheel was rolling along on its own on her side of the car.

"Dinnie, look!" she shouted, startled.

"What the hell," he said, gaping at it. The wheel sped ahead. He registered that it was a wheel off his car. At the same moment, the wheel hit a pothole and careened in front of the Morris.

"Hold on!" he yelled, and his left hand shot out to protect Addie.

"Shan't!" replied Toad, with great spirit. "What is the meaning of this gross outrage? I demand an instant explanation."

Dinny's eyes fluttered open. He saw his Great Aunt, seated, and reading aloud to him.

"Auntie Em," he said. "What…" His words were cut short by a spasm of searing pain in his head and another down his left side.

"Lie still," said Foxy gently. "You were in a terrible car accident. You have been in a coma for two days." She blinked back tears. "I was reading from one of your favorite books as a child."

"Was it *Wind in the Willows?* I was having a dream about Toad in driving goggles."

"Yes," said Foxy, smiling. "I thought reading you a familiar story about cars would help bring you around. I wanted to stimulate your prefrontal cortex."

Dinny smiled weakly but with real affection at his great-aunt. *Leave it to her to invent her own cure for a coma.* "Toad was a terrible driver," he said, and the question about his own driving was implied.

"Yes, his friends had to put a stop to it," she paused, then grasped the implication. "No, Dinny, this accident was not your fault. You differ from Toad in that regard, and for that I am deeply grateful. Do you remember anything that happened?"

Dinny closed his eyes and tried to remember. His eyes snapped open. "Addie, is she…?"

"She is fine. She is just down the hall. William is with her. She has a dislocated finger and a bump on her head. The doctor assures us she will recover with no complications. You are the one we have all been a bit worried about. The doctors had no idea when you would come out of your coma."

"Hence Toad and his driving goggles," said Dinny, smiling.

"Yes," said Foxy, "I bought it at a treasure of a second-hand bookstore I found here on the High Street. I wanted to hurry things along a bit. I was getting impatient with how long you were comatose." She knew her effort to hide her worry would not fool Dinny.

"Where am I?" asked Dinny.

"You are in the Warwick Hospital with a concussion and several broken ribs. The doctor said that once you came out of your coma, you would be fine, but you will need to rest for about six weeks until your ribs heal."

They heard the swish of the starched, white apron before they saw the nurse. "Morning visiting hours are over," she said. "Patient needs his rest."

"Yes, of course," said Foxy. She leaned over and gave Dinny a gentle kiss on the cheek. "William and I will be back this evening."

As she left the ward, she spoke quietly to the Sister on duty. "You will be sure to tell Dr. Collard that Dinny is awake now and seems to remember the accident."

"Yes, I shall," said the Sister, using her crisp, professional voice. Then, more gently, she said, "He will be relieved to hear it."

Foxy nodded her thanks. She saw William coming down the corridor from Addie's room. "How is she today?"

They had taken the earliest train after the call from the Warwick police station in the early evening on Friday. Since arriving, they had either been at the hospital or trying to grab some rest in their rooms at the Royal Arms. They had eaten quick meals at a pub near the hospital.

"Her head hurts a bit, but that's to be expected. Her finger is fine. She is a very, very lucky young woman," he said.

"The same is true for Dinny," said Foxy, grimly. "He came out of his coma while I was with him."

"Why, that's wonderful," said William, smiling with relief. "The doctors thought it might be weeks or months."

"Yes," she said, managing a bit of a smile, too. "He is lucid and alert and remembers the accident. His first concern was for Addie."

"And she has been asking about him since yesterday," said William. Noticing that Foxy looked positively haggard, he said, "Why don't we have a decent meal for once. We should keep up our strength."

"Good idea," she nodded. "Then, let's go talk to the police. We only know what the officer told me on the phone. One of the wheels came off the car. Most peculiar, to say the least."

Several hours later, they were shown into the office of Inspector Lynch. He was in his early forties, broad-shouldered, straight-backed, with deep-set dark eyes. He was stout, and his neck bulged slightly over the high collar of his uniform. He was delighted when William offered him his Capstan Medium Navy Cut pouch. The mood became informal, even congenial, as blue smoke arose from their pipes.

"How are the two patients?" asked Lynch. "They were in bad shape when the ambulance took them." He spoke with the clipped consonants and nasal vowels of the West Midlands. "Terrible, it was."

"They are both coming along fine," said Foxy. "We have been so worried. This is the first opportunity we have had to talk with you to find out what happened."

"Yes, of course," said Lynch. "Fortunately, we have a witness. Dr. Collard happened to be coming along behind them when he saw the back wheel come off on the passenger side. He said he blinked his lights, honked his horn, waved, and hollered, but there was just not enough time to warn them. The wheel went spinning along, and then it must have hit something in the road. It bounced in front of them. It looked like Mr. Custus swerved to avoid it, and the car went into the ditch and flipped over on its side. It's a wonder they both weren't killed outright."

"Yes, indeed," said William, "Dr. Collard told us that as well. It was fortunate that he was right behind them."

Collard had flagged down the next passing car and sent the driver on to Stratford to call for an ambulance and to inform the district police. He had given what immediate aid he could to both Dinny and Addie and followed the ambulance to the hospital. He impressed William and Foxy as an excellent physician.

"There's none better than Dr. Collard," nodded Lynch, his head wreathed in smoke.

"By the way," said Foxy, who had felt a cold chill creep up her spine while imagining again the scene of the accident and had until then been unable to speak. "What happened to the wheel?"

"We went looking for it, naturally, the next morning. It took the constables a while to find it. It hit the ditch, then bounced up and over the hedge row and kept on rolling across the field of stubble for about fifty yards before it finally fell over. None of us has ever seen the like," said Lynch, shaking his head before taking another puff on his pipe. "That car must have been going at least thirty-five miles per hour, maybe forty, when the wheel came off. That Morris Oxford has a top speed of forty-five, though why anyone would want to go that fast is beyond me. There ought to be a law against it."

"What do you think might have caused the wheel to detach?" asked William.

"The mechanic who worked on the car ought to be given a stiff talking to," said Lynch with a tinge of anger. "He must not have properly tightened the wheel nuts. Gradually, they worked loose, and off came the wheel," he said with the confidence of an experienced investigator. The explanation seemed obvious to him. "The dozy bastard might have been up for manslaughter. Sorry, M'lady, for the language. He still might be liable for criminal negligence."

"There seemed to be nothing suspicious about it?" said William, in as offhand a manner as he could manage.

Lynch's bushy eyebrows shot up. "Suspicious? What, you mean as if someone had fiddled with it? No, nothing like that. What made you think of that?"

"Nothing, really," said William, "I just thought the question needed to be asked, that's all." He hurried on. "I am arranging to have the Morris taken back to the garage where Mr. Custus keeps it. Can you send the wheel and lug nuts along, too?"

An expression of relief and understanding came across Lynch's face. "Oh, I see," he said, "you were wondering if we would be keeping it for evidence. No, you can have it. We are recording this as an accident and closing the file." He sat back in his chair, looking quite complacent.

"I guess that's all then," said William. He glanced at Foxy and saw that she was white-knuckled, gripping the arm of her chair, her body tensed.

"Yes, thank you, Inspector," she said. "You've been most helpful."

Out on the street, Foxy hissed between clenched teeth, "I'll bet he didn't even ask that the wheel nuts be checked, or the wheel frame, or the tire, either." She was angry at the Inspector's complacency and at the situation because she could not suggest to the Inspector that the case might not be as straightforward as it seemed without disclosing why someone might possibly want to harm Dinny and Addie.

"Yes, quite," said William. "Competent enough in his own way, I suppose, but not willing to look beneath the surface of things."

"A nice man, but stupid, you mean," said Foxy with a sharp edge in her voice.

"Come along," said William, gently. "Let's stop at the pub near the hospital before evening visitor hours start."

"Knott, tell Tumbler to summon the Turquoise Ghost," said Foxy into the phone at the Royal Arms.

"Certainly, M'lady," said Knott, who knew she meant she wanted the chauffeur to drive the Rolls-Royce Silver Ghost Limousine somewhere. She had it painted turquoise, naturally. "What destination?"

"He'll need to stop at Lord Ainsworth's house in London to rest because he will be going on to Warwick. I will speak to Cook about what food to pack. Lord Ainsworth will tell the house in Chelsea what to get ready and to expect Tumbler. Tell Tumbler we will meet him at the Warwick Hospital. He can call and leave a message at the Royal Arms from the Chelsea house, so I know when to expect him. We will be driving back to London as soon as possible after he arrives. And tell him to bring my shotgun and plenty of shells."

Knott did not ask why. It wouldn't have been appropriate. It worried him, though. In a shaking voice, he said, "Please give Dinny our best. Everyone is worried about him and wishes him a speedy recovery."

"Thank you," said Foxy. She had warm feelings for Knott and knew he was genuinely concerned. "I will."

When Foxy and William returned to the hospital that evening, they met Dr. Collard on his rounds. He confirmed he was releasing both Addie and Dinny. "I see no sign of permanent damage in either of them. Mr. Custus's concussion is worse than Miss Gold's, obviously, but I find no signs of confusion or slurred speech. His grip is good, his physical responses show no sign of a lack of coordination, his eyes track a light without wavering, and he is alert. He will have headaches for about a week. No strenuous physical activity for six weeks. Addie has no remaining symptoms and just needs rest." He recommended a visiting nurse to tend to Dinny's broken ribs and to monitor his recovery from his concussion.

William and Foxy agreed that Addie needed to come to stay in the Chelsea house. Her only living relative was her ailing grandmother, who lived in Norwich. Addie accepted William's invitation because she wanted to be close to Dinny while he recovered. She did not suspect that both Foxy and William thought she would be safer at the Chelsea house rather than in her own flat, just in case the wheel coming off the car was no accident.

The drive home saw Dinny and Addie swaddled in down-filled comforters and nestled into large, soft feather pillows in the commodious seat behind the driver. Dinny had been given a final injection of morphine to dull the pain of transferring to and riding in a car with broken ribs and a headache. "This will be the last one," said Dinny. Wounded friends of his had been released from military hospitals addicted to morphine, and he did not want to depend on it to ease his pain. He would take Aspro and use ice packs. Other than that, he would just have to grit his teeth.

Dinny wore clothes Tumbler had brought. Addie wore a new periwinkle blue dress, with new shoes and stockings. Foxy bought them for her, along with new lingerie, at a boutique the hotel's concierge recommended to her. She thought the blue would set off Addie's dark eyes and hair. "Thank you so much," Addie said as she opened the box and folded back the tissue. Her eyes sparkled as she held up the dress. "It is so lovely. I was dreading having to wear hospital pyjamas and dressing gown home. And blue is my favorite color. I have tried not to think of my clothes scattered all over a muddy field."

Foxy said, "We will have the clothes sent on to be cleaned. They were actually in better shape than either you or Dinny."

As the Silver Ghost pulled smoothly away from the hospital, William and Foxy, seated behind Addie and Dinny, talked cheerfully about the arrangements awaiting them at the Chelsea house. Their voices lulled Dinny into the arms of the chemical Morpheus, and Addie was soon sleeping as well. An hour later, Dinny roused and pronounced himself thirsty and hungry. Addie woke up at the same time.

There was a hamper of what Foxy called Brain Food, "to assist with curing the concussion, and "Bone Food," to help Dinny's bones knit. It was packed with cherries, peaches, hard-boiled eggs, sheep's milk cheese made on the Butterschloss estate, two kinds of sandwiches—salmon spread and ham— cut into triangles with no crusts on the bread, "the way Dinny likes them." To drink, there was bottled Schweppes Malvern-Seltzer, "to settle your tummies, if necessary, on the long ride."

The Silver Ghost came with a large chest that attached to the back of the car to make sure everything was available for impromptu, roadside picnics. Tumbler had arranged the plates, glasses, and silver cutlery in a second hamper and placed it inside the car.

"What, no sardines?" asked Dinny, teasing. "I thought fish was an excellent brain food."

"The salmon will have to do," said Foxy, shooting him a mock-repressive look with one cocked eyebrow.

Dinny did not ask how his great-aunt had arrived at the conclusion that the food would aid specifically in curing concussions and making bones heal. He decided he couldn't care less. He was very hungry. He and Addie happily sampled everything in the hamper and sipped from the bottles of Schweppes. Tumbler drove the powerful, purring Rolls through the countryside toward London, his own small hamper by his side and a thermos of tea as well.

Seeing that Dinny and Addie were fully refreshed by the picnic meal, Foxy leaned forward from the seat behind them. "I have some good news for you. You have both been reinstated in your jobs."

They looked at each other, their mouths open, and began talking at once.

"But how?

"What did you do?"

"I had a little talk with McCreedy and convinced him that you two were best suited to find out what had happened to the missing files."

Dinny chuckled. "Don't make me laugh, Auntie Em. It hurts." He pressed his palm against the area of the broken ribs."

"I am being quite serious, my boy," said Foxy, a little primly. "I simply reasoned with him. Punishing you two would not bring the files back, and you both would work like the Devil gathering souls to find out who had taken them." She paused to consider her last words. "I did not use that exact metaphor, but he got my meaning."

"And so you reasoned with him, and that was all it took?" said Danny, skeptically.

"Why, yes," said Foxy, with mock innocence.

Dinny didn't believe her for a minute, but he knew he would have to pry it out of her another time. "Auntie Em, you are a force of nature," he said, with a broad grin on his face.

'I don't care a fig how you did it," said Addie. "Dinny can't turn around to give you a kiss without screaming in pain, so I will do it for both of us." She gave Foxy a gentle kiss on her cheek, then sat back against the pillows, laughing.

"And that's not all," said William, who was seated next to Foxy. "She got McCreedy to hire her to assist in the search as well."

At this, Dinny began coughing and laughing at the same time, concluding with "Ow, ow, ow," and pressing his one palm against his side and the other on top of his head.

"I am so sorry, my dear boy. I shouldn't have sprung it on you like that," said William apologetically." He handed him an open bottle of Schweppes. "Drink a sip of this. It might help."

Dinny took a sip and said, "No, it is fine. Really. The pain doesn't last long. It only hurts when I cough, or laugh, or move," he said.

"How on earth did you talk him into hiring you?" asked Addie, taking Dinny's hand.

"I suppose he wanted me to keep an eye on you two," said Foxy, with a mischievous grin. "It isn't as if I am inexperienced. I have worked at the old Admiralty before, as you both know. I knew him during the war."

Addie looked at Dinny, who had a plaster over the stitches at his hairline and whose ribs, she knew, were bound in tight bandages. She asked anxiously, "When were we supposed to start back to work?"

"I had thought we two might go in on Tuesday, the day after tomorrow, to give you time to settle in," said Foxy.

"I should be fine by then," said Addie.

"Are you sure? You will tell me if you are not one hundred percent?" asked Foxy. "And Dinny, I will make sure you are given medical leave."

Dinny moaned, "What will I be doing, lying around the house all day?"

"Nonsense," said William. "You and I will try to discover who, who..." He faltered.

"Who tried to kill the two of you?" said Foxy flatly. There was a dead silence. "Oh, come now. You must have thought that it was too much of a coincidence that your wheel just happened to come off the day after someone swiped your research, and you were suspended?"

William intervened. "We don't know for certain that your car was sabotaged. The police are sending it to your garage, Dinny. We both agree, though, that it is a possibility that the disappearance of the files and your accident are linked."

Dinny said, "I have to admit it occurred to me, but I tried to put it out of my mind as an overreaction. What made me think about it was the motorcycle."

William said, "What motorcycle?"

"A motorcycle sped past just as we saw the wheel come off. It was odd. It didn't stop or slow down. If anything, it put on speed."

"Do you remember what make or model it was?" asked William.

"Or what the driver looked like?" said Foxy, almost talking over him in her excitement.

"I think it was a recent model of the AJS," said Dinny, "but I cannot be certain. I really couldn't see the rider. He wore a leather helmet, goggles, leather jacket, gloves, the whole kit."

"How can you be sure it was a he?" asked Foxy. "I drove motorcycles even before the war and during the war as well."

"I can't be one hundred percent certain, except the rider was built like a man in good shape." He paused. "Why don't I call Dr. Collard tomorrow? He must have seen it, too. Maybe he remembers more details."

Addie, who reacted to the suspicion that someone had tried to kill them with a cold fear, squeezed Dinny's hand. "I remember something, too. Just as the car swerved, you put out your arm to protect me. When we landed in the ditch, I landed on you, which is why you got such a bang on the head and broken ribs, and I came out of it with a mild concussion and a bent finger." She stopped. "Thank you," she said softly.

Dinny looked at her, his face filled with tender admiration and the gentle budding of love. "Think nothing of it," he said.

Chapter Eleven

Tea in the Garden

Foxy invited Addie to sit with her in the back garden in the late morning. Over tea, they discussed the problem of the missing files. "We must get the timing down as precisely as possible," said Foxy. "How did that day unfold?

Addie explained that Dinny knew she would be working in the archives that morning. He asked her to locate the decrypts from the week before the *Lusitania* attack until it was sunk and just after. At about ten o'clock, Jan Gruter directed her to the correct stacks. She saw that the space was empty where the cardboard box files should have been. She asked Gruter if anyone had checked them out. He said that no one was allowed to take them. Slightly alarmed, he had gone to the stacks to see for himself. He had returned, shaking his head, and muttering that they must have been misshelved. Addie called Dinny. He came down immediately and stayed for perhaps fifteen or twenty minutes. When he returned to his office, he found that the reports on the *Lusitania* had been taken. He reported everything immediately to McCreedy.

"And that," concluded Addie ruefully, "is when McCreedy rolled the muck spreader over us."

Foxy looked up from her notebook and smiled at the image. "At ten o'clock, the files were on Dinny's desk, and by what—10:30 or 10:40, they were gone? It must be someone familiar with the Admiralty building," she mused. Her first thought was of Fishy McCreedy. He could easily have stepped into Dinny's office while he was downstairs in the ARO. But why would McCreedy do it? Because he was a piece of pond slime who simply wanted to have a reason to get rid of Dinny? But again, why? Or could the librarian have slipped away long enough to take them? That did not match Addie's story. And again, why would he do it? Who had access to Dinny's office?

Foxy asked, "The librarian, Jan Gruter, is he from the Netherlands?"

Addie nodded, "Yes, he has relatives there, but was raised in England. Why?"

"Just curious. It is an unusual name."

They decided, when they reported later that day for work at the Admiralty building that they would need to interview the couriers who brought the files to Dinny. They agreed to ask Jan Gruter for information about anyone interested in the *Lusitania* files and the security measures in the ARO. They divided these assignments between them. Each then fell silent, appreciating the warm day, the cooling breeze, the colors of the autumn leaves.

It occurred to Foxy that she might be going about this the wrong way, assuming Dinny was the target, when it could be Addie, who, after all, was working on current decryption assignments. Maybe someone followed Addie to the ARO and decided to take the *Lusitania*'s decrypts as an act of misdirection. Whoever he—or she—was might have heard the concerned exchange between Dinny, Addie, and Gruter, and acted on impulse to go to Dinny's office and take the files. That would get them both in hot water and lead both of them to think that someone was interested in the *Lusitania* when the real concern was for whatever it was Addie was working on. It was a clever way for a spy to get the two innocents accused of being, at worst, unreliable or, at best, (from the perspective of the spy)—spies.

"Addie," she said, breaking the contemplative quiet, "may I ask what brought you to the ARO in the first place?" When Addie hesitated, Foxy said, "If you are worried about divulging secret information, you needn't worry. I am still bound by the Defense of the Realm oath I took during the War, and McCreedy gave me full clearance for the work I will be doing in the ARO."

Addie decided she could tell Foxy. "A German company is marketing a very clever encryption device to businesses. The thinking is that it might be useful for military purposes. I was asked to look into the electrical decryption and decoding devices used by Room 40 during the war to see if the plans still existed and how that machine could be improved upon."

A wide grin broke across Foxy's face. "And how far have you gotten with that?"

Addie sighed. "Not very far, I'm afraid. The machines were dismantled, and I cannot locate any plans."

"I can help you with that," said Foxy, pouring them each another cup of tea. "Have you ever heard of the women who were part of Room 40's operation?"

Addie looked at her. "The only thing I've heard is that there were women hired to do clerical work."

"Typical," snorted Foxy. "I hope I don't shock you too much when I tell you that we were a group of highly educated women working on decryption."

"Doesn't surprise me one bit," said Addie, aware of how often women's intelligence work was demeaned. "You were working on the decryption machine?"

"Yes, along with a number of other women. We started in May of 1916. The machine would have reminded you of the Hollerith machine," said Foxy.

Addie's face lit with recognition. "Yes, I was asked to learn about it, as a matter of fact, but haven't had a chance. It was used in the late 1880s to compile census data in the United States. Herman Hollerith devised a machine using punch cards and an electromagnetic circuit to sort the information."

Foxy nodded. "Yes, that's right. It was clever." A needle punched holes in a card to correspond with the answers on one census report. The punch card was placed in a "reader," or a press with two plates, closed by a lever. There were needles in the upper plate. When any needle went through a hole, it made contact with mercury, creating a current, which registered the count for each census question on forty counting dials mounted on a wooden frame. Then, the cards were automatically sorted into slots on a long table. The machine "read" the punch card data on the dials, and then indicated into which slot that card should be placed. The slots sorted duplicate responses to the questions about age, race, sex, citizenship, occupation, etc. An experienced tabulator in 1890 could process eighty cards a minute.

Addie said, "You know, Hollerith continues to work on advanced machines that sort data. He changed the name of the company this year. It's called IBM, for International Business Machines. The man must be worth a fortune."

"Yes, no doubt, and the women who operate his machines will be known as nameless faceless 'clerks,' too, I suppose," said Foxy, dryly. "What we used was a more advanced punch-card sorter for codes. It was called the "pianola," or "hat-machine", and we who worked it were called grinders."

Addie wanted to know more. "How exactly did it work?"

Foxy said, "At first, we used a punch-card machine to decipher messages sent in codes that were already known. But it became much trickier when the code was not known. These were 'hatted' messages, and we used the sorting machines to reduce the guesswork. The cipher machine registered all the occurrences of a particular cipher sequence in all received messages. By a process of sorting and analysis, we initially could categorize twenty correlations per day. At our peak, we could categorize one hundred a day, which essentially made them readable to the decoders we sent them to," said Foxy, with a smile of satisfaction. "We also managed to break at least one code, in addition to decryption."

"Holy cats!" exclaimed Addie. Murky, who had been rolling in the grass at their feet, stopped and stared at her with big, yellow eyes, then licked her little, dark nose, shook her dark head, and lay on the ground again with a sigh. "You were doing electromagnetic *codebreaking* during the war? Somehow, I had it in my head that the machine was only for deciphering." She stared at Foxy with surprise and admiration. "But what did you mean when you said you sent them on? Weren't you in Room 40?"

"'Room 40' is an *omnium gatherum*. There were offices and staff spread out over several floors. We were in Room 229, dealing with diplomatic codes. There was a vacuum tube that communicated with Room 40. We would put compilations in the carrier, stick that into the tube, and send it on its way. I can still hear the "WUMP!" Foxy's exaggerated sound effect made Addie giggle. "The room is empty now. Would you like to see it?"

"Are men jealous of Rudolph Valentino? Of course, I would love to see it, even if it is choked with dust and hanging with cobwebs," said Addie. "Just to be where you and the other women cracked the German ciphers and codes. I'll summon their spirits."

"We're not dead yet," said Foxy, laughing.

"I meant it metaphorically. Obviously," said Addie, also laughing but just a little bit embarrassed.

"But you haven't told me much about this new machine you are researching," said Foxy.

"It is a rotor cipher machine. There are four cipher wheels, twenty-eight electrical contacts on either side of each wheel, and a cog wheel to advance each of the cipher wheels. The initial position for each wheel can be set by knobs on the side of the machine. There is a five-digit counter for the characters. The keyboard operates much like a plain text keyboard."

It was Foxy's turn to stare in astonishment. "It seems there would be an infinite number of combinations. That would make it impossible to decipher a message if a different cipher were used daily to reset the machine."

Addie nodded. "That's what has the top brass worried. It was shown at a trade fair for the first time this year. The advertising is for businesses that want to keep their wireless messages secret from their rivals. But the Swedes are negotiating a purchase for their military. And, everyone is worried about the Germans."

"Of course," said Foxy. She fully endorsed the view of the brilliant economist, John Maynard Keynes, that the peace had been built on foundations of sand. "What is this device called?"

"The generic name is *Die Handelsmaschine.* It is sold under the brand-name *Enigma.*

Addie left to call Josie, leaving Foxy alone with her thoughts. They were anything but coherent. If the Germans found out about the hat machine she used during the war, they would certainly want to know how it worked. Maybe there was a spy who wanted to find the information before Addie did, possibly to destroy it, certainly to make off with it. But if Addie were the target, surely there was no need to try and kill her. That made no sense. On the other hand, it made no sense to try and kill Dinny for poking around the records of the *Lusitania* disaster, either. Then again, it was entirely possible that the accident was actually an accident, and not related at all to the work either Dinny or Addie were doing for the Admiralty. Foxy sighed in frustration. She looked up to the sky and cursed. It was clear and blue, so no chance of being hit by a thunderbolt and waking up with the answers. She thought of Hercule Poirot and his "little grey cells." All he had to do was think about the "clues" which magically presented themselves to him without much effort on his part. She found him slightly insufferable.

She launched herself from the chair. Better to be up and doing. She went to the kitchen to discuss dinner with Cook. Mrs. Flowerdew was a large, florid-faced woman with a genial disposition who ran her kitchen more efficiently than most captains ran their ships. They sat at the long, scoured, wooden table that was the center of operations for the kitchen.

"I wonder what you would think of having dinner a bit early," she asked. "Say seven. I want Dinny to be able to enjoy it before the nurse hurries him off to medications and bed."

Mrs. Flowerdew was especially fond of Dinny, and she was used to Foxy serving as hostess whenever she was staying as a guest. "Of course," she said. She was from the Scottish highlands and spoke a clear, crisp English. "And I think it's best to keep the dinner light. He should not be stuffing himself with rich foods." She quickly wiped a tiny tear from the corner of her eyes with the hem of her crisp, white apron. Foxy often brought Dinny along when she and her late husband visited William in London, and Mrs. Flowerdew remembered fondly serving him his favorite ice cream in the kitchen while he told her of his many inventions, some of which, like his flying machine, hadn't worked out. He had shown her the bruises to prove it.

Mrs. Flowerdew produced a menu written in her neat hand. Most of the ingredients came from the Butterschloss and Ainsworth estates. "I've had a lovely salmon sent up and will make a mousseline with cucumber. That's nice and light."

"No soup course?" inquired Foxy.

"If you don't mind, M'lady," said Mrs. Flowerdew. "It's just that Master Custus made it quite clear that he is sick of soups. It seems that one night a week, he and Master Tris have to cook for themselves, and all they can think to make is soup. So, if it's all right with you…"

"Say no more," laughed Foxy. I am sure we will do fine without soup, especially as it will make Dinny happy."

They agreed on lamb roast, new potatoes, green beans, and a salad course. "And I want to make a peach melba for Master Custus, if that suits you. The peaches have come on a treat this summer, and he adores my vanilla ice cream." Foxy agreed happily. "And make sure there is a good supply of Schweppes. Dinny should not have any alcohol. Is there anything you need?"

Mrs. Flowerdew finished making a few notes on her menu. "I've asked the maid, Katherine, to help out with Maisy in the kitchen. That won't leave her time for flowers," she said in her blunt, simple manner.

"I would be delighted to bring in some cut flowers and arrange them. It will give me something to do, and I certainly need the distraction," agreed Foxy, not bothered at being made a subaltern to Captain Flowerdew. She went off in search of secateurs and a trug. "Then I'll go over to the townhouse to get the clothes I have left there and invite Tris to dinner."

Chapter Twelve

Clues

William hailed a cab for the journey from Brick Lane to Bermondsey. Sparky Stryder's garage extended under one of the railroad bridge arches like the undercroft of a cathedral. Sparky was a sprightly seventy-year-old with short, white hair parted neatly on one side. He wore a flat-topped hat with a narrow brim and worn, but spotless, blue overalls. The garage floor was swept clean, the tools hung neatly along the wall. Sparky's dark eyes were alert and keen. His thin lips looked ready to break into a grin at the slightest provocation or offer of a pint. He spoke with an East London accent.

William introduced himself. "A pleasure to meet you. Master Custus called to say you was coming. How is he?"

"Dinny sends his best, and wants you to know he is healing quite well," replied William

Sparky took his hat off and shook his head. "That were terrible, it were. I've been right worried, I have."

"Yes, it was quite a bad accident," said William. "Dinny is lucky to be alive."

"T'weren't no accident," said Sparky grimly. "Come with me. I've somethin' to show you." Far back into the cavernous shop, Dinny's car sat in a sad heap. "See that there?" Sparky picked up a set of lug nuts from a tray. "Just have a feel of 'em."

William reached out and took them. "They are oily," he said in surprise.

"But, why…"

"Yeah, that's what I'd like to know," said Sparky. "They came off that wheel hub, they did," he said. "Coppers sent 'em down with the car. Oiled lugs like that, bound to come loose sooner or later."

"And you did not oil these, I take it?" said William, just for confirmation.

"No, course not," said Sparky with a hard note to his voice. "You put oil on lugs if there is rust and they seized. Which they hadn't, of course. That car is only a year old, and I keep it in top condition. Somebody snuck in here and had a go at it, that's what."

William was unnerved. "When was the last time you serviced the car before Dinny picked it up for his trip to Stratford?"

"Me and Doug went over it the night afore. And we checked them lugs, of course. Then, I came in the morning to give it a quick polish before Master Custus picked it up."

"I see," said William. "And did you check the lug nuts then?"

"'Course I did," said Sparky, with the same edge in his voice. "I checked to make sure they was tight. The thing is, though, that even if you tighten lug nuts, if they was oiled, then they won't hold, see? They works their way loose, like. Crikey, I'd like to get me hands around the neck of the bastard what did that. Master Custus could have been killed. Lucky he wasn't."

"Lucky indeed," said William, feeling his anger rise along with Sparky's. "How do you lock up at night?"

"I use a big padlock with a chain," said Sparky. He fetched it for William, who saw the tiny scratches indicating the lock had been tampered with. "Someone has picked your lock," he said matter-of-factly.

"That's right," said Sparky, with disgust. "I didn't notice it until after I saw them lug nuts had been tampered with. Then I looked at the padlock. Someone had to have broken in. Thing was, though, nothing was taken, and the padlock was locked when I came in the morning when Master Custus came for the car. Whoever did it only oiled the one set of lugs. He must have worried that someone would see the padlock was open, so he were in a hurry."

"That makes sense." Holding up the lug nuts, he asked, "Can I take these along?"

"'Course," said Sparky, "anything that will help catch the bastard what did this."

"Dinny may want to notify the police, too, so they may come around," said William.

"I ain't never had no trouble with coppers, and I don't suppose I will now."

"By the way, has anyone on a motorbike, possibly a newer model AJS, come here asking questions, possibly about Dinny or his car?" asked William

Sparky was momentarily taken aback. "Now that you mention it, yes. A young feller came by around the time Master Custus asked us to get his car ready for him." He scratched the back of his head. "Let's see. I think it was the same day. He came round to say that Master Custus spoke highly of me and had recommended I service his motorbike. And like you say, it was an AJS, maybe a year old."

"Did he leave his AJS to be serviced?" asked William.

"No, he did not. He said he just wanted to know what our hours were and if he needed to make an appointment for service. Things like that. He looked around for a bit, too. I think he was a man in his late twenties or early thirties."

"You think? Didn't you get a good look at him?" asked William.

"No, I didn't because he kept his helmet and goggles on the whole time. I found that odd. He was shorter than you by a bit, I can say that. But that's about all. Spoke with a posh accent, but then, you would expect that of someone who owned an AJS."

"What about the bike. Can you remember anything about the AJS? What about the license plate?"

"I don't remember the numbers, but it were an 'A'" said Sparky. "That is what I can say for sure."

"So, a London license," said William. "Thanks, Sparky. You have been of enormous help."

"I hopes so. I want to help lay hands on this Stoke-on-Trent," he said emphatically. Seeing the confused look on William's face, he said, "That's rhyming slang for 'bent,' means criminal, see?"

William didn't see, but he reassured Sparky that everything would be done to discover who had sabotaged the car, and no blame would fall on him. "Dinny knows how loyal you have been to his family."

Sparky's face broke into his familiar grin. "Oh, right you are," he said, "I took care of the Old Governor's cars when Master Custus was just a kid. Give my best to Lady Butterschloss, will you?"

"Yes, certainly. And I promise to keep you informed on Mr. Custus' recovery. I will definitely let you know when we catch the bastard who did this." William shook Sparky's hardened, calloused hand. "That's a promise," he said.

Foxy came through the door of the Chelsea house in a great rush. She was clearly agitated. As Maisie helped her off with her coat and hat, she said, "Send my apologies to Mrs. Flowerdew and tell her there will be one less for dinner, and bring me a gin and tonic. I'll be in the Conservatory." She was unusually abrupt because she was preoccupied and worried.

After gathering flowers for the dinner table, Foxy had Tumbler drive her to her Mayfair townhouse. She left some of her clothes there when she offered the residence to Dinny and Tris, and wanted to pick some out to wear to the ARO. She felt a wrench when the Turquoise Ghost arrived at the familiar 19th-century detached three-story townhouse with its brick façade, sash windows, shutters, and mansard roof. For many years of her marriage, Foxy loved the house. Now she called it The House of Last Nights. From his tiny cot, Timmy, gasping for air, had been rushed from the nursery to the ambulance. He never returned from the hospital. She and Robin spent their last night together in this house. She never saw him alive again. She took a deep breath, exhaled slowly, and returned her memories to the imaginary shrine where she kept them. She used her key and entered the tiled entry hall. She hesitated. The house felt unlived in, with an elusive quality of cold air, silence, and an inexplicable sensation of prolonged emptiness. She called out, "Tris! It's Foxy! Are you in?" There was no answer.

She climbed the stairs to a large wardrobe on the first landing and selected several items that would suit her for working in the dusty archives of the ARO. She slung these over the cast-iron balustrade. She went to Dinny's room. It was neat, the bed made, everything in its place. She gathered some books and drawing materials he had asked for, as well as some clothes and his uniform. She decided to leave a note inviting Tris to dinner. This gave her a good excuse to snoop in his room. She opened the door and was taken aback by the rumpled bedclothes and the open, gaping wardrobe. A note stood against a glass on the bedside table.

"I've been ordered north. Cannot say more. Don't worry. Tris."

Foxy crossed the room to the wardrobe. It was empty except for a few civilian clothes. His uniforms were gone, as were his shirts, socks, and underclothing. Foxy picked up the shot glass and sniffed it. Scotch whiskey. All that was left was a residue on the bottom and sides, the result of evaporation. In the bathroom, there were no toiletry articles. She turned off a dripping tap in the sink and noticed a rust-colored circle around the drain. She found no identification or money. The alarm clock, which had stopped, was set for 7:00.

Foxy went to the back of the house, where Nora Wright, the housekeeper, lived in the Carriage House. Foxy hired her as a maid when she and Robby were newlyweds who had just moved into the townhouse. Nora was pleased to see Foxy and asked after Dinny.

"He is doing fine, Nora. He will soon be back to his old self."

Nora's face brightened. "When you called to tell me he would be staying with you until he was better, I can tell you, my heart sank. Automobiles. I can't see the good of them. You will tell him I hope he is better very soon."

When Foxy asked about Tris, Nora said she hadn't seen him since he went out Thursday night. "No, he wasn't down for breakfast Saturday morning," she said. "I saw a car that looked official with a Royal Navy insignia on the side of the door. I thought maybe he had been called away. That would have been before seven o'clock, when Tris usually gets up. It's odd, though, because both of them usually leave me a note when they are going away for a few days, but this time, Tris didn't." She furrowed her old, wrinkled brow. "Is there anything wrong?"

Foxy reassured her, even though she was unsettled. "You're probably right, Nora. He just got called away suddenly and didn't have time to leave you a note."

Chapter Thirteen

Mrs. Flowerdew's Triumph

Josie arrived with clothes for Addie, and the two sat in the Conservatory over drinks before dinner. Addie caught Josie up on events and reassured her that she was fine. When everyone was called to dinner, William said in a low voice, "Cook has worked very hard all day to prepare a special dinner. Let's not spoil it by discussing anything about the accident."

"Or why Tris isn't here," said Foxy, intimating that she had important news on that front.

The table was beautifully set. The plates were pre-war blue and white, embellished with sailing ships of the line on the border and the Royal Navy crest in the center. The silverware gleamed in the light from tapers in silver candle holders. Foxy's flowers had been discreetly moved to the sideboard by the maid, Kathleen, who was following Mrs. Flowerdew's orders. Foxy had conformed to much of what had been expected of her as the daughter of the aristocracy. She could shoot waterfowl with deadly accuracy; she rode horseback as if she and the animal were one. She loved to read and excelled at German, French, and mathematics. But flower arranging had never caught her fancy. It required too much patience to achieve the necessary symmetry and color balance. She had plunked the flowers she had picked that morning in a flower bowl. She called it a rustic look. It resembled what a small child might rip from a garden and proudly present—clutched in grimy hands—with a sunny smile to her mum.

As the roast and vegetables were served, the conviviality was lubricated by frequent pourings of a Châteauneuf-du-Pape. Addie accepted a slice of lamb and said to Foxy, with a mock lamentation, "I do hope one of the sheep from your estate wasn't slaughtered just for us. I remember the lambs hopping about this summer."

"Don't worry, dear," Foxy came back with a faux aristocratic hauteur, "I am sure this one was struck down by a bolt of lightning."

The Peach Melba arrived. Individual servings in footed, clear-glass dessert bowls held the two halves of a poached peach, embracing a generous scoop of vanilla ice cream swimming in a raspberry sauce. Dinny's face lit up as it had when he was a boy, and Mrs. Flowerdew had made it for him. Everyone was transported by the ambrosial taste, perfectly paired with a Muscat de Frontignan. As he finished the last spoonful, Dinny said to Kathleen, "Could you ask Cook to come in?"

The serving maid reappeared, holding a reluctant Mrs. Flowerdew by the wrist and pulling her gently into the room.

Everyone burst into loud applause. "A toast! A toast!" said Dinny. He recited an extempore poem:

> As I've been confined to bed,
> My spirits began to droop
> But, tonight, heaven be praised!
> I say it without more ado,
> All glasses now be raised
> To Mrs. Flowerdew!

"To Mrs. Flowerdew!" everyone chimed in.

Mrs. Flowerdew beamed. Everyone clapped. And as always, when overcome with emotion, Mrs. Flowerdew wiped her eyes with the corner of her apron.

After dinner, they gathered in comfortable chairs and a sofa around a low Chinese table of carved elmwood. A fire burned brightly. The coffee service was already on the table. William urged the company to serve themselves and offered brandy to everyone except Dinny. "Time for our debrief," said William, taking out his pipe and striking a match. "I know these will interest you." He puffed his pipe. "I draw your attention to the lugs from Dinny's car." He pointed to a small clay bowl he had taken from the kitchen. "If you pass those around, you will feel they are oily. You can wipe your fingers on that clean rag the bowl is resting on."

"They *are* oily," said Dinny. He was instantly agitated. "But Sparky would never…this can only mean they were tampered with." He looked with dismay at Addie. "It was no accident. You…we…could have been killed. But who would…?"

Foxy and Josie were equally alarmed. "The wheel came off because someone oiled the lugs before the drive to Stratford. This was attempted murder, then," said Foxy. She felt a cold anger sweep over her.

Josie looked at her two friends. "I can't believe this. Who would do this? Why?" Her fear for them showed in her face, which drained of blood.

Foxy asked, "Dinny, who knew you and Addie were driving to Stratford?"

"I booked the tickets," said Addie. "That is, I asked the secretary if she would mind booking them for me. The secretary at GCCS, I mean. Her name is Bridgett. I went back to my office after I was barred from the ARO. I thought my boss would have some questions. He didn't, as it turned out."

"Was there anyone else around?" asked Dinny.

Addie's brow furrowed. "I don't know. The pigeon-holes for all of us are in the adjoining room, and there is no door. I asked her on Thursday morning. I said I needed two tickets for Friday night's performance of *Much Ado.* We got to talking, the way women do, and she asked if we were driving or taking the train. And she wanted to know who the other person was. So I told her it was with the person I had been working with at the ARO. She asked if he—you—" (she looked at Dinny) "were handsome."

"And what did you say?" inquired Dinny.

"That you were old, with one foot in the grave, and as ugly as sin, of course, but very, very wealthy." They laughed. "Actually, she already knew about you. She met you once when you came to give me a ride. We were kidding around. Anyone could have overheard us mentioning you by name if they happened to be in the next room. I stopped by later to ask if she had made the booking, and she said she had put the confirmation number in my pigeonhole. I suppose anyone could have seen it. It was just a note saying there were two tickets reserved for *Much Ado About Nothing* at Stratford for Friday night."

"But that would not explain how anyone would know where Dinny's car was kept," said Foxy.

"I don't think that is so very hard to explain," said Addie. "Dinny mentioned to me several weeks ago that Sparky could use a few more customers. I posted a note on the bulletin board in the office. It had Sparky's address and phone and said anyone wanting to know about Sparky's Garage could call Dinny."

"I posted notices on bulletin boards in the Admiralty break rooms. I gave my name for anyone who wanted references for Sparky's work."

Foxy glanced at William, who smiled ironically. "That certainly narrows things down," he said. After a pause, he continued, "There is no doubt someone entered Sparky's garage the night before Dinny picked it up. Earlier that day, the owner of an AJS came by saying Dinny recommended Sparky as a good mechanic. Sparky did not see his face but was definite that it was someone in his late twenties or possibly early thirties. The rider who passed you when your car went off the road was the same person who was asking questions at Sparky's garage. He must have come back later in the dead of night, picked the lock, and sabotaged the car. Sparky remembered that the license was issued in London, but not the numbers."

Dinny was listening with intense concentration. He nodded his head, "I spoke on the phone with Dr. Collard today. He remembered the motorcycle and saw the London registration. He thought it outrageous that the rider suddenly passed him and sped up when my car swerved. He was very clear on that. He also remembered something else. When the ambulance was ready to leave, Dr. Collard walked to his car to follow the ambulance to the hospital. He noticed a small medallion or pin on the road. He thought it probably dropped from the motorcycle. He picked it up because he wanted to report the rider for causing a possible hazard at the site of an accident.

He thought the insignia might be for a cyclist's club, and a membership list might help the police find the rider. He doesn't recognize the insignia, and neither did the police when he showed it to them. When I said I might have better luck since the cycle is registered in London, he said he will send it to me immediately."

Josie moved her armchair closer to the sofa where her two friends sat, clutching one another's hands tightly. She reached out to hold Addie's other hand. The three were clearly alarmed and frightened. "But why," asked Addie, "Why would anyone want to harm…?" Her voice quavered.

William refreshed the brandy in everyone's glasses. "I have some information about that, but it is pretty slim. I had lunch today with Clive Edgerton, who worked with me at the Naval Intelligence Division and is now working for MI5. I thought he might throw some light on why anyone would be interested in making sure nothing about the *Lusitania* ever came to light. Clive said the only person he could think of was Winston Churchill.

His listeners gasped. "What do any of us have to do with him?" asked Addie, who was by this time quite agitated.

"Hear me out," said William. "I said it was a slender thread. Churchill intends to leave the Liberal Party and join the Conservatives, and they are planning to force the Labour Party to call a General Election in the next few months. They are determined to get rid of Ramsey MacDonald as Prime Minister. The problem for Churchill is his record when he was the First Lord of the Admiralty. I amusingly thought his Achilles' heel would be the Dardanelles disaster, but what do I know? Just because I was actually there. Clive says no, that the real problem might be a cover-up intended to shift blame from Churchill over the sinking of the *Lusitania.* He said there have been rumors circulating about his role in the disaster ever since it sank. He pointed out that Churchill persists in placing all the blame on Captain Turner—who was, as you know, exonerated. Clive recommended I read Churchill's account of the sinking in *The World Crisis,* so I purchased a copy from Nevin Belltower's bookstore on the way home today. I haven't had a chance to look at it yet, but perhaps it will prove worthwhile to study it."

There was a silence as this information was absorbed. Foxy said with a note of incredulity in her voice, "What you are saying, if I understand you, is that Winston Churchill is powerful enough to arrange for the files to be stolen from Dinny's desk, the decrypts removed from the ARO, and the sabotaging of Dinny's car in order to make sure he is elected in the next General Election. Is that about it?"

William relit his pipe and shook out the match. "Sounds very far-fetched, I realize," he said. "But it is the only reason Clive could suggest."

Foxy cleared her throat. She hesitated to suggest what she was about to put forward. "There is another possibility," she said, looking at Addie. "And that is that Addie and not Dinny is the target. Addie told me earlier today that her assignment for the GCCS is to look into encryption devices. The Germans have developed a rotor device for protecting business messages sent by wireless transmission, but they are in the process of selling it for military purposes to the Swedes." She suddenly became aware that she might be violating the secrecy law. She looked at Josie, "I know we can trust you that this information stays in this room. We have security clearances, but you don't."

"Of course!" said Josie. "My lips are sealed. This is too serious for me to talk about with anyone outside this room." She gave a reassuring look to Dinny and Addie.

Addie smiled at her friend. "I know that perfectly well. Anyhow," she said, "I was sent to ARO to see what I can find out about the decryption device used in Room 229 for decoding diplomatic messages during the war. I asked about the *Lusitania* decrypts because Dinny wanted me to help him, but it has nothing to do with my assignment from GCCS. Foxy's idea is that stealing the *Lusitania* files and removing the submarine decrypts was an opportunistic move to hide the real motive, which is either to prevent me from finding out anything about the decrypt device used by Room 229 or maybe to stop my inquiry into decrypt devices entirely. It worked, too, since I was barred from the ARO and would have faced a hearing at the GCCS. In other words, the Germans are behind the thefts because they don't want us to get ahead of them in ciphers or codes."

"Or possibly the Bolsheviks," said Foxy. "They wouldn't want to let anyone get ahead of them in ciphers and codes after their losses to the Germans in the war." She sighed heavily. "They learned that lesson when they insisted on using outdated and easily broken codes for wireless transmission during the war. The Germans had no trouble breaking the codes. It cost the Russians dearly in terms of losses."

Dinny frowned. He said slowly, "But none of this explains why someone would want to kill either of us, and make it look like an accident. It all should have ended when the files went missing, I faced court-martial, and Addie was barred from the ARO. It would have seemed to anyone who wanted to stop either of us as if his plan worked. If the accident happened after we were reinstated, then it might make sense. But the timing doesn't work. No one could have known we would be reinstated when we left for Stratford. Not even us."

Josie spoke up tentatively, unsure whether her information would be helpful. "This all leads back to what happened the day the files were stolen, and the decrypts could not be found. My professor told me today he has been doing research at the ARO. I don't know what he is researching, but he seemed to recognize you at least by sight, Addie, when I mentioned you were doing work there, too."

Addie looked up, interested but uncertain. "You talk about Professor Arensdorf often enough, but you have never told me what he looks like?"

"Bald head, pale skin, wire-rimmed glasses, in his sixties. Ring any bells?" asked Josie.

A flash of recognition crossed Addie's face. "Sure. I have seen him. I would have introduced myself if I had known who he was. He is a regular at the ARO."

Foxy leaned forward and asked Addie, "Was he there Thursday?"

Addie frowned. "He may have been. He usually sits at a desk back in the stacks. There is a half-window that lets in light and a hanging lamp just over the desk. You can't see him from the front desk, and I had no reason to go back there Thursday." She saw the disappointment in Foxy's eyes. "We could ask Jan Gruter, the librarian, tomorrow when we go there."

"And I could ask Professor Arensdorf. Or even better, I could see if he would agree to meet both of you," said Josie.

"That's a splendid idea," said Foxy, eagerly, "If you wouldn't mind going to the trouble."

"Not at all," said Josie. "I want to be involved. I will ask him tomorrow. What shall I tell him?"

"Good question," said Foxy. "If he happened to be there on Thursday when the files went missing, he will know your friend Addie is in trouble over it. Perhaps he saw or heard something that might be useful in finding out what happened. He doesn't need to know more than that."

"Done," said Josie. "I will let you know what he says."

"And now," said Foxy, "I have some very odd news about Tris." Dinny looked alarmed. "When did you last see him?"

"Friday morning, before I left for Stratford. Addie and I left here together the night we came here. We rode in the same cab. It dropped her off first. When I arrived at the Mayfair house, I went straight to bed. I wanted to get an early start the next day. I was up and dressed by 6:00 am. I opened Tris's door to see if he was up, but he was passed out in his evening clothes on the bed. I assumed he had a late night of it and decided not to wake him. I had tea and a slice of bread and jam. Nora wasn't up yet, so I left her a note. The cab came at 6:30 or perhaps a little earlier to take me to Sparky's, where I picked up my car. That was the last time I saw Tris. Why has something happened to him?"

Foxy said slowly, "I think he is probably fine. I took these from his room." She placed the alarm clock, note, and glass with the evaporated Scotch whiskey on the low table.

A silence fell. Everyone was unsettled. Holding the small glass up to the light, Dinny said, "For one thing, Tris would never in a million years pour himself a glass of this Scotch whiskey and not drink it. He has expensive tastes and keeps a bottle of Highland Park in his room. He would not waste a drop, much less leave it to evaporate. Any more than I would," he said. "It borders on the sacrilegious."

Foxy nodded because his answer added to her concerns. "Then, there is the note. Why does he write 'Don't worry'? If he were simply ordered to a base in the north for a secret research project, he would have no reason to think you would worry. He might write, 'I'll be in touch as soon as I can,' but he doesn't. What if the real meaning is the opposite of 'Don't worry'?

William asked, "And the alarm clock?"

Foxy replied, "Tris would have received advanced, written orders. It is highly unlikely he would be careless about the time when the car would arrive. Nora says she saw an official Royal Naval car outside the townhouse before 7:00. And yet, his alarm clock is set for 7:00 am, and that is the time he usually gets up, isn't it?" she asked Dinny.

He nodded. "Tris certainly would have reset the alarm if he knew he was being transferred to another base and a car was coming to pick him up."

Foxy remembered with a pang when Robin departed for the last time in a car sent for him.

"He seems to have left in a hurry. He left a slow drip of water running in the bathroom sink," said Foxy. "It left a rust ring around the drain."

Dinny, who had become increasingly agitated, looked at William. "Could I trouble you for a brandy? I think I need a stiffener."

Foxy and Addie admonished Dinny, but William thought the brandy would do him more good than the negative side effects might do him harm. Dinny said, "Tris would never leave the tap dripping. Nora has been especially clear on that point because the rust ring makes more work for her. Tris is as fond of her as I am and would not forget to tighten the tap."

As William handed Dinny the snifter, he said, "I'll ask around at the club, get in touch with Tris's CO in the submarine research division, and get a message through to Clive. Somebody must know what this is all about. Until then, try not to worry."

Foxy's heart went out to Dinny. She wanted to reassure him that Tris was probably fine, but realized her words would sound hollow. She spoke in a sharp tone that betrayed her frustration. "What I want to know is what this has to do with what has happened to Dinny and Addie. It is too much of a coincidence, and I don't believe in coincidences."

This hit everyone like a thunderbolt out of the blue. The shock triggered

Dinny's memory.

"Hold on," he said. "I just remembered something Tris said to me before we parted Thursday morning at the Admiralty." He turned to Addie. "Did Tris ever tell you he was related distantly to Churchill?"

Addie nodded. "Yes, on more than one occasion," she said dryly. Then her eyes opened wider. "Oh, I see," she said.

Dinny went on hurriedly. "You don't know this," he said to Foxy and William. "Tris went to Egypt for a fortnight with two elderly aunts from that side of his family—the Churchill side, I mean. He returned late Wednesday afternoon. While we walked to work Thursday, I told him I would be reading the *Lusitania* files and that I asked Addie to help. He said he learned something from one of his aunts while he was in Egypt that might be useful for my research." He looked at the eager faces, all eyes fixed on him. He let them down. "I don't know what it was. He never had the chance to tell me." His voice was taut with worry. He took another swallow of the brandy.

"And now, conveniently for someone, we cannot contact Tris to find out what it was he wanted to tell you about Churchill and the sinking of the *Lusitania*," said Foxy. She was irritated because she felt helpless. She thought for a moment. "I don't suppose you know how to contact his aunts, do you?"

Dinny hung his head and said, "No. All I know is they did not return to England with Tris. They got off the ship to stay with friends in Nice. Evidently, they vowed never to endure another winter here. I have no idea how to contact them."

They fell into silence at this dead end. William said again emphatically, "I will find out where Tris is. There was an official insignia on the car they took him away in. Someone knows what Naval base he has been sent to. And someone very high up must have pulled strings to arrange for his transfer to get him out of the way."

Addie had not said anything about Tris coming in his drunken state to see her. She did not want to upset Dinny more than he already was.

Josie leaned over and said in a low voice, "I think you better tell them."

Addie was looking down at her lap. She nodded slightly. Dinny, who had overheard Josie, said, "What? Tell us what? Do you know something about

Tris?"

Addie looked up at him and took a deep breath. "It probably means nothing. Tris showed up drunk at the apartment Thursday night. I think he was upset that we had not met him at the Above Board after work. I didn't have a chance to explain. He went on and on about how I had turned him down when he asked me to marry him."

Dinny groaned. "Not that again. I thought we were past that."

"Yes," said Addie. "So did I. But," she paused, "but he said the most terrible thing. He said I would be sorry if I chose you over him."

Dinny sat back on the sofa, one hand over his broken ribs. He looked pale and drained. "He couldn't have meant it, not the way you are thinking."

Josie said quietly, "I heard him," she said. "He was very, very drunk."

"Why didn't you tell me this before?" asked Dinny, not in irritation but in sadness.

Addie said, "I frankly thought it was just Tris going off, as he sometimes does, and then apologizes. I thought he would send me flowers and chocolate and call himself an ass, and we would be friends again. Then, we were in that crash, and you were unconscious for days, and, well, I couldn't see that it was important because I didn't know Tris was gone." Her eyes welled up, Dinny took her hand, and Josie put her arm around Addie's shoulder.

Just then, there was the familiar swish of a starched uniform as Sister Parker entered the room. She wore a nurse's watch pinned upside down on her blouse. She held it up and glanced at it— right side up for her to read it. She tsk'd.

"I agreed to allow Mr. Custus to stay up a bit late for the special dinner tonight," she said crisply. "Now, it is past eleven." She saw the empty snifter in front of him. She glared at the assembly as if they were all in league with the Devil. "I see," she said brusquely. Then, more sympathetically, she said to Dinny. "You seem to be in pain."

Dinny nodded. "It is playing up just a bit. Nothing to go on about."

"Come along," said Sister Parker. "I'll rewrap your ribs and give you some Aspro. It will ease the pain and will not react with the brandy."

Dinny's nickname for the efficient Sister was Torquemada. He usually chafed under her rigid rules and schedule, but had to admit to himself he ached, felt exhausted, and was unnerved by what Addie had told them. William helped Dinny into his reclining wheelchair, and Sister Parker wheeled him away.

Josie said, "This evening has been a strain on all of us. Except for that wonderful dinner. Please tell Mrs. Flowerdew how very much I enjoyed it."

William saw how exhausted she was and offered to call her a cab.

Josie said to Foxy, "I honestly think, I mean, I know in my heart that Tris would never do anything to harm either Dinny or Addie."

Addie and Josie said their good nights and hugged one another. "You know I will do anything for you and Dinny and Tris," said Josie.

"I know you will," said Addie.

William helped Josie on with her coat. She stepped into the chilly night and the waiting cab. Addie went to sit with Dinny.

William and Foxy looked at one another with the grim determination earned by experience and fueled by protective instincts.

"We'll sort this out," said William.

"You bet we will," said Foxy with a steely edge to her voice.

Chapter Fourteen

Foxy Goes Bang in the Night

Foxy was restless. She tossed and turned in her bed, unable to sleep. The story of Tris, escorted by two men in Naval uniform to an official car, opened the shrine where she kept her last memories of Robin.

In the pre-dawn darkness, he moved quietly about the bedroom in the Mayfair townhouse. Foxy stirred.

"I didn't want to wake you," he said.

"I couldn't sleep," she said.

They spoke in whispers to avoid waking Dinny, who was asleep in the next room.

"I'll be back before you know it. Three days at the very most." He hugged her tightly to him. They kissed intensely, passionately. No more words passed between them. He walked into the dark hall and was gone. From the upstairs window, she watched him get into the waiting car with the Royal Navy insignia on the door. Then it drove away. The sky was clear in the false dawn, the last stars fading. Standing at the window, she quietly sang the Sailor's Hymn:

> Eternal Father, strong to save,
> Whose hand does bind the restless wave,
> Who bidst the mighty ocean deep

Its own appointed limits keep;
Oh, hear us when we cry to Thee,
For those in peril on the sea!

Her voice broke.

Three days later, she was absorbed in her work, waiting for Miss Robertson to call, "Tea Break, Ladies," and trying to reassure herself that Robin would surely be home that evening. Someone came in the door. It was William. His face was drawn, pallid. Miss Robertson looked up, expecting a courier. William did not even glance at her but searched for Foxy.

"Foxy, I…" he stammered. Their eyes locked. She saw his tears well up.

She stood up to walk to him. *It's over. He's gone.* Then her world went white.

Foxy wept quietly into her pillow, not the soul-rending wails that overtook her in the days following the news that her Robin was killed when a German plane strafed the car he was driving with other officers inspecting the Naval base at Dunkirk. No one in the car survived. She fell into an uneasy sleep. She awoke suddenly. Murky sat on the sill of the bay window, bathed in bright, blue moonlight. She did not look as if she were lost in philosophical cat musings. She was very alert, her body tensed, looking down through the side pane, making the "ceck, ceck" sound she made at birds flitting in the trees on the other side of a window where she perched herself to watch them. Something was moving in the front yard. Foxy got quietly out of bed and padded to the window. Following the cat's gaze, she saw a leg disappear over the sill into the library. Where Dinny was.

She moved quickly to the closet. Her 12-gauge shotgun, its dark metal barrels shining like living things, awaited the call to action. The cartridges hung from a canvas bag. She slid the lever sideways, broke the barrels, clicked in two cartridges, slung the bag over her shoulder, and went out the door. The entire maneuver took less than thirty seconds.

She was aware from reading mysteries that any detective called from bed to an emergency took time to put on a dressing gown over his—or her—nightclothes. She thought this a ridiculous waste of time. She was wearing perfectly modest satin pajamas. Even if she were naked, she would have shot out that door like the proverbial bat out of the equally proverbial Hell.

Shotgun held, still broken, over one arm, she tread silently down the steps. She snapped the barrels into place, slipped off the safety, threw open the library door, and clicked on the light switch next to it. In the split second that it took for her to aim at the figure sitting on the edge of Dinny's bed, she recognized the intruder. She swung the gun away from him just as she pulled the trigger. Blue-grey smoke streaked from the barrel. Glass shattered from the spray of birdshot against the window. Dogs in neighboring houses erupted into urgent barking. Lights came on in houses up and down the street.

As the smoke cleared, she saw two frozen faces: Dinny was one, Tris the other. "What the hell do you mean by crawling in here through the window!"

Dinny said with a shaking voice, "It's all right, it's all right. Tris heard we had been hurt."

Tris's lips moved, but no sound came out. At last, he found his voice, "Ye-es, ye-es, that's right. I came to see if they were okay."

Foxy, her hands trembling, put the safety back on, slid the catch, and broke the barrels. She leaned against the door frame, looking grim. "Were you unaware that there is a knocker on the door?" she said with controlled fury.

"Yes, yes, of course," stammered Tris, relieved to see the gun was disarmed. "But, I, ah…"

They were interrupted by the arrival of the entire household.

"Ah, oh, hello Tris," said William with aristocratic *sangfroid,* as if Foxy regularly fired her shotgun at unexpected guests arriving in the middle of the night. He had taken the time to put on a silk dressing gown over his pajamas. Foxy was shaking. He placed a reassuring hand under the bent forearm Foxy was using to hold the shotgun. She leaned against him in relief, unconscious of how definite she was that she needed him at that moment.

Addie, in a long, flannel nightdress, hurried down the stairs, alarmed by the gunfire. "What...?" Then she cut herself off. "Tris!" She said, remembering the last time she had seen him. "What are you doing here?" Then, seeing the shotgun said, "What happened?" She felt a confused dismay come over her. *Had Tris tried to hurt Dinny? No, no, that just couldn't be...*

Sister Parker, wrapped in chenille, shook her head in dismay. "Honestly," she said, conveying in that one word a cargo of approbation heavy enough to sink a dreadnought.

Mrs. Flowerdew, bringing up the rear, was too short to see the shotgun, but aware that something must be going on that was jangling nerves. She said helpfully, "I'll just make up some cocoa, shall I?" Kathleen and Maisy, asleep in attic rooms, did not wake up.

After assuring herself that Dinny was fine and accepting Foxy's word that she would look after him, Sister Parker retired, with straight-backed umbrage, to her room. Clanging bells warned that someone in the neighborhood had called the police. Aware they had only moments to spare, Foxy said to Tris, "Hide under the bed." Then she took Addie by the wrist. "Are you ready to put on a little show?"

Foxy had already decided to take Addie under her wing. For one thing, she saw that Addie and Dinny loved each other. For another, Addie was a genius at cryptography, and Foxy wanted to mentor her as much as she could.

Addie, with a glint of mischief in her eye, nodded, "Of course. What do I need to do?"

"Pretend I have fainted, and you are soothing me. I'll take care of the rest." She turned to William, who nodded, showing that he understood. "Ask Mrs. Flowerdew to bring in that cocoa as soon as possible."

She stretched out on the sitting room sofa. Addie plumped the ornamental pillows under her head and covered herself with the blanket, which was kept in a hassock for chilly evenings. There came a heavy knock on the door. William opened it and said genially, "Good evening, Sergeant. I assume you are here because my neighbors reported hearing a gunshot?"

He ushered in a sergeant and two police officers whose combined bulk filled the hallway. "Yes, Sir, that is correct," said the sergeant in heavy, solemn tones.

"I must apologize for getting you out on such a chilly night and at such an early hour," said William, laying on with a trowel his practiced upper-class charm laced with a hint of the class condescension he rarely used. "There's been an accident. No one was harmed, thankfully."

He led the policemen into the room where they could witness Foxy playing the role of a distraught, foolish, old woman, stretched out on the sofa, while Addie stroked her forehead and soothed her with calm words. "Here is your culprit," he said. "Please do not upset her any more than she already is over her foolish mistake. She is mortified."

The sergeant took out his pad and pencil. After establishing Foxy's full name, address, and that she was a guest of Lord Ainsworth—she was careful to use her title and his—he said, "Now, can you tell me what happened here? I understand you fired a gun by mistake."

In a high-pitched, quavering voice, Foxy said, "I am such a silly fool. Such a fool. My bedroom is upstairs, and something woke me up. A noise or some such. I looked out the window and thought I saw someone trying to get into the house. I have a shotgun in the closet upstairs."

She paused, noting with a quick, sidewise glance the question forming on the Sergeant's lips. "I'm going on to Scotland in a few weeks for a grouse hunt being held at the lodge near Inverness at the invitation of my dear old friend, Admiral Sir Archibald Leonard Arbuthnot and his wife." Foxy seemed to warm to her subject as she played the role of a garrulous, shallow, name-dropping snob. "You see, officer, er, Sergeant, my husband was an Admiral, and we met the Arbuthnots long ago in India. I don't suppose you've heard of them. No? They have a lovely lodge, and even though I am widowed, I so love fall grouse hunting, once the midges die down, as they do in early September. I hate midges, cannot abide them. I don't suppose anyone likes them. Except other midges, obviously." She paused. "Where was I?"

"You were going to tell me why you fired your shotgun, Lady Butterschloss," said the patient Sergeant.

"Was I? Oh, yes, of course. Well, I saw something moving out in front of the house, and I immediately thought it must be an intruder, so I loaded my shotgun—it's a 12-gauge—with birdshot to frighten him off. You know, birdshot might sting at that distance, but I wasn't shooting to kill. I save that for the grouse." Here, Foxy tittered, as if she had made a joke. "That shot woke everyone up, I'm sorry to say, and set every dog in the neighborhood barking. It turned out," here she laughed coquettishly, "you won't believe this, it was just the cat, Murky. She's usually in the house at night, so I didn't expect her to be outside."

As if on cue, Murky jumped up on the blanket and began to give herself a good wash behind the ears. "And here she is now," said Foxy. "You naughty girl, giving me such a scare. Were you afraid of my little gunny-wunny?" Never having been addressed with baby talk, Murky stopped in mid-ear swipe and gave Foxy an appalled glare with her yellow eyes.

Addie stopped herself from rolling her eyes. William nearly choked but managed to say, "You see, Sergeant, it was just a blunder. I have encouraged Lady Butterschloss to keep her shotgun in the locked gun case where I keep mine until it is time for her to leave for Scotland."

"Yes, I have been such a silly fool to cause all this trouble," said Foxy, her voice quavering again.

Addie stroked her brow. "There, there, you were just trying to protect us all. I call that brave, not foolish," she said as if talking to a six-year-old." Addie tapped a finger alongside her temple to signal to the sergeant that Lady Butterschloss wasn't all there.

Mrs. Flowerdew entered with a tray of mugs and steaming cocoa. William said, "Won't you and your constables have some cocoa to warm you on such a chilly night?"

The two young constables began to reach for the mugs. "No, thank you," said the Sergeant firmly, giving them a quelling glance. "That is most kind of you, Lord Ainsworth, but I think we have finished here." He wanted nothing more than to get as far away from the silly, dangerously irresponsible Lady Butterschloss as he could. As William saw them out, the Sergeant said, "I'll report this as an accidental discharge, and that will put an end to it. But please, keep that gun locked up."

"Yes, I certainly will," said William. "And thank you for your understanding." He waited until he heard the police car drive away and came into the sitting room. He looked steadily at Foxy and asked, "The gunny-wunny?"

Addie, Foxy, and William burst out laughing. Dinny heard them from across the hall. "What's going on? Can Tris come out from under the bed? He's had quite a scare in case you forgot."

The three stopped laughing and rushed to the library. William looked under the bed. "Can I help you get out from there?" he said. Tris crawled out and stood up. He was pale and still a bit shaky. "Good Lord," said William, "you do look all in. Are you hungry at all?" Tris nodded.

Mrs. Flowerdew soon brought two kinds of sandwiches—salmon mayonnaise and thinly sliced lamb—and tea biscuits into the sitting room. William handed Tris and Foxy "stiffeners" of Scotch to help settle their nerves, and one for himself. Addie declined. After bringing the fire back to life and placing Dinny in his reclining wheelchair close to it, William sat down and waited with the rest to hear what Tris had to tell them.

Tris downed his Scotch in two gulps and fell on the sandwiches. "I'm famished," he said, apologizing for his apparent gluttony.

He looked at Foxy with a combination of sheepishness and awe. "I am so sorry I frightened you," he said.

"And I am sorry I fired at you," said Foxy. "I must have taken ten years off your life." Foxy's life had been shortened by a decade as well. She was badly shaken and trying not to show it.

Tris tried to seem calm but found he couldn't. "I am very grateful that you did not blow my head off."

"Oh," said Dinny, in an effort to lighten the mood, "she would never have done that. She always looks before she shoots."

Foxy said emphatically, "Dinny is quite right. I am not an American, after all. That said, I for one would like to know why you came like a thief in the night."

"Yes," said William, lighting his pipe. "Where have you come from?

Perhaps you should start there."

"I left Invergordon yesterday, and…"

His listeners said as one, "Invergordon?"

"What were you doing in the back of beyond?" asked Addie.

"You must have really riled an officer," said Dinny, half-joking.

"There was more to it than that," said Tris, grimly. "Remember that Thursday when we were going to meet at the Above Board?"

"Yes," said Dinny. "I haven't seen you since."

Addie said steadily, "And then you came to my place later. You were very drunk and said quite a few things I didn't understand."

Tris nodded and blushed a beet red. "I was very drunk and frightened." He recounted the ham-fisted interrogation by Agent Knuckle Dragger. "I could tell something dark and possibly dangerous was behind the questions. I was worried about Dinny and my aunts." He turned to Addie and said lamely, "I didn't know how much to say and not to say, or what was behind the questions Agent Knuckle Dragger asked. And I really was far gone with booze. I guess I just went to pieces." William quietly and efficiently poured him another scotch. "I'm so sorry, Addie."

Addie said to herself, *"That's what it was all about. He wasn't threatening Dinny. He was warning me."*

"I made quite an ass of myself, I admit," said Tris, taking the glass from William with a grateful nod. "The next morning, I was rousted by two officers who said I had been ordered to Invergordon to work on what turned out to be a bogus, top-secret project. I tried to find ways to let you know I was in trouble, Dinny."

"You did a very good job of it," said Foxy. "And you can thank Nora for being the inquisitive person she is. She saw the car take you away. And I took away some of the clues you left." Tris saw them on the table and gaped.

Dinny said, "I got the messages, loud and clear. Especially the glass with the evaporated Scotch. You would never have left even a drop in the glass except under extreme duress." The two friends smiled at one another. Dinny explained that he had understood Tris's other clues. "I was a bit thrown off course when Addie told me what you said to her."

Tris blushed again. "I wrote to you to tell you I had been an ass, but I wasn't allowed to send any messages from the base." He paused. "Or receive any either."

William said reassuringly to Tris, "We put most of the story together after dinner. I was planning to try and find out tomorrow where you were and who ordered you there." He took a draw on his pipe. "Foxy and I mistakenly thought you had something to do with the accident, but of course, that turns out to be nonsense."

Tris was dumbstruck. He thought he might weep. He had felt so alone and helpless since he was put unceremoniously on a coastal cruiser and then held as if he were a criminal at Invergordon.

"Tell us the rest of the story," said Addie. "It all sounds so horrible."

Tris told them he was not allowed to leave the base and was ordered to stay at Invergordon until December. "Yesterday, I picked up a week-old local Warwick paper and read an article about the accident. I knew if I asked for compassionate leave, it would be denied. So, I just left the base through a weak spot in the perimeter fence we use when we want a night out at the pub."

A silence fell over his listeners. Dinny was the first to speak. "You mean you are AWOL?"

Tris nodded. "I was fed up with the lies and nonsense that were keeping me at Invergordon, and I needed to know you and Addie were all right. I also needed to tell you why I thought you were in trouble."

"I took the train from Invergordon to Edinburgh and then to London. I didn't want to wake the whole house when I saw the lights were out, but I didn't want to sleep on the front doorstep, either. I saw the window was open on the ground floor and decided to take a chance. It was foolish, I admit." He looked sheepishly at Foxy. "Anyhow, Dinny woke up when I threw my duffel bag through the window. When I tumbled in, I know I gave you a start," he said to Dinny. "We only had time to say a few words…" He broke off.

"Again, I am very sorry I gave you a fright," said Foxy. "We are all on edge. We know that someone tampered with Dinny's car, and we are keeping a close eye on Dinny and Addie. I thought someone was coming to harm Dinny."

Tris took another sip of Scotch. "I was afraid to think that might be true," he said somberly. "I mean, about it not being an accident. Because of what happened to me, I couldn't help wondering. I knew there was something underhanded going on."

"I quite agree," said William. He sounded much calmer than he felt. "Someone has gone to great lengths to make sure something about the sinking of the *Lusitania* never sees the light of day." He turned to Dinny. "By the way, why was your window open? I went around to make sure everything was battened down before going to bed."

"It was stuffy in the room. I wanted fresh air. I can move more than Torquemada permits, even though it hurts like hell. I climbed out of bed and opened the window. My only excuse is that the possibility that either Addie or I might be a target had not really sunk in." He looked at Addie, who tried to give a brave smile. "Sorry," he said to both Foxy and William.

"In the end, there was no harm done," said William. "Think no more about it. We must all be very careful from now on."

Dinny said to Tris, "What was it you were going to tell me? Something your aunts told you while you were in Egypt? The Knuckle Dragger questioned you about it, so it must be important somehow. You said it might help with my research on the *Lusitania*."

Chapter Fifteen

What The Aunts Said

It was sunset in Aswan. The sky and the Nile were a deep, carmine red. Silhouetted against the last light of the sun, children splashed in the water as felucas, their sails tinged red, headed for their docks. Tris sat on the upper deck lounge of the elegant dahabiah, its sails furled, at anchor for the night. His aunts, Alice Dashwood and her sister-in-law Daphne, sipped sherry; Tris had a whiskey and soda. They felt the heat of the day begin to abate as a breeze drifted into the lounge. All three sat in reverential awe at the sanguine sky and river. In front of them, built solidly on boulders that lined the shore, rose the red brick façade of the Cataract Hotel, its windows, reflecting the red light, outlined in white casings. Built by Thomas Cook in 1899, it offered British and Continental tourists the exotic Egyptian décor, ultra-luxurious accommodation, deferential service, and pampering expected by the privileged classes and the crowned heads who stayed there.

The two women were in their late sixties. Alice had a penetrating gaze, a straight nose, thin lips, and short, white hair. Daphne was plump, her face unwrinkled, and her eyes conveyed both warmth and a hint of mischief. One reason for this trip was Alice's desire to visit Alexandria, the port where her husband embarked with the men in his command on his last journey. He died in the sands of Gallipoli. She called on her favorite nephew, Tristan, to come on this trip because Alice's two sons were away, one assigned to the

British embassy in Washington, D.C.; the other a Naval attaché in Moscow. Tristan was very fond of his two aunts, whose vigor and intelligence drew him to them like magnets.

The dahabiah had taken them on a leisurely and restful cruise from Luxor, where they visited the Valley of the Kings to see for themselves where Carter had discovered King Tut's tomb. All three were struck with the wonder of Karnak, its immense columns thrusting into the clear Egyptian sky, and the Temple of Luxor, guarded by two colossal, seated figures of Ramses II.

"When was it that Winston stayed there?" Alice asked her sister-in-law, pointing with her chin at the Cataract Hotel.

The Dashwoods descended from Robert Dashwood, who was made a baronet by Charles II, and were related, albeit distantly, to Churchill through his paternal relatives. Daphne looked up from reading the book by Howard Carter and A.C. Mace, *The Tomb of Tut. ankh.Amen.* Although never married, Daphne evaded the usual fate of a spinster: she was never tied to an elderly, dying relative or obliged to move in with a sibling to help raise nieces or nephews. She attended Lady Margaret's Hall in Oxford, where she studied Classics. Finding the British aristocracy stifling, she used her sizable inheritance to set herself up in Paris, where she studied painting, involved herself with the avant-garde, and held very popular salons. When the war broke out, she volunteered as an ambulance driver but was soon recruited into the espionage network in German-occupied Belgium, *La Dame Blanche.* It was organized by British Military Intelligence Branch 6, or MI6, with headquarters in Rotterdam, to run a network of spies in Belgium and northern France. After the war, she maintained ties with those who ran the operation in both Rotterdam and London, but she never spoke of her espionage during the war to anyone outside that network. Tris knew only that Daphne was on the Continent during the war as an ambulance driver.

Daphne placed a bookmark in her book, took off her wire-rimmed glasses, and looked at the hotel. "Wasn't it 1902? He came here to attend the opening of the Aswan Dam."

"Yes, that's right," said Alice. She fell into a meditative silence. "Shall we tell Tristan about Winston and the *Lusitania?*"

Tristan was taken by surprise.

"Yes, I think so. Tristan might as well know about the stain on that quarter of the escutcheon," replied Daphne. "What about you, Tristan? Are you in the mood for a bit of family history?"

"Yes," he said, "Of course. It sounds very hush-hush and scandalous. Is it?"

"Oh, I can assure you it is both," said Alice. "Why don't you tell him, Daphne? You are closer to the source."

"Yes, I will, but Tristan, you must not ask me how I came to know this," she cautioned. "I shall begin by introducing you to Edward M. House, or Colonel House as he prefers to be called. Have you heard of him?"

"Very little. He was in the American delegation at the conference on the Treaty of Versailles, wasn't he?"

"Yes, but this part of his relationship with Wilson is earlier than that. House has never been in the military, and I doubt he has ever been anywhere near a battlefield in his life. He is an American from Texas, and it is the habit of the governors of Texas to grant the honorific Colonel essentially to anyone of any standing who applies for it. Colonel House was, throughout the war, Woodrow Wilson's closest, most trusted advisor. Wilson sent him to the UK as his emissary during the war, before America finally decided to join us, to try to broker a peace settlement. House wasn't well-educated by any means, and had no diplomatic experience, but you know how brash these Americans can be, especially those from Texas." She gave a shudder of horror, "God help us. Tris, I think I need something a bit stronger if I am going to do this story any justice."

All three ordered Tuxedo Cocktails. After taking a sip, Daphne continued her story.

"The Government, naturally, was far more interested in bringing America into the war than in chasing Wilson's imaginary rainbows of peace and goodwill with the Germans. In point of fact, Wilson thought the ambitions of both Germany and Britain were equally improper and culpable, and he did not trust the British. He relied heavily on House to find a way to bring these two imperialist nations to their senses. It soon became obvious that House might be highly useful to our Government in bringing America into the war."

Daphne took another sip of her cocktail and lowered her voice to a dramatic *sotto voce*. "On May 7, 1915, House was in the company of Edward Grey, who was Foreign Secretary at that time. Grey was showing House around Kew Gardens prior to an appointment House had with the King. While discussing casually the various specimens and listening to House go on about the flora of Texas, Grey worked the conversation around to the war and asked—hypothetically, mind you—what the reaction in the United States would be if an ocean liner with American passengers were struck by a torpedo and sunk. House did not hesitate. He said it would make Americans so angry that America would enter the war on the side of Great Britain."

"What!" exclaimed Tris. Then he lowered his voice. "But that was the day the *Lusitania* was attacked."

Daphne nodded her head. "Yes, it was. But that's not all. House then met with King George. Again, the conversation turned to America and the war, and the King asked House what he thought would be the reaction if a cruise ship, say the *Lusitania,* were sunk with hundreds of Americans aboard. House told the King that Grey had just asked him the same question, and he would give the King the same answer. It would bring America into the war on the side of Great Britain."

Tris choked and coughed in mid-sip of his cocktail. "The King said that to House? I find this extraordinary. I mean to say, I trust you, of course, Aunt Daphne, but it is so difficult to take it in. What was Colonel House's reaction when he learned the *Lusitania* had been sunk by German torpedoes?"

His Aunts cackled with laughter. "At first, he didn't believe it," said Daphne. "I mean, both the Foreign Secretary and the King asked him on the same day on two separate occasions how America would react, and yet when he heard about it later in the day, he was just baffled."

"Thick as a plank," said Alice. "It didn't take him long, though, to urge Wilson to declare war. He left London and went back to Washington to convince him."

"But," said Tris, "Wilson did not declare war, did he? He warned the

Germans he would unless they called off unconditional submarine warfare against shipping in the war zone. The Germans did, at least for a few years." He paused. "Are you saying that the Government *intended* for the *Lusitania* to be sunk, that they were aware it would be attacked? That is horrifying to contemplate. Horrifying."

"Let's just say that the Germans made no secret of designating the *Lusitania* a target before the ship left New York. There was an arrogant belief that the ship could outrun any German U-boat, but the U-boats were active in the area and sank several merchant ships just prior to the sinking of the *Lusitania*."

"To err on the side of caution, then, that means that the King and those in the Government may have *hoped* it would happen, but not that they knew for certain it would," offered Tristan, thoughtfully.

"And that is what the King told House a few days later," said Daphne. "He told House it was quite an extraordinary coincidence that the sinking of the *Lusitania* happened just after they discussed the hypothetical possibility. And House seems to have accepted that. Did I mention he was a dolt?"

"Yes," said Alice in mock reassurance, "I think we have established he was dense and arrogant at the same time."

For a time, they were silent, watching as dusk turned to darkness and stars began to appear. Tris said, "But you said Winston was somehow implicated in all this."

"Yes," said Alice gravely, "we did. The question you need to ask yourself is, where were the promised escorts? Why didn't Admiralty gunships accompany the *Lusitania* once it entered the Irish Sea? Cunard liners expected the escort and received protection on previous voyages."

"Winston was First Lord of the Admiralty," said Tris, recognizing the implications.

"Yes, he was," said Alice, with a bitter tone. "At the time the *Lusitania* sank, he was in France discussing plans for joint operations in the Dardanelles. When confronted with a wave of criticism for failing to protect the *Lusitania*, that was the excuse he and his supporters used. They pointed out he wasn't even at Admiralty when the *Lusitania* entered the Irish Sea. As if Winston were entirely cut off from the Admiralty, as if he could not receive or send coded wireless communications while he was overseas. He could have decided not to provide an escort for the *Lusitania* before he left for France. Pshaw!" she uttered vehemently.

"You see," said Daphne, reaching her hand out to take Alice's wrist to calm her, "there were no escorts, presumably because ships were being sent to the Dardanelles. At least, that is one excuse. But the reality is that Germany made a public threat against the *Lusitania,* and no one told the Cunard company there would be no escort. Nor did the Captain know, or the passengers. They assumed the opposite."

"At the very least," said Tristan, moved by his aunts' account, "Winston was guilty of inaction, of criminal negligence."

Daphne gave a cynical chuckle. "When he was questioned in Parliament about why there were no escorts, Winston said he couldn't discuss the disposition of naval forces because it would give information to the enemy, and besides, the Admiralty could not supply destroyer escorts for every merchant or passenger ship—even though they had been providing them to civilian cruisers. He chose not to explain that sudden, unannounced change in policy." She paused. "It didn't do him much good. He had to resign as First Lord of the Admiralty," she said without satisfaction.

The darkness had settled around them. Alice sat rigidly in her seat and said between clenched teeth. "I think those escort ships were not available because of Winston's damned idea that the Navy could force the Dardanelles with Naval power alone. When that didn't work, they thought they could destroy the Turkish resistance using ground forces. And that's where your uncle Henry died. On the bloody sands of Gallipoli." Daphne put her arm around Alice. The two sat silently. Then Alice said resignedly, "I'll be all right. I didn't know I would react this way. I said my final farewell to Henry when we were at Alexandria."

The river flowed on in the darkness. They heard its eternal force lapping against the hull. It flowed as it had past kingdoms that had risen and fallen, past the pharaohs in their tombs, past Alexandria, where Alice's husband had embarked on the journey to his death. Tristan felt he was being dreamed by a dreamer, one who must never wake or the world would end. The Nile was like a thread pulled by the inexorable needle of Time, stitching together eons of lives, until the thread came to his uncle, to the *Lusitania,* to all who died in the war. The monumental columns stretching to the sky, the colossal Ramses who guarded his own temple, the gilded mummies, all were a great boast, a cry to Time that feeble men could defeat death, outlast their own endings. The monuments remained, crumbling, but death was not defeated. What remained unchanged were the enveloping night, the cold, distant stars, and the mocking sound of the river that flowed on. It mocked the grand plans of men eager to make the world malleable to their will. He heard his Aunt Daphne hiss as she held Alice in her arms: "Damn Churchill. Damn him to hell."

Chapter Sixteen

Code Wodehouse

The fire crackled. It was the only sound in the room after Tris finished his story. His listeners were stupefied as the implications took hold and ramified in their minds. The appalling conclusion was that through the sin of omission, the *Lusitania* became a staked goat to bait the U-boat wolf packs and bring America into the war. It was impossible to imagine, and yet there was the evidence: the missing files and transcripts, the oiled lugs that showed someone wanted Dinny and Addie out of the way or dead, the Knuckle Dragger from MI5 who interrogated Tris, and his orchestrated exile to Invergordon. Aunt Daphne's account was not the addled surmise of a frustrated spinster entering her dotage. She had a source she trusted, and William and Foxy understood immediately that she must have been in the intelligence service during the war and had connections in high places. Very high places. Whoever was behind this also knew that about Daphne. Agent K. Dragger made it glaringly obvious when he wanted to know what Tris's aunts had told him about the *Lusitania*. Peril threatened Addie, Dinny, and Tris. Addie and Dinny were safe with William and Foxy. That left Tris.

William said briskly, "I think the first thing is to get Tris back to Invergordon." His pragmatic call to action brought the others out of their stunned silence.

"Yes, I quite agree," said Dinny. To Tris, he said, "You missed morning muster yesterday. When you miss it again this morning, you will have officially been AWOL for twenty-four hours." He asked William, "Couldn't you do something to smooth the way for Tris?"

"I'll call your Commander. My rank should carry some weight," said William. "And he sounds like the kind of bootlick who will not want his Masters to know you have been off base, not when it was his job to keep you tied up there until December. You should be all right. Certainly, nothing will appear on your record. I don't think you should travel alone at any rate. I'll go with you."

"Thank you, Sir," said Tris. He hadn't thought of himself as in any physical danger, but Dinny's state convinced him that William had a point. "Let me call my mate tomorrow morning. He said he would cover for me. I may not have been missed."

"That may well be, but I will come with you. Now, it is getting on toward two o'clock. Tris, I'll show you to your room," said William.

Foxy cleared her throat. "I have been thinking," she said.

Everyone turned to look at her. "Foxy Thinking" always meant something portentous was soon to be announced.

"Shouldn't we try to find out who this MI5 agent is? His interrogation—and intimidation—of Tris gave his hand away. We now know that Dinny and not Addie is a target for whatever is going on, and that powerful people do not want information about the *Lusitania* to come to light. We also know that Tris had to be gotten out of the way to make sure he told no one about the interview with the MI5 agent. How long have they said you will be assigned to Invergordon?"

"Until December, just before Christmas, if I don't freeze to death or die of boredom first," said Tris, glumly.

Foxy said, "In other words, whatever information it is about the *Lusitania* has to be kept under wraps until Christmas at the latest. That is a very definite schedule. Why does MI5 want a blackout on information about the *Lusitania* between now and December? Something must be going to happen here in the next four months that makes it crucial that the *Lusitania* is kept out of the public eye."

"Possibly a General Election?" ventured William.

Foxy nodded. "Your commanding officer must realize that there is no real reason for your assignment to be treated as top secret," she went on. "There is no reason for you to be confined to base with no contact allowed with the outside world. Your commander must have received orders to keep you *incommunicado* and is not willing to go against whoever issued them, even if it is obvious that the whole thing is as flimsy as Betty Blythe's costumes in *Queen of Sheba*. Who gave him those orders, I wonder?"

She looked intently at Tris. "Could you find out?" she asked. "I know I am asking a great deal, and if it means landing you in hot water, then I wouldn't ask you to go that far. But if there is any way for you to get your hands on the orders that sent you to Invergordon, it might tell us a great deal about who is behind this."

"I have tried sweet-talking the secretary who has access to the personnel records. But I haven't had much luck."

"What?" said Dinny. "You, the Rudolf Valentino of the Royal Navy Volunteer Reserve?"

"Scoff all you want," said Tris. "Molly Sinclair knows her worth. She is a flirt."

"Batting eyelashes, top button of her blouse undone—that sort of thing?" asked Dinny.

Addie shot him a sidewise glance. Josie tried to hide a grin.

"Something like that," said Tris, looking sheepish. "But she will have nothing to do with any man who cannot bring her gifts or take her out to have some fun. I cannot do either." He looked thoughtfully at William. "Could we find time to do a little shopping before the train leaves? It will soften her up if I bring her some gifts."

"Of course," said William. "An excellent idea."

Tris turned to Foxy. "But how would I get word out to you if I find out who had me posted to Invergordon?"

Foxy smiled a knowing smile. "I've thought of that. Is there a local newspaper?"

"Yes, the *North Star and Farmers Chronicle*. It's a daily," said Tris. "I am an avid reader. No news is too trivial when you are bored to the point of insanity."

"Do you think you could get permission to place an ad in it asking for donations of books to the base?" asked Foxy.

Tris nodded. "If I can't get permission, then I can ask a pal to do it. But why?"

"I'm coming to that in a moment," said Foxy. "William, while you are there, could you take out a subscription to this paper and have it delivered to your brother at Thornberry?"

"Certainly," said William. "I take it this involves a code?"

"Yes, of course," said Foxy. "The thing is, though, if you take out a subscription and have the paper sent here, it could tip off the MI5 agent who questioned Tris if this craven commanding officer tells him Tris went AWOL. It wouldn't take even an ape like him long to figure out Tris would want to see his injured mate."

She looked at Addie. "I was thinking we should send Tris home with a book. A recent one and very popular, one that would not seem a curious choice or out of place. Let me think. What about the second Jeeves book? *The Inimitable Jeeves?* It came out almost a year ago."

Foxy turned to William. "Do you think Mr. Belltower has it in stock at his bookstore? Tris needs a copy, and so do I."

"I can do better than that. I have a copy in the library," said William. He soon retrieved it. "Tris can take this, and we can get a new copy."

"Now what?" Tris asked.

"Now, we pick a page to use as the code," said Addie.

"Except," said Foxy, "I am going to pick the first sentence in a chapter just in case the pagination is different in a later edition." She flipped through the pages. Her eyes fell on Chapter Eight. She read aloud, "'I had met Sir Roderick Glossop before, of course, but only when I was with Honoria.' Addie and I will write down instructions on how to use this sentence to create a substitution code."

Tris nodded. "And when I know the name of the bloke—and I really mean the bastard, if you will pardon my language—who sent me off to prison at

Invergordon, I will take out an ad in the *Northern Star.* But how will you know which of the letters I use refer to the code?"

"You use a coded letter only as the first letter in each sentence. The rest of the words don't matter, as long as each sentence makes sense and seems to be about getting donations of books to the base library," said Foxy.

"Then, my brother receives a copy of the *North Star and the Farmer's* whatsit. He finds an ad soliciting books and sends it on to me," said William.

Addie asked, "Why not have the paper sent to a fake name, care of your brother's estate? That way, anyone who is too curious would think it was for someone from Invergordon who is in service at Thornberry."

"Good idea," said Foxy.

"Excellent," said William. "And now, I think, it really is time to get to bed. Tris, you will find a pair of my pajamas laid out for you in an upstairs bedroom."

"Addie and I will write out the instructions for a substitution code using a constrained text. It shouldn't take too much time." Foxy turned to Addie, "Is that all right with you?"

Addie replied with a wide grin. "I was hoping you would ask."

With that, they said goodnight for a second time, agreeing to meet at seven for breakfast.

Addie and Foxy each poured another cup of cocoa and sat down at a small writing table with *The Inimitable Jeeves.*

Addie and Foxy met Tris at breakfast. After they ate, they pushed aside their plates. Foxy laid a piece of paper in front of Tris.

- I = A
- H = B
- A = C
- D = D
- M = E
- E = F
- T = G
- S = H

- I = I
- R = J
- R = K
- O = L
- D = M
- E = N
- R = O
- I = P
- C = Q
- K = R
- G = S
- L = T
- O = U
- S = V
- S = W
- O = X
- P = Y
- B = Z

"Now, Tris," said Foxy, "the left column is the first twenty-six letters, in the order they appear, in the first sentence of Chapter Eight. The right column lists the letters of the alphabet in order. You take the letter you need to encode from the right column and use the corresponding letter from the left column. So 'C A T' is 'A I L.'"

Tris nodded.

"What you need to do," continued Addie, "when you send a message, is start each sentence in your message with the code letter for the corresponding letter in the word you are spelling. For example, the message might be this: 'A thought has occurred to me. I need to write a letter to my sister. Livia will wonder what has become of me.'" She showed what she had written to Tris. "The first letters in these sentences are A-I-L. They decode as C-A-T."

Tris nodded again. "I get it. It is quite simple. What about the doubled letters in the code? There are two Rs and two Ss. Won't that be confusing to you when you try to decipher the message?

Foxy smiled reassuringly. "No, because there are only two choices for each doubled letter, which will make deciphering easy for anyone with the code. Anyone trying to break the code will count the frequency of letters—how many times any given letter is used—so to have two of the same letters in the code will throw them off."

Tris nodded, "Can I just keep this paper?"

"No," said Foxy. "It could be stolen, or you might mislay it. In that case, if it is found, you will be asked questions about it. Or if it isn't found, you will worry yourself sick wondering if someone else has it. It is the most important principle of security: use your codebook, not a key to the code that you carry around with you. Just don't forget that the code is Chapter Eight, the first twenty-six letters. Make the message as short as possible to be completely clear."

"I will remember that," said Tris. "Thanks. Both of you. I won't let you down."

"If we can find out who sent you to Invergordon to cool your heels, it will give us a lead on who is targeting Dinny and Addie," said Foxy.

"I know that, too," said Tris, looking with concern at Addie. There was nothing he would not do to protect her and Dinny. "My plan is to woo Mary Sinclair, but I don't want to lead her on to thinking I want something more serious than a flirtation. No jewelry, no perfume, but something that says LONDON POSH. I thought we could stop at Fortnum and Mason's and pick up chocolates in one of their boxes that has their name blazoned on it, a box that is not too small, and not too large, but just right."

"I think you are confusing Miss Sinclair with Goldilocks," said Addie, teasing, "but that sounds just the ticket. A couple of pounds of mixed chocolate with the famous Tristan charm should be worth a peek at your file."

The awkwardness between them was gone. Before going to bed, Tris had sat with Addie and Dinny. Tris described to Dinny his drunken visit to Addie, explaining his confused state of mind. He apologized repeatedly.

Addie said, "It wasn't like you, Tris, but I was at a loss to know what was behind it. I realized tonight that you were actually worried about Dinny, not threatening him, and that Agent really put the wind up you."

The three agreed to put Tris's lapse behind them and concentrate on finding out why Tris and Dinny were targets.

Tris said to Foxy, "I would also like to purchase a gift for Mrs. Sweet, the base librarian. She lives up to her name. I would have gone insane without her suggestions for what I should read to stave off the boredom. I want to win her over to the scheme of a book drive. She is in her late sixties and lives off base, alone as far as I can tell, except for her cat."

Foxy thought for a moment. "For a librarian, something practical but also special. How about an Eversharp propelling pencil in gold plate?"

"Yes," said Tris with a relieved smile. "I know she would like to have one."

"I think gold plate would please Mrs. Sweet, and she would use it, I'm sure. I rely on having it with me at all times," said Foxy. She glanced at her watch. "You and William will need to leave soon if you are going to purchase the gifts and catch the 10:00 express. Fortnum opens at nine. There is a very fine stationers next to it, where I purchased my Eversharp. It's called Cables. If I call ahead, I know they will have one ready in a lovely gift box. You could find what you need at Fortnum, and William could pick up the propelling pencil. That should leave you enough time to get to the station, which is about twenty minutes away from Fortnum, and buy your tickets.

Tris found his uniform had been brushed and steamed. He bathed and dressed and met William in the sitting room. "I'll call ahead to see what might be waiting for me at the base."

He placed the call and asked for Allen, his best friend, drinking partner, cribbage player, and companion in sneaking out of camp. "How are things?" Allen asked cheerfully when he came to the phone.

"I finished my business, and I will be back at the base tomorrow night," said Tris.

"Your business, you call it," said Allen. "That's a funny name for it, I must say."

Allen thought Tris left base in pursuit of a woman. Confused, Tris said, "I can't really talk about that now. What I want to know is how much trouble am I in for missing muster?"

Allen chuckled. "None at all. None at all. I told you I would cover for you, and I did. I volunteered to take over the roll call yesterday and this morning. You were recorded as present both times. None of your mates have said a word. Since you are officially supposed to be in what they call a lab doing top-secret work, your absence has not been noticed by anyone else."

"I really owe you for this," said Tris.

"Don't forget my tea and coffee," said Allen, "and keep on losing at cribbage. That will be payment enough."

"I'll be arriving late tonight. Can we meet at the Shipping Out? I'll have someone with me."

"Oh, so that's it?" said Allen, assuming he was going to meet Tris's lover, bride, fiancé, or sweetheart. "Someone special, I take it?"

Tris, still confused, said, "I guess you might say that. Anyhow, can you meet us and reserve a room for the person I am bringing?"

"Of course, of course," said Allen cheerfully. "Nothing would give me more pleasure."

Soon after breakfast, Foxy asked Mrs. Flowerdew to pack a small basket with berry preserves, rich butter, and a bit of cream—all sent from the Butterschloss estate. She also asked for an empty Thermos. After saying farewell to William and Tris, Foxy and Addie set off in a cab for their first day of work. Foxy had the cab stop at the Pâtisserie Chelsea. She purchased half a dozen croissants, still warm, and had the Thermos filled with hot, strong coffee. These she snuggled into her basket, which she carried over her arm as they entered the Admiralty. After they had checked in with the Porter and picked up their ID cards, Foxy handed the basket to Addie. "This is to break the ice with Jan Gruter," she said. "I am going to report to McCreedy, and then I will find you in the ARO."

"You can't come to work wearing that!" was how McCreedy greeted her.

"Wearing what?" said Foxy with mock innocence. She was dressed in an ensemble Coco Chanel designed for her: flare-legged trousers in a dark navy knit jersey, topped by a crisp, white cotton blouse that came to just below the waistline. A linen navy-blue short jacket completed the suit. Years earlier, Foxy met Coco at an embassy party and discussed with her the need for designs suitable for the older, zaftig woman.

"Those, those trousers," he spat out.

"McCreedy, where have you been? Women wore trousers during the war in the factories and on the farms, as you very well know," said Foxy.

"The war is over, or hadn't you heard?" said McCreedy with snide sarcasm.

"Yes, but then along came Coco and truly liberated us all," said Foxy, laughing.

"Coco? Who or what is Coco?" snarled McCreedy. "Sounds like a hot drink for children."

"She is the French woman who designs clothes women can wear," said Foxy. "I would love to fill you in on the history of women's fashion, but I understand there is work to be done. I just stopped by to report to you. I'm off to the ARO," said Foxy. "I'll let you know if we find out anything useful about the *Lusitania* records."

"'We?'" blustered McCreedy. "What do you mean? I know Lt. Custus is on sick leave. Some kind of car accident," he said, evincing no sympathy.

"Don't you remember? You very generously reauthorized Adelaide Gold to use the ARO. She is with me today. She will also need authorization from you to question the messengers involved in getting the files from the ARO and delivering them."

"Yes, yes. She can pick that up from my secretary, Seaman Ridley, anytime." He paused. "Well, see to it there are no more missing files. And remember, you are reporting directly to me." Foxy turned to go. "Dismissed," said McCreedy in one last effort to assert his control. *And I hope you stay in the basement, so no one else can see you in that ridiculous outfit.*

Foxy took the elevator to the basement. It was an hour before the ARO would open for the day. Addie had spread the croissants, jam, butter, and cutlery on the blue tea towel Mrs. Flowerdew included. The coffee was served in the mugs reserved for the staff. Jan Gruter was seated behind his desk. Addie sat facing him. Gruter rose when Foxy entered the room. "How do you do?" he said formally. "Allow me to introduce myself. I am Jan Gruter. And you must be Lady Butterschloss. Welcome to the Records

Office." He pulled an oak office chair on wheels close to Addie and held it for Foxy.

Foxy reminded herself that Gruter was from the Netherlands, which was a hotbed of espionage during the war. William, too, had wondered if Gruter had been a spy during the war, which would account for him being assigned to the post of librarian—a civilian posting with few responsibilities and good pay—as compensation.

Gruter was in his mid-fifties. He was tall, slender, and had a long face with a high forehead and a mouth that drooped slightly. His full head of blond hair was combed back from his face. His clear, blue eyes showed a shrewd intelligence, perhaps with a hint of acerbity. His bearing was dignified, certainly reserved, and he seemed perpetually wary.

"Thank you," said Foxy, taking the offered seat, "It is a pleasure to meet you. Addie has told me how very helpful you have been." What she wanted to say was, *How did you get this job? Were you a spy in Holland for the Admiralty during the war?* Instead, she accepted a cup of coffee and a croissant. "I hope I can be of some help to you, especially in finding the missing files."

"Certainly," said Gruter. "By the way, I want to thank you for this. The coffee and croissants remind me of home."

"Do you mean Holland?" asked Foxy, who brought the coffee and rolls in the hope they would make Gruter nostalgic and provide her an opening for probing his past.

"Oh, no," said Gruter, quietly. "I meant Colchester. My father was from Amsterdam, but my mother was English. I spent my school years in the UK, and my summers in Amsterdam with my grandparents. Pa and mam both loved croissants and very strong coffee for breakfast."

So much for the food-of-your-people gambit, thought Foxy. But at least she understood why Gruter spoke English without a Dutch accent. "I am so pleased you enjoyed it," she said. "Now, perhaps, you wouldn't mind if I asked you a few questions about the files?"

"Not at all," said Gruter. This was Addie's cue to excuse herself and find the messengers who had delivered Dinny's request for the *Lusitania* files to the ARO, and who brought the files from there to Dinny.

"Were you here when the request arrived from Dinny for the *Lusitania* files?" asked Foxy.

"No, actually. I found the request under my paperweight just before I locked up for the night. I was making my last round to check that there was no one at any of the reading desks. This usually takes me about half an hour, sometimes a bit more, because I also pick up any stray material left on the desks to place in the reshelving carts. And when I returned, I saw the request under this." He held up an eleven-inch marlin spike with a steel shaft honed to a fine point. "I tell the Messengers to leave the requests under this if I am not at my desk. This is a ceremonial spike," he said with a hint of nostalgia, "given to me by a friend when he retired from the Navy. You see? It has copper and brass around the top of the shaft and is engraved with the name of the ship that was his last command." He set it down and seemed lost in memories for a moment. "Then, I took the keys, turned out the lights, and left. I locked the door, as usual, of course."

Foxy was familiar with the ARO. "If I recall," she said, looking around, "you could not have seen the desk for most of the time you were checking the reading desks. The shelving would have blocked your view. Did you hear anyone come in?"

Gruter took a sip of coffee and nodded toward the far wall hidden behind tall shelves. "Yes, yes, of course. I was just over there when I heard the door open and then close again soon after. I assumed it was a Messenger delivering a late request."

Foxy nodded. "So, you assumed you were right when you saw the request on your desk. Tell me, did you say anything to the Messenger—I mean, call out a greeting or anything of that sort?"

"Good heavens, no, nothing of that sort," said Gruter, who clearly thought it would be an undignified breach of Naval protocol to call out a familiar greeting to a mere Messenger.

"Naturally," said Foxy, who thought Gruter stood on his dignity. "Was there anyone lingering at any of the reading desks?"

"Yes, there were one or two, as I recall. But if I can anticipate your next question, I think they left before I heard the Messenger come in. I know them both. They are regulars here. I can get their names for you, if you wish," offered Gruter. Foxy thanked him and asked if anyone had ever requested the files before.

"Absolutely not," said Gruter, "at least not since I started here. I am sure of that because the next morning, I had to enter the request. The files came to the ARO in 1916."

"And there was nothing unusual or out of place when you came in that morning?" asked Foxy.

Gruter shook his head. "I came in as usual around 8:00, I made tea, went through the requests, and gathered one or two of the more frequently requested items. I checked in the card catalogue to confirm the location of the decrypts, but I did not go to see if they were there. I located the *Lusitania* files, signed them out, as I said, and I called a Messenger to take them upstairs to Lieutenant Custus. That would have been about 9:30."

"And that was about the same time Addie—I mean Miss Gold—came to ask you for the decrypts?"

Gruter confirmed the files were missing and had never been requested. Then, Lieutenant Custus called to say the files were missing from his desk.

"It is all quite shameful," said Gruter, shaking his head.

"No one could blame you," Foxy said. "As you say, you followed the correct procedures." She paused. "And I assume you did not mention the request for the *Lusitania* files to anyone."

Gruter smiled his gentle smile again. "I assure you, once I close that door behind me, the last thing I want to do is think about this office."

"Quite understandable," said Foxy, "and I assume your wife would not want to hear about…oh, I am so sorry. That was quite unforgivable. I did not mean to pry into your private life." Of course, that is exactly what she had wanted to do.

"I am a widower," said Gruter, matter-of-factly. "I lead a very quiet life."

Foxy rose to clear away the cups and repack the jam, butter, Thermos, and tea towel. She smiled brightly. "You have been very helpful. If you don't mind, I would like to come back tomorrow at the same time to have a look around at the shelves just to double-check that the files have not been misshelved. Perhaps fresh eyes might spot something your assistants missed."

"I would be most grateful," said Gruter. "And will Miss Gold join you?"

"Yes, she and I will be working closely together to find out what happened to those files."

"In that case, permit me to return the favor and provide coffee and rolls," said Gruter.

Chapter Seventeen

Foxy and Addie Investigate

After she left the ARO, Addie found McCreedy's secretary and picked up the authorization to question the Messengers. Seaman Rigley directed her to the office of the Clerk for Office Staff Management. There she was shown to a small room with a table and chairs.

The first Seaman was Chauncey Caxton, who was blonde-haired, blue-eyed, with small, foxlike features. He was fit and wiry. Addie couldn't help asking about his family because his name suggested an aristocratic lineage, and his speech was educated. "My father," he said in an arrogant, upper-middle-class tone, "is related to an officer in the upper echelons of the Admiralty—no one you would know, obviously—and wanted me to learn some military discipline before taking over the family business. He thought a few years as an ordinary Seaman would help me learn the ropes, so to speak."

How serving as a Messenger in the Admiralty would help with that, Addie couldn't imagine. She asked him about the day the files went missing.

"There was nothing exceptional about it," said Chauncey, who adopted a bored attitude. "I was sent to Lt. Custus about 16:45 the previous day. He handed me an ordinary requisition form. They are pink, for some reason, by the way, I assume to make it clear where they are supposed to be taken, just in case some of us cannot read 'Requisition' and 'Record Office' across the top of the page. And, between us, I think there are any number of Seamen who could not. Read it, I mean." Addie gathered that Chauncey did not agree with his father that a stint as a Seaman Messenger could help him prepare to run a large business.

"You took it straight to the basement, I assume?" said Addie neutrally to avoid revealing she was not enchanted with Chauncey's manner.

"Yes, I took the elevator, as a matter of fact. Usually, I would take the stairs, of course," he offered, wanting to assure Addie of his athletic fitness. "But my watch ends at seventeen hundred, and I wanted to be off."

"Did you see or encounter anyone?" asked Addie.

"I was in a bit of a hurry as I said, and as I opened the door, I bumped into Professor Arensdorf. He dropped the papers he was carrying. But what else would you expect?"

"What do you mean?" asked Addie. "Is he nearsighted?"

"No," said Chauncey mildly. "Just Jewish. A clumsy oaf."

Addie stood up and smacked Chauncey hard across his face, bringing tears to his eyes. Then she bashed him over the head with her notebook and pushed him over backward in his chair. That is what she wished she could do to this loathsome toad.

"Anyhow, he knocked the requisition out of my hand. There it was, on the floor, with his papers. He bent over to pick his up, and I did the same to get the requisition," said Chauncey.

"You didn't help him pick up his notes?"

"No, why should I? They weren't mine."

Addie was willing to bet that Chauncey was a bully, among other odious aspects of his character, and had pushed or bumped Arensdorf on purpose.

"What you are suggesting is that Professor Arensdorf saw the requisition for the files," said Addie, dryly.

"Yes, I suppose he might have seen what files were being requisitioned. Why? Oh, I see what you mean. Those are the files that have gone missing. Something about the *Lusitania*, was it?"

Addie was not taken in by Chauncey's disingenuousness. He knew perfectly well why he was being interviewed. "How is it that you know Professor Arensdorf?" she asked.

"Because the ARO seems to be his second home. He is always there, looking things up. I have heard Gruter refer to him by name. He is a professor at the LSE. That's all I know about him."

"Then how do you know he is Jewish?" asked Addie.

"Oh, you can always tell," said Chauncey breezily.

Well, obviously, you can't, thought Addie, "*or you would have knocked this chair out from under me by now, by accident, of course.* "What happened next?" asked Addie.

"Nothing, really. I put the requisition on Gruter's desk, placed the marlin spike on top, and left. I saw Professor Arensdorf get into the elevator. Rather than wait for the elevator to come back down, I took the stairs. I came here, signed out, and was on my way at seventeen hundred hours exactly."

"And you saw no one else in the ARO or coming out of it?" asked Addie.

"No," said Chauncey. "I assumed Gruter was doing his regular routine of checking the reading tables, so I did not expect to see him."

Addie wanted nothing more than to be rid of Chauncey Caxton. "Thank you," she said, "that will be all."

"My pleasure," said Chauncey, cockily pushing his chair back and giving Addie a wink. Addie felt her flesh creep.

Alone again, Addie asked for a cup of strong tea to wash away the taste of bile her interview with Caxton left in the back of her throat. She then interviewed Seaman Sidney Field, who was tall, slim, with red hair, laughing, brown eyes, and an open face. He was more than willing to assist with her inquiries.

"Aye, right," he said in his lilting Edinburgh accent. "I took the file up to Lt. Custus. He seemed quite pleased to receive it."

"Did you happen to see if there were any other people around when you delivered the files or when you left the office?

"Aye, I did, I had to give a right smart salute to Captain McCreedy. He is quite strict on such matters." Sidney gave an exaggerated salute and smiled at Addie. He was confident she would understand what a pillock McCreedy was. "He was coming down the hall to my right. I had to pass him to get to the stairs."

"So, he must have seen you leave Lt. Custus' office?" asked Addie.

"He must have, unless he is blind," said Sidney.

"You didn't happen to be near Lt. Custus' office when he left not long after?" she asked.

"It happens, I did. I had to pick up papers from the Office of the Comptroller. I saw Lt. Custus come out of his office and rush to the stairs. He looked all peely-wally." Noting the confused look on Addie's face, he said, "Sorry. I meant he was very pale, like the blood drained from his face. Then, he just skedaddled. Pushed right past me and headed for the stairs." Sidney pantomimed being pushed and rocked his body back in the chair. He clearly enjoyed telling a story. "He left the door open. I didn't think that was right. So I pulled it closed."

"Did you happen to see what was on his desk?" asked Addie.

Sidney suddenly became serious. "Nothing except the file I delivered. I didn't chore anything."

"Chore?" asked Addie.

"I mean steal. I didn't steal anything."

"I wasn't suggesting anything like that," said Addie calmly and with a smile. She was taken with Sidney's charm. "Did anyone else see Lt. Custus rush from his office?"

Aye, McCreedy was in the hall at the time. Lt. Custus went right past him. Probably forgot to salute. That would have really put him up to a high doh. That means—"

Addie laughed. She realized he was flirting with her now by using words she didn't recognize. "You don't have to translate. I am sure I understand. Is there anything else you can tell me?" Field shook his head. "You have been most helpful," she said. "Thank you so much."

"Any time, any time at all," said Sidney as he rose and left, giving her another of his broad smiles. "Lang may your lum reek," he said. "That means 'may your chimney smoke for many years.'"

"Thank you, I think," said Addie, smiling at him as he left the room.

Foxy hesitated at the door to the Above Board where she and Addie agreed to meet for lunch. She had been here with Robin the night before he shipped out for the last time.

"Foxy, we're over here," she heard her husband call. Her face lit into a wide smile as she crossed the room to the table where William, Dinny, and Robin sat.

"Hello, Robby," she said, giving him a quick kiss on the cheek. Robin was handsome and in his late forties. Foxy adored the crinkles around his eyes, the slight greying of his dark hair just around his temples, the healthy tan from his times at sea.

"Hello, Foxy," he said with the light in his blue eyes that he always had for her. He shifted slightly as she slid onto the bench beside him.

"Auntie Em," said Dinny, "Can I get you a cider?"

"That would be lovely, Dinny," said Foxy.

"You're looking good, William," she said. "I haven't seen much of you at NID this past week.

William smiled at Foxy. "Yes, I'm sorry to say, it's true. Blinker has kept me quite busy these past few weeks."

Dinny returned and placed Foxy's cider in front of her. "Well, I see we all have our drinks," said William. "I propose the first toast, which is to Robin." He held up his glass, "To our ships at sea and all who sail on them, especially Admiral Paganel." Foxy took her husband's hand as she drank. She was determined to put on a brave face.

Dinny raised his glass next. "Fair winds and an even keel, Uncle."

Foxy felt her throat start to close and tears well up. *"Damn,"* she said to herself. She cleared her throat and said huskily, "Go out safe and return safe." Her husband squeezed her hand. They dared not look at each other.

Robin cleared his throat. "Thank you all. I'll be buying you a first round in a few days. Meanwhile, here's to ourselves."

"To ourselves," they said in unison.

Foxy took a deep breath and tried to swallow the lump in her throat. When she felt able, she entered the Above Board and spotted Addie, head bent, writing up the notes from her interviews. They each ordered a ploughman's lunch with a cider. As they ate, they compared notes.

"Hmm," said Foxy. It sounded like a deep-throated growl. "So, McCreedy might be the culprit after all. He takes umbrage at Dinny for forgetting to throw him a salute or doing it carelessly. He wants to find a more serious reason to place Dinny on report. He realizes his office is empty, goes in with a vague idea of finding some sort of contraband—whiskey in his desk drawer, for instance—his eye falls upon the file marked 'secret,' and he swipes it. It would be just like him."

Addie took a bite of her pickle and chewed thoughtfully. "But what about the decrypts? They have disappeared, too."

Foxy took a drink of the cider, set it down, thought for a second, and said, "Yes, that's a good point. But they might have disappeared at any time since 1915 or 16. No one but you has ever requested them. Who knows how long they have been gone? It could be just a strange coincidence."

"'To use a phrase by which things are settled now,'" said Addie, delighted with herself for remembering the line from Byron's *Don Juan.*

"I agree," said Foxy, getting Addie's point. "I don't believe in coincidences either. The two are connected. Maybe McCreedy's strings are being pulled by someone higher up. What else did you come up with?"

"I think," said Addie, we need to ask Professor Arensdorf about the day before. It seemed obvious to me that the little worm Caxton wanted to cast suspicion in his direction. Josie said she would help arrange a meeting with him. I'll call the flat and tell her I'll be there for dinner after work. I'll bring her up to date and then come to Chelsea House."

Over their meal in the flat that evening, Addie told Josie what happened the night before, after Josie left.

"You cannot be serious," she said. "Foxy shot at Tris at close range? You must be joking. This really isn't funny, Addie."

"It is not something I would joke about," said Addie, seriously. "There was blue smoke, shattered glass, and Tris and Foxy were white as sheets."

"Do you mean to tell me that Foxy could have blown Tris's head off last night?"

"Not Foxy. She came very close, though. If she had less steel in her nerves, she certainly would have. She shifted her aim just as she fired. I mean, after all, what do you expect? She saw someone climbing into Dinny's window in the dead of night," said Addie.

"But, why a gun? Did she think someone meant to harm Dinny? I mean, it might have been a burglar who was only interested in the silver," said Josie. "People aren't usually tucked up in bed in a downstairs library."

"Because of what we found out last night while you were there. Remember, the car wreck wasn't an accident. Someone tampered with Dinny's car."

Josie gave a little shiver. "Yes, I can see why that would put her nerves on edge. She thought someone was trying to finish what they intended to do when they loosened the lugs. But you haven't said why Tris was sneaking in the window at 1:00 in the morning. And where has he been?"

"You will find that hard to believe, too," said Addie.

Addie told Josie the story of Tris's interrogation by an MI5 agent, his exile to Invergordon, and his decision to go AWOL. Josie understood for the first time the full meaning of being struck dumb. Finally, she found her voice.

"I don't know what to say? Why would anyone care what Dinny might have told Tris about the *Lusitania?* Or, for that matter, what his Aunt told Tris? And he went AWOL. Do you think he will be in a lot of trouble?" she asked. She was distressed, alarmed, and felt helpless. Tris and Dinny were two of her oldest friends, along with Addie, and Josie was still shaken by the thought that Addie and Dinny could have been intentionally killed or badly injured.

"I am not sure if Tris will be in trouble or not," said Addie. He thinks not, but William has gone with him to Invergordon just in case," said Addie. "I'll make some tea. I bought a Madeira cake on my way home."

Fortified by a steaming cup of tea and a slice of cake, Josie could focus her thoughts better. "And you are saying that all of this—what happened to you and Dinny, and what happened to Tris—is because Dinny wanted to find out more about the *Lusitania?*"

Addie nodded. "Yes, and I am helping Foxy find out what happened to the files at Admiralty. We started working there today."

Josie froze with her cup midway to her lips. "Foxy is working at Admiralty?"

Addie smiled at the look of surprise on Josie's face. "She pulled some strings of her own. We are authorized to ask questions about what happened the day I couldn't find the decrypts, and someone stole the files from Dinny."

Josie took a sip of tea. "This is a lot to take in all at once," she said. She thought another slice of cake would help her piece together all the information Addie had given her.

Addie also took another slice. "I know it is overwhelming. And we need your help."

Josie stared at her. "Me? What can I do?"

"I know you offered to set up a meeting with Professor Arensdorf. He was there the evening Dinny sent a messenger to the ARO requesting the *Lusitania* files. Arensdorf literally bumped into the messenger. Maybe he remembers something important, or maybe he was there the next day when the files disappeared, and he saw or heard something that can help."

"Of course," said Josie. "I will see if I can get an appointment with him tomorrow. I know he is giving a morning lecture. If he agrees, how can I reach you?"

Josie had the phone number for the house in Chelsea. Addie gave her the number for the Porter at Old Admiralty. "By the way," said Josie, "why did you decide to stay on at the Chelsea house? Does it have anything to do with Dinny?" She raised an eyebrow, quizzically.

Addie blushed ever so slightly. "William and Foxy wanted me to stay for my own safety. You don't mind, do you, being here on your own for a few days?"

Josie shook her head as she got up to put on water for more tea. "No, not at all. It gives me a chance to search for your love letters or diary and to try on all your clothes to see if they suit me. If they do, I can 'borrow' them without you being any the wiser." They both laughed.

"If you find any love letters, they were for someone who lived here before I did," said Addie.

"Seriously," said Josie, "I miss you, but I would rather know you were safe at the Chelsea townhouse." She gave a sly smile. "And of course, with Dinny laid up, you have a real opportunity to work your charms on him. He can't run away even if he wanted to, which I don't think he does, judging by how you two were making eyes at each other last night." She poured two fresh cups of tea. "How did things go with Tris? Did you settle your quarrel with him?"

Addie said, "Josie, he lost his head. He was rattled by the interrogation. He wanted to find Dinny to tell him he might be in danger. When he didn't find him, he thought Dinny had pushed him aside and wanted to be alone with me. That triggered his old feelings of jealousy. If he hadn't added a drinking spree to his fear, confusion, distress, anger—all of it—he might have been able to handle himself better. As drunk as he was, he needed to let off steam. The three of us talked it all over last night, and we are fine now."

Josie pretended to look disappointed. "So, no chocolate?"

Addie said, "That reminds me. I didn't tell you. Tris is going to try and sweet talk one of the civilian secretaries on the base to check his file and tell him who ordered him to Invergordon. He planned to buy her the biggest box of chocolates at Fortnum's before he boarded the train with William this morning."

Josie smiled. "I pity her. When Tris turns on his charm, the night sky lights up like the opening night of a Hollywood movie. Mr. Irresistible, that's what he is." She started to clear the table. Then paused with dishes in her hands. "Wait. How is he going to let anyone know once he finds out the answer? You said he cannot leave the base or receive or send messages."

Addie replied matter-of-factly, "Foxy and I worked out a simple code for him to use. When he finds out, he is going to take out an ad in the local paper using the code to send us the name. William will take out a subscription for it when he is in Invergordon. He is having it sent to a false name at his brother's estate."

"You two made up a code just like that?" said Josie.

"Yes, just like that," said Addie. "It isn't hard once you know how, and there doesn't seem to be much about codes and ciphers Foxy doesn't know."

Josie was affected by the seriousness and complexity of the efforts to find out who was behind the threats and intimidation of her friends. "There's nothing I wouldn't do to help," she said gravely.

"I know that," said Addie, grateful to have Josie as a friend. They trusted one another's resolve because of the ordeal by jeers, humiliation, and outright intimidation they had endured at Cambridge. "Now let's do the washing up."

When Foxy arrived at the Chelsea townhouse that afternoon, she found Dinny on the sofa, reading. He was restless and bored. Foxy pulled one of the armchairs close to him and took his hand in hers.

"I wanted to talk to you about last night, I mean, about firing my shotgun. I wish I could tell you how wretched I feel. I know better than to rush around with a loaded gun, never mind fire it without being certain of the target. I have no excuse. None. I was so terrified after William told us the lug nuts had been greased. All I could think about was not losing you. I cannot let anything happen to you." She broke off.

Dinny said softly, "I know. I understand. Don't forget, I still feel Uncle Robin's absence every day, too. He is always in my thoughts. I didn't know Timmy, but how could you not ache for him still? I still feel the loss of my parents, so I understand."

Tears came into Foxy's eyes. "Yes, that's it. I was so afraid of losing you, and the pain of losing Robin and Timmy just welled up, and then I was like a, like a—"

"Grizzly protecting her cub?" said Dinny, smiling.

"Yes, yes, I think at some level, I was acting on pure animal instinct. And that is not a good idea when I have a loaded gun in my hand. That is what haunts me. I was in an irrational state."

"What you need to think instead, Auntie Em," said Dinny, "is that you acted far more rationally than someone less experienced with a loaded shotgun would have. You didn't just pull the trigger. You looked and saw you were about to shoot at someone you knew, and you reacted quickly. There are very few people I know with such reliable reflexes. I would say your rational side was firmly connected to instincts and your trigger finger."

Foxy felt a profound gratitude for having Dinny in her life. She always had, but at that moment, it was deeper and stronger than she could have thought possible.

"I've never said this to you before, but you have always been my anchor," said Dinny. I miss Uncle Robin terribly, but he was so often away at sea. When we were on our own at Butterschloss, you were just as enthusiastic about exploring the estate as I was. You were so fascinated by everything I found and encouraged me to bring everything that I liked back to the house. I don't know where you found all those display cabinets for everything I collected—rocks, insects, bird feathers, skeletons of fish found washed up by the ocean, fossils, and shells." He laughed at the recollection. "I thought I had a treasure hoard."

Foxy smiled at the memory. "I had Knott organize search parties in the attics to find those cabinets. I think any number of people who lived at Butterschloss before us must have been amateur naturalists."

"Your enthusiasm for my treasures meant so much. You made me feel confident because what I liked was what you liked, too. You gave me what I needed. I felt lost, bewildered, and frightened after Mother and Father were killed. You pulled me out of my shell. Every day became a new adventure— searching for things to add to my collections, horseback riding, reading poetry at night with cups of hot cocoa, learning to shoot clay pigeons, sailing in the dinghy—and it brought me back to life. That is why it pains me so much to see you feeling the same way I did when I arrived at Butterschloss. I want you to know I am very proud of you. Don't lose your confidence in who you are. I know last night you wanted to protect me, and you didn't kill or harm anyone. Although I have to admit I stopped breathing until the blue smoke cleared and I realized the only thing you hit was the window."

"Thank you, Dinny. You have no idea how much that means to me." She wished she could say more, but didn't want to embarrass Dinny with a display of emotions. She said with determination and steel in her voice, "And we are going to move heaven and earth to find out who did this to you, and who has interfered with Tris, too."

"That reminds me," said Dinny. "This came today from Dr. Collard." He pulled a small, enameled medallion from the pocket of his dressing gown. "It's what he found in the road after the accident."

He held out a round, enameled medallion. It bore three concentric circles.

The largest, outer circle was black. The second circle was white with the words, in black text, "For King and Country" surmounted by a white York rose with green leaves and a black Christian cross in the center. The inner circle was black with a large, white capital "F."

"Is it some kind of service badge?" asked Dinny.

"It's not one I've ever seen. Perhaps it is used by a volunteer organization helping veterans," said Foxy, "but I don't know of one that starts with the letter F. Of course, there are so many of them now."

"Do you think it might help us find the motorcycle rider?" asked Dinny. "Obviously, it belongs to the same person who was asking questions about my car at Sparky's garage."

"Yes, you are certainly right. We will show it to William when he returns. He can ask his contacts to help us track it down."

Dinny sighed and said, "At least I've done something to help, even if I have no idea what this is. I feel useless. I just sit around waiting for Torquemada to come at me with her next torture."

"You need to remember our motto," said Foxy.

"No moping," said Dinny. "Yes, I will try hard to remember that."

"Addie will be here after dinner. She can tell you what she found out today. William should be back tonight. Tomorrow, we will convene a Council of War."

"Will I have an assignment?"

"Without a doubt. I just don't know what it is yet."

"Is it just the two of us for dinner?" asked Dinny.

"Yes, just like old times," said Foxy. "Which is rather nice, I think."

"Absolutely," said Dinny. "And you can tell me what you found out today."

"I look forward to telling you about Fishy McCreedy. Be prepared to laugh."

"Ouch!" said Dinny in mock pain.

Chapter Eighteen

Back to Invergordon

Allen sat in the *Shipping Out* and awaited with anticipatory impatience the arrival of Tris and his "friend." He admired Tris's audacity in bringing her to Invergordon, but worried it would bring trouble in its train, given that Tris could not leave base and could not have visitors. *Was he planning on spending every night off the base? How long was she staying?* His musings were interrupted when Tris entered the pub, followed by an older man in officer's uniform. Allen's jaw dropped at the same moment he leapt to his feet and saluted.

William returned the salute automatically, smiled, and said, "No need for that." He extended his hand. Allen shook it and turned a baffled look on Tris.

"Allen, this is Lt. Commander Sir Ainsworth. He is a close friend of my best mate. That's who I went to see."

"Call me William," he said, releasing the handshake.

"William, I've told you how grateful I am to Lt. Allen Franklin."

"Yes," said William, "you helped Tris when he needed it. I can't thank you enough."

"But," blurted Allen, "I thought, that is, why exactly was it that you had to leave base?"

The three sat down. Ewan, the pub owner, knew Tris and Allen well. He brought over two ales and said hello to Tris. "Welcome back," he said with a wink. "And I've lit a fire in your room, Sir," he said to William. "I hope you will be comfortable. And anything you need, you only have to ask."

"Thank you. I understand you offer excellent accommodations."

Ewan smiled with a publican's pride and took William's order for a Scotch.

After he left, Tris said to Allen, "I owe you an explanation. A mate of mine was in a terrible car accident. I knew I wouldn't be given compassionate leave. I had to find out how he was. I didn't tell you why I had to leave because I thought the less you knew, the less you would have to lie for me."

"Oh, I see," said Allen, struggling to regain his composure. "And how is he?"

"He's doing fine now," said Tris. He saw Allen looking at William with an implicit question.

William saw it, too. "I came along just in case Tris was in any trouble, to help smooth things over if necessary. As Tris said, I am a close friend of the family."

Allen understood he had taken the wrong end of the stick. "That is very kind of you," he said. "I'm afraid you have come all this way for nothing. I can take Tris back to the base, and no one will ever be the wiser." He turned to Tris. "I've asked Ewan to set aside a bottle of his best just in case we run into a guard." Both Tris and William smiled appreciatively at Allen's foresight.

"And I have tea and coffee for you in my kit. From Fortnum's," said Tris, with a broad smile.

"Well," said William, getting to his feet, "everything's in order, thanks to you. Tris, you'd better be getting back. If you need me, I'll be here until my train leaves tomorrow morning. And good luck, Tris." He gave him a final handshake.

"Thank you for everything you have done," said Tris. And with that, Allen, Tris, and a bottle of Scotch whiskey left the Shipping Out.

The next day, Tris had lunch and went to the base barbershop for a trim and a shave. He took a long, hot shower. He dressed very carefully in his uniform and settled his hat in the precisely correct manner. Giving himself one last look in the mirror, he left his room with the box of chocolates and headed for the office of Molly Sinclair.

It was late in the day. With nothing else to do and no one around to supervise her, Molly was adjusting her makeup. She held a mirror in one hand and put on fresh lipstick. She checked to be sure her carefully plucked eyebrows had no stray little hairs. She gave her dark, bobbed hair a little shake and patted her curls into place. She put the mirror away and took out a file to smooth her nails.

She sighed. She was not actually pining for Mack McCullough, she told herself. She had resolved to give up on him. He had been away at sea for months, and she had no word from him for three whole weeks. She was sure that somehow mail could be sent even from a battle cruiser roaming somewhere around the Atlantic Ocean. Maybe not the Pacific. But surely, there must be post office boats or something like that in the Atlantic. He sent her letters from various ports, but then they stopped. No, she had decided she was worth more than having to sit around waiting for Mack McCullough to take it into his thick head to write to her. Even so, she liked Mack, with his very broad shoulders and cute little nose, and the way he always gave a strong shove to any man who even looked at her in the pub. He was a real he-man, she thought. Like Douglas Fairbanks in *Thief of Bagdad.* Mack had taken her to see it and even put his arm around her while they were watching Douglas Fairbanks and Julianne Johnson on their magic carpet as they flew past minarets and out over the ocean. She sighed again. No, she had to be resolute. She was done with him.

The door opened, and there stood Lt. Dashwood, looking handsome and smart and like such a gentleman. Her heart skipped a beat.

"Hello, Miss Sinclair," said Tris.

"We've been missin' ye, we have," said Molly, a bit breathlessly. "A have nae seen ye for a day or twa."

"Yes, I went off to London without letting anyone know. I brought you back something from London, as a surprise."

Molly blushed, and her dark eyes danced with delight. "A present? For me? Oh, A couldnae..."

"Oh, I hope you will," said Tris. He smiled his best high-wattage smile and handed her the package wrapped in brown paper and tied with string.

"Well, A wad nae want tae be rude," said Molly, snatching the package. She reached into her desk drawer, pulled out a pair of scissors, snipped the string, and quickly dispatched the brown paper. She saw a very large, oval box. She could only stare at it.

On top of the chocolate box was an illustration of a pretty young girl seated on the grass under a rose bower. She had curly, dark, bobbed hair. Her rose-patterned skirt billowed on the grass; her black strapless camisole had large, puffy short sleeves. A straw hat lay beside her. Her head was tilted as she fixed a rose to her curls, and she looked sideways out of her dark eyes, a come-hither look that was both flirtatious and innocent.

"You see?" said Tris. "I thought the picture looked just like you. I couldn't resist."

"What's in it?" asked Molly, as she gazed at the charming image.

"Why don't you open it and see?" asked Tris.

She removed the top and stared open-mouthed. It was more chocolate than she had ever seen at one time.

"They are chocolates made at Fortum and Mason's in London," said Tris, hoping she would be impressed.

"Oh, A'v heard of them. Quite posh they are. These must have cost ye a fortune. I really cannae accept such an expensive gift," she said, half-heartedly.

"Well, you could think of it more as a gift to you and anyone you might like to share it with, then," said Tris, thinking fast.

"Aye, I guess that would make it aw right," she said. Having made up her mind, she plucked a dainty chocolate from where it nestled in the box. As the chocolate gave way to the creamy, caramel filling, her eyes lit up with delight.

"I am so pleased you like them. It gave me something to look forward to. Coming back here, I mean. I guess you can tell I am feeling pretty useless."

"What do ye mean?" she said, taking another one, and discovering with ecstatic delight that it was filled with a cherry.

"I think somebody sent me here from London just to get even with me for something he thought I did to him. I don't know who it was. But the thing is, I don't really have anything to do, and I am not allowed to leave the base. I had to sneak away. I am going crazy with boredom," said Tris, appealing to her sympathy. "I can't even take you out. Or get regular passes to London to buy you little gifts."

"I thought ye were here to do hush-hush, top secret somethin' or other," said Molly. "A hope I dinnae have chocolate all o'er ma face." She took out her mirror and checked. She was fine. "What were ye sayin'?"

"It's just that, well, I wish I knew who had ordered me here, that's all. If I knew, I might be able to straighten everything out. But I can't if I don't know…" he trailed off, and looked at her with what he hoped was the expression of a puppy lost in the pouring rain on a very dark night.

"That should nae be a problem," she said. "Wait here a tick." She went into the back room, brought out a folder, looked at him in a way quite similar to the flirtatious girl on the box, sat down, and wrote out a name and folded the paper. She handed it to Tris. "This is the officer wha ordered ye here," she said.

Without looking at the folded note, Tris felt a wave of relief wash over him. "Thanks, thanks so much. I really appreciate this."

Molly said, "It's nothin'. Think of it as my gift to ye in thanks for chocolate. Makes us e'en."

"You are the best," he said.

" Ye're no sae bad yourself," she said.

"I guess I'd better be going," said Tris. "Enjoy the chocolates."

Molly sighed as she watched him go out the door. And to think, just a little while ago, she had been missing that big lug Mack McCullough. She bit into another chocolate.

Once alone in his quarters, Tris took out the folded paper and read the name on the note Molly had given him. He was more determined than ever to get a message through to Dinny and the others.

Early the next morning, Tris saw from his window the gray ships of the returning battle group emerged from a dense fog—powerful and sinister. The tenders bringing ashore officers and seamen with leave would soon start ferrying them. He checked his watch and saw it was time for the library to open.

Mrs. Sweet presided over the one large room. When she saw Tris, Mrs. Sweet's plump face broke into her typical kind, friendly, open smile. She took off her gold, wire-rimmed glasses to greet Tris.

"Welcome back," she said. "It is so good to see you again."

"I've been to London to visit a sick friend," he said, returning her smile. "Don't worry. He is doing fine. I brought you back a little something, he said. I hope you like it." He placed on her desk a slim, white box with Eversharp printed on the top. She was quite surprised. "An Eversharp?" she gasped. "You didn't—"

"Yes, I did," said Tris.

She took off the ribbon and opened the box. Inside, there gleamed a short, gold-plated self-propelling pencil, with rows of machine-worked chevrons running the length of the barrel. She took it out gently, twisting the top knob to see the thin lead come out.

"Lt. Dashwood," she said, "I am so very pleased. Thank you. I am sure I will use this every day, and when I do, I will think of what a thoughtful gentleman you are." She was obviously moved.

"Mrs. Sweet, you certainly deserve it. Your books have kept me sane." Tris was quite sincere. "I think I have read just about everything you have. That has given me an idea. If we put our heads together, do you think we could have a book drive? I was thinking that if we advertised in the local paper with instructions on how to donate used books, you will add some new titles, and with any duplicates, you will be able to replace some of the books that really need to be retired."

Mrs. Sweet was, not surprisingly, quite keen on the idea. "I would have to talk with the officer in charge of supplies and acquisitions, but I could do that early tomorrow morning." They talked for some time about what kinds of books would be needed, whether to accept paperbacks, how to set up a drop box at the gate, and the numerous other details that would have to be taken care of. Mrs. Sweet was glowing with delight, energized by this plan. She agreed to place the notice in the *North Star and Farmer's Whatsit* as Tris now thought of it.

Tris felt guilty about leading Molly on. He thought she had really fallen for him. Well, how could she not? The big box of chocolates. His charm. Not to mention his looks—blonde hair, blue eyes, strong chin—and of course, there was the uniform. She may even have seen just a hint of Douglas Fairbanks in him. He felt like a bounder. He needed to let her down gently. Tell her she was too good for him. Or that there was a hereditary disease in his family. No, that was taking it too far. What if she said she was willing to sacrifice herself for him and nurse him through his last days?

He went to see her when he knew she would be getting ready to take her lunch break. When he entered her small office, she was stirring a cup of cocoa with a small, silver spoon topped with a windmill at the end of the handle. She blushed when she saw him.

"Oh, it's ye," she said, haltingly and with a noticeable lack of enthusiasm. "How nice."

Tris was too preoccupied with his own embarrassment to notice hers. "Yes, hi," he said. "Look, there's something I need to…"

Molly interrupted him hurriedly. "Look, A am sae sorry, but ye see, thare is someone else. A hate tae have tae break it tae ye like this, but he'll be here any minute now because we are havin' tea together here i' the office. A didnae tell ye before because we had broken up. Well, really, A was gonna' break up wi' him. On account o' his no writin'. But he tells me when the ship is steamin' for home there is na way tae send letters. Which A did no know. Anyways, he gave me this clever little spoon from Holland. See, the windmill spins." She gave it a spin. "And this cocoa from Galle an' Jessen (she pronounced this Golly an Jayson) i' Denmark." She showed him the red tin. "An a Spain shawl wi' long, black fringe an embroidery wi' flowers. An perfume from France. It is Rose Rêvée (ree-Vee, as she pronounced it), which he says means dreamy rose, an he thinks A am just dreamy. Is nae he sweet?" Here she smiled as if Tris should enjoy the compliment to her as much as she did. "But he doesnae know aboot the chocolates comin' from ye. Or from anyone. A telt him A won thaim i' a contest i' a magazine. Sae, ye wonae tell him, will ye. Please?"

Tris, who had done his best to follow this rapid-fire explanation, which Molly delivered without apparently taking a breath, just nodded. Then, seeing she seemed to need more reassurance, he said, "Sure, mum's the word."

"A knew ye wad be a sport aboot it. Now, A think ye better leave. He is very jealous an A wouldnae want ye tae get hurt."

A Seaman striking a superior officer did not seem a likely threat to Tris. On the other hand, the encounter with Molly had gone much better than he could have hoped, even though his vanity had taken the kind of beating Molly imagined her gift-bearing sailor would give him. "Right," he said, "I'm off before my blood is spilled."

"Na hard feelings?" she asked without it being a true question.

"No, none at all," said Tris, and he genuinely meant it.

Chapter Nineteen

Foxy's Fashion Sense

Over coffee in the conservatory the next morning, William and Foxy briefed each other. William arrived late the night before, too late to tell Foxy anything about the trip to Invergordon. "Tris will be all right," William reported. "And I've taken out a subscription to *The North Star and Farmers Chronicle.* I'll tell everyone about getting him back into Invergordon after dinner."

"Good idea. Let's have a Council of War," said Foxy. "Addie and I have information to report, too. And then there is this. Dr. Collard sent this to Dinny," said Foxy. It arrived yesterday. Any idea what it is?"

William looked it over carefully. "Some kind of membership badge, but I've never seen it before." He turned it over. "It has a maker's mark and issue number. 'Birmingham Medal Company 14233.' That might lead somewhere. I'll see if Clive knows anything about this organization. I am going to have lunch at the club today. I want to ask if anyone knows where Captain Turner is living. I think it might be helpful if we could ask him about the effort to cover up what happened by making him a scapegoat. If he will see me, will you come along?"

"Of course. I can read Churchill's account of the sinking of the *Lusitania* if we need to take a train to wherever he lives."

"You will find it most instructive," said William, ironically. "By the way, where's Addie. A bit late, isn't it?"

Addie and Dinny had talked into the early hours of the morning. Addie crawled out of bed with great difficulty and dressed hurriedly. She quickly downed toast and tea and found Foxy ready to depart for the ARO. She noticed that Foxy was wearing the Chanel deep blue jersey knit instead of her pantsuit and was carrying a messenger bag familiar during the war instead of her usual handbag.

"What's in the bag?" she asked.

"Just a few necessary bits and bobs for what we will be doing today," answered Foxy briskly. This left Addie puzzled, but she was too fuzzy-brained to ask any questions.

When they arrived at the Old Admiralty, they signed in, and after inspecting whatever they were taking into the building and handing them a ticket for their checked items, the Porter handed Addie a message from Josie setting up a meeting at Arensdorf's office after lunch.

While Addie went down to the ARO, Foxy reported to McCreedy.

"I'm glad to see you came to your senses and are dressed as a proper woman ought to be," he snapped.

"I haven't the foggiest idea what you are talking about," replied Foxy. "This morning, we are going to inspect the shelves systematically to see if the decrypts have been misplaced.

"Surely Gruter and his crew have already done that," said McCreedy. "Sounds like a waste of time to me."

"Possibly, possibly," said Foxy, as if she were making an actual concession to McCreedy's reasoning. "On the other hand, we are much more motivated to find them, and will therefore be more eagle-eyed, so to speak. And since you are just as eager to get the files back, probably more so, I think you will agree it is a good idea to make a careful search."

"Yes, I suppose so," he half growled. Foxy turned to leave. "Dismissed," he snapped.

Gruter laid out a small feast—or what he referred to as an ordinary breakfast in the Netherlands—of thinly sliced ham, hard-boiled eggs, sliced apples, cheese, dark bread, gingerbread, butter, and jam. He had a large Thermos of strong, dark coffee, a bottle of cream, and a container of sugar.

As they ate and settled into relaxed conversation, he again gently deflected any of Foxy's questions about his past. They discussed how the materials in the library were organized, and Gruter gave them a map of the shelves, each marked with the call number ranges. Addie and Foxy walked along the shelves for two hours. Addie was yawning frequently. Foxy called a halt, saying her eyes were glazing over and she was sure she was becoming less alert. They left Gruter the map marking the shelves they had searched and pointed out the "strayed" items they had placed in the shelving cart.

"We'll pick up where we left off Monday morning," she said.

"Why did we leave so early?" asked Addie. "Didn't we plan on working until lunch?"

"You are exhausted. And I promised I would show you where the 'hat girls' worked, and we have to find time for lunch before we go to meet Arensdorf. Come on. It's this way." She led Addie upstairs. "There probably isn't anything left in it," she said. "But I can tell you how everything was set up. And I want to get a look at it, too. I haven't been in there since the war ended."

They arrived at the door to Room 229 and found it locked. "I was worried about this," said Foxy, "although why anyone would think it important to lock an empty room is beyond me." There was no one else around. The post-war budget cuts meant the offices were unoccupied.

"What should we do now?" asked Addie. "See if McCreedy will give us the key?"

"I didn't ask him in the first place because he would have said no, just because that is his mulish nature. He would have accused me of violating the DORA by even telling you the room existed or some such nonsense." She began rummaging in the messenger bag.

"That would be ridiculous. I was assigned to find out if there is any information kept here about the decoding machines you were using," said Addie.

"He is a ridiculous man," said Foxy, who had removed several items from her bag, "and he would have said that it was one thing for you to be sent to find out about what I, among others, were doing, but a violation of my oath to tell you."

"What are you looking for?" asked Addie, quite thrown off by the rummaging and unpacking.

"These," said Foxy, pulling what looked like a set of keys from the bag. This is my old messenger bag. I used it to carry papers during the war when I had to deliver something hush-hush to someone in another building. It has several hidden pockets. I knew I could get these past the Porter.

"And they are?" asked Addie.

"These are called two-lever mortice try-out keys. She knelt down. "Now, let's try the first one." Nothing happened. She tried the second key. "Ah, that one bit ever so slightly." The fourth try-out key turned in the lock. "We're in," said Foxy.

The musty, drab, windowless room seemed larger than Foxy remembered, now that it was empty. In her mind's eye, she saw herself and other women bent over plain, wooden tables, absorbed in decrypting messages. They worked in silence, taking their breaks outside the room. She recalled the punch-card machines that produced such breathtaking results by the later years of the war. It had been the most stimulating and rewarding time of her life. She was glad the war was over, but she missed the work she had done in this room, the people, and the camaraderie.

"Is this the pneumatic tube you told me about?" asked Addie.

"What did you say?" asked Foxy. "Yes, that's it. We would load a cannister with…"

"There's something stuffed in here," said Addie, bending over and probing with her fingers.

"Careful, it might be a rodent's nest," said Foxy, crossing quickly over to Addie, who pulled out a rolled-up set of papers.

"This is no rat's nest," said Addie, holding out the papers to Foxy. She took them, carefully unrolled them, and studied them for a moment.

"They were put there by a human rat," said Foxy. "These are the decrypts we've been looking for. Dinny was interested in any messages from U-20—the submarine that torpedoed the *Lusitania*."

And that's what these are?" asked Addie, feeling a thrill of excitement.

"Look," said Foxy. At the top, typed in red, was: U-20. "These are Minute Sheets. They record every intercepted wireless transmission from the U-20." She riffled through them until she found the entries for May 1915. "Here it is," she said solemnly, pointing with her finger. "'Sank British s.s. Lusitania by torpedo without warning 20' S of Old Head of Kinsale.'" They both took in the stark entry. "Almost twelve hundred people lost in less than twenty minutes," said Foxy. There was nothing more to be said. They were dumbfounded.

Addie pointed to the entries at the beginning of the Minute Sheet. "These begin in April. They look like they record the route of the U-20."

Foxy nodded. "Room 40 was tracking it."

Addie was stunned by the implication. "But that would mean…"

"That they knew the U-20 would endanger the *Lusitania*? Yes, possibly. But let's not get ahead of ourselves. Dinny needs to look at these. He'll know what to make of them."

"But he can't come here, and you can't take the papers…" said Addie. "What are you doing?"

Foxy was lifting her skirt. Around her waist was a slim, cotton belt with two cotton pockets sewn to it, one on each of her hips. "That should do it," she said, eyeing the packet of papers. "Let's divide them in half, roll each up, and slip them into these pockets." They set to work. "Why not hide them in one of the hidden pockets in your messenger bag?"

"I am afraid they might crunch when the Porter examines the bag. The try-out keys are wrapped in felt, so I know they won't rattle," said Foxy, lowering her skirt. "How does it look?" she asked Addie, smoothing the dress.

"No one could ever guess you are smuggling secret papers," said Addie, giving Foxy's dress a critical eye. "That dress drapes so beautifully. Are the hidden pockets from your days working here?"

"No, these are my own invention—reinvention, I should say. I find, when I travel, it is so much easier to get around if I don't have to carry a handbag or worry about pickpockets. These were quite common until toward the end of the 18th century. McCreedy prefers me in this dress to my pantsuit.

He thinks it makes me look more like a proper lady. If only he knew."

"Why did you wear them today? You didn't know we would find these," said Addie.

Foxy smiled. "Why, to steal—or should I say borrow—the *Lusitania* file and the decrypts if we found them. If we didn't find anything today, I would simply wear them every day we searched. But let's get out of here."

Addie opened the door. There was no one in the hall, and the two were soon walking arm in arm on Spring Gardens Street to the Above Board for lunch.

It was a fine fall day, and they decided to walk off their pub lunch. They made their way to the Victoria Embankment, where they stopped to watch the sunlight dazzle on the Thames. Then, they strolled to the Strand and from there to the LSE. They found Professor Arensdorf in his office talking with Josie.

He spoke with a soft voice and Dutch accent. "Miss Devereux tells me you are trying to solve something of a mystery." Foxy noted his keen, penetrating gaze. "You, Miss Gold, have fallen under suspicion over the disappearance of some decrypts. And your grandnephew, Lady Butterschloss, is blamed for the loss of the files on the *Lusitania*."

"I have been authorized to look into the matter," said Foxy. "I worked at Admiralty during the war."

He gazed steadily at her. "What office did you work for, if I may ask?"

"I am afraid I couldn't say," said Foxy, gazing steadily back. "You understand, I am sure."

Arensdorf bowed his head. "Of course."

"So, we understand each other," thought Foxy.

"How can I help?" asked Arensdorf.

Addie spoke up. "I understand you had a run-in with one of the messengers on the day the files were requested. His name is Chauncey Caxton."

Arensdorf's face showed his contempt. "Yes. A most unlikeable young man. He bumped into me, intentionally, I think, late one afternoon as I was leaving. Is that the day in question?"

Addie nodded. "Caxton dropped the requisition form for the *Lusitania* file. I wondered if you noticed it when you were picking up your papers."

Arensdorf thought for a moment. "I recognized the requisition form by its color, but I did not notice what was being called for. I was busy picking up my own papers and wondering if I should reprimand Caxton, and decided it wasn't worth it. I took the elevator and left for the day. I can tell you that Gruter—what is the phrase?—ticked off Caxton earlier in the day. I was working in my carrell after lunch. It is against the wall, behind the shelves. I usually cannot hear anything being said at the front desk. But on that particular day, I was aware of Gruter talking with two men. Their voices were raised. I heard Gruter protesting about something. And the name Zinoviev."

Foxy expressed surprise. "Zinoviev? Grigory Zinoviev?" He was one of the most powerful men in the Soviet Union and was the leader of the Comintern, whose mission was to foment Communist revolutions around the world.

"I can only assume so. Although why Gruter should be discussing him— or arguing about him—with two men, I could not guess," said Arensdorf, looking straight at Foxy.

"*Of course, you can guess. And so can I,*" thought Foxy. "*You either know Gruter was a spy during the war, or suspect he was, and think he probably still is.*"

"Gruter must have caught Caxton lurking about. I heard him reprimand Caxton in very strong terms. One of the men who was there said something too low for me to hear, but it sounded conciliatory, as if he were trying to smooth things over. After that, everything went quiet. I think the two men left shortly after Caxton."

"Any idea who the two men might have been?" asked Foxy.

Arensdorf shook his head. "I couldn't say. I was well out of view, behind many rows of stacks. I only heard their voices, not any words, until they raised them briefly when they were arguing."

Arensdorf could have said more, but he would have given himself away as more than a war refugee and professor of Economics. He could have said the two men were well known to him. One was retired Admiral Sir William

Reginald Hall. The other was Major Sir George Joseph Ball, head of MI5 Investigation Division. They were plotting with Gruter to smear Ramsey MacDonald as a puppet of the Soviets. He knew Gruter was a dangerous spy during the war, a thug employed by the British.

"I am afraid I have not been of much help.' said Arensdorf. "But something did occur to me after Miss Devereux approached me yesterday. Our library received a recent bequest that might interest you. They are the papers of Philip Teague. He was a secretary to Lord Mersey, the Wreck Commissioner who heard the evidence for both the *Titanic* and the *Lusitania*." Arensdorf chuckled. "We are not supposed to have them. Teague wanted them kept in the family, as I understand it, but did not stipulate that in his will. His widow did not want them 'cluttering things up,' as she said to our head librarian. Her father is an alumnus, and he suggested she donate them rather than destroy them. The librarians have finally finished cataloging them." He turned to Josie. "I can see to it you have access to them, if you want to take the time to find out if there is anything worthwhile about the *Lusitania* investigation in them."

Foxy and Addie looked expectantly at Josie, who immediately agreed. "I think I can divert my attention from my research for a few days," she said as nonchalantly as she could manage, inwardly bursting with delight.

They thanked Arensdorf. Foxy gave him her card and said they would undoubtedly meet again in the ARO.

Foxy said she needed to make a phone call. Josie led her to the department office and the telephone. Then, she walked Foxy and Addie out of the building.

"That was certainly a surprise," said Josie. " About the Teague papers. What should I look for, do you think?"

"Anything related to the *Lusitania* that has never been reported, or that someone would not want to come to light now," said Foxy.

"One thing we know for sure that has never been disclosed is that Naval Intelligence was decoding the wireless messages from the submarine that sank the *Lusitania*," said Addie.

"We do?" said Josie. "How do we know that?"

"We found the decrypts," said Addie, beaming. "And Foxy has them hidden under that gorgeous dress."

"You can't be serious," said Josie. Then she saw that Addie was not kidding, and all three of them burst into gales of laughter.

When they calmed down, Foxy said, "Dinny was interested only in finding out if there were wireless decrypts from U-20 on the day it sank the *Lusitania*. It seemed improbable, but he wanted to check. What he didn't know was that there were wireless decrypts tracking the U-20 since April. And someone did not want him to find out about them."

Addie said, "Gruter said that no one had ever requested them before, even though they were cataloged."

"But someone knew they were there, knew they had a tale to tell, and knew you had requested them," said Foxy. "We need to find out exactly what those decrypts can tell us about the details of the route of the U-20. Dinny will need help with that because the charts are large. That's why I made the phone call. I asked William if he could go to the Hydrographic Office to get them." She saw the bewildered looks of Josie and Addie. "Dinny will need the charts of the English Channel, the North Sea, and the Irish Sea to plot the course, but they are large and unwieldy. They need to be fixed on a flat surface. He has limited reach. Because he is in a wheelchair." She realized her brain was spinning plans faster than she could easily explain. She felt embarrassed. "Sorry," she said. "I was getting ahead of things. Addie, if you work with Dinny tomorrow, the two of you can chart the route of U-20. And Josie, if you can join us for dinner Sunday night, you can report on anything you find in the Teague papers."

"Certainly. I'd be delighted." Turning to Addie, she said, "If you need me to bring you anything from the flat, let me know." The two friends gave each other a hug. Foxy and Addie got into the cab, and Josie watched them drive out of sight. She was eager to be of help, and the idea of being the first to explore an archive about the *Lusitania* excited every one of her scholarly nerves. Nothing suited her better than a day tucked away in a library ferreting out information.

Arensdorf watched them from the window in his office. He mentioned

Zinoviev's name because he was certain Lady Butterschloss had worked in Naval Intelligence during the war. He needed her as an insurance policy in case anything happened to him before he could reveal the Zinoviev letter as a fraud.

Chapter Twenty

Foxy Says "2ocks"!

William and Foxy were alone in a first-class carriage on the train to Liverpool. They had been invited to visit Captain Bill Turner and his long-time companion, Mabel Every. After inquiring at the Club and learning from a mutual friend where Turner lived, William sent a telegram asking to visit him because his father had always spoken so highly of Captain Bill. As he scanned a page of the *Times*, William's mind drifted to the incident he mentioned in the telegram.

When William was ten, he and his father often went out in a small sailboat, his father at the rudder and William setting the sails. His father's clear blue eyes looked out from his chiseled, tanned face over the calm sea and clear sky in the sheltered bay. He spoke to William in a calm, level voice. "You see that cottage on the headland? My friend Tad lived there. We grew up together. His father was the local baker and a friend of my father's. Tad and I loved the sea. While I was training as a midshipman, he joined the crew of a merchant ship. He sent me a letter telling me he was aboard a barque sailing out of Liverpool. There was a very heavy fog. Suddenly, out of nowhere, loomed the prow of the Cunard liner, *Cherbourg*. It rammed the barque. Tad picked up a cabin boy, who was about eight, and scrambled up the mast where they clung to the first cross tree as the barque sank. He was rescued by a man named Bill Turner. He was third officer on the Cherbourg and part of the rescue party. He plucked them both off that crossbar and into the rescue boat. Tad was convinced he and the boy would have drowned if Turner hadn't done what he did. Four crew and the Pilot drowned that day." He turned to look William in the eye. "Tad's letter made me think for the first time about death, about losing a close friend, suddenly. I was a cocky midshipman, and my head was filled with romantic notions of sea battles. I had never thought about death, my own or anyone else's. It also made me think about what true heroism was. Tad picked up that cabin boy without a second's thought for himself. And Bill Turner was calm and steady as he lifted them from the crossbar to safety while their sinking boat could have overturned his rescue boat. I've never forgotten it."

It wasn't until he was in the Dardanelles that William was hit with the full force of the moral of his father's story. In his mind's eye, he saw Walter's small shroud slip into the sea.

"Bollocks," said Foxy, snapping closed Churchill's *Times of Crisis*.

William, roused from his meditations, raised a questioning eyebrow. "You disagree with Churchill on some finer point of history?"

Foxy replied, "He was so upset with Wilson for not bringing America into the war after the sinking of the *Lusitania*. Listen to this: 'What he did in April 1917 could have been done in May 1915. And if done, then what abridgment of the slaughter; what sparing of the agony; what ruin, what catastrophes would have been prevented; in how many millions of homes would an empty chair be occupied today; how different would the shattered world in which victors and vanquished alike are condemned to live!'" Foxy snapped the book shut in irritation. "He claims that something like the American soul, or will, or spirit really wanted to be in the war in 1915, but Wilson was so isolated he could not gauge the resolve of the people. As if Wilson had not been re-elected on the slogan, 'He kept us out of War.' And as if the reason the war went on so long is that America wasn't in it; otherwise, I gather, he thought it was conducted brilliantly by the Allies, who could not prevail just because of a lack of more human bodies to throw into the trenches. Bah! He knows that Wilson's warning to the Germans after the *Lusitania* led them to stop their unconditional submarine warfare, at least for a time. And that meant that there was a freer flow of goods to the UK. But he doesn't mention it."

"You have to admit he has great command of parallelism and synecdoche," said William. "Product of a Public School education and all that."

"The real key here," said Foxy, calming herself, "is the reference to May 1915. Obviously, Churchill hoped the sinking of the *Lusitania* would bring America into the war because there were almost two hundred Americans aboard."

"I agree. Churchill thought it ought to have done. Did you notice how he laid the blame on Turner?"

"He lays it on with a trowel," said Foxy. "According to him, Turner willfully ignored the warnings of submarine activity. He did not follow instructions to steer a course away from headlands, to go as fast as possible, and to lay a zigzagging course." She opened the book and read, "'In spite of these warnings and instructions, for which the Admiralty Trade Division deserve credit, the *Lusitania* was proceeding along the usual trade route without zigzagging at little more than three-quarter speed when, at 2:10 pm on May 7, she was torpedoed eight miles off the Old Head of Kinsale...'"

Foxy looked up from the book. "What made no sense to Robby or me at the time is why Admiralty—or really the First Lord of the Admiralty, Churchill—would be so intent on distracting attention from Germany as the culprit. Blaming Turner watered down the condemnation of the Germans for attacking an unarmed civilian ship."

William nodded. "Turner was not only exonerated by the Mersey Review Board, but his honor was fully restored, as if it needed to be. Later in the war, he was captain of the SS *Ivernia,* another Cunard ship. It was taken over by the Navy and used for transporting troops in the Mediterranean. On the first day of 1917, a U-Boat torpedo struck off the coast of Greece. There were twenty-four hundred troops aboard. Twenty-four hundred. Just imagine the chaos. They lost some crew and fewer than a one hundred troops, thank God. Could have been much worse. The ship went down very quickly. Turner was the last one off the ship. He received the OBE at the end of the war."

"Yes," said Foxy, "I remember that. But then, Churchill had to publish this personal history and blame Turner. Obviously, there was more to the story than Churchill wants the public to know. But what does it have to do with the missing files?"

William fussed with his pipe. "Whatever it is, someone does not want it known even now, enough to try and harm Dinny and Addie." William felt the dragon within him open its yellow eyes and bestir itself. He had to check his anger. Again. He took a puff on his pipe to steady himself. "And to kidnap Tris."

Obtuse though Foxy admittedly was when it came to recognizing William's love for her, she had an infallible understanding of him. She knew the dark moods that threatened to overcome him and the suppressed anger, both caused by the war. He saw too much in the Dardanelles, and learned too much, had to hold too many secrets from his service in the Naval Intelligence Division. The increasing likelihood that military intelligence was being used for purely political purposes struck at the core of his moral code. The misuse of intelligence to endanger those close to him would test his deeply inbred habit of keeping his emotions under the firm lock and key of rationality, detachment, and objectivity. Foxy decided to distract him.

"Anything in the *Times*?" she asked.

William nodded. "It appears Clive was correct in predicting that the Campbell Affair would lead to a vote of no confidence in the MacDonald government," said William, who understood that Foxy was taking care of him by changing the subject. He was grateful. "The Conservatives are proposing a vote of censure against MacDonald for instructing the Attorney General to withdraw the prosecution against Campbell and the *Worker's Weekly*."

"Will they win? It seems a rather flimsy reason to force another General Election. We've had two in the past three years," said Foxy.

"We'll know by Thursday morning, I should think," said William. "Clive seems all but certain that it will work."

They arrived by cab at the two-story, semi-detached townhouse in a quiet Liverpool suburb. Mabel Every, a woman in her sixties with snow-white hair swept back into a bun, opened the door to greet them. Her large, dark eyes, soft features, and comfortable plumpness suggested a steady, sincere, and friendly disposition.

"Come in, come in," she said with a wide smile as she showed them into the sitting room. "Bill has been waiting for you. I'll just go fetch him."

Foxy and William were shown into a cozy living room, with two deep-seated tan leather chairs and a sofa upholstered in deep blue. The arms were inset with carved oak panels of sailing yawls on a sea blown by a fresh breeze. On the opposite wall was a glass display cabinet filled with neat rows of Bowler hats. It was well known that Commodore Turner, otherwise known as Bowler Bill, bought himself a new Bowler every time he was given command of a new ship.

From the back garden, Foxy and William could hear a fiddle playing a lively sea chanty. It stopped suddenly, and soon a robust, silver-haired man in his late sixties, carrying a fiddle and a bow, entered the room with a broad smile on his weathered face. "So, this is Gideon Ainsworth's son, is it? You are the spitting image of your Da," he said in a strong and cheerful voice. "I know you've met Mabel already. You must be Lady Butterschloss. I knew your husband. A fine man, God rest his soul."

Mabel disappeared and reappeared with a tea tray, teapot, cups, and a dark, round apple-cinnamon cake, fresh from the oven. "The apples are so good this year," she said, "I couldn't resist baking this."

As cake and tea were served, the four settled into a congenial conversation about life in Liverpool. At last, William mentioned the ostensible reason for the visit. "Thank you for seeing me on such short notice. My father was a great admirer of yours."

"He wrote me after I rescued Tad. We became regular correspondents and met when we could during the war," Turner said. "I saved the letters your father sent me. I have them in my study. I thought perhaps you would like to read them."

The two men disappeared into Turner's study. Foxy helped Mabel clear the dishes, then joined her in the clean, tidy kitchen for another cup of tea at the round table with two chairs.

"It's good seeing Bill enjoying company. He has become reclusive, especially after Churchill—save me from calling him what I think of him—published that history raking up all the old accusations about the *Lusitania*." Mabel's lips tightened, and she spoke bitterly.

"Yes, I was reading it on the train here," said Foxy. She wanted to use the word "bollocks" again, but restrained herself because she had just met Mabel. Instead, she said stiffly, "I cannot imagine what would lead him to rehash those accusations that were not upheld at the time."

Foxy's tone encouraged Mabel. She took a sip of tea and set the cup down gently on the saucer. "The sinking of the *Lusitania* just about ruined our lives, I can tell you." She sighed, "After the war, we went into beekeeping at a lovely place in Devon. It was our little paradise, just the two of us living a quiet life of retirement. Then, the reporters found out where we were living and descended on us. They couldn't stop questioning Bill about the *Lusitania*. Bill just couldn't take it, after all those years had passed and after what they tried to do to him, blaming it on him, I mean. He had enough. So, we sold up and went to Australia. He was looking for his two grown sons. His wife, Alice, took them there in 1915, right after Bill faced the Admiralty charges. She deserted him when he most needed her. Don't get me started on her," said Mabel sourly, taking a sip of her tea. "When we arrived in Australia, we discovered Alice was not there. She moved to Canada with their sons without sending any word to Bill." She shook her head in disgust.

"How terrible," said Foxy, who recognized the banality of the phrase and wished she did not sound so insipid. It was terrible to her; there was no other word. Well, there were, but she wasn't sure enough of Mabel to know how she would react to them. She could not help herself from saying the least offensive of them. "Execrable."

Mabel seemed to warm to Foxy. She nodded, feeling understood. "We stayed on there for eighteen months, but our hearts are here. We haven't been back in Liverpool for all that long. It's where Bill was born. I grew up here, too, of course. And then Churchill published that book, raking up the allegations that Bill was incompetent."

"It must be so very hard on him not to see his sons. And for all of this about the *Lusitania* to be back in the public's eye," said Foxy, quietly.

"That isn't the half of it," said Mabel, looking up with alarm in her eyes. "He has terrible dreams. What worries me is that he has such painful stomach cramps now, and he's always been so hearty. It's worn him down, and that's the truth of it."

Foxy, whose feelings about Churchill were growing colder by the minute, asked, "Do you think Churchill believes what he says, or is he trying to cover up the Admiralty's failure to prevent the sinking of the *Lusitania*?" Foxy was trying not to push too hard or be too obvious and hoped she did not strike Mabel as a gossip hound. She needn't have worried. Mabel would have gladly shouted the story from the rooftops.

Mabel set her cup in its saucer and looked Foxy straight in the eyes. "For one thing, Churchill doesn't want anyone to remember that the Royal Navy provided no protection for the *Lusitania*. That's what they had been doing. That's what they did the time before when the *Lusitania* crossed with a different captain. Bill expected Navy ships to escort the *Lusitania*, especially since there had been sinkings and submarine sightings right before he arrived off the coast of Ireland," she said. "That's what Churchill doesn't want anyone to think about now."

"I remember," said Foxy, nodding her head. "When Churchill was asked questions about that in Parliament, he said that His Majesty's Navy was too busy with war operations and that commercial traffic had to take care of itself."

"Well, that's a load of bilge, isn't it?" said Mabel with disgust. "There were destroyers at Milford Haven that could have met the *Lusitania* at Queenstown, but they were not ordered out. I don't see how sending a destroyer out would have slowed the war effort. Bill says the submarine might have sunk both the destroyer and the *Lusitania*, but how likely is that? A destroyer would have scared the submarine off, is what I say."

"I also remember wondering why the *Lusitania* wasn't given orders to put in at Queenstown or sent north?" said Foxy, acting now as a chorus to Mabel's disgust. "Churchill doesn't mention that possibility, either."

"And well you might ask," said Mabel, who was visibly upset. "He did not receive orders to change his route." She paused. "You should have seen him at the time of the hearing. He was dazed; he talked in one-syllable words. He said he couldn't even think about it. And there they were, cross-questioning him, pushing him, and pushing him to try to make it out that he had not followed the advice of the high-and-mighty Admiralty." Mabel snorted to indicate her indignation.

"Churchill says in his book that Turner ignored the advice of the Board of Trade," said Foxy, who no longer felt like she was egging Mabel on to divulge information she would rather keep to herself.

Mabel's voice took on a sharp edge. "Oh, I am well aware of that. The same as what they said at the hearing. The truth is, the advice to Bill was the same advice they gave to all merchant ships. Everyone thought the big passenger liners could outrun any U-boat. So the advice was just general. Stay clear of headlands, run down the center of channels, ram a U-boat if you see it on the surface—as if—and then they threw in the advice to zig-zag. That was where they tripped poor Bill up. They read out the detailed description of how to zig-zag and asked him if he had received the order. He said that it didn't sound like the advice he received. Of course, it didn't. Those detailed orders weren't issued until a week after the *Lusitania* was sunk. They were trying to deceive the judge, see. There was only general advice, and Bill thought zig-zagging meant what to do if a U-boat was actually sighted."

"I remember the reassurance that passengers on liners were safe because they could go so much faster than the U-boats. It seems to have been a misplaced confidence," said Foxy. "But then, no one thought the Germans would attack a passenger liner, even though the Germans published warnings in the American newspapers at the time the *Lusitania* sailed."

"They said he wasn't going as fast as he could, and that showed he was not following advice. He told them that he was doing eighteen knots because he did not want to have to drop anchor waiting for high tide to cross the Mersey Bar, here at Liverpool, the final destination, because that really would make the ship a sitting duck. Eighteen knots is still fast enough to outrun any submarine. But Churchill makes it out that he was going too slow. That's what they tried to say at the trial, too."

"So Churchill is as good as lying about that," Foxy said slowly. Her anger was reaching the boiling point, but she tried not to show it.

"You said it," said Mabel decisively. "That and a lot else. At the trial, they claimed Bill was only eight miles off the Old Head at Kinsale, ignoring orders not to sail too close to land. But Bill said he was thirteen to fifteen miles from land, and that is the truth, because that is where the wreck of the *Lusitania* lies at the bottom of the sea. I don't know what other proof anyone would need. And the reason he wasn't any farther away is that he got a message on May 7 in the evening that there was a U-Boat just south of Coninbeg light vessel. See, Bill thought if he went any further out, he would be in the path of that U-Boat."

"So, another outright lie that Churchill repeats," said Foxy, trying not to sound shrill.

"I'm not half through," said Mabel. "That night, Bill got a message to avoid headlands, pass harbors at full speed, keep to the mid-channel, and there were U-Boats off Fastnet. They sent that message seven times that night. So what does Bill do? He does what any Captain would. He ordered the lifeboats swung out, doubled the men on watch, had the bulkheads locked, and ordered that all the cabins be checked to make sure the portholes were closed. Of course, some passengers opened them again, and the Admiralty wanted to make it out that Bill was incompetent because of it. Can you imagine? Anyway, the next morning, they were in fog, so Bill slowed the ship. He did not see Fastnet in the fog, but he thought that because he passed it, that they were out of danger. Then he gets a message late that morning that says there was a U-boat in the southern part of the Irish Channel. And it also said, 'Make sure *Lusitania* gets this.' Turns out, the reason Bill got it was because the agent for the Cunard company in Ireland knew U-boats had sunk a ship and insisted that the *Lusitania* be warned. Bill signaled that he wanted to know exactly where the U-boat was operating. Later, he got a message saying a submarine had been sighted off Cape Clear at 10:00 am. Bill thought they were well past that danger by then, and the fog had saved them. The fog cleared. Bill and his officers started looking for the Naval escort. Of course, we all know that never happened." She rose abruptly. "All this talk is making me upset and parched," said Mabel, who put the kettle on.

"What about the order to keep to a mid-channel course?" asked Foxy, emboldened to ask questions by Mabel's willingness to talk.

Mabel was standing by the hob, waiting for the kettle to boil. "Bill wasn't in a channel when he was torpedoed. He was in the Irish Sea. The next landfall south was Spain. There was no way to steer a "mid-channel" course, and they knew it at the time, and Churchill knew it when he wrote that book." The kettle started to steam, and Mabel busied herself brewing a new pot. Seated again, and with fresh tea in both cups, Mabel continued her indictment. "All Bill had to go on was the same general instructions sent out every night to all merchant ships and one additional sentence, which was that there was a submarine operating off Fastnet, which he had passed by safely. Later in the morning, he received a message that there were submarines in the South Irish Sea with no further details. What was he supposed to do with that information? He sent a message asking for more specific information, and what he got back was not much better. He had no headings, nothing to go on except vague information."

"And Admiralty knew all of that, obviously," said Foxy. "And still Churchill persists in laying the blame on Turner for incompetence. Unforgivable." She was far more upset than she showed.

"That's one word for it," said Mabel. "I apologize for going on so. You must think I'm a raving lunatic."

"Please, don't think that," said Foxy. "I am very grateful to you for telling me all you have."

Mabel looked toward the closed door of the room where Bill had taken William. "I wanted you to know, so you could tell Lord Ainsworth, because if I know Bill, he will not talk about it at all, even with the son of his old friend. You will tell him what I told you, won't you? I want him to understand. I hate the idea that he would believe Churchill, especially since his father and Bill were so close."

"I will tell him. But really, there is no chance that he would think less of the Commodore." They heard the men talking as they emerged from the study. Foxy and Mabel got up from the table and gave one another a meaningful hug. "The Commodore is lucky to have you," said Foxy.

"I'm the lucky one. We take care of each other."

In the living room, Foxy found William looking at his watch. "We need to think about catching the train back," he said. He looked ashen and a bit shaken, which surprised Foxy.

"I'll phone for a cab," said Turner, who went back into his study.

"Let me give you something to eat on the train. You won't get back until after tea." Mabel brought them neatly wrapped sandwiches and slices of the cake.

They put on their coats and said their goodbyes just as the cab arrived. Turner gave William a hearty handshake and invited him to come again. Mabel and Foxy hugged again with promises to stay in touch.

They spoke little in the cab, and once they were in the First Class carriage, Foxy retrieved the copy of Churchill's book from her handbag, along with her propelling pen and notepad. She was preoccupied with quickly noting the details she had learned from Mabel before they faded from memory.

"Bollocks," she said under her breath as she rapidly noted the information that contradicted Churchill's account. Across from her, William rose to open the window a little, then sat down and began to fill his pipe. Foxy looked up as he struck a match and saw his hand shake. This was not normal.

"How did your conversation with Turner go? Did he discuss the *Lusitania*? she asked.

William looked out the window at the twilight. "Not directly. We talked for the most part about Father." He took a draw on his pipe. "I found out what it was McCreedy did to prevent Father from being promoted."

Foxy was surprised. "What was it?"

"It was in one of the letters he wrote to Turner at the time he was facing charges of incompetence. Father told Admiral Hall—Blinker—that he wanted to write a letter in support of Turner, attesting to his character. Hall ordered him not to get involved, but Father wrote it anyway. McCreedy somehow found out. He told Hall. You know how vindictive Hall could be. He put a stop to Father's promotion."

Foxy was taken aback. "Typical of McCreedy," said Foxy, "but petty on the part of Hall. It wasn't that great an infraction and should have been understood as an act of personal conscience."

"Yes," said William. "It makes one wonder. How much difference could a letter supporting Turner's character have made?"

"You will understand when you know what Mabel told me about Admiralty's effort to heap all the blame for the sinking of the *Lusitania* on Turner's head. As the train gained speed, Foxy told William all she learned from Mabel.

When she finished, William shook his head in disgust. "Words fail me," he said. "How underhanded and vicious. And for what? To save Churchill's reputation?" He paused, bringing his anger under control. After a time, he said to Foxy, "I've waited a long time to find out what McCreedy did to stop Father's promotion. He would never tell me. He must have been under tremendous pressure not to defend Turner in any way, including attesting to his character and courage. I have always looked up to him, but now I respect him even more. I hope I can live up to him."

You already have in so many ways, thought Foxy. She surprised herself with the thought.

Suddenly, William's mood brightened. "I found out why McCreedy was not promoted until after the war. Father told Turner in a letter."

"Oh, goodie," said Foxy. "You can tell me over sandwiches and cake." She brought out the wrapped food, and William pulled out the two bottles of cider, one from each pocket of his overcoat, he purchased at the station. As they settled into their picnic, William said, "It has to do with the Battle of Jutland."

Chapter Twenty-One

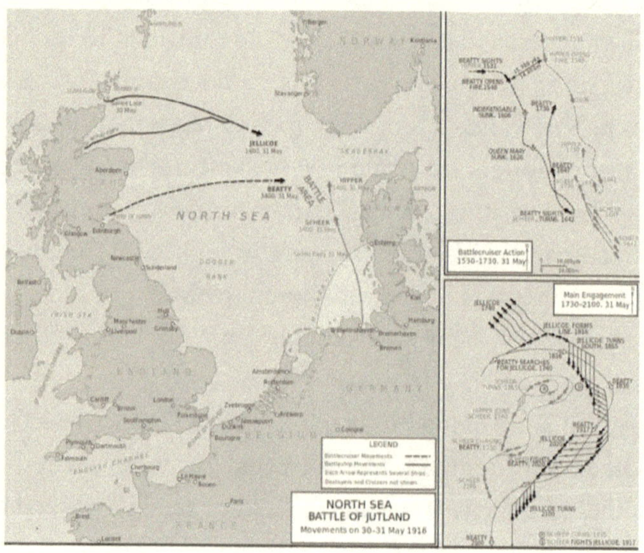

Winning By Not Losing

Seated in the railroad car hurtling to London, neither William nor Foxy needed to be reminded that the largest naval battle of the war could have been lost because of the Naval Intelligence Division's sins of omission and commission. The British Grand Fleet, based at Scapa Flow in Scotland, was the largest fleet in the world. Its primary objective was to keep the German High Seas Fleet—the second largest in the world— bottled up at Wilhelmshaven in Jade Bay. The High Seas Fleet was the mouse quivering inside the mousehole; the Grand Fleet was the cat waiting outside. Without even having to engage German battleships, the Grand Fleet imposed a highly effective blockade, strangling the supply of necessary food and war materials to Germany. Admiral Carl Friedrich Heinrich Reinhard Scheer, commander of the High Seas Fleet, grew tired of being the mouse. He planned to become the cat through a clever ploy that would lure the Grand Fleet into his jaws. This set in motion the largest naval battle of World War I, the Battle of Jutland, pitting Admiral Scheer against Admiral John Rushworth Jellicoe, commander of the Grand Fleet.

The cryptographers of Room 40 had the codebook of the German High Seas Fleet and knew Admiral Scheer would steam up his warships and come out of Jade Bay in the early hours of May 31. That afternoon in the cafeteria, Foxy saw her friend Olive Rickward, who worked for Room 40. Olive was thirty-two. Not only did her polished sophistication, green eyes, and thin lips belie a crack cryptographer, but she was also the wife of one of the most brilliant civilian codebreakers. Olive took her work very seriously. With her, it was personal. She wanted to honor the memory of her brother, Robert, who was killed in action in Belgium in 1915. Foxy found Olive in the cafeteria, struggling to stay awake by downing cups of coffee and taking a bite from a second Chelsea bun.

"What's happened?" asked Foxy. "You look half dead."

"Understood," said Olive. Her wavy hair, pulled into a bun at her neck, stood at odd angles because Olive had been running her hands through it while she worked. "Room 40 has been frantic. The Germans changed their encryption key about the same time the High Seas Fleet left Wilhelmshaven. We've been working since before sunrise, living on coffee and cigarettes. But we just cracked it," Olive said triumphantly. "It was a one-key slide. But before we cracked it, we missed the transfer of the D/K code."

"The what?" asked Foxy. "I am afraid I don't know that one."

"It is the name of the code Admiral Scheer uses. When he sets sail from Wilhelmshaven, he transfers it to land for security reasons. We knew we would be able to tell when he led the fleet out because we would recognize the different code he used when he transferred it."

"So, you didn't know when he set sail?"

Olive smiled grimly, squashed her cigarette butt in an ashtray, and immediately lit another one. "We had plenty of other intelligence that the High Seas Fleet would come out in the early morning hours today. The problem was that Jellicoe got misleading SIGINT because of that bone-headed fool, Captain Jackson, and some knuckle-headed watchkeeper. I don't know who he is. Have you ever had a run-in with Captain Thomas Jackson, Director of Operations?" Olive sat up straight as she pronounced his name pompously.

Foxy shook her head. "I have certainly heard of him, though." From what was said about him behind his back, Foxy knew Jackson was what might charitably be called "unenlightened" when it came to understanding the value of a bunch of civilian eccentrics in Naval reserve uniforms working in Room 40.

Olive took a sip of her coffee. "Until today, he has only come to Room 40 twice. Once, he came in beet red and fuming because he cut himself on the red, iron box we use to send him decrypted messages. Imagine a Naval officer complaining about a tiny cut. You would have thought he had an arm blown off in battle, and it was our fault. A second time, he came around to learn that the flow of messages was halted because we were trying to work out a new code. He said, 'Thank God! I shan't have any more of that damned stuff!'"

"That's the man himself, in all his glory, as I've heard him described," said Foxy, laughing.

Olive said, "Jellicoe was ordered last night to bring the fleet out of Scapa Flow ahead of the German fleet's departure. Jackson came to Room 40 before noon today to find out if the German fleet had left Wilhelmshaven. He asked the watch officer where the call sign D/K was. The watch officer told him that the signal was coming from Wilhelmshaven. He didn't offer any other information, such as, one, that when Scheer put to sea, he transferred the call sign to the land base in Wilhelmshaven to confuse the enemy; two, because of the change in German encryption, which we had not yet deciphered, it was impossible to know whether the signal had been transferred, but it probably had been because, three, all the available intelligence indicated that The High Seas Fleet set sail very early today. He told Jackson none of this." Olive was disgusted.

"What happened?" asked Foxy. She knew the battle at sea was raging as they spoke.

"Jellicoe was supposed to be sailing south to rendezvous with Vice-Admiral Beatty's Battle Cruise Squadron off the Danish shore, at Jutland. Beatty came out of the Firth of Forth sailing east and was supposed to turn north to meet the Grand Fleet." Jazzed up on coffee, cigarettes, carbohydrates, and sugar, Olive spoke rapidly with grim outrage, keeping her voice low, in a hoarse whisper. Foxy leaned forward, caught up in Olive's account.

"But, when Jellicoe got that incorrect message, he thought the German fleet had not left Wilhelmshaven, so to conserve fuel, he *slowed down,*" said Olive in a whisper.

Foxy felt a cold stone in her stomach. William's father was sailing with Beatty's squadron. "What's going to happen?" she asked in a whisper. "Could this cost us the battle?"

Olive looked at her wristwatch. "I don't know, but it is a terrible mistake. I have to run."

Early in the morning of June 1, Foxy went to the cafeteria. She saw Olive, bags under her eyes, a pencil stuck in her rumpled hair, smoking a cigarette, and drinking a cup of coffee. She looked with little interest at the soft-boiled egg standing bravely at attention in its little cup. She took a bite of toast and chewed. She was obviously disconsolate. Foxy brought a cup of coffee to the table and sat across from Olive.

Olive looked up. "Oh, hello, Foxy. I didn't see you come in. I am exhausted. I was here all night."

Foxy was desperate to know the progress of the battle

"It is all so very discouraging," she said. "I don't know if we lost or won, but the battle is over. Scheer slunk away from Jellicoe in the dead of night and made it to home port. Jellicoe lost him in the dark and couldn't find him when the sun came up. By that time, Scheer was long gone."

"That sounds like Scheer fled with his tail between his legs," said Foxy, cheered by the news and not understanding why Olive was so out of sorts.

Olive sighed and took another sip of coffee. "It's not that simple."

Olive lit another cigarette and blew out a stream of blue smoke. She put the cigarette in the ashtray. She held up all five fingers of one hand and four of the other. "We decoded nine—count them, nine—messages between 10:43 last night and 2:00 this morning. They revealed Sheer's course, position, and the route for his escape. None of them was sent on to Jellicoe. None. Of. Them," she hissed. She picked up her cigarette, took a drag, and exhaled as if firing a torpedo. "We even intercepted Sheer's request for Zeppelin reconnaissance off Horns Reef, which turned out to be his route of retreat."

Foxy stared at her. *Messages not sent? And Scheer escaped? What was wrong with Operations?"*

Olive said in a hoarse whisper, "We had the key intelligence needed to convince Jellicoe where the hell Scheer was going last night, and it was never sent!" She shook her head in disgust. "Honestly, I don't know why we even bother."

Foxy felt gutted, "Why didn't Operations send the message to Jellicoe about the request for Zeppelin reconnaissance?" She was asking the question as much of the Fates as she was of Olive. "Was it the fault of Operations or Oliver?" Admiral Sir Henry Francis Oliver was Chief of the Admiralty War Staff. He had to approve any message transmitted to the fleet before it could be sent.

"We don't know," she said. "Someone said Oliver was sleeping at the time. But he must have given responsibility to someone in Operations to wake him up if any significant decodes came in. He must have turned it over to someone in Operations who can't tell the difference between his arse and a hole in the ground. And this time, it can't be Jackson because he wasn't even in the building. Of course. Why would he be when the largest naval battle in the war is going on?" She looked at her soft-boiled egg, standing in its cup, bravely waiting for its execution by spoon, the dead stubs in the ashtray, the crumbs from the toast, and the empty cup of coffee. She looked at her watch. "I'm going home," she said, "for a bath and then an afternoon getting my hair done."

Foxy smiled. "Good idea. You might want to take the pencil out of your hair first, though."

Olive smiled for the first time and reached for the pencil. "Thanks, Foxy, I'll see you tomorrow."

In their first-class carriage, Foxy opened a bottle of cider and passed William another sandwich. "What does the Battle of Jutland have to do with McCreedy?" she asked.

He took the bottle and sandwich. "Remember how that buffoon Jackson bungled the information about when the High Sea Fleet left port?"

Foxy nodded, chewing her sandwich.

"Remember, it was as much the fault of the man on watch when Jackson came to ask him where the D/K code was, but we never knew who that was?"

Foxy was taking a swallow from the bottle of cider. She nearly choked as she gasped, "You don't mean it was…?"

William nodded, "McCreedy. Yes, it was."

Foxy had a coughing fit. She recovered herself. She saw William's ironic grin. "I am not surprised. He always prides himself on his correctness. He wouldn't answer a question he wasn't asked, even if his silence would cost Britain control of the North Atlantic."

William agreed. "Father found out from Beatty, who was furious about it when the Destroyer Fleet returned to the Firth of Forth. So was Jellicoe when he returned to Scapa Flow."

"McCreedy's part never made it into his record, though, because Jackson was promoted to Rear Admiral the next month. Too many questions about the D/K transfer might have scuttled that."

"I remember," said Foxy. That must have stuck in McCreedy's throat. I know it did in mine at the time. On the other hand, McCreedy certainly benefited from the cover-up. He wasn't promoted, but evidently the real reason did not appear on his record."

After finishing Mabel's cake, they fell into a companionable silence. Foxy's thoughts returned to the Battle of Jutland. She did not want to share them with William because there was no need to remind him of battle and return him in his mind's eye to the Dardanelles. Or to make him think about how close his father had come to being maimed or killed. He was aboard Beatty's ship *Lion.* It was hit fourteen times; ninety-nine men were killed, and fifty-one wounded.

The Battle of Jutland was the greatest naval battle of the war. There were one hundred thousand British and German sailors deployed in two hundred and fifty warships when the battle started. In the end, twenty-five ships and eight thousand five hundred men were at the bottom of the sea. The Germans at first claimed victory. The High Seas Fleet sank fourteen ships. The British casualties numbered six thousand, seven hundred and eighty-four. By comparison, the Grand Fleet sank eleven ships and inflicted three thousand fifty-eight casualties. But the German fleet never again dared to come out of Wilhelmshaven. The cat stayed in Scapa Flow, watching the mousehole at Jade Bay. *We won the battle by not losing it,"* she thought. A paradox.

Night had fallen. As she looked at her reflection in the window of the carriage, brief flashes of her memories of serving as an ambulance driver lit her mind like lightning. One night, she was driving her ambulance filled with wounded men through pouring rain. The road was a slurry, a slimy mix of clay, motor oil, and blood. When she reached the aid station, she helped carry in one wounded soldier with a leg wound. He was quiet because he had been given morphine. She was told to take the stretcher directly to the operating theatre. The doctor ordered her to get ready to assist. "We are short-handed," he said, sharply. "Scrub up, put on a gown, mask, and gloves, and stand at the end of the table. Nurse, help her, and give her a towel to hold." Another nurse removed the dressing from the soldier's leg and quickly cleaned it while the anesthetist dripped ether on a mask over the soldier's face. Foxy saw the wound. It looked like minced meat. In two smooth circular moves, the doctor cut the skin away, then the muscle tissue. He sawed through the bone. He lifted the severed limb and handed it to Foxy, who now understood the reason for the towel. Absurd thoughts raced through her mind as she tried to understand what just happened. *So, when the leg is amputated, it can never be put back on. It is a separate thing. This thing I am holding. This thing that was on that man just seconds ago. Whose is it now? Is it his? Should I keep it for him?* She might have stood lost in the surrealism of the moment if the doctor hadn't barked at her. "Don't just stand there. Get rid of it." She stared at him. *Get rid of it? Get rid of it? How?* The assisting nurse nodded her head toward the tent wall behind Foxy. Foxy turned and saw a large bucket. As if in a trance, she walked toward it. She looked in and saw a mass of legs and arms. She quickly dropped the leg into the bucket, raced outside, and vomited.

It was dark outside the railway carriage now. She saw herself reflected in the window. Her face distorted, crumpled the way a baby's did when it was frightened, just before the mouth opened and let out a wail. This distorted expression took hold of her from time to time when the grief and agony of the war came over her. It passed quickly. She neither wailed nor cried.

Winning by not losing seemed to sum up the entire war. The bitterness and the demand by those on the winning side to take their revenge on the losing side laid the way for disastrous, harsh penalties doled out to Germany, which laid the way for the next war. Foxy was sure of it. She needed to protect those she loved. And after hearing Mabel's account of lies and deception, she feared the gathering forces of darkness.

Chapter Twenty-Two

Council of War

Josie copied the final entry from the journal Phillip Teague kept on the inquiry into the sinking of the *Lusitania*. Her jaw was clenched. With studied resolution, she closed her notebook, took off her glasses, and rubbed her tired eyes. She returned the Teague journals and other related material to the librarian's desk. She had been invited to supper at the Chelsea townhouse, to be followed by a Council of War. She had much to report.

Dinny and Addie bent their heads over the Admiralty charts William had procured, marking the route of the U-20 and noting the messages sent by the Captain to his base. They often stopped their work to exclaim over the information they discovered.

Sunday was Mrs. Flowerdew's day off. She left instructions for Maisy to reheat the beef stew, prepare the tomato salad, and serve the apple pie. Maisy brought coffee *mit schlag* and tea after dinner as everyone gathered for the Council of War around the fireplace. The large nautical chart was pinned to a burlap-covered board on a substantial stand.

"Who would like to start?" asked William when everyone was seated.

Addie and Dinny quickly volunteered. Addie positioned the board where everyone could see it.

"I knew you wouldn't mind, William," said Dinny. "I borrowed your father's charting board."

"Excellent idea," said William.

Addie took up a pointer. "Dinny read me the coordinates from the decrypts, and I pinned them and connected them with ribbon. The red ribbon is for the wireless transmissions of the outbound journey of the U-20, and the blue is for what we think the route was once the U-20 went around Scotland and stopped transmitting. The black is for the return. We have marked the point where the torpedo struck the *Lusitania* with this X."

"As you can see," said Dinny soberly, "Room 40 knew what the route was of the U-20 from the time it left Emden the morning of April 30, 1915. The U-20 signaled its positions to its headquarters fourteen times in the first twenty-four hours as it headed into the North Sea. Then it stopped transmitting, probably to avoid detection by the Admiralty ships at Scapa Flow. From its course to that point, it is obvious that the U-20 went round the northeast tip of Scotland at Fair Isle."

"Right under Jellicoe's patrol boats," observed William.

"Exactly," said Dinny. "U-20 must have proceeded down the west coast of Ireland. As we know from the position of the *Lusitania,* he must have reached the southern coast of Ireland, probably off Kinsale Head, in time to sink the *Lusitania* on May 8," said Dinny. Addie pointed to the large, black X. "Remember that the U-20 would have maintained radio silence once it rounded Scotland because of the assumption that radio wave transmission could not reach beyond several hundred miles."

Using her pointer, Addie said, "We assume the U-20 retraced its route. The next time it sent a message was on May 12, when it was two hundred miles from the home base at Wilhelmshaven."

"This is the message the Captain sent," said Dinny, reading from his notes. "'Have sunk one sailing vessel, two steamers, and *Lusitania.*' In a later message, he said he sank the *Lusitania* with one torpedo."

Foxy and William exchanged glances. "One torpedo?" asked Foxy. "Are you sure?"

"Quite sure," said Dinny. "About five hours later, the Commander-in-Chief at Wilhelmshaven signaled back: 'My highest appreciation of commander and crew for success achieved, of which the High Seas Fleet is proud, and my congratulations on their return.'"

The five fell silent.

"For killing over a thousand civilians, including women and babies," said Foxy. This wasn't news, but the stark congratulations hit home with a new realism. The celebrations in Germany moved a private citizen, an artist named Karl Goetz, to cast a commemorative medal depicting, among other things, artillery pieces and airplanes on the *Lusitania's* deck, a falsification to "justify" sinking the *Lusitania* because it was armed.

"Tell them about the earliest decrypt," said Addie to Dinny.

"Oh, right," he said. "The first decrypt is from March 3. Room 40 intercepted a message from the German headquarters at Norrdeich to all ships—meaning particularly the U-Boats—that the *Lusitania* was expected to reach Liverpool from London on March 4 or 5."

"Ah," said Foxy. "Mabel told me yesterday that the Admiralty had sent out a destroyer to accompany the *Lusitania* on its previous sailing before Turner took over as Captain. So, Admiralty had no doubt the *Lusitania* was a target for submarine command."

William lit his pipe. His face was wreathed in smoke. "They would have known that at any rate. Remember, the German Embassy in the US placed notices in prominent newspapers just below Cunard's ad for the sailing date of *Lusitania,* warning passengers of the danger of a German submarine attack. It was very clear that the *Lusitania* was a target." He looked at Dinny. "What no one knew, except for Churchill and one or two others, was that Room 40 could track the U-20, and presumably any other submarines, coming from Wilhelmshaven and heading for the Irish Sea. But the most significant information is that the U-20 Captain transmitted the message that he fired only one torpedo."

"But at the time, the Admiralty insisted there were at least two torpedoes," said Foxy. "Why?"

Josie was almost quivering with anticipation, eager to report what she had learned. She had to wait, however.

"Since you mentioned Mabel, why don't we debrief what we learned yesterday?" asked William. Foxy recounted Mabel's condemnation of the case presented against Turner by the Board of Trade in June 1915. She concluded, "Mabel is absolutely certain that the Admiralty did not explain why the Royal Navy failed to provide protection for the *Lusitania*, while claiming that Turner ignored Admiralty advice about zig-zagging or maintaining speed or the course he should take. Churchill repeats these allegations in *Times of Crisis* even though he has every reason to know better. He can do that because much of the hearing was held behind closed doors, and he repeats these allegations against Turner even though he was exonerated from them at the time." Foxy's disgust showed in her tone of voice.

"It's all rotten," said William, also bitterly. "Turner is a decent, honest man who was awarded the OBE. Churchill wants to clear his own name before standing for Parliament as a Conservative. That's how I see it," he said, clamping his teeth firmly on his pipe stem. He had enjoyed his time with Turner and was outraged at Churchill's villainy in trying to climb back into office by heaping a mountain of abuse on Turner.

Dinny was also moved by Foxy's account. He looked at the chart with its ribbons and the X where U-20 sank the *Lusitania*. "Churchill certainly would have known that the German U-boats were ordered to seek out the *Lusitania* as early as March, and he would have known that U-Boats were heading for the Irish Sea. The decrypts make that clear."

Josie cleared her throat. "I think you ought to know what I found in Teague's papers. He provides a detailed account of what went on behind closed doors at the hearing, and some things that even Turner didn't know."

William turned to her and nodded. "Please tell us."

Josie's straight, dark hair was parted in the middle and drawn back into a bun. Her thin features bore an expression of serious concentration. She put on her glasses and consulted her notebook. "Let me tell you something about Charles Dyce Teague. He was born in 1835, the second son of a wealthy tea merchant. He studied law at the University of London and, by 1880, made a name for himself in commercial law. In 1895, he accepted a position with the Wrecks Commission attached to the Board of Trade. He was the official legal secretary to Lord Mersey during the *Lusitania* Enquiry, which everyone now calls the Mersey Enquiry. Teague retired in 1917 and died in 1921. I copied the last entry from his journal on the *Lusitania* Enquiry.

> "I have written this in the hope that sometime in the future, after I am dead, it will be read by someone with a passion for the truth. I am constrained by my obligation to maintain confidentiality about the proceedings, most of which were conducted behind closed doors. As those who may read the preceding account must agree, the Board of Trade was most eager to condemn Captain Turner as either incompetent or as working on behalf of the Germans. There is no doubt their prosecution of the case reflected the wishes of both the Admiralty and the Prime Minister. It is due to the integrity of The Right Honorable John Bigham, 1st Viscount Mersey, that, despite considerable pressure placed upon him, he declared Turner exonerated of any charge of incompetence. He was, in fact and to his credit, disgusted by the manipulation of evidence by the prosecution, which became clear, as I have described, in the course of the hearing. I am also concerned about the censorship of news reports coming from the wire services and hope that will be looked into as well."

Josie looked up. As her words sank in, a stillness came over her four listeners. She continued. "The Germans gave five reasons to justify sinking the *Lusitania*. They claimed the British government paid for the building of the *Lusitania* in 1904 to be used as an auxiliary cruiser during times of war. True, but it was never called into service. The captain was an officer in the Naval Reserve. True, but irrelevant. The *Lusitania* was armed. Not true. Canadian troops were on board. Not true. The *Lusitania* was carrying explosive ammunition and other contraband," Josie paused for effect. "True."

William was startled. He asked, "You mean it was carrying more than rifle cartridges? I recall they admitted the cargo included about five thousand cases of cartridges, which could not have exploded. It was legal for a neutral nation to ship cartridges to a belligerent nation."

"Yes, I do," said Josie, matter-of-factly.

"God Almighty," said William.

"Damnation!" said Foxy. "I for one need a stiffener."

William nodded his agreement, rose, and offered brandy or whiskey. "Do go on," he said grimly.

"The government wanted the public to believe that at least two and possibly more torpedoes had been fired, which accounted for the rapid sinking of the *Lusitania*. It went down in eighteen minutes, which is extraordinarily quick and not likely to have been caused by one torpedo."

"That's right," said Addie. "They knew from the decrypts that only one torpedo was fired."

"Were the munitions armed?" asked Dinny. "Would they have exploded?"

Josie consulted her notes. "The evidence presented at the closed session of the Enquiry was that there were four thousand, two hundred cases of rifle cartridges, which would not have exploded. There were also twelve hundred and fifty shrapnel shells, which they claimed were not armed. There were eighteen cases of percussion fuses stowed separately, they said, so they could not have touched off the explosion."

Dinny thought for a moment. His course on metal stresses at Cambridge included the effects of various explosives. "Those fuses were made of fulminate of mercury," he said slowly. "If they were stored with the rest of the munitions, they could have caused an almighty great explosion."

"Quite right," said William, who had firsthand knowledge of the potential for ammunition to explode if it caught fire. "And if the shells were filled, even without fuses, they could have caused an explosion as well, if there had been a direct hit on the hold where they were stored."

Foxy took a deep draught of the Scotch whiskey. "This is inconceivable," she said.

Josie turned a page in her notebook and cleared her throat again. "Admiralty claimed that the heavy munition shells were stored on one of the decks right under the Bridge, forward of the first funnel. They had witnesses who said the first torpedo hit between funnels two and three—so not near the stored munitions—and the second well aft of that."

William rose to pour himself another drink, which he downed quickly. This was unusual for him. He was a man who sipped his single malt. "Nonsense," he said. "The *Lusitania* went down bow first. There is no question of that. If there had been two torpedoes—which there weren't—-hitting that far aft of the Bridge, it could not possibly have gone down bow first, as any seaman worth his salt would know." He paused. "Who else needs a refresher?"

Josie continued, "Mabel Every is right about the orders Turner received, but the head of the Admiralty's Board of Trade, Captain Richard Webb, tried to make it seem otherwise. In Teague's papers are two different memos about the sinking of the *Lusitania*. Webb prepared both of them. They included different accounts of what those orders were. In the second memo, which was the only one submitted in evidence, Webb said that all ships had been warned to 'keep well off the land.' Since Turner had not done that, Webb accused Turner of 'almost inconceivable negligence' and that he was 'forced to conclude that [Turner] is either utterly incompetent or he has been got at by the Germans.'"

'So Mabel was right about that," said Foxy. "What a terrible thing to do to Turner."

"It gets worse," said Josie. "According to Teague, Mersey was thoroughly provoked when he found out there were two different orders, one presented as evidence and the other not. Mersey was deeply concerned and asked Teague to get to the bottom of it. This is what he wrote in his journal:

> "It didn't take me long to discover that it wasn't until a week after the Lusitania was sunk that the orders for staying offshore and zig-zagging were approved, and that was the memo Webb presented in evidence. Mersey was more than a little angry.
>
> He confided in me that Admiral Ingelfeld, who is one of the four assessors hearing the case, approached him and said, 'It would please the government if you were to find Turner guilty of incompetence.'

Mersey told me how he replied: 'Have you considered that if the blame is laid on Turner and not the U-boat, it will encourage the Germans to continue to attack commercial liners?'

'Nevertheless,' replied Ingelfeld, 'the government wishes a finding that Turner had received written instructions which he had failed to follow. And if you need more reassurances, I have been authorized to invite you to Number 10 to hear it from the Prime Minister.'

Then Mersey said to me, 'And after what you found out, Teague, it is as clear as day that Turner never received the orders presented to the hearing. I won't have it. I just won't have it.'"

Josie continued reading her notes. "Mersey adjourned the inquiry in June. He asked the assessors to give their opinions on whether to find Turner guilty of incompetence in sealed envelopes. Only one assessor voted to find him guilty. It was, not surprisingly, Sir Frederick Ingelfield. When the inquiry ended in July, Mersey resigned. He waived his fees and wisely confiscated the master court file. It remains in his private collection. His last words to Teague were, "That was a damned, dirty business."

Josie looked up. "There's more. It corroborates what Mabel Every told you about the false claims that Turner was too close to the headlands and not in mid-channel. I have just a few more notes to take tomorrow, and then I will type them up."

Foxy said angrily, "I don't know how much more of this I can stand."

"If you will bear with me, there is one more item I should report," said Josie. "Teague collected newspaper clippings and magazine articles from the US about the sinking of the *Lusitania*. Teague commented on one in particular: 'On May 8, there was a wire report from the US that Cunard had been assured there would be destroyers sent to accompany the *Lusitania* once it entered the war zone.' That report was censored. It was never reported in the UK papers."

Josie closed her notebook and took off her glasses. Four pairs of eyes stared at her. No one knew what to say.

Chapter Twenty-Three

Whose Ox Is Gored?

Dinny broke the silence. "Josie, it must have been so difficult for you to sit there alone, reading this, I mean." *I have pulled Josie and Addie into deep, sinister waters.* He felt both guilty and frustrated because he could do so little from his wheelchair.

Josie smiled her cheerful grin. "Oh, come now, Dinny. You don't seriously think that I had to be coerced into being the first person to read a primary source written by a witness to a major scandal affecting the war." She paused. "Honestly, Dinny, I have felt so useless after what happened to you and Addie." She cleared her throat. "I can't even talk about that."

Addie said briskly, "Hey, let's not rake that up. We survived, and now we are on the hunt for the misbegotten louse that messed with the car."

"And stole the files and decrypts," said Dinny, "That could have destroyed both our careers, don't forget that."

Dinny, Josie, and Addie had instinctively drawn closer to one another, reviving the sense of invincibility they felt when they faced down the prejudices and threats women faced at Cambridge. "I wish Tris were here," said Josie. It seemed to be a *non sequitur* to anyone who did not know them.

"Yes, well, you can bet he does, too," said Dinny. "Or if not here, anywhere but Invergordon."

William felt his anger rise at what these young, close friends were going through, but he didn't want to give even a hint of how he felt. "I, for one, don't think I can start to put all of this together without a raid on the kitchen. There must be a slice or two left of Mrs. Flowerdew's lemon pound cake from yesterday's tea."

Foxy, who had also been lost in thought about what Dinny and his friends were having to face, quickly agreed, "Excellent idea. And the fire is perfect for buttered toast."

After a slice of lemon cake and a cup of cocoa, Foxy said, "Right. Now that we're fortified for battle, let's consider whose ox would be gored if the information in the *Lusitania* archive and the decrypts came to light. There's no doubt in my mind. Everything points to Churchill. In his *Time of Crisis*, he repeats the allegations against Turner. He repeats the lie that two torpedoes hit the *Lusitania*. Churchill makes such an effort to rake up the allegations against Turner again. He must be afraid something will come to light about the *Lusitania* sinking and his handling of it. He couldn't care less what accusing Turner will do to Turner himself, or how the accusations just don't jibe with either the findings of the Mersey Commission or the honors given Turner after the war." She uttered a sound of disgust. "Makes me sick."

"Yes," said Addie, buttering the bread she had toasted in the fire on the end of a special fork. "It really is heartless." She paused. "The thing is, he published *World Crisis* just recently. That's the important thing, isn't it? Not what *really* happened, but what Churchill *says* happened."

"Yes," said William, "you've hit on something, Addie. The Conservatives plan to force a General Election very soon. They want Labour out of power. They think of Labour as socialists aligned with the Bolsheviks, which is nonsense. The Conservatives oppose the trade treaties MacDonald is about to sign with the Soviets. Above all, they want back into power. Churchill wants to leave the Liberal party—he, too, despises their efforts to secure treaties with Russia—and return to the bosom of the Conservatives. He must clear his reputation of his failures while he was First Lord of the Admiralty. One is the catastrophe of the Dardanelles, which he does by blaming Kitchener for not providing land forces at the beginning of Naval operations. The other is the *Lusitania*, which he does by blaming Turner.

Foxy, still upset, said, "Yes. And the one issue he can avoid if he places the blame on Turner is the question of why in God's name there was no protection from the Navy once the *Lusitania* entered the war zone."

Josie, who was just finishing her buttered toast, nodded vigorously. "Yes, that is clear. The question of why there was no protection never came up in the Mersey Commission. And remember that wire-service report that was censored, stating that Cunard received assurances that there would be protection."

"Yes!" said Foxy, agitated. "That's it. Churchill is so vehement in his condemnation of Wilson for not coming into the war after the sinking of the *Lusitania*, it is obvious that is just what he *hoped* would happen at the time."

"And then there's Tris' Aunt," said Dinny, who felt the energy in the room like a gathering of static electricity. "I mean, you know, there's the Foreign Secretary AND the King asking Colonel House what the American response would be if the Germans sank a liner with Americans aboard. The King mentioned *Lusitania* specifically. So," he went on excitedly, "that is why the decrypts had to disappear. Not just because Room 40 is still a secret, but also because the decrypts made it very clear that Admiralty *knew* U-20 was heading for the Irish Sea and had received standing orders issued in March to sink the *Lusitania*."

William lit his pipe. "That explains why Churchill would want the *Lusitania* archive to disappear, in case there is something there that is damning to him, and why the decrypts disappeared, for the same reason. It also explains why Tris is shivering and dying of boredom on Invergordon." He paused and reached into his pocket. "But I don't think it explains this." He held up the membership badge Doctor Collard found at the site of the accident.

Dinny sat up straighter in his wheelchair. "Oh, yes. Did you find out what that is?"

"Yes, I certainly did, from Clive. It is the badge of a group called the British Fascisti, founded a year ago, in May, by a fanatical woman named Rotha Lintorn-Orman. She was weeding in her garden, thinking how awful it was that the communists were growing in their influence here, when she suddenly got the idea of using Mussolini's Fascist Party as a model for a resistance movement."

"So, she wanted to weed out communists rather than sticking with the boring business of weeding her garden," said Foxy.

"Yes, something like that," he said, smiling slightly. "The point is, this was dropped by the motorcyclist who passed Addie and Dinny when the car went off the road, the same person who was snooping around Sparky's garage."

"What exactly does that mean?" asked Addie. "This group wants what, and why would they target Dinny and me?"

"That's what I cannot understand," said William. "Rotha Lintorn-Orman is anti-communist, anti-Semitic, anti-immigrant, and to the right of the Conservative Party. Her adherents seem to be drawn from the ranks of retired military officers and members of the aristocracy. It is her mother who finances the operation."

At the mention of anti-Semitism, Addie felt a cold chill in her spine. "That creep Caxton, one of the Messengers I interviewed, is openly anti-Semitic," she said. "Remember, he pushed Arensdorf and made him drop his papers?" Foxy and Josie nodded. "But what would that have to do with sabotaging Dinny's car?"

At the mention of Arensdorf, Foxy remembered something, too. "When we met with Arensdorf, he seemed very keen to let me know he overheard two men in a meeting with Jan Gruter. It seems to have been heated. At one point, he heard the name Zinoviev. He made it very clear he wanted me to know that."

Josie chimed in, "I remember now. He said that one of them—was it Gruter? —saw Caxton lurking about and gave him what for, but one of the men at the meeting said something to calm Gruter down."

Addie felt they were onto something, but didn't know what. "Yes, that's right. I remember that, too. I couldn't see why Arensdorf mentioned it, though."

Foxy said quietly, "Arensdorf understood that I must have worked for

Naval Intelligence during the war, just as I understood he must have been involved in espionage. My guess is that Jan Gruter was, too. He may have been testing me or warning me. I don't know if there is a connection with the *Lusitania* papers or not." She shook her head in exasperation.

"You know, there is something fishy about Caxton," said Addie. "He told me his father is in business, and he wanted Caxton to acquire some discipline or something like that before he took over the company. So he got his brother—Caxton's uncle—who is an officer in the Navy, to pull strings and get Caxton enlisted and assigned to Admiralty. Who does that? It makes no sense. Except that I could understand any parent wanting to get Caxton out of the house." She paused and looked at Foxy. "I think we should find out if he rides a motorcycle."

"Good idea," said Foxy

"It seems a bit far-fetched to me that Churchill would be involved in trying to harm Addie and Dinny, though," said William. "Although getting Tris well out of the way makes sense now that we know what his Aunt told him. It wouldn't do for Tris to make any of this known. That is what the fear seems to have been."

Dinny said, "I for one have my head too stuffed full of information—"

"And your tummy with tea and toast," said Addie, giving him a little smile.

"Yes, that, too. Anyhow, I cannot make any more sense of this tonight."

William called for a cab for Josie. Addie sat up with Dinny while William and Foxy retired for the night.

"I seem to have landed you in the Dismal Swamp by asking you to help me," said Dinny.

"I wouldn't have missed out on this intrigue for the world, except for the accident, of course."

"'Apart from that, Mrs. Lincoln, how did you like the play?'" joked Dinny. Addie laughed.

"Come here," he said, pulling her toward him. They talked no more that night.

Chapter Twenty-Four

There's a dead man

Murky was on top of the bedclothes, kneading energetically with her front paws.

"Hello, you," said Foxy, reaching out to give her a scratch behind the ears. The clock on the bedside table said 5:30 am. "I was having a bad dream." She had dropped off to sleep about 2:00 a.m.

Murky jumped off the bed, headed for the door, stopped, looked over her shoulder, and mewed. "All right," said Foxy, "I might as well get up." She put on her red satin dressing gown over black, striped satin pajamas, slipped into her curly-toed, embroidered slippers, and followed Murky down the stairs. Murky led her to the Conservatory, where she jumped onto the grooming table, sat down, stared with yellow eyes at Foxy, and mewed once.

"I have been neglecting you," agreed Foxy.

She had not groomed Murky in several days. She laid Murky gently on one side, slid her arm under the cat's head, and grasped her two front legs. She began to stroke the grooming brush through the long, black fur on Murky's side. Murky purred loudly. Foxy's thoughts returned to the previous night, matching the rhythm of her strokes. Lost in thought, she brushed Murky very briskly, too briskly. Murky bit the end of the brush. A nimbus of dark fur floated on the air. Fur festooned the leaves of the nearby aspidistra. Foxy sneezed. Murky sneezed.

"Sorry, Murky," she said. "I got carried away." She released the cat. Murky sat up, gave herself a shake, jumped off the table, shot a highly judgmental look at Foxy, and headed to the kitchen for her breakfast with her tail cocked in its typical question mark.

Foxy followed her. She asked Maisy for a cup of coffee rather than her usual tea.

"Sorry to hear you didn't sleep well, Madame," said Maisy. "Shall I bring it to you in the Conservatory?"

Foxy sat surrounded by plants, watching the false dawn gradually cast a grey pall over the sky. No birds sang. Murky jumped up, apparently seeking an apology in the form of a scratch behind the ears prior to falling asleep on Foxy's lap. Foxy sipped her coffee and thought about Churchill and what he had to prevent from ever seeing the light of day if he expected to be elected to Parliament again.

William joined her as Maisy brought more coffee. "Couldn't you sleep, either?" asked Foxy.

William was impeccably dressed in this uniform, but looked tired, and he, like Foxy, usually had tea first thing in the morning.

"I admit I tossed and turned. A penny for your thoughts," he said.

"I was thinking about Churchill's failures as First Lord, not only the *Lusitania* but the Dardanelles, of course, which was a much more obvious calamity in terms of what the public knew," said Foxy

Foxy immediately regretted mentioning the Dardanelles, but for once, William didn't fall into a profoundly distressing interior recollection. "I agree with something Clive said," replied William. "The Dardanelles is a huge blot on his record, but it is a matter of record, and Churchill exonerates himself. But the whitewashing, the secrecy, the lies and half-truths about the *Lusitania*—all that would do him irreparable harm if it became known now. Imagine what the Americans would say if they knew the chicanery behind the Mersey Report. And the Germans, too."

"Do you think that is, would Churchill's political ambition drive him to harm or even kill two people he doesn't even know?" said Foxy, who found it incredible.

"You have just given an excellent definition of war," said William grimly.

"Isn't it about powerful individuals killing thousands, even millions, of faceless people in the name of some ambition or other?"

"Granted," said Foxy, quietly. "But this is about Dinny and Addie."

The sun came up, casting its weak, golden rays into the Conservatory. Looming clouds threatened rain. Foxy's coffee had gone cold. "I must dress for breakfast. Addie and I are off to the Admiralty today, of course," she said.

"I would like to come with you," said William.

"How delightful," said Foxy, "but why?"

"I wanted to discuss with McCreedy what I learned from Turner about what he did to Father," said William, mildly.

"Oh, I see," said Foxy. *Guns for two, tea for one at the Admiralty,* she thought. She gently set Murky down and rose to go.

William drove them to the Admiralty and parked in the reserved lot on the side of the building where Foxy worked during the war.

"That brings back memories," she said to Addie, pointing to the fire escape. "We hat girls used to have our smoke breaks there. We weren't supposed to, of course. Breach of security and all that."

They parted company after signing in. William went to find McCreedy. Addie and Foxy took the stairs down to the ARO.

Foxy and Addie froze halfway down. At the bottom of the staircase lay a man, quite still. On the stair just above him stood Chauncey Caxton, his face white as a sheet, his body rigid. He gripped the handrail so tightly his knuckles were white. He was staring at a body. Papers and file folders were scattered on the stairs.

Addie and Foxy clambered down the stairs. "It's Arensdorf," they said in shocked unison. Addie searched for a neck pulse. There wasn't one. She stood up and yelled at Chauncey, "You murdering bastard! What did you do, give him another one of your little anti-Semitic shoves?"

Chauncey could not respond. He stared at her, his eyes popping from his sockets. "You're coming with me!" said Foxy. It took a bit of time to loosen his grip on the handrail.

"You stay with Arensdorf," said Foxy. "And don't let anyone near the body.

Where's Gruter? You think he would have heard the commotion." She grabbed Chauncey by the wrist and dragged him up the stairs.

William, who had told McCreedy he knew about the stupid error that could have lost the British fleet, was quietly but efficiently giving McCreedy a piece of his mind for snitching on William's father. Foxy burst in, Chauncey firmly in her grip.

"What is the meaning of this…" said McCreedy querulously.

"There's a dead man…" she began, puffing, "at the bottom of the stairs to the ARO…it's Professor Arensdorf…Chauncey here was standing over the body when we came upon it…you should hold him for questioning…and come see for yourself…I need to sit down."

"What are you saying?" said McCreedy. "There can't be a dead body in the Admiralty!"

William stood up and pulled his chair over for Foxy. She still clung tightly to Chauncey's wrist.

"But there is one," said William, "evidently. You should see to it. Can you give Foxy some water?" He spoke like a ranking officer to a subaltern.

McCreedy, obviously irritated, rang his secretary. "Can you bring Lady Butterschloss some water? And send someone down to the ARO. There is a report of a dead body. Yes, that's what I said," he snapped. "A dead body."

"This young man is known to have pushed Arensdorf once before. He was proud of it. He dislikes anyone who is Jewish," Foxy said, regaining her breath. "Addie and I found him standing over the body. He needs to be questioned. He seems to be out of his wits at the moment."

McCreedy looked bewildered. "Call the Master-at-Arms," said William, taking charge. Again, McCreedy buzzed his secretary. "Can we count on you to hold Chauncey until he is taken into custody?" asked William. McCreedy nodded, gradually taking in the gravity of the situation.

William and Foxy found Addie conferring with a physician from the Chief Naval Medical Service. He introduced himself as Dr. Lionel Hawkins. He looked to be in his sixties. He had a slight stoop, which made his crisp, white lab coat hang slightly askew. White hair framed his bald head, and he wore gold-rimmed glasses. His nose was red, his eyes rheumy and yellowish, his skin wrinkled.

"I understand you were one of those who found the body," he said to Foxy. "It must have been quite a shock. This is indeed a most unfortunate accident." He spoke briskly, as if he wanted to have this messy business over and done with as quickly and efficiently as possible.

Addie, who was standing behind Dr. Hawkins, looked up sharply. She shook her head and mouthed, "No," at William and Foxy.

"How can you be certain it was an accident?" asked William calmly.

"Because I have been a Naval doctor for thirty-five years, and I have seen more than my share of falls," he said sharply. "There is no sign of an altercation, and the wounds are consistent with a fall caused by a slip. He was an older man, probably unsteady on his feet, and couldn't grasp the handrail quickly enough, probably because he was carrying so many files. I will know more after the Coroner's report, but I think it will confirm my first impression."

"Come along," said William to Addie and Foxy. "I think a pot of hot tea is in order." He led them to the Wardroom on the ground floor. It was muffled from the noise of the city by heavy curtains, plush carpets, and thick mahogany panels. The hot tea—heavily sugared—was restorative, as were the warm, buttered scones and jam.

"I can't believe this. We just saw him Friday," said Addie, her voice shaking.

"When you're ready, can you tell us why you don't think his fall was an accident?" asked William.

She had a bit more tea and another bite of scone. "I saw head injuries caused by all kinds of nasty things when I worked in hospital during the war. A fall like that would not have caused all that fresh blood to pool around the head. A fall would cause internal bleeding. And I pushed up his pant leg and sleeves. I know I shouldn't have," she said hastily. "I was looking for bruising. There didn't appear to be any, and there usually would be if he had fallen. And for that much blood, he must have had a severe blow to the head, a deep wound, on the side that I couldn't see. I don't know what that doctor was thinking."

"But his neck looked broken," said Foxy. "I agree, though. There was too much blood for a bump on the head." She, too, had seen many head injuries during the war.

Addie nodded. "I agree his neck was broken. But maybe it was done after the blow to his head," said Addie. "I hope the Coroner's report is more exacting than the doctor's examination. It seemed very cursory. He seemed in a great hurry."

"He also seemed to be a heavy drinker," said William.

"How so?" asked Addie

"That bright red nose, for one thing," said Foxy.

"And his yellowish eyes for another," said William.

"Not to mention his skin looks like he should order Pond's Vanishing Creme by the crate," said Foxy.

"I did wonder about his shaking hands," said Addie. "I wanted to believe it was that creep Chauncey who pushed him down the stairs, but could there be more to it?"

Foxy said, "Even if Arensdorf did not die from being pushed, Chauncey might have been involved in some way. After all, he was standing right next to Arensdorf. Maybe he saw who killed Arensdorf, but isn't willing to say. I think I'll see what I can find out about his father and his connections to Admiralty." She took a sip of tea.

"We definitely need to find out about what Chauncey has to say for himself. I'll get McCreedy to tell me what the Master-at-Arms finds out when he interrogates Chauncey," said William.

"How will you get him to do that?" asked Foxy.

William gave a half smile. "I told him what I knew about the battle of Jutland and how he almost lost us the war in the North Atlantic. I imagine he will be quite tractable once I assure him that I, at least, am not a snitch. Unlike what he did to Father."

"Do you want to go home?" Foxy asked Addie. "You have had quite a shock."

"So have you," said Addie. "I think we both want to get on with our investigation more than ever. This may have something to do with the car wreck."

They were restored by the tea and drew on the resilience they learned during the war.

Foxy said, "I suggest we find out where Gruter has been all this time. Shall we three meet at the Above Board for lunch and compare notes?"

Addie and Foxy took the elevator to the basement. Arensdorf's body had been removed, and the doctor was gone. The area at the bottom of the stairs had been cordoned off. Oddly, the door to the ARO was locked. Addie rattled the doorknob and knocked on the door, calling for Gruter. It was still too early for the rest of the staff to have arrived.

"We'd better ask the Porter if Gruter called in sick," said Addie.

They took the elevator up to the ground floor. "No, Lady Butterschloss," said the elderly Porter, Mr. Gibson. "There's nothing wrong, I can assure you. Mr. Gruter told the Night Porter he would be working late and would stay overnight. He has quite a cozy apartment down there, you know. It was set up during the war, when many of those working here had to stay overnight, the archivist included. By the bye, I heard Professor Arensdorf had a terrible fall. Killed him. Terrible thing, that," he said, shaking his head. "I liked him. He was always so polite."

Had Gibson been better at reading people, he would have understood that Foxy was barely able to suppress her impatience.

"The thing is," said Addie sweetly. "We are very worried about Mr. Gruter. He is usually at his desk by this time, but the ARO is locked, and he didn't come to the door. We want to make sure nothing has happened to him."

Gibson smiled, "As it's you, I'll see what I can do to set your minds at ease." He was condescending to what he supposed were the jangled nerves of a sensitive young woman.

A junior Porter went with them to the ARO and unlocked the door. There was still no sign of Gruter. "Can you show us where his apartment is?" asked Foxy, who hid her agitation.

The door to the room was unlocked. It was small but quite comfortable, set against a far corner of the ARO. It was simply furnished with a bed, a rocking chair, side table, a lamp, hot plate, electric heater, and a small bathroom in a second room. There was no sign of Gruter. The bed was neatly made. The room contained no clothes or any other signs that anyone had been in it recently.

Foxy and Addie burst into McCreedy's office without knocking. "Jan Gruter is missing," said Foxy. She stopped suddenly, and Addie nearly bumped into her. "I apologize," she said, I didn't realize..."

"This is Master-at-Arms Fletcher," said William as the men rose. He introduced Foxy and Addie.

"How do you do," said Fletcher. He was in his early forties and had kind, dark eyes and a pleasant smile. "I understand you found Professor Arensdorf. Most unpleasant. And what is this, now, about Mr. Gruter?"

Foxy quickly explained that he was supposed to have slept in his apartment, but he was not there. Nor had he signed out anytime last night or that morning.

McCreedy had been subdued up to this point, a result of his discussion with William about the battle of Jutland. "There must be some perfectly simple reason why he isn't in the ARO," he said, with just a hint of his old asperity.

"Yes, most likely," said Fletcher. "But I'll have the lads search the building, and question the Porters, too, just to make sure."

"We had best be going, too," said William. "Thanks, McCreedy, for your assistance."

"Think nothing of it," said McCreedy, quietly and without a hint of sincerity.

It was a despondent trio seated at the Above Board.

"Never mind the food," Foxy said to William. "Make mine a gin and tonic."

"May I have a Pimm's?" asked Addie.

William ordered a Doom Bar Amber Ale for himself.

Addie sipped her Pimm's. "Poor Professor Arensdorf. I liked him, and I know Josie did, too. Gosh! Josie! I need to tell her."

"I'll drive us home after lunch," said William in his reassuring way. "You can call her then."

"What did Fletcher have to say about Chauncey?" asked Foxy after taking a deep swallow of her gin and tonic.

"We are not going to learn much from him, I'm afraid," said William. "Chauncey was admitted to Queen Alexandra Hospital and sedated. All they could get from him was incoherent babble. He kept repeating, 'Thanks, No Thanks,' and he couldn't stop shaking his head."

"Sounds like shell-shock," said Addie. "He certainly isn't the smug, upper-crust, anti-Semite he was a few days ago."

"What do you suppose happened to Gruter?" asked Foxy.

"I don't suppose it is a coincidence that he disappeared at the same time Arensdorf was murdered," said William, "any more than you do."

"No, I don't," said Foxy. "Addie, did you notice anything odd about the apartment?"

"Only how shipshape and Bristol fashion it was. It had a cold, un-lived-in feel to it."

"I agree," said Foxy. "What struck me was what wasn't there. There was no shaving kit, for instance, and no sign the towels had been used. Nothing that said, 'Gruter was here.' There wasn't even a set of keys to the ARO or a key to the apartment itself."

"And what, if anything, does it have to do with the missing *Lusitania* files and sabotaging Dinny's car?" asked William, frustrated.

Chapter Twenty-Five

Posthumous Messages

J osie was talking with Dinny when Addie, William, and Foxy arrived home. They were surprised to see her.

"Josie has something for you," Dinny said to Foxy. "And she is a bit worried about Professor Arensdorf."

William stepped into the kitchen to ask for tea, anticipating what was to come. Foxy and Addie exchanged glances.

Josie said, "I found this in my pigeonhole this morning. It is from Professor Arensdorf for you, Lady Butterschloss." She handed a long, brown envelope to Foxy.

Inside was a paper filled with random letters. She realized she was probably holding Arensdorf's last words, a message he thought so important that he needed to send it in cipher, and that he knew she had worked for Room 40. She looked at Josie. "You say you found this in your pigeonhole. When exactly?"

"It was just before 9:00 this morning. There was also a message from the librarian. I put in a call for the Teague papers to work on them today. The diary has gone missing," she said. "What is going on? Did you see Professor Arensdorf at the ARO?"

William returned, and he glanced at Foxy. "We, that is, Foxy and Addie, did see Arensdorf, and I am sorry to say, we have bad news."

Josie looked at them. "Why? Has something happened?"

"Yes, I thought you looked pale," Dinny said, looking at Addie. "Are you all right?" He reached out a hand to her.

"Addie and I found Arensdorf's body at the bottom of the stairs to the ARO," Foxy said quietly.

"What! Is he all right? Is he in hospital?" asked Josie, alarmed.

Foxy shook her head. "I'm sorry, Josie."

"What? You don't mean…" she said. "I can't believe it. Was it an accident?" Tears filled her eyes.

"We don't think so," said Addie softly. "Someone…" her voice broke.

Maisy came in with the tray and set it down quietly. "I'll take care of this," said William.

It took some time, but the tea, murmurs of understanding, and gentle reassurances gradually calmed Dinny and especially Josie enough that they could discuss the terrible news. When they understood all that had happened that morning, they became somber.

"That cipher must be very important," said Josie. "It might tell us who wanted to, to murder him." She forced herself to say the word.

"Can you decipher it?" asked William. "Arensdorf obviously thought you could."

Foxy looked at the rows of letters again. "Not without a keyword," she said. "He would have sent that separately. "

William said, "I am a complete ass! Mrs. Flowerdew told me flowers came for you this morning." He hurried to the kitchen and brought out a lovely bouquet in a vase.

Foxy took the little card out of its envelope. "It is from Arensdorf," she said. "'To Lusi Tania. I know you will understand.' It is signed 'A.'" She looked at William. "Could you ask Wilkinson to step in for a moment?"

Foxy had been raised to be a Victorian lady. At least, every effort had been made in that direction. She knew that she was supposed to learn not only how to arrange flowers—which she obviously had not—but the "language of flowers" as well, the subtle messages that could be sent as a gift, or worn in the hair, or pinned to a gown, or displayed as an arrangement on a dinner table. Foxy preferred considering how a spider's web could hold so many drops of dew without breaking, how to ride a horse blindfolded, and how to shoot clay pigeons. She knew there was a "language of flowers," but she did not have the key to understanding it. If anyone would, it would be Wilkinson.

"Ah, Wilkinson, how are you this afternoon?" She asked as he came into the sitting room with William. "I wonder if you would look at the plants in this bouquet. You would do us a great favor if you could tell us what these mean."

Wilkinson, who had been busy removing the tufts of Murky's hair from the aspidistra, set aside his irritation, "Yes, of course, Madame." He took the head of one of the flowers gently in his rough hands. "This one is a white Camellia. It means 'my destiny is in your hands.' And this one he said, pointing to a cluster of white flowers, is the Mock Orange, which means 'deceit.'" He took delicate, pale pink blooms on a stock between two of his fingers. "This is the tuberose," he said. "It comes from Mexico. The Admiral has some specimens. It means 'danger, or dangerous.' Now, this one means something different from that," he said, pointing to a pink flowerhead. "It is the pink Zinnia, and it means, 'lasting affection.' Let me not forget the fern. It might be ignored, beautiful though it is, because it has no blossom. It is Maidenhair, and it means 'discretion.'"

To his surprise and gratification, his audience applauded. "That was marvelous," said Foxy. "It was just what was needed."

"Thank you. Madame," said Wilkinson, "And Lord Ainsworth. I hope I have been of some assistance. And now, if you will excuse me, Sister Parker and I are meeting in the Conservatory. What she doesn't know about the medicinal qualities of plants, well, it doesn't bear considering."

"What you two have come up with has been very helpful to me," said Dinny.

"I am pleased to hear it, and will tell Sister Parker as well," said Wilkinson, taking his leave.

"That seems clear," said Foxy. "Arensdorf has a secret he wants me to keep, he wants me to use discretion once I decode the message, he warns me of danger, and he wants me to know he is sincere."

"I suppose there is little doubt he was a spy for one side or another," commented William. "And his assignment required him to be in the ARO."

"I agree. It sheds some light on Gruter's disappearance," she said. "I don't want to jump to any conclusions, however. First, we need to decipher the message he sent me." She studied the rows of numbers. "This is a Polybius Square," she said, thinking out loud. "The Germans used it during the war." She smiled and thought, *This is a hatted code. Arensdorf saw my pin and understood. It is the ADFGX cipher.* She remembered the day she had noted the "V" that was added to it. It was an important find as it turned out the Germans changed the cipher to ADVGVX." She looked up, "Addie, have you learned this?"

"Of course. I haven't practiced it very much. though" said Addie.

"Good," said Foxy, "that will make it easier. Addie and I will need to work on this on our own. Otherwise, we would be violating the DORA oath. Not that I don't trust all of you, but we are treading on dangerous territory, and if this came to light, I wouldn't want to have to face a charge for treason."

"Of course," said William. "Understood. Josie, join us for dinner, will you? And I'll have Mrs. Flowerdew send something to both of you. Will that be all right?"

"Splendid," said Foxy. "By the time you are ready for coffee and brandy, I think Addie and I will be able to tell you what the message is. Is it all right if we use the Admiral's study?"

Addie and Foxy settled themselves at the big desk, facing each other. Foxy unrolled one of the large Admiralty charts and placed it face down.

Foxy said, "We'll use this to work out the message. This is a hatted code, so we have to unlock what letters the numbers refer to, and then what message the letters conceal."

Addie nodded. She drew a grid with five rows across and five rows down. She added one horizontal row and one vertical column, each numbered one to five. She wrote the word "Lusitania," beginning at the top row, omitting the second "I" and "A." Then, she filled in the remaining spaces in the grid with the rest of the letters in the alphabet in order.

"Right," said Foxy. "I'll read the pairs of numbers, and you write down the letters. The first paired numbers in Arensdorf's message are five and two."

"That is a 'W,'" said Addie, consulting the second letter in the fifth row.

There was a gentle tap on the door. Foxy opened it and saw William holding a tray. She smiled, thanked him, took the tray, and closed the door. "Watercress and butter, and cheese and pickle sandwiches," she said. "And coffee and biscuits. Very nice."

Nibbling the sandwiches, they bent their heads over their work.

They emerged looking solemn and joined the others around the fire. Addie sat next to Dinny and held his hand.

Foxy read from the paper she held, "Walls have ears. I am watched. Lusitania file taped under Gs desk. CC handed G the file. G is White Russian. Zinoviev is fake."

Dinny gave a soft whistle.

William said, "Arensdorf was obviously a spy who knew his cover was compromised. He wanted you to know that the missing *Lusitania* files and whatever is meant by the fake Zinoviev memo are somehow connected. Gruter is a spy for the White Russians, which means Arensdorf was probably working for the Soviets."

"It also makes it more likely that Gruter killed Arensdorf, does it not?" said Foxy. "Or at the very least, that he was complicit in some way."

"Which raises the question of why Arensdorf went to the ARO today. He knew Gruter was a spy for the Russian anti-communists—and some of them are Loyalists to the Czar."

"He seems to have thought he was in some danger," said Addie, "judging from the flowers. What was the flower…?"

"The tuberose," said Josie. "Perhaps he knew he was in danger, but something in the ARO was so important he felt he had to go back."

"Or," said Dinny, "he was warning *us* of danger."

"I wonder if the *Lusitania* file is still taped under Gruter's desk," said Foxy.

"Unlikely," said William. "Gruter probably took it with him when he disappeared."

"Do we agree that CC is Chauncey Caxton?" asked Addie.

"Certainly," said Foxy, "or else Arensdorf would have spelled out the name."

"Chauncey could have slipped into my office and taken the file when I bolted out the door after I got the message from Addie that the decrypts were missing," said Dinny.

"That would mean he knew Dinny would be called away suddenly," said Addie.

"Which means," said William, thoughtfully, "that what happened the day Dinny's files went missing was planned. Everything was staged."

"My request set off a chain of events earlier than the day they happened. Is that what you mean?" asked Dinny. He thought for a moment. "That is entirely possible. I sent the request for the files late in the afternoon, assuming they would come the next morning. Then, I notified Gruter that I would ask Addie to take a look at the decrypts."

"And I left a request for them. That would mean Gruter took the decrypts and hid them in Room 229 before he left the night before," said Addie

"We still need to find out who is behind this. If Gruter murdered Arensdorf, why? And how is it linked to the missing *Lusitania* file and this Zinoviev memo, whatever that is?" said William.

"And why, once the *Lusitania* file and decrypts were well out of reach, and Dinny and Addie suspended, did someone sabotage Dinny's car?" added Foxy.

"Yes," said William, "that is curious. It was unnecessary, since neither Addie nor Dinny had any opportunity to see what was in the files or decrypts.

It was dark. The rain pattered on the windows. The fire burned brightly.

Josie felt drained and wanted to go home. "I will try to find out about the florist, if that will help, and also who might have taken the Teague diary." She asked William to book a cab.

"Are you sure you don't want to stay?" asked Addie. "We could bunk together."

"Yes," agreed William, "it would be no imposition."

"You are so kind. But honestly, I need to be alone." She and Addie hugged and agreed to meet the next day.

"Do be careful," said Foxy.

William held an umbrella for Josie and walked her to the waiting cab.

"Good night," he said. "Get some rest. You have had quite a shock." She thanked him, and William watched as the cab drew away into the rain and gloom.

Foxy felt depleted. "I find it difficult to think clearly. I keep seeing Arensdorf lying in a pool of blood. Still, we must crack on. What shall we do tomorrow?"

William said, "We need to find out what the Zinoviev letter is. I'll try to arrange to meet Clive for lunch."

"I have an idea about how Gruter got out of the building," said Foxy. "I will investigate that and see if by any chance the file is still taped under his desk."

Addie paused. "If I am not needed, I should check in at the GCCS," she said.

"And I'll be left here with nothing at all to do," said Dinny morosely.

William cleared his throat, "If I might make a suggestion, you could spend some time tomorrow finding out exactly what it is that Wilkinson and Sister Parker are concocting for you."

Dinny smiled a cheerful grin. "Good idea. No telling how much eye of newt and toe of frog Torquemada is setting to boil and bubble."

Chapter Twenty-Six

Do You Have Any Books?

Kathleen interrupted breakfast the next morning with a letter for William. "I know you usually read your morning mail in your study, Sir," she said, "but you told me to bring you anything from Thornberry as soon as it arrived."

"Thank you, Kathleen," he replied. "You did the right thing. It is from Henry," he said to Foxy, Dinny, and Addie. They looked at him like eager dogs waiting for someone to toss a ball for them chase.

Inside the envelope, he found the clipping of an advertisement in the Invergordon *North Star and Farmer's Chronicle.* Henry included a brief, handwritten message. "Do you have any books you would like to donate?"

"That didn't take Tris long," said William, handing the clipping to Foxy.

Foxy retrieved the key she had made from *The Inimitable Jeeves* and returned to the breakfast table with paper and pencil. Dinny, Addie, and William watched intently as Foxy worked out the message hidden in the first letter of each word in the ad:

Do you ever wonder what to do with books you no longer need? A solution is at hand. Knitwear is always appreciated, but the Invergordon Naval Base also needs books for our library. Make sure your books are in good condition, please. Most titles will be gratefully accepted. Donate by postal service, care of the

Library, Invergordon Naval Base, Invergordon. Donations will be accepted at the main gate during daylight hours. Packages left at the gate before or after hours should be well wrapped in waterproof material or placed in a well-sealed wooden box.

Her eyes flashed angrily as she held up the paper she used to write the name revealed in the ad: McCreedy.

There was a moment of shocked silence.

"Why would McCreedy send Tris off to Invergordon on a fake secret mission?" asked Dinny, angrily. "He can damn well order him back to London! I wish I weren't stuck in this wheelchair!" Dinny banged the arms of the chair with his fists in frustration. Then, he winced at the pain in his ribs. Addie reached out to comfort him.

William clamped his lighted pipe between his teeth. He looked at Foxy, who looked back.

"I think we better both see him this morning," said William, quietly.

"I couldn't agree more," said Foxy. "Just let me go and change into an outfit that will truly offend his sensibilities."

William, wearing his Naval Reserve Uniform, and Foxy, wearing one of her Chanel jersey knit pants and tops along with her "hat" pin, brushed past Able Seaman Rigley and entered McCreedy's office without knocking.

"What is the meaning of this!" shouted McCreedy, nearly choking on his tea.

"Sit down, McCreedy," said William evenly, "and tell us all about Lt. Dashwood."

"Who? I don't know what you are talking about! How dare you come into—"

"SIT DOWN," said Foxy, cutting sharply into his rant. "We need to talk to you." McCreedy looked from one face to the other. He saw the set of jaws, the glint in the eyes. He sat down. Foxy closed the door. She took a chair next to William.

William began filling his pipe. "Perhaps you would care to tell us why and how you seconded Lt. Tristan Dashwood to Invergordon on a false secret mission." William lit his pipe.

A flash of recognition crossed McCreedy's face. "Oh, that, yes. You know Dashwood, do you?" he said resignedly.

"Yes, as a matter of fact, we do," said Foxy, levelly. "He is a very close friend of my nephew. Remember him? The one you wanted to court-martial?"

"Dashwood's related to Churchill, as a matter of fact," said William, dryly.

McCreedy stared at him stonily for a moment. "Yes, well, as a matter of fact, that is why Dashwood is in Invergordon."

"Because he is related to Churchill?" said Foxy, not sure she understood.

McCreedy sighed. He looked at William. "You aren't the only one who knows about Jutland," he said in a lowered voice. Blinker Hall does too.

William and Foxy exchanged glances.

McCreedy continued. "He came to me not long ago and said he wanted me to order Dashwood to Invergordon on some trumped-up mission. He threatened to leak my role in the Jutland business to the Press. He told me Dashwood was related to Churchill, and he wanted Dashwood 'out of the way' until Christmas."

"Did he say why?" asked Foxy.

"No, he did not," said McCreedy, crisply, still smarting from his meeting with Blinker. "I assumed it had something to do with Blinker being an old pal of Churchill's. Probably something to do with getting Churchill elected. He told me to get on the horn to Dashwood's commanding officer, requesting that Dashwood be temporarily assigned to me for a top-secret project."

"Were those his exact words—that Churchill wanted Dashwood 'out of the way'?" asked William.

McCreedy smiled wryly. "You know Blinker. He would never be so direct. He did not say that the request came directly from Churchill. He might have meant that, or he might have meant that he, Blinker, thought it best to get Dashwood off to Invergordon for reasons that would suit Churchill's interests. He left it just that vague." He paused. "How on earth did you find this out?" he asked, testily.

Foxy replied with pointed asperity, "I couldn't possibly say."

William puffed on his pipe. "Listen here, my dear chap," he said as blue smoke rose, "you seem to have been drawn into something that you don't understand, and unless I miss my guess, you are well aware you might be left holding the bag if any of this becomes known. I don't imagine Dashwood's CO was too pleased that you pulled him away from his assignment to send him off to the back of beyond."

"That is one way to say it. He went up like a volcano," said McCreedy. "I had to tell him the assignment was vital to the defense of the nation and that I couldn't tell him any more than that."

"I am sure you understand the implications," said William, still calm.

"Well, of course, I do!" shouted McCreedy. He lowered his voice. "I am not stupid, man! If it becomes known that I used my rank to protect a political figure, I may be cashiered. It won't matter that I had no idea how it might benefit Churchill. What will matter is that I did it at the behest of a Retired Admiral who is a former Conservative MP. And if I have to tell why I did what he said, the whole Jutland matter will be unearthed. That is what you are trying to tell me, isn't it?" He had gone quite pale.

"Why not join forces, then?" asked William coolly.

"What do you mean?" said McCreedy, impatiently. How on earth can you help?"

"This all started when the *Lusitania* files went missing," said Foxy. "MI5 questioned Dashwood about what Dinny may have told him. Then, Dashwood is packed off to Invergordon so he cannot tell anyone about the interrogation. And, there may well be a link between Arensdorf's death, the theft of the *Lusitania* files, and Gruter's sudden disappearance."

A stillness filled the room. McCreedy stared at Foxy as if she were mad. "What in God's name are you babbling about?" he asked peevishly.

"You had better take her seriously," said William sternly. "You are tangled in a web of theft of government documents and decrypts, attempted murder or intent to harm, abuse of the authority of your rank for political purposes, murder, and a missing Admiralty employee, who may well have murdered Arensdorf.

All the mettle went out of McCreedy. He seemed deflated like a forgotten balloon a week after the birthday party. "You are right about Arensdorf. He was murdered. I read the Coroner's report this morning." He paused. "What do you suggest?" He asked.

"Let's start at the beginning. What do you know about the theft of the *Lusitania* files and the decrypts?" began Foxy.

"I thought I made that perfectly clear," snapped McCreedy, his temper threatening to erupt. He regained control of himself. "I knew nothing about it. I thought Lt. Custus had been incredibly careless, and I suspected a conspiracy involving him and Miss Gold. I now know I was wrong in that."

"What about Gruter? What do you know about him?" asked William.

"Only that Blinker told me he had given valuable service as a spy during the war after the Bolshevik Revolution in '17, and that he needed a job," said McCreedy. "He was anti-Bolshevik, apparently. Hall was the one who got Gruter the job. I had very little to do with him."

"What was in the Coroner's report?" asked Foxy. "How was Arensdorf killed?"

McCreedy opened a drawer in his massive desk and handed her a file folder. "As you can see, he was struck with a blunt instrument just behind his left ear. His neck was broken after he was struck, very efficiently. That's what killed him." McCreedy was sober and direct.

Foxy grimaced. "Brutally murdered." She read the report and handed it to William. "The weapon has not been found, I take it."

McCreedy shook his head. "The Master-at-Arms ordered the building searched, but found nothing."

"Has Scotland Yard been called in?" asked William, although he anticipated the answer.

"No," said McCreedy. "MI5 contacted the Master-at-Arms. They will conduct the inquiry."

And that means it will be covered up, thought William. He asked, "The best witness is Caxton. How is he?"

"He is still at Queen Alexandra. He was sedated yesterday, but the report I had this morning is that he is awake, angry, and unwilling to tell anyone what happened," said McCreedy with a sour tone.

"What do you know about him?" asked Foxy. "His story about his father wanting him to get some experience as an ordinary seaman is wafer-thin."

"That's down to Blinker, again," said McCreedy, the resentment returning to his voice. "Caxton is the nephew of Vice-Admiral John Armstrong."

William's eyes registered his surprise. "Spanky Armstrong. Isn't he Vice-President of the British Fascisti?"

McCreedy nodded. His face showed his disgust. "I can think of nothing that violates Naval decorum more than for a serving officer to openly associate himself with any politics, never mind the Fascists in Italy. It seemed very odd to me at the time, but Blinker had me over a barrel, so I had orders cut for Caxton to be assigned here as a Messenger. I can't say I will miss him. He was an arrogant little bastard and had a mean streak in him."

"Said the Pot about the Kettle," thought Foxy, keeping her face impassive.

Aloud, she said, "We found that out when Miss Gold interviewed him. He is virulently anti-Semitic. Did you know he recently accidentally-on-purpose shoved Arensdorf hard enough that he dropped the papers he was carrying?"

McCreedy looked surprised and irritated. "When was this? I never heard anything about it?"

"The late afternoon of the day Dinny—Lt. Custus—requested the *Lusitania* files. Caxton brought the requisition to the ARO. Arensdorf was coming out the door as Caxton was going in. Arensdorf decided not to mention it," replied Foxy.

"I wish he had told me. I would have put the little weasel on report," said McCreedy, sharply. "The anti-Semitism comes from his father. Blinker told me Caxton's father was a member of the BBL before the war."

William's face registered recognition. "I thought I recognized the name. He was indeed active in the British Brothers' League, stirring up workers to bring pressure for the passage of restrictions on immigrants. Virulently anti-Semitic. They succeeded in getting passage of the 1905 Alien Act restricting the numbers of Eastern European Jews."

"When did Blinker ask you to assign Caxton as a Messenger?" Foxy asked.

McCreedy thought for a moment. "It was several days before Lt. Custus requested the *Lusitania* files. You think there is a connection?"

"I can't see Blinker mixed up with that Fascisti crowd," mused William. "His politics are traditional Conservative and rock-hard anti-communist." He paused for a moment. "Ask the Porter to give you the names of anyone signing in to go to the ARO from the time just before the *Lusitania* files went missing until yesterday."

"Why? Is it important?" said McCreedy, who felt he had lost the thread.

Foxy explained, "Arensdorf overheard two men talking to Gruter. Their voices were raised at one point. Then, Gruter noticed Caxton lurking about. Gruter was angry at him, but someone spoke in a conciliatory tone. Arensdorf said he heard them say the name Zinoviev. Does that mean anything to you?"

"Only that he is the head of the Soviet Comintern and wants to destroy our country and way of life," said McCreedy archly. "I can understand Gruter taking an interest in the Soviets, but who was with him?"

"Exactly," said Foxy.

McCreedy gave the order to his secretary. Not long after, an assistant to the Porter arrived with the sign-in registry. Foxy and William looked over McCreedy's shoulders as he turned the pages to the previous weeks. "There they are. It must be," said Foxy, pointing to two names. "Admiral Hall and Major Joseph Ball to see Mr. Jan Gruter, ARO."

There was a dead silence for some moments.

"Obviously," said McCreedy with his usual arrogance and gift for stating the obvious, "Blinker must have been the one to protect Caxton when Gruter spotted him eavesdropping."

"Agreed," said William. "But why was the head of MI5's counter-espionage division with Blinker and why were they discussing Zinoviev with Gruter?"

McCreedy closed the Registry with a distinct thud. "I have done all I can to assist you in this matter," he said with his usual note of asperity. "And we agree that nothing about my role in this goes any further than this room?"

"You can count on us," said William. *Since neither of us is a snitch, unlike you, Fishy,* he thought. Aloud, he said, "And we are counting on you to keep mum, too."

"Yes, of course," said McCreedy. "You have my word."

Foxy thought, *Your word and one shilling six pence will buy a pound of tea.*

William and Foxy stood outside the entrance to Old Admiralty. Rain poured down. William opened his umbrella and walked Foxy to his car.

Where to?" he asked as he opened the passenger door for Foxy.

"I was going to snoop around the ARO, but I think I will go see Caxton instead. Perhaps he will open up to me. After all, we both suffered the same shock—seeing Arensdorf dead, I mean."

"But Addie and you as much as accused him of killing Arensdorf. He might remember that and have some resentment about it," said William dryly.

"There is that," said Foxy. "I will try my Kindly Grannie wiles on him. You always told me that the best way to get a spy to talk was by becoming friends. It is worth a try."

As he put the car in reverse, William laughed. "I wish I could be a fly on the wall to witness your Kindly Grannie act."

"Don't be such a skeptic," she said, laughing along with him. "You are off to meet Clive for lunch, aren't you?"

"He has pulled strings and reserved us a table at the Indian Pavilion at the Empire Exposition. I am looking forward to it."

"Drop me off, and I'll make myself a sandwich and change into a Kindly Grannie dress. I can take a cab to Queen Alexandra," said Foxy.

Chapter Twenty-Seven

Mrs. Flowerdew's Orders and Complaints Day

"You startled me," said Kathleen, who was dusting the balusters when Foxy entered the house. "We didn't expect you back for lunch."

Foxy hung her emerald green gaberdine rubberless raincoat on the hallway tree, along with her waterproof burgundy rain hat, which was shaped like a bell and shielded her face. "Change of plans," she said, pleasantly. "Let Maisy know I'll make myself a sandwich. I don't want to trouble her. I know it is Mrs. Flowerdew's Orders and Complaints Day."

Every Wednesday morning, Mrs. Flowerdew went to the shops to place food orders for the week and register any complaints she had about the previous week's deliveries. Her rounds completed, she would treat herself to a light lunch at a tea shop. It was up to Maisy to serve the family their lunch.

Foxy changed into her Business in the City dress she wore when she saw McCreedy for the first time. She went downstairs and telephoned to book a cab. She entered the kitchen and discovered to her delight that Maisy had set out a plate of thick-sliced buttered bread, wedges of cheddar and Lancashire cheeses, a slice of smoked ham, mustard, sliced apple, and a pickle.

"There was no need to interrupt your schedule," said Foxy, aware of the long list of cleaning and prep Maisy did every day. "I could have made myself a bite. This does look delicious, I must say."

"It was no problem at all, M'Lady," said Daisy, setting a fresh pot of tea on a trivet. I am pleased it suits you. I'll leave you to it, then."

She went into the large pantry to arrange the dry goods, putting them to the front of the shelves so the new orders could be put behind them in neat rows when they arrived. Foxy finished her lunch. As she stood to place the dishes in the sink, her eyes fell on half-a-dozen freshly baked Chelsea buns on the counter. *Perfect. Kindly Grannie would naturally bring along some baked goods.* She located Mrs. Flowerdew's stash of baskets for all occasions in the utility closet, lined one with a colorful tea towel, put all the buns into it, folded the corners of the tea towel over it, and called to Maisy.

"Tell Mrs. Flowerdew I am sorry to be taking the Chelsea buns. It is for an emergency. I will bring her some from the bakery when I come back," said Foxy.

She was already through the kitchen door when Maisy called from the pantry. "But M'Lady, they're not Mrs. Flowerdew's buns. They were made by Sister Parker." She emerged into an empty kitchen and heard Foxy closing the front door behind her. She looked through the glass panel to the side of the door just as the cab drove off.

Dinny spent a highly instructive morning with Sister Parker and the gardener, Wilkinson, in what was called the Potting Shed. It looked like a guest house, built in the Edwardian style to match the main house. Attached to it was a glass greenhouse, used for growing plants from cuttings and seeds taken from plants in the Conservatory. Dinny wanted to know what ointment or salve Sister Parker was using to ease the pain of his broken ribs. She had readily agreed with him when he said he did not want to rely on morphine and risk addiction.

He sat in the wheelchair as Wilkinson pushed it into the long greenhouse. "These are what Sister Parker and I are using to make your salve," he said, pointing to a small forest of dark-green plants with green, serrated, palmate leaves. They are from an original specimen Admiral Ainsworth brought from India."

"It is called *Cannabis indica* but is much the same as *Cannabis sativa,* which grows naturally in Britain," said Sister Parker. "We have been distilling them.

Their medicinal properties have been recognized for centuries, but their use in Great Britain was introduced by Sir William O'Shaughnessy Brooke, who was a Professor at the medical college in Calcutta in the last century. I have been reading his work. He researched local plants for their medicinal value and brought *Cannabis indica* to Great Britain. His publications led to investigations into the medicinal uses of cannabis throughout Europe, and the popular medications available at any pharmacy were first developed by him."

Wilkinson wheeled Dinny into the Potting Shed. He took in the tied bunches of the different varieties of cannabis hanging from the hooks on the wall to dry, a large, marble pestle and mortar, and jars of oil.

"I am impressed," he said. "I see you have set up a still."

"I built it." Wilkinson beamed as he pointed out the features of the glass beakers and rods.

Parker, who obviously admired Wilkinson's ingenuity, continued the explanation. "I mix the distilled cannabis oil with mineral oil and melted beeswax to give it the consistency of a salve."

"It certainly has helped with the pain," said Dinny, "sometimes more than at other times."

"That's why we are experimenting with different varieties," said Wilkinson. "We keep track of how well each batch eases your pain. We are learning as we go along."

"The ice packs and aspirin also help," said Parker.

"I must admit I am awestruck," said Dinny. "Where did you learn so much? And where did you get the equipment?"

Sister Parker spoke in the same short, clipped sentences she used to instruct patients, but with none of the usual authoritarian tone of voice. "My father was a chemist. He ran his own pharmacy. My mother is a chemist, too. She is interested primarily in herbal remedies. I qualified as a nurse and learned a great deal about the treatments for wounds and for pain during the war. I was assigned to Queen Alexandra's. I came to the same conclusion as you. Morphine is a wonder drug when it comes to alleviating pain, but it is also addictive. I began researching alternatives and was quite ready to put my ideas to use when I came here," she said.

"Isn't she a wonder?" said Wilkinson, his voice betraying his admiration. "We have been working together since the day she arrived. I have been growing varieties of cannabis for a considerable time to keep the Admiral's Conservatory stocked, but never knew anything about possible medicinal uses."

"The results are commendable," said Dinny. "I wonder why cannabis oil works—what are its properties?"

"I am not sure. O'Shaughnessy found it alleviated seizures when ingested. That suggests it interferes at some level with the nervous system. He also found it has intoxicating properties. I thought if I could isolate the chemicals that cause intoxication, I might have a better understanding of why the topical oil works to alleviate pain."

"We have been working on that for the past several days," said Wilkinson, "and are at the final stage of our experiment." He sounded very eager.

"How do you mean?" said Dinny, surprised. "It sounds as if you have been experimenting with hash or hashish."

"That's just it," said Wilkinson. "We made an extract of just the buds of *Indica* by simmering them in *ghee*."

"It's clarified butter," said Parker. "It is an adaptation of a recipe O'Shaughnessy includes in his book.

Wilkinson grinned happily. "And this morning, Sister Parker used the butter in her recipe for Chelsea buns."

Dinny gaped. "You are going to try them on yourselves?" He was intrigued and alarmed.

Parker grinned. "I started the yeast dough this morning because I knew Mrs. Flowerdew would be out. She has absolutely banned me from her kitchen since the first time I put a pot on her stove, and she got a whiff of the cannabis I was trying to extract. That was before we set up the still."

"But why Chelsea buns?" Dinny was especially fond of the buttery, sweet, rolled buns laced with spices and raisins and topped with a sugar glaze.

"To mask any disagreeable or strong taste from the cannabis butter," said Parker. "I baked them about an hour ago. I put on the glaze and left them to cool." She glanced playfully at Wilkinson. "They should be ready to try."

Wilkinson closed and locked the Potting Shed. Parker permitted Dinny to walk slowly down the path to the house while she wheeled his chair behind him.

"Are they safe? What about the dosage?" asked Dinny.

"We are going to take it slowly," said Parker. "I recommend cutting each bun into quarters, eating one quarter, and waiting to experience the effect. It takes anywhere from thirty minutes to an hour, according to my research. Then we can judge how much more to eat—if at all—from those effects. It should induce a state of euphoria."

Maisy came into the kitchen to find them staring blankly at the empty plate. "I am so sorry," she said. "I tried to stop her, Lady Butterschloss, I mean. She said it was some kind of emergency and took them all with her." Maisy was agitated, fearing she would be blamed for the purloining of the Chelsea buns.

Dinny looked at her sympathetically. "Never mind, Maisy. I am sure you tried your best to explain they were Sister Parker's. Auntie Em doesn't always listen when she has an idea in her head."

"Thank you, Sir," said Maisy, becoming calmer. She looked at Parker, hoping to mollify her. "Lady Butterschloss did say she would stop at a bake shop and buy some Chelsea buns to replace the ones she took."

"I don't blame you," said Sister Parker. "Lady Butterschloss was not to know..." her voice trailed off. "Do you know where she went?"

Maisy shook her head. "She wasn't expected for lunch. I was in the pantry when she called out that she was taking them buns. I called after her, but she was out the door and in the cab before I could explain." Maisy returned to sorting in the pantry.

Sister Parker sighed, "I just hope no one eats more than one and no one has a severe reaction. I don't know what the effects will be." She looked anxiously at Dinny.

"How many were there?" asked Dinny.

"Six," said Parker. "I made a short batch." She looked haggard, nothing like her usual crisp, commanding, confident self.

"You cannot blame yourself," said Dinny. "It was a perfectly reasonable—"

"What's going on in here?" demanded Mrs. Flowerdew archly from the kitchen door, back from her Complaints and Orders Day, and none too pleased to find intruders in her domain. "Sorry, Sir," she said to Dinny, "I didn't see you at first."

"Everything is fine, Mrs. Flowerdew," said Dinny. "We were just leaving. We haven't touched anything." They retreated to the conservatory.

Sister Parker slumped into a chair. "I wish a hole would open up and swallow me," she said.

His former resentment of Sister Parker's brusque efficiency was gone. Dinny wanted only to reassure her. "I will square everything with Lord Ainsworth and Lady Butterschloss," he said, gently. "They will be understanding, I am sure, and no word of this will reach your employer."

She smiled at him wanly. "Thank you. The worst of it is that I acted so irresponsibly. I should never have left those laced buns in the kitchen to cool."

"There now," said Wilkinson in a soothing voice. "You were not to know they would be snatched away. What's done is done. Come with me now, and I'll fix you a bowl of my soup. We can sit by the fire and have some tea, too." Wilkinson did not live on the grounds, but he had a sitting room, with all the amenities, in the Potting Shed. He led Parker gently through the French doors of the Conservatory and across the lawn.

Chapter Twenty-Eight

Chelsea Buns

Under the portico of the imposing red Edwardian brick Queen Alexandra Military Hospital, Foxy shook out her umbrella before closing it. She steeled herself as she entered. The odor of carbolic stirred memories of field hospitals and, later, of visiting friends who were injured in the war. The corridors echoed with the whispers, cries, and groans of ghosts—the wounded and maimed, the blind, those with gangrene, trench fever, head injuries—an unending list of pain, injury, dying. But now, she was coming to see a young man who had never seen war, who was seemingly little more than an upper-class, arrogant bully, who had been shocked out of his wits by the sight of a dead man.

She remembered the enthusiasm of young men who rushed to join up after war was declared. Entire sports teams, entire classes from university, groups of young men who had grown up together in villages and towns. *They were off for the Great Adventure, their heads filled with the propaganda of knights in shining armor rescuing the damsel Europe raped by Germany, of returning as heroes. War was an intoxicant. Then, they were stupefied out of their pain from the horrible wounds of war by heroin, that opium compound named after the German 'heroisch'—strong, heroic. It was not supposed to be addictive. But it was. Highly addictive. War itself was a kind of heroin—powerful and addictive—to millions of young men and the politicians who led them into war.*

Is imagining himself a hero what lay behind Caxton's swaggering, bullying arrogance? Caxton had been too young to go to war but had been raised to be xenophobic and anti-Semitic by his anti-immigration father. His uncle was intent on making Italian Fascism a political force in the UK. His mentality had been shaped by fear and hatred and fueled with notions of a great cause—to defeat communism in all its forms, which included Jews, socialism, and the labor movement.

Blinker Hall, that sly fox, put Caxton in Admiralty for a reason. To spy? Probably. Hall wanted to make sure nothing about the Lusitania would come to light if it would damage Churchill's chances in the next election. What notions of being a heroic spy for the great Conservative cause had Hall put into Caxton's head? And what, if anything, did it have to do with Arensdorf, and something called the Zinoviev letter?

Caxton was in one of the few private rooms. A nurse knocked on his door and told him he had a visitor. Without waiting for his reply, Foxy swept into the room. Caxton, wearing hospital pajamas and a dressing gown, was staring out his window. He turned to see who had come to visit.

"Oh, it's you," he said, his rudeness fully restored.

"Good afternoon, Caxton," she said. "Good to see you are up and about. Nurse, might I trouble you for some tea if any is available?"

Foxy took off her coat and hat and hung them on a hook on the wall. She settled herself in one of two chairs, her basket on her lap.

"I came to see if you had recovered from the terrible shock you—well, we—had yesterday," she said, her voice filled with what she hoped was grandmotherly sympathy.

"You as much as accused me of having something to do with Arensdorf's death," he said bitterly with a sneer.

"I must apologize for that. I was shocked, of course. I must have been out of my mind a bit," she said, introducing a quaver into her voice. "Oh, how nice. Here is the tea. Thank you, nurse. Shall I pour? I brought along some freshly baked Chelsea buns. I thought you might like them. The food in hospital can be so dreary."

Caxton took the tea and bit greedily into the bun. He didn't bother to say thank you. "Yes, the food is bloody awful. I hope I can get out of here today.

The doc is supposed to check me over later."

Foxy took a bite of her bun. It was light and sweet with undertones of spice and orange, and something else she couldn't place. "It is terrible, I know, being in hospital. Have you had many visitors?"

"Yes, as a matter of fact, I have. I told them how rotten I've been treated, too. It might interest you to know that my uncle is Vice Admiral Armstrong. He visited me. So did Admiral Hall," he said, haughtily.

"Ahh," she said. "I used to work for Admiral Hall. Is he a particular friend of your uncle?"

"You worked for him?" said Caxton, surprised, his mouth stuffed with Chelsea bun.

"During the war," said Foxy off-handedly. "I was just a secretary. But everyone had to do their bit. I rarely even saw Hall, but we all respected him so very much." She adopted a deferential tone.

"He is an old friend of the family. I told him how I was questioned by the Master-at-Arms and then dragged here and sedated," he said with a smirk. "Someone's going to be in deep trouble."

Caxton either did not recall that he had been babbling incoherently or had chosen to forget it. He continued to be arrogant and petulant. After half an hour, Foxy despaired of getting anything useful out of him. Caxton was biting into a second Chelsea bun when his mood suddenly lightened.

"I know a lot about Reggie Hall you probably don't know," he said slyly. Then, he started to giggle. It was a high sound, piercing and unpleasant.

Foxy doubted Caxton knew more about Hall than she did. "Oh, do tell me," she said, feigning the eagerness for gossip she assumed Caxton would think typical of a silly, old woman. In point of fact, she was starting to feel like a silly old woman and had to suppress a giggle.

"Once, he was outraged at Judge Bray. Bray," said Caxton, with his high giggle. "Good name for a Judge."

Foxy found herself laughing, too, and not just because she was playing a role. She found it genuinely funny.

"Anyhow," said Caxton, regaining control, "Hall was outraged because Bray let off a German spy with a light sentence. Hall was involved in catching him. Bray said that even though he was a spy, he had not succeeded in actually damaging anything of military importance. Hall knew Bray's manor house was in Shere in Guildford. There was a gunpowder factory near there as well. He gave Bray's address as the site of the gunpowder factory to a German double agent, who passed it along to the Zeppelin command. Bray's house was bombed, but he escaped with his life." Caxton was overcome with laughter. "Then, Hall made sure he was seated next to Bray at a dinner. Bray told him the whole story and how frightened he was. Hall said, 'Oh, well, at least it wasn't a target of military importance.'" Caxton doubled over with laughter and had trouble catching his breath.

Foxy had heard this story. Robby had been at the Club one evening when Hall told it to a few trusted friends. He didn't find it funny, and neither did Foxy. The raid over Guildford had not resulted in any casualties, but it damaged homes and terrified the residents. There was nothing amusing about the Zeppelin raids. But Foxy found the story funny now, as if looking at it from an entirely different perspective. She felt cut loose from moral considerations and saw only the creative genius behind the story. She laughed along with Caxton, although part of her brain was wondering why.

Foxy was in sufficient control of her faculties to remember why she had come. "Did Hall help you get assigned to Admiralty as a Messenger?"

Caxton, who had finished his second bun, gave her a giddy smile. "Yes. He wanted me to be a spy," he whispered loudly. He put a finger to his mouth. "Shhh, don't tell anyone. It is hush-hush. I was supposed to find out why someone wanted to know about the Loose-Loose-Loose…"

"*Lusitania?*" prompted Foxy.

"Yes, that's it," said Caxton, with an exaggerated nod. "Hall told me it was a top-secret mission and would help our country keep out the communists." He was still whispering very loudly. "That's what I did." he suddenly became very relaxed and pleased with himself. "I stole the files and gave them to Gruter to hide. That's what Hall told me to do. But then I had another idea. You'll like this, 'cause it's just like what Hall used to do. I found out who had asked for the files. Then, I found out what kind of car he drove, where he kept it, and when he was going on a trip. I overheard him talking to his girlfriend. Very, very pretty car. I knew where it was kept because he had posted the address on the bulletin board to recommend the mechanic. At night, I broke into the garage and put grease under the lug nuts on one tire." Here, he giggled again with delight at his own genius. "I followed him—them—until the wheel came off. I didn't want to kill him, or them, I mean," he said, looking up with wide eyes and a solemn look on his face. "Nooo, noo. I just wanted him out of the way for a while. To help Hall. I wanted him to be proud of me." He grinned a silly grin.

Foxy felt suddenly morose. All the giddiness drained from her. She knew she needed to continue to play the part of a sympathetic listener. "Weren't you afraid of being court martialed?" she asked as if she cared about his well-being.

"No," Caxton replied, entirely relaxed and suffused with well-being. "I can't be. I am not really in the Navy. Uncle Armstrong fixed it up. My papers are all fake." He ended with his annoying high-pitched giggle.

"But, my dear," said Foxy, "you might have been arrested."

Caxton was again relaxed and close to a state of lassitude. "No need to worry about that. My dad, uncle, and Hall have connections with Scotland Yard and the newspapers. They hush things up all the time."

"You were very upset yesterday when Arensdorf was lying dead at the bottom of the stairs," said Foxy, risking a change of subject.

Caxton suddenly became unsmiling, downcast, and glum. "I-I-I just gave him a tiny push. He was on the last step. I was surprised when he fell to his knees. That scared me. I thought for sure I would go on report."

"Then what happened?" prompted Foxy. "He was alive and on his knees. He wasn't dead."

Caxton took a long, shaky breath. "Then, Gruter appeared. He had his heavy, brass marlin spike, the one he kept on his desk as a paperweight. Arensdorf had his back to him. Gruter looked up at me, put his finger to his lips to tell me to keep quiet. Then, he hit Arensdorf on the back of his head, hard, with the round end of the spike. It knocked Arensdorf out, I think. Before Arensdorf fell over, Gruter grabbed him and twisted his head. When he let go, Arensdorf fell to the ground." Caxton's entire body was shaking.

"Then, he said to me, 'Thank you,'" and disappeared.

"Is that why you kept repeating 'Thank you, No, thank you' when you were questioned?" asked Foxy quietly.

Caxton was slumped forward. He was weeping. "I just gave him a little push. I didn't want him to die."

"Why didn't you tell the Master-at-Arms yesterday?" asked Foxy, again quietly.

"I don't know," said Caxton desperately. "I thought maybe they would blame me. Or, or that Gruter was acting for Hall in some way. I knew they were plotting together. I wanted Hall to be proud of m,m, me." Caxton was blubbering.

Foxy had enough sympathy for Caxton to help him from his chair to his bed. She folded the remaining Chelsea buns in the tea-towel, put on her coat and hat, picked up the basket and her purse, remembered to take her umbrella, and left Caxton, attended by a nurse, his body shaking with sobs.

She felt detached from what she had learned and witnessed. In the cab, she rolled down the window. The cold, wet air revived her. She remembered she needed to stop at a bakery to replace the missing Chelsea buns. She tried several times to count how many remained, getting a different sum each time. She settled on three. She had the driver stop and wait while she went into Goodey's Bakery, not far from hospital. She ordered the Chelsea buns and realized she was quite hungry. She took away a dozen shortbread fingers, two Eccles cakes, two scones, and a half-dozen almond crescent cookies covered with icing sugar. In the cab, she munched on the baked goods she had purchased for herself and fell into a happy reverie while noticing how vivid the colors were on the trees, lawns, and flowers passing by the window.

When the cab pulled up in front of the Chelsea house, she awoke from her reverie. She was surprised that there were crumbs and sprinklings of white icing sugar down the front of her emerald-green raincoat. She was equally surprised to find she had eaten everything from Goodey's except for the Chelsea buns. She paid the driver, hefted herself awkwardly from the cab, and brushed off the crumbs which smeared the icing sugar. She marveled at what a bright green her coat was. How had she never noticed that before?

Dinny was in the library reading, anxiously awaiting Foxy's return. He heard the front door open, and then a loud "VIEW HALLOO! VIEW HALLOO!" Dinny rose stiffly and went slowly to the library door. He was taken aback by Foxy's appearance. White powder spackled the front of her raincoat. Her rain hat was askew. She was clumsily trying to hold onto her purse, umbrella, keys, basket, and two small boxes from a bakery. Kathleen, startled by the commotion, hurried into the hall and tried to assist Foxy in getting her coat off. Foxy was unable to realize that she had to let go of what she was holding. After some fruitless gymnastics, Kathleen suggested that she take these items from Foxy, who said Kathleen should be sure to give the basket of Chelsea buns to Mrs. Flowerdew, along with the buns from Goodey's bakery.

Once Katherine managed to relieve Foxy of her coat, hat, and other impediments, Dinny guided her gently down the hall. He deftly took the basket of Chelsea buns from Kathleen and said, "Could you ask Sister Parker and Wilkinson to meet us in the Conservatory? I think you will find them in the Potting Shed."

He led Foxy to the wicker chaise lounge in the conservatory and gently helped her to recline. "How are you feeling?" he asked, lowering himself gingerly into a rattan chair next to her.

"I am feeling fine, just fine, dear boy," she said languidly, passing her palm gently along his cheek. "How are you feeling?"

"Much better now that you are here. I have been worried about you."

"About me? Why?" said Foxy, smiling. "I am fine. Just fine."

"Auntie Em, there's something you need to know—" Dinny said.

He was interrupted when Sister Parker and Wilkinson came through the French doors.

"How is she?" asked Parker, anxiously. She took Foxy's wrist and timed her pulse.

"She seems very happy and relaxed," said Dinny. "Is that a good sign?"

"Yes, it is," said Parker. "How many of the Chelsea buns did she eat?"

"I was just about to tell her about them," said Dinny.

"Let me. It was my fault," said Parker.

Foxy followed this exchange with a benign grin. "Tell me what? That reminds me, I have something to tell you, Dinny. It's about that creep Caxton."

"Lady Butterschloss," began Parker. "Those Chelsea buns you took today…"

"It's all right," said Foxy. "I bought some to replace what we ate. I didn't want Mrs. Flowerdew to fret."

"How many did you have?" said Parker.

"Oh, let me think. One."

"That's where you were? You saw Caxton at Queen Alexandra?" asked Dinny, surprised.

"Yes, that is what I need to tell you…"

Parker counted the Chelsea buns in the basket. "Caxton must have had two," she said. "Is that right?"

"Cor-rect," said Foxy. "You have it." She smiled beatifically.

"Lady Butterschloss," began Parker. "They weren't made by Mrs. Flowerdew. I made them."

"Did you? Did you?" said Foxy, jovially. "Well, I need to ask you. What did you put in them? I tasted the orange and the spices. But there was a taste I couldn't identify. Not that I minded."

"They were laced with cannabis," said Parker. "It was an experiment—"

"Cannabis? Cannabis?" said Foxy, confused. Then her face lit with recognition. "You mean hashish? You put hashish in the Chelsea buns?" She started to laugh. "Why on Earth…?"

Parker blushed bright red. "I thought, maybe, there might be a medicinal benefit, to help Dinny. I meant to eat them, not to give them to anyone. It was irresponsible of me to leave them in the kitchen to cool."

Foxy stared at her for a moment or two. Then she burst into a very hardy laugh. Wiping the tears from her eyes, she said, "You wonderful, clever girl."

"What do you mean?" asked Dinny, hoping Foxy was not permanently demented.

"It's what I have been trying to tell you. Caxton told me everything after he had those Chelsea buns. It must have been the hashish, because I couldn't get anything out of him before he ate them." She looked at Parker. "It was about half an hour before they took effect," she said. "Then, he sang like a canary, as the Americans say." She turned to Dinny. "He put the oil on your lug nuts," she said. "He said he didn't want to kill you, though."

"Thoughtful of him," said Dinny, dryly.

"I will tell you the whole story. But first, I need a cup of tea, I think."

"And then, I recommend sleep," said Parker.

"An excellent idea. I shall sleep here, in the Bower of Bliss," she said, gesturing to the overhanging leaves and jasmine vine. "Honestly, Wilkinson, I don't know how you get such vivid colors."

"Thank you, Madame," he replied. "And may I say I am happy to see you are none the worse for wear. We were very worried the whole time you were gone."

As Dinny headed haltingly for the kitchen, Parker followed him out of the conservatory. "She should recover soon. Certainly, by morning." Then she sighed heavily. "I need to call Queen Alexandra to tell them they have a patient recovering from ingesting cannabis."

"No, you will not," said Dinny, firmly. "That little sod was responsible for these broken ribs. Addie could have been seriously injured or even killed. You are not going to lose your reputation over that piece of slime. Let him sleep it off. He was put in there under observation for shock. They will think he had a relapse."

"But they might give him medication that will be affected by the cannabis in his bloodstream," she said.

"Good," said Dinny. "I hope it gives him nightmares. Now, no more about this, Sister Parker. I won't have it."

Tears filled her eyes. "Thank you" was all she could manage to say. She turned to attend to Foxy while Dinny went to ask Maisy for tea.

Chapter Twenty-Nine

Lunch at the British Empire Exhibition

William drove to the British Empire Exhibition in Wembley. This gave him time to think about what they had learned from their meeting with McCreedy. Blinker Hall and Joe Ball had met with Jan Gruter and were overheard by Arensdorf discussing the Zinoviev letter. William knew Major Joseph Ball only slightly, but nevertheless heartily despised him. Ball had been assigned to the domestic intelligence agency—Parliamentary Military Security Department No.2—during the war. They were concerned primarily with spying on socialists, labor organizers, and conscientious objectors. They also wanted to discredit that branch of the suffrage movement that remained pacifist. *Disgraceful agency. The Wheeldon Case was an absolute outrage."* Alice Wheeldon, her husband, son, and two daughters regularly hid conscientious objectors in their homes. Herbert Booth, who was a top official at PMS2, pretended to be an army deserter. Booth agreed to spirit her son and another CO away to America to avoid conscription if she procured poison Booth would use to kill guard dogs at CO prisons in a plot to free the COs.

When PMS2 raided Wheeldon's home in January 1917, they found the poison and charged Alice, her two daughters, and her son-in-law with intending to murder the Prime Minister by firing a curare-tipped dart at Lloyd George when he was playing golf. *"Ludicrous. If I had been told to use that prosecution, I would have shot myself rather than appear to be such a malicious fool."* When Alice, her daughter Winnie, and her son-in-law Alfred were found guilty of conspiracy to murder, there were immediate protests against the verdict. Alice went on several hunger strikes and was force-fed. By the end of the year, the Prime Minister was informed that Alice's condition was critical. *It gave the PM an excuse to yield to common sense, without political risk.* Alice was released, but her health was broken. She died of influenza in 1919.

The outcry over the Wheeldon trial had been the death knell for PMS2. *Good riddance. I would never have agreed to work for PMS2. But Ball did, and he continued to work for MI5 throughout the war. And now he is working for Blinker Hall, who is trying to protect Churchill. Everything always comes back to Churchill.*

Although he had read a good deal about it, William was unprepared for the immense scale of the temporary city set in two hundred and sixteen acres. The architectural styles of six nations and fifty-two colonies, protectorates, and territories were juxtaposed in a dizzying mélange. Pleasure boats carried visitors along the man-made lake and under arched bridges. At the far end of the waterway, there rose like a dream the stark white exterior of the exotic India exhibition hall. The British architects called it Indo-Saracen, the hybrid style they invented. It struck William as a hyperbolic blend of the Taj Mahal and the set of *Thief of Baghdad.* He passed under the elaborate archway and stopped in his tracks, taking in the stunning courtyard, with its long pool flanked by low, potted palms, leading to an ornate entrance. William made his way through the exhibit halls to the restaurant. He gave his name to the Head Waiter, costumed in turban and long tunic, who led him to Clive's table.

"What do you think of it?" asked Clive. "Around the World in a day for one shilling six pence."

"Except for the Queen's Dollhouse, Palace of Arts, Admiralty Theatre, and the Amusement Park," replied William, dryly. "You have to pay extra for those."

"Well," Clive replied with a wry smile, "you can't have everything."

"Bearer! Bearer!" A man in his fifties, with a flushed face, high forehead, close-set eyes, drooping mustache, and thinning hair—one lock of which stood to attention on the top of his head—shouted to one of the costumed waiters, who hurried over to him.

"Yes, Sahib," he said, bowing slightly. "May I help you?"

"I would like ale," said the officious diner, "and the memsahib would like tea. And don't take all day."

"Of course, Sahib." The waiter bowed again and went to put in the order.

"And that," said William, "is why India wants Dominion Home Rule."

"No wonder the nationalists want rid of the Raj, if that blustering popinjay is any example of how they are treated by us," said Clive.

William said, "They deserve Home Rule. The King promised it if India contributed troops to the war. Over one million served, and they had one hundred and thirty thousand casualties." William felt the glowing coal of anger again. Had the carnage been only to preserve the Empire for horrible little men like the former colonial at the next table?

Their waiter, in a turban, white tunic, sash, and loose trousers, came to the table to hand them menus. He was the same waiter who was serving the man and woman at the next table. Clive said, "I had a word with the Chef when I made the reservations. He is preparing us a special menu."

"Yes, of course, Sahib," said the waiter, "I will see to it directly."

"No need for the 'Sahib," said William. "I wonder how you stand it."

"For the tips," said the waiter, smiling, and dropping his lilting "India" accent. "Such men tip well. It makes them feel superior to flash their money around." He took their orders for ale and left.

"Wouldn't you want to be a fly on the ceiling if that oaf at the next table tried it on with the waiters at Vilner's?" asked Clive, and his face broke into a broad smile.

William laughed. "I would pay a good deal for a ticket." Then, he eyed Clive suspiciously. "What did you mean about a special menu?"

Clive looked back innocently. "It's just that the dishes here are Anglo-Indian, tamed for the British palate. I thought you would enjoy some authentic, regional food. You will find it has quite a different flavor."

William looked around at the tables with their crisp, white tablecloths and gleaming cutlery. "You are right. This is certainly an Anglo-Indian production. The food concessions are controlled by the Lyons company, and not by India."

Clive nodded. "The chefs are Indian, though. The Indian government insisted on that."

William said, "I thought it shameful that Lyon and Company didn't support the Trade Union Council when it asked that the workers be allowed to form a Labor Council to alleviate the working conditions and low salaries when the exhibit was being built."

Clive nodded. "And when workers organize for better conditions, they are tagged communists, and I am assigned to spy on them. A waste of time in most cases."

"I am sorry to hear that. You are too valuable to have your talents wasted," said William, quietly. He was overheated. Then he realized it was not caused by his anger, but by the sticks of fried okra he was nibbling. The waiter had brought them with the ale.

"Good God, what are these?" he said, reaching for the ale, and drinking it in great gulps.

Clive gave him a mischievous grin. "Fried bhindi," he said. "It is okra, coated in a batter with spices and chilies, then deep fried. How do you like it, Crumpet?"

"It's a bit like having a fire in my mouth," said William, emptying his glass.

"It's a taste of the real India," said Clive with an innocent expression.

Their waiter arrived. "This is Vathoo Vindaloo. It is duck prepared with spices and chilies. It is a favorite of the Chef's, but he has not served it here before. He has prepared a special naan bread with coconut to balance the flavor. Please enjoy."

William ordered another ale. "If I may ask, what exactly did my friend here ask the Chef to prepare?"

The waiter missed the 'keep mum' gesture from Clive, who put a finger to his lips. "He said his friend—you, I presume—was especially fond of the spicy and hot chili dishes. This made the Chef very happy because he does not cook those dishes for the British."

William stared at Clive. "It was very thoughtful of my friend," he said blandly. He was determined not to let Clive see any sign of distress when he ate the duck dish, which he assumed would have more heat than the fried bhindi. He was right. But he smiled broadly, nodding his head appreciatively at Clive while blinking back tears, and taking a big bite of the sweet naan bread.

Clive enjoyed the trick he had played, although he also had to disguise his reaction to the burst of heat when he bit into the duck. "What did you want to see me about?" he asked as casually as he could, given the constriction in his throat.

William was grateful for an excuse to put down his fork and stop eating. He took a gulp of the ale. "I want you to tell me if you know anything about the Zinoviev letter," he said.

Clive had a coughing fit, and not because of the chilis. "How on earth do you know about that?"

"I don't know anything about it, as a matter of fact, except that it may be connected to the missing *Lusitania* files and to the murder of Josef Arensdorf," he said. "I take it you can tell me what it is."

"I can, but I don't know how it can be connected with the theft of the *Lusitania* files. I can make a guess how it might be connected to Arensdorf," said Clive.

"What can you tell me about him?"

"During the war, he spied for the Russians. Blinker turned him into a double agent, as he did with any spy he could." William nodded. He was familiar with Hall's tactics and his successes.

"After the war," Clive said, tearing himself a piece of naan bread, "Blinker saw to it Arensdorf was given a position at LSE. But then, Arensdorf upset Hall when he became an advocate for the Soviets. He has been under surveillance by us since the end of the war. We know he has ties to the Reds, but he wasn't in a position to pass along any high-level secrets. He has—I mean had— excellent contacts with academic economists who are advising the Government. This made him useful to the Bolsheviks because Arensdorf explained to them why the Labour government wanted to approve the loan to Moscow. He also informed the Soviets about the exiled White Russians, the Conservative Party, and a number of meddlesome private business groups who oppose the loan. He was a loss to the Foreign Office and the Labour government.

"And this has something to do with the Zinoviev letter?" asked William.

"Yes," said Clive, lowering his voice. "At the beginning of the month, a copy of the so-called Zinoviev letter landed on Morton's desk at MI6. You remember Sir Desmond, of course," said Clive.

"I know him, but didn't work with him often. He's head of the anti-Bolshevism division, isn't he? I know he is very close to Churchill," replied William. *Churchill, again.*

Clive took a sip of his ale and nodded, "The copy of the Zinoviev letter was part of a report from MI6 operatives in Riga. Morton didn't see anything unusual in the message from Zinoviev to the British Communist Party. He sees them all the time. The usual stuff, encouraging the British Communist Party to organize the military and workers to overthrow the government. Morton sent it on to the usual distribution list—Admiralty, Air Ministry, MI5, the Foreign Office, and Special Forces at Scotland Yard. The Foreign Office heads also saw it as the usual sort of message, but had concerns because of the timing. It urged political action to ensure that the loan agreement with the Soviets would pass in Parliament despite the opposition from the Conservatives. The loan, it said, would ease the way for organizing the international uprising of the workers."

William looked up sharply. "Surely, the letter is a fake. It seems to me particularly obtuse to think the Bolsheviks would send such an incendiary message just at the moment the loan agreement is about to be approved. They would have been aware of the consequences if British intelligence learned of the letter."

"Eyre Crowe at the Foreign Office was worried the letter, if leaked to the Press, would provide ammunition for the Conservatives in the run-up to the General Election at the end of the month. As you are well aware, forgeries done by anti-Bolsheviks arrive at MI6 on a fairly regular basis. Crowe decided to find out if the copy was legitimate before drawing it to the attention of the Prime Minister. He asked Morton about it. Morton's spies in the British Communist Party confirmed the letter had been received. Based on that, Crowe advised the PM to issue a public rebuke, and has sent him a draft—MacDonald is away on a campaign tour."

The waiter cleared their dishes and served a purple dish he called Tho-Thole. "For dessert," he said. "It is made especially for you with black rice flour. Enjoy."

Black rice flour? Is it made of gunpowder? Will it explode in my mouth? He tasted it warily and was relieved to find it was sweet with a hint of coconut and almonds. "This is delicious," he said to Clive. "Go on with your news. Are you saying Crowe thinks someone inside MI5 or MI6 might leak the letter for political reasons, to influence the election? Is that what you mean?" William asked somberly.

"Yes, it is a very real possibility," Clive said. "Especially now that you tell me there is good reason to think it is a forgery. The only reason for a forgery to turn up now would be to paint MacDonald as either a fool or a knave in his dealings with the Bolsheviks right before the General Election."

"You say Morton received a copy of the letter in a dispatch from Riga. Has anyone seen the original?" asked William.

"Excellent question, old boy," said Clive. "I see you are still as sharp as ever. No, no one has seen the original, as far as I know."

William frowned. "That complicates it for anyone who wants to leak it to the Press. An editor would want to see the original. Or, have absolute assurances of the authenticity of the copy. And the only way to get that would be if someone inside MI5 or MI6 confirmed it."

Clive nodded. "It's a dirty business," he said grimly. "Why do you think it is a fake?"

"The day he was murdered," William said, lowering his voice, "Arensdorf sent Foxy two messages. He described the two messages and how Foxy had deciphered them, one with the help of Wilkinson.

"Clever about the flowers," said Clive. Why did Arensdorf send the message to Foxy?"

"They met each other for the first time the day before," answered

William. "Foxy and Arensdorf each guessed the other had been involved in intelligence work."

"That makes sense," said Clive. "Arensdorf was being handled by Blinker during the war."

William described Arensdorf's coded message.

"What made him think Foxy would know about the Zinoviev Letter?" asked Clive.

"When they met him—I should explain that the meeting included Josie and Addie, and they met at his office at LSE—he told them he had overheard Gruter talking with two other men at the ARO, and he heard the word Zinoviev."

"But what made that important? Who were the two men?" asked Clive.

"Foxy and I just found that out this morning. The two men were Blinker Hall and Joseph Ball," said William, calmly, and watching Clive for his reaction.

Clive was surprised into a stunned silence. After a moment, he said, "How on earth did you find that out? And why would they be discussing Zinoviev with Gruter?"

William explained that Tris had managed to send a message saying McCreedy was the one who ordered him to Invergordon.

Clive was surprised into another stunned silence. "Hang on a moment, Crumpet. I thought you said that Tris was not allowed to communicate with anyone outside the base."

William accepted a cup of tea from the waiter. He smiled and dazzled Clive with the brilliant plan that led to identifying McCreedy.

Clive shook his head. "I hope you and Foxy stay on our side," he said.

William chortled with deep satisfaction. "We barged into McCreedy's office a few hours ago. He told us that Blinker blackmailed him into ordering Tris to Invergordon, and Blinker made it clear that it was an effort to make sure no scandal touched Churchill before the election, just in case Tris learned something damaging from Dinny or from his Aunts."

"His Aunts? Where do they come into this?" asked Clive.

William recounted the story Tris heard on the dahabiya.

Clive lit a cigarette. "I assume you agree it was Ball who interrogated Tris." William nodded. "Which means Blinker and Ball are at the center of the unsavory campaign of getting the Conservatives elected, including Churchill."

William said, "It is one thing to know that Blinker is working for the Conservatives to help recruit members to stand for office. He is retired. But Ball is highly placed in MI5. I always pegged him as unscrupulous from the time he was working for PMS2 during the war. What has he been up to since '18?"

Clive inhaled deeply and leaned back in his chair. "As you know, since the war, the budgets for intelligence work have been cut drastically, and quite a few officers have been retired, again, due to budget cuts. Many former agents and officers are now working for banks, commercial firms, and the like. They have been, well, for the lack of a better word, organized into a civilian intelligence agency by Ball. They call themselves the I.P. Club."

William interrupted. "What does I.P mean?"

Clive shook his head. "That's not clear. It means either Important Person or Intelligence Person. I know," he said, seeing the look on William's face. "Ridiculous. They meet regularly, at least once a month. All of them are staunch Conservatives—some of them even farther to the right than that. Some of us at MI5 have been concerned that Ball may be crossing the line and using domestic intelligence for political purposes—passing information on to his Club members and using information they pass on to him for political rather than security reasons."

William, who filled his pipe while Clive talked, lit it and took the first few puffs. "It isn't outside the realm of possibility, then, that Blinker and Ball are planning to release the Zinoviev letter to the press before the General Election next week."

"Or, that they are part of—or at least aware of—a plan to do that," said Clive. "There are rumors flying that there will be some kind of document that is harmful to MacDonald in the Press very soon. That is why Crowe was pressing MacDonald to publish the information first, along with a strong rebuttal."

William said slowly, teasing out the most important information, "Arensdorf, who knew the letter was a fake, is dead. And Gruter, who met with Blinker and Ball to discuss the letter, is missing," said William.

They sat in silence, finishing their tea, two veterans of the Intelligence war, the unseen war that defeated Germany and preserved the Empire. They knew much—too much—about the clandestine workings that brought America into the war, and that cost the lives of agents and double agents, some of whom had been considered expendable. They had wrestled with their survivor's guilt, conscious that they had been spared the killing fields of the Western Front, but consoled by the knowledge that much of what they did brought an end to the war and resulted in the peace, regardless of how flawed it was. To be confronted with highly placed individuals who had been their superior officers and who now used the power of secret intelligence to manipulate an election made them angry and threw a mantle of despair over them. They felt betrayed. Each knew how the other felt, and each knew they lacked the words to express it.

The waiter presented the bill to Clive. "It has been a pleasure to serve you," he said, and seemed to mean it.

"Please give our warmest compliments to the chef. The lunch was superb," said Clive, opening his wallet.

Outside in the late afternoon gloom, the two men could hear the faint sounds of music and the machines in the massive amusement park, people laughing, some screaming with delighted fear. They shook hands.

"I will keep you informed," said Clive.

"I will do the same," said William

"My best to Foxy," said Clive.

The two parted, Clive to take the train from the station near the amusement park behind the India Pavilion, and William to return to his car at the opposite end of the Exhibition grounds.

Chapter Thirty

Final Council of War

William hitched up the collar of his overcoat. The dark clouds told him the rain would start again soon. He decided to ride the novel Never-Stop Railway: driverless, with open-sided, covered cars pulled along continuously by an enormous screw under the cars, which was turned by a cable. William was carried slowly past a reconstruction of the old London Bridge with squat turrets and Norman arches at either end. Its neighbor was the elaborate Burma exhibition hall—six rising stories of pagodas, each one smaller than the one below it, with delicate carving rising into the sky from each pointed corner. The juxtaposition of the old London Bridge with the Burmese architecture struck him as surreal, a compression of dream and reality, of time and space, a revelation of the desire for the power of Empire mingled with an antic spirit, a need for spectacle and entertainment.

He drove home slowly through the downpour and rising mist. The monotonous slap-slap of his windshield wipers underscored his sense of irritation with the British Empire Exhibition. The cultivation of a lumpish fascination with spectacle in the name of imperialism seemed intentional, a way of distracting the public from the realities of the broken world the war had engendered.

He arrived home dripping and in a foul mood. He noticed the house seemed unusually quiet. He found Dinny in his wheelchair, sitting by a crackling fire, a whiskey decanter and one glass on a small table next to him.

"Hello, William," said Dinny. His cheerfulness struck William as a little forced. "We have had quite a day around here. I need to tell you about it. How was your visit to the British Empire Exhibition?"

"I'd rather not talk about it," William replied tersely. He took the whiskey Dinny offered with a nod of thanks and sat down wearily. "What is it you want to tell me?" he asked, making an effort to soften his tone.

"I, uh, took your advice and spent the day with Sister Parker and Wilkinson finding out about the pain medicine Sister Parker distills from plants in the Conservatory."

"And what did you find out?" asked William, somewhat warily.

Dinny cleared his throat. "It's all quite interesting, actually. Admiral Ainsworth had several specimens of cannabis…"

"Yes, I know," said William. "He told me he brought them back from India and collected some from Europe."

"Then you'll be interested to know Wilkinson has been growing them in the greenhouse."

"Has he now?" said William. "And why is that?"

"Sister Parker and Wilkinson distill an oil from the cannabis plants for a salve, which she uses to ease the pain of my broken ribs. Sometimes it helps quite a bit, and other times, not so much. She and Wilkinson have been experimenting with different varieties to discover the most effective distillate," said Dinny.

"That sounds quite interesting, and I cannot see how it can be harmful," said William. "My pharmacist sells potions and tinctures containing cannabis.

"Yes, well, Sister Parker was interested in the psychoactive effects. She knew it had been found to be highly efficacious for the treatment of a number of disorders when taken internally," said Dinny. "She wondered if it might be useful as a non-addictive painkiller, so she and Wilkinson used the flowers to prepare an extract." Dinny paused, aware the rest of the story would disturb William and quite possibly result in Sister Parker's dismissal.

"Here, let me refresh your drink."

William sipped his second whiskey. Dinny explained that Sister Parker used the extract in preparing a batch of Chelsea buns, which she left to cool in the kitchen, intending to test the effect on herself. As he recounted the events that followed, and particularly, how Foxy had reacted to eating the buns, William's face drained of blood.

"Where is she? How is she?" He asked, rising to his feet.

"She's fine, she's—" said Dinny.

"Where is she?" repeated William in clipped tones.

"She's resting in the Conservatory," said Dinny. "But I tell you, she is fine."

"No thanks to Parker," said William. "She'll have to go." He was angry and frightened for Foxy.

"But, that isn't quite fair..." expostulated Dinny. He was talking to William's back.

William found Foxy asleep on the chaise under a pale, green coverlet. She was surrounded by the green leaves of elephant ear and philodendron. The white flowers of jasmine, trained on a trellis, released their sweet fragrance. William knelt by Foxy's side. She opened her eyes, which registered her delight at seeing him.

"Oh, hello, William. Wait until I tell you what I found out today," she said. She was relaxed and smiling.

"What I want to know is if you are all right?" said William, looking at her intently. "Dinny told me you had a dose of cannabis—"

"I am absolutely fine. Better than fine," said Foxy. "I just needed a little nap and..."

"Sister Parker will have to go," said William. "This was totally irresponsible."

"No, no, William. You have it all wrong. I should not have taken the Chelsea buns and rushed off. You know how impetuous I am. I dive into the pool without waiting to find out if it has any water in it," she said.

"Yes, but it might have been much worse. Sister Parker was experimenting with a dangerous drug, and—"

"Don't be Bottom to my Queen Titania here in my bower," she said, smiling very sweetly. "Be my Oberon instead." She reached out and stroked his cheek. She withdrew her hand suddenly. *What has gotten into me? And what am I doing, calling him an ass? And then a king? Why am I babbling about Midsummer Night's Dream?*

"I must apologize," she said. "I guess the effects of the cannabis have not quite worn off."

William felt a thrill flood his body when Foxy stroked his cheek. She had never done that before. She had taken his arm to be led into dinner or helped into a car, but never had there been any indication from her that she reciprocated his feelings for her. He saw her blush, and heard her apologize, but decided—or hoped—that the psychoactive properties of cannabis made people speak the truth they otherwise would not.

Foxy sat up and rang for tea, clearly eager to change the subject as well as the mood. "Did Dinny tell you what I found out from Caxton? No? Caxton confessed to stealing the *Lusitania* files and sabotaging Dinny's car," she said grimly. "And that Blinker put him up to stealing the files. He also told me that it was Gruter who killed Arensdorf."

"Did he, indeed?" William was taken aback, utterly speechless.

"Yes, and it was because he ate two of the Chelsea buns. It is an intoxicant, you see, and…well, never mind about that for now. The point is, he idolizes Blinker. Caxton was supposed to spy for Blinker, to find out what Dinny and Addie wanted to know about the *Lusitania*. Caxton thought it would impress Blinker if he got them out of the way. That is why he sabotaged the car. It was his idea," said Foxy. "He is a horrible young man, filled with the toxic concoction of anti-Semitism—which means he believes in his own racial superiority—and the delusion planted in his head by Blinker that he is a warrior against communism. But for all his cocky bravura, seeing Gruter kill Arensdorf threw him into a catatonic shock."

"What do you mean, he saw Gruter kill Arensdorf? Why didn't he say anything at the time?" asked William.

"That little degenerate pushed Arensdorf again, this time off the bottom step going down to the ARO. Gruter must have seen it, grabbed that spike he uses as a paperweight, and before Arensdorf could get to his feet, knocked him out and broke his neck."

"No wonder he was a blabbering idiot yesterday," said William. "You need to know that Gruter killed Arensdorf because Arensdorf found out about the Zinoviev letter. Clive told me today about a plan to use it to smear MacDonald before the election."

Maisy brought in the tea. Foxy poured them each a cup and took a sip before going on. "Caxton would not have confessed if it hadn't been for the Chelsea buns. He ate two as if food had just been invented. So, you see…"

"Yes, yes, I will grant you that," said William. He knew he would have to concede the point. "You simply have to understand I was very worried about you, concerned that there might have been serious side effects."

"There was never any chance of that. And it has worked out for the best. Sister Parker meant no harm and never intended anyone but herself to eat the Chelsea buns. The entire incident was an accident," said Foxy. "She felt terribly guilty. She was willing to ruin her career by calling Queen Alexandra's to tell them Caxton had eaten a bun laced with cannabis. Dinny wouldn't allow it."

"Very well," said William, "Sister Parker can stay, but with some constraints on her enthusiasm for experiments. They will have to be confined to the Potting Shed."

Foxy sighed with relief and smiled. "Thank you. And now, how did your lunch go with Clive? What exactly did he tell you about the Zinoviev letter?"

"I'd like to hold off on what I learned until we can have a Council of War after dinner," said William. He was feeling worn out and decided to rest for an hour before tea was served at 4:30.

Josie called to say she had information to report. Dinny invited her to join them for dinner.

By the time the Council of War convened, Foxy's head had cleared, William's mood had lifted, and Dinny was pleased because he had delivered the news to Sister Parker that she would not be fired. Dinny told Addie the Adventure of the Chelsea Buns when she returned from the GCCS. Josie arrived with an enormous bouquet.

They convened after dinner around the crackling fire. Maisy served coffee, and Foxy began her account of Caxton's confession, including the details of Arensdorf's murder.

The blood drained from Josie's face. "This is horrific," she said, looking at the others. "It is so vicious. Why would Gruter kill Arensdorf?"

William said, "That is a question we have all wanted to know." He recounted what he learned from Clive. He concluded, "The Zinoviev letter will be given to the Press sometime this week." He paused. "Obviously, this information can go no farther than this room."

Josie's brow furrowed. "They are plotting to legitimize a fake document?"

William nodded, agreeing with her concern. "Either Arensdorf was wrong, and the Zinoviev letter is authentic, or he was correct, and an agent of MI5 and a former Director of Naval Intelligence are about to release a forged, inflammatory letter to the Press to influence the election. That would be shameful enough if the letter were authentic."

"It must be a fake. Why else would Arensdorf have been killed?" asked Josie, grimly. "He overheard them discussing this Zinoviev letter. Somehow, they found out, probably because Caxton told them he was in the ARO at the time, and that was Arensdorf's death sentence."

Dinny chimed in. "If I understand this, the plan has two parts. One is to suppress any information about the *Lusitania* which might reflect badly on either Churchill's conduct as the First Lord of the Admiralty in 1915, or on his effort in his history of the war to exonerate himself from any responsibility for the sinking of the *Lusitania* by putting the blame on Captain Turner. The second is to defeat the Labour Party by making them seem to be either in the back pocket of the Bolsheviks or too blind to realize that they are playing into the hands of the Bolsheviks. Blinker and Hall are involved in both plans."

"That sums it up," said William. "But only one of them has enough authority to arrange for Gruter to kill Arensdorf.

"You mean Ball," said Foxy, matter-of-factly. "Blinker is retired. Ball is head of an intelligence division of MI5.

"And, as I learned today, he has organized his own private, civilian intelligence group from ex-officers and intelligence agents. But you didn't hear it from me," said William, lighting his pipe.

"It is reasonable to suspect Ball of getting Gruter to kill Arensdorf and then spiriting Gruter away," said Foxy.

William took a puff on his pipe and seemed lost in thought momentarily. "Yes, Major Ball is the type who would have offered Gruter a sizable amount of money, a passport to some far-away country, and letters of introduction that would assure him easy entrée into at least the outer fringes of power in that country. If Gruter proved reluctant to leave the country, Ball could have threatened to betray him and have him hanged as a spy. Similar operations were carried out during the war when a spy became expendable. For the Greater Good, of course." His voice took on a sour and sardonic tone.

"From the description Caxton gave and the autopsy report, I would hazard a guess that this wasn't the first time Gruter had killed someone," said Foxy.

William nodded. "I quite agree. He seems to have had professional training to know just how to break a man's neck so efficiently. He would have learned that and other deadly tricks of the trade when he trained as a spy if he didn't know them already."

Foxy was unfazed by William's chilling suppositions because she had been aware of such dismal operations during the war. Dinny, Addie, and Josie, however, were catching a glimpse for the first time into the darker side of the life William led in Naval intelligence during the war. A deep silence followed his account. Aware that he needed to dispel the pall he had created, William stood up and walked briskly to the liquor cabinet. "Time for a stiffener, I think." Josie and Addie accepted the brandy. Foxy thought she had better not, after the Chelsea buns, and Dinny still could not drink alcohol because of his medications.

Returning to his chair, snifter in hand and gently swirling the brandy, William said, "Josie, what have you learned?"

Taking a sip of her brandy to steady her nerves after William's speculations, she explained that she had gone to the LSE library, asked for the Teague journal, and was told it was missing."

"I knew there was no point in asking if anyone had checked it out," she said. "It wasn't supposed to circulate, and anyway, librarians are not allowed to give out information of that kind. But my friend, Charlotte Langhorne, works at Circulation part-time. You met her, Addie, remember?" Addie nodded.

"She was there this morning," said Josie. "I asked her if anyone came in yesterday morning looking for the Teague Collection. She said she remembered very well a man who seemed to have some kind of tic in his eyes because he blinked so often, and he looked like Punch from Punch and Judy—you know, a long nose that almost reached his prominent chin."

"Blinker Hall," said Foxy and William in unison.

"So, our old boss, Admiral Sir William Reginald Hall, has stooped to stealing from a library, I mean, honestly," said Foxy.

William laughed. "Indeed."

Addie said thoughtfully, "He must have read about the donation of the collection in the newspapers, checked the catalogue, and decided the one item he had to steal was the Teague diary." She turned to Josie, "It is a good thing Arensdorf arranged for us to see the collection before it was officially available to the public."

"We owe him a great deal," said Josie. "He is a great loss." It took her a moment to regain her composure. She took a sip of her brandy. "I also visited the florist who sold Arensdorf the flowers, *Roses' of Bloomsbury.* Its owner is Betty Rose," said Josie. She was heartbroken over Professor Arensdorf's death. I asked if I could send flowers to his funeral. She said that in Jewish custom, flowers are for the living. When she visited his grave, she would bring a stone to put on it so others would know that he was remembered. She also had a torn piece of cloth pinned to her dress, to signify that she was mourning Arensdorf's death as if she were a member of the family."

Addie nodded, "Yes, those are both Jewish rituals of mourning."

"She and her husband knew the Arensdorfs before the war," said Josie, a note of sadness in her voice. "She taught him the code of flowers. He used it every time he sent a bouquet to anyone."

"I take it that was fairly often," said William.

"Yes, he was a regular customer," said Josie. "And according to Mrs. Rose, he always wrote funny or whimsical names on the cards. They made no sense to her. She assumed they were private jokes or nicknames."

Foxy said gently, looking at Josie, "Arensdorf probably wanted to make sure she knew nothing to protect her in case he was discovered, and the authorities questioned her."

Josie nodded, "I thought so, too." Her eyes brimmed over with tears. Addie went to sit by her and handed her a handkerchief.

After a pause, Foxy said, "Josie, we owe a great deal to Arensdorf. And to you. What you learned today was that Arensdorf was evidently in frequent contact with comrades here in London. He was undoubtedly being watched by MI5."

William, who was affected by Josie's sadness, said quietly, "Yes, Clive told me that today."

Addie said, "Doesn't that lend weight to his claim that the Zinoviev letter is a fake? I mean, if he had frequent contact with the Communist Party members, wouldn't he know whether Zinoviev actually sent a letter about the loan and fomenting revolution?"

William said, "I agree. But top officials in Intelligence are willing to verify its authenticity. The problem is, not one of them has either the original or even a signed copy. What is in circulation is a copy of a copy of what is purported to be a typed translation."

"Which is why," said Foxy, with irritation, "the word of Blinker or Ball or both would carry such weight with the editors of the Conservative newspapers. Still, you would think that even they would want to see an authenticated, signed copy."

"One question I still have," said Dinny, "is why Blinker and Ball were talking with Gruter about Zinoviev. It had to have been about the letter, but what reason would they have to raise it with him?"

"And," Addie added, "Arensdorf said they were speaking in raised voices. Were they arguing? If so, about what? Or were they excited about something to do with the Zinoviev letter?"

Foxy burst out, "OH! Why didn't I think to ask that when I was with Caxton? He was eavesdropping on their conversation. Maybe he knows why they were discussing Zinoviev."

"Could you see him again?" asked Josie. "He certainly opened up to you today."

Foxy knew Josie had not been told about the Chelsea buns. "Perhaps," she said vaguely. "I suppose he will be released from Queen Alexandra's and held for questioning by the Naval authorities. At least, I will do everything in my power to make sure that happens after I tell the Provost Marshall what Caxton confessed to me today."

"Are you planning to go to the old Admiralty tomorrow, then?" asked William.

"Yes, and not just to file a deposition about Caxton," said Foxy. "I also want to know if the *Lusitania* file is still taped to the underside of Gruter's desk. And I have a few other hunches." She left the mystery float in the air.

"I won't be going with you," said William. "I plan to visit Blinker tomorrow to ask him some very pointed questions. I have no doubt McCreedy has kept him updated on our investigation, until we put a stopper in his bottle today, that is. Blinker will want to know what I know and will warn me off the investigation."

"I wish I could come with you," said Addie, turning to Foxy, "but I have been given a special assignment, and I am working against a deadline."

Josie looked bereft. She said to Foxy, "Could you find out when Professor Arensdorf's body will be released? Mrs. Rose is very unsettled because no arrangements have been made. He had no next of kin. The body could be released to their rabbi," she said softly. "I had her write the details for me. I can give it to you before I leave."

"Certainly," said Foxy, "I will do what I can."

Addie knew her friend was grieving. "I was hoping we could get together for lunch tomorrow. I was thinking of that little place near the river. We could take a walk after."

Josie smiled a half-smile, putting on a brave face. "I would like that," she said.

Dinny said, "Terrific idea, Addie. I wish I could join you. I also would like to give you a hug, Josie, but…" He reached out his hands to Josie. She rose and took his hands in hers. "I am very sorry," he said. "I want you to know that."

Josie's eyes brimmed again. She smiled and nodded. "Thank you, Dinny. She turned and said, "Thanks to all of you for…" Her voice broke.

Chapter Thirty-One

When I sup with the Devil

The next morning, Foxy was brushing Murky's long fur as the cat purred, lying on the table in the Conservatory. William, wearing his Naval Reserve uniform, joined her and quietly laid on the table his Colt .45 service revolver. Murky nuzzled the gun and turned her large, amber eyes on William. *I can't eat this. Why is it on my grooming table?*

Foxy frowned and stopped brushing Murky. "What...?"

"You are going to the ARO today. The last time you were there, Arensdorf was killed. I am worried about you," he said in his usual reserved voice.

"And I am worried about you seeing Blinker," she said.

"I've arranged to meet him at the Naval and Military Club," said William. "I've booked a private room. He did not seem at all surprised when I called and asked if we could meet."

Foxy was gently brushing Murky's tail. "I'm just finishing this. Why not order coffee for us, and we can talk things over?" she suggested. She released Murky, who sniffed the gun, gave William a disgusted look, and voiced a hoarse meow. *You disappoint me.* She jumped from the table and walked sedately from the room, her tail held high in its question mark. *Why must I be surrounded by nincompoops?*

Maisy brought the coffee *mit schlage* to the Conservatory.

"You start," said Foxy to William. "Why should I take a sidearm to the ARO?"

"Arensdorf's killing seems to have been calculated," William said, "and if I am correct, Gruter was either ordered to do it or paid to do it. It seems Ball will stop at nothing to make sure no questions are raised about the authenticity of the Zinoviev Letter. If he finds you snooping around there today, I worry about what he might do to you. The letter is due to be in the papers very soon."

"I will take precautions, then," said Foxy. "I will ask the Porter if Major Hall has signed in, and I will tell McCreedy I am in the building and when I expect to leave. And I will hide the gun, but not loaded. I'll take the cartridges in case I need them, but I will not carry a loaded gun around, even with the safety on. Not after I almost shot Tris."

"Fair enough," said William. "Now, why are you worried about Blinker Hall?"

Foxy took a sip of coffee. "Caxton reminded me of what Blinker did to Judge Bray—or claimed to have done."

"Oh, yes," said William. "I remember. I often wondered if that were true, or if he made up the story after the bombing."

"I think it was probably true," said Foxy. "You have to admit he could be ruthless. Robby told me what Ed Bell said to him about Blinker over dinner one evening. Did you know him?"

William nodded, "Bell was Second Secretary to the American Embassy, which was a cover for his being their top man in intelligence in London. We weren't supposed to know that, obviously."

"Yes, that's right," said Foxy. "Bell admired Blinker's genius but said he had never met a colder-hearted individual. His exact words were 'He'd cut out a man's heart and hand it back to him.'"

William lit his pipe. "Yes, I can believe someone saying that of Blinker." He did not elaborate.

"And he could sometimes be violent," said Foxy. "You know Essie—Blinker's wife—played bridge regularly with the Naval officers' wives. One day, Blinker came in so frustrated by something that had gone wrong that he knocked over the bridge table in anger. Sent the cards, teacups, and biscuits flying all over the place. The story went around like wildfire."

"I remember it," said William.

"You take my point," said Foxy. "And remember, Blinker is untouchable. Not only is he a retired Admiral and a former Conservative Member of Parliament, he is also a Knight Commander of the Order of St. Michael and St. George and the Order of the Bath. There is no higher honor than the KCMG."

"Which he deserved. He was brilliant as the Director of Naval Intelligence. The KCMG was in special recognition of this key role in bringing America into the war by intercepting the Zimmerman Telegraph," said William.

Foxy smiled. "That was a great coup, I admit. I remember when we decrypted the message from Zimmerman—known to us as a top official in the German Foreign Office. He offered to give Mexico back territory in the southwest United States in exchange for invading America if America entered the war. After that, Wilson had no choice." Foxy reflected, remembering how it had all played out. "It really was Blinker's finest hour."

"I take your warning seriously," said William. "Hall is brilliant, ruthless, and influential with an untouchable reputation and is involved in highly questionable political intrigue."

Foxy nodded emphatically. "Remember, 'softly, softly, catches monkey.'"

William dropped Foxy at the old Admiralty Building. She said she would take a cab home in time for lunch, around 1:00. It was raining again. As she shook out her umbrella, she thought about asking the Porter if Major Hall was in the building, but decided against it. *What if he came later and the Porter told him I had been asking about him?* She turned her hat, waterproof coat, and umbrella over to the Porter, who gave her a claim check. She made an appointment to meet with the Provost Marshall in an hour. She went to McCreedy's office, her courier bag over one shoulder. She felt the Colt .45 hard against her thigh in one pocket, the bullets in the other in the contraption she tied around her waist under her skirt. It was not noticeable because she was wearing Coco Chanel's dress, designed to hide multiple bulges.

Seaman Ridley told Foxy that McCreedy was called away suddenly to a meeting in Bristol and would not be back. He did not hesitate to give her the key to the ARO. She opened the door to the Records Office, closed it behind her, and switched on the light. She crossed over to Gruter's desk, knelt down, and to her surprise saw two Manila folders glued to the underside of the desktop. She hadn't really expected to find anything. She pried the envelopes loose. She sat at Gruter's desk, turned on the desk lamp, and gasped when she realized one of the folders contained a typed letter to the Communist Party of Great Britain, with Zinoviev's name at the bottom. She put a piece of blank paper into Gruter's typewriter and typed several sentences from the letter.

> Dear Comrades,
>
> The time is approaching for the Parliament of England to consider the Treaty between the Governments of Great Britain and the S.S.S.R. for the purpose of ratification. The campaign raised by the British bourgeoisie around the question shows that the majority of the same, together with reactionary circles, are against the Treaty for the purpose of breaking off an agreement consolidating the ties between the proletariats of the two countries.

Foxy pulled the paper from the typewriter and saw that on the original and her copy, the "e" was darker than the rest of the letters, the "B" and 'i" were smeared, and the "S" was faint. There was no doubt that both had been typed on Gruter's machine. She then studied the marginal notes and compared them with Gruter's handwriting on the notes on his desk. They matched. He indicated that "concluded" should be inserted after "Treaty," and "fierce" before "campaign."

She read the most inflammatory sentence, the one included to ensure Labour lost the election:

> It is necessary to stir up the masses of the British proletariat to bring into movement the army of unemployed proletarians whose position can be improved only after a loan has been granted to the

S.S.S.R. for the restoration of her economics and when business collaboration between the British and Russian proletariats has been put in order.

Gruter had crossed-out "necessary" and written "indispensable" in the margin.

Arensdorf was right. The Zinoviev letter is a fake. Gruter composed it and typed it in this room. He must have typed a fair copy and given it to Hall or Blinker, and then glued the draft under his desk. Why? Probably as insurance, in case he wasn't paid off as promised.

Foxy needed to hurry to get this information to William. She glanced at the second manila folder and confirmed it was part of the missing *Lusitania* archive. *Just one more thing to check.* She unrolled cotton wool she stole from Sister Parker, wrapped the files in it, and stuffed them into the hidden pockets in her courier bag. *That should stop them from crackling when the Porter inspects the bag.* She took the elevator to Room 229. She thought that since Gruter hid the decrypts there, he might also have stashed the spike he used on Arensdorf. She worked out that Gruter must have left the building using the fire escape, the one she and the other women in Room 229 used for breaks. That explained why the Porter did not see him leave the building after he killed Arensdorf. She took the elevator to the second floor. As she expected, the hallway was empty. What surprised her was the doorknob to Room 229 turned easily. The door was not locked.

Unlike the heroines of far too many novels, Foxy did not open the door and say, "Hello? Is anybody there?" She stepped back and pressed herself against the wall, hoping whoever was in the room had not seen the doorknob turn or heard her footsteps. She decided to slink silently down the hall, with her back pressed against the wall, hoping to reach the stairway. Suddenly, the door was flung open. She saw a fleshy face with drooping jowls and large, round glasses. He pressed his large hand over her mouth. The other hand was raised and held Gruter's spike. She registered the sudden pain. Then, her world went black.

William arrived at the Naval and Military Club fifteen minutes early.

Blinker Hall was a stickler for punctuality. William arranged for coffee and scones to be sent to the quiet room he reserved. Raindrops coursed down the large windows overlooking Green Park. William rose from the armchair when Hall entered the room.

"Thank you for agreeing to see me," he said. He did not salute. He might have, given they were both in uniform, but William was disgusted with Hall. He knew Hall would notice the slight, the breach of courtesy.

"Not at all, old boy. I knew we had a good deal to talk about," said Hall, his eyes blinking involuntarily. His voice was the same surprising, slightly high-pitched tenor. William thought Hall had aged well. He was lean, his hair gone gray, his eyes still bright, alert, and intelligent. With his hooked nose, he reminded William of a kestrel about to plummet from the sky on its prey.

Hall poured himself a cup of coffee. He offered William a Turkish cigarette. William declined, preferring his pipe. Hall lit his cigarette with a lighter, snapped it shut, blew a stream of smoke, and, seated in the armchair opposite William, said, "How can I help you?"

William took his time filling and lighting his pipe. He assumed the bland, expressionless face he adopted when involved in intelligence work. Poker face, the Americans called it.

"First of all, I want to be certain I haven't misjudged you," said William quietly.

"How so?" asked Hall blithely.

William sounded indifferent. "You have been working on behalf of Winston Churchill to bring him over to the Conservatives and to assure nothing interferes with his election to Parliament next week." It was a statement, not a question.

Hall looked highly self-satisfied. "Why, yes, I have. Nothing wrong with that. I very much admired Churchill when he was First Lord. I liked him, liked him very much. I admired his genius, his dash, you see?" Hall warmed to his subject. He leaned forward, his face animated. "He was very approachable and always ready to back me up as far as he could. He had so much energy. He worked without ever seeming to tire." Hall's voice rose to a higher register in his enthusiasm. "And the stream of information and ideas he sent at all hours of the day and night was astounding, and not just in volume, but in how informed he was. It was a bit frightening, really, when one comes down to it. He had courage and vision. His one flaw was that he wanted to make all the executive decisions, take all matters into his own hands. We need him in the Conservative Party. He is just what we need," he concluded emphatically.

William took a sip of his coffee. His passive expression did not mirror Hall's enthusiasm. "And your thinking is that nothing from the past should rise up now and prevent his election." He did not wait for a reply. "And that brings me to the *Lusitania* file and the decrypts of U-20. You learned that Lt. Custus had requested the *Lusitania* file and the decrypts. Who told you that, by the way? Gruter?"

"I see no harm in telling you now," said Hall, mildly. "It was Major Hall. He handles—or handled—Gruter after I got him the job at the ARO. He was a valuable double agent during the war, and when I left Naval Intelligence, I turned him over to MI5 with a very strong recommendation."

"You blackmailed McCreedy over the Jutland affair to get him to hire Chauncey Caxton to steal the *Lusitania* file," William said levelly. He did not let his eyes stray from Hall's.

Hall said airily, "I advised him that I would add a letter to his file about his dereliction of duty during the Battle of Jutland and reminded him how often such matters come to the attention of the Press. He seemed to understand what I meant. Hiring Caxton was more like a favor to me, rather than something as sordid as blackmail," said Hall, blandly, his eyes blinking rapidly.

"Young Caxton idolizes you," said William, his face taut. "He wanted to impress you."

"You can't blame a young man for his idealism," said Hall, complacently.

William went on gravely. "To impress you, he sabotaged Lt. Custus' car. He and his passenger were injured and hospitalized. They have been recovering in my home in Chelsea. "We—that is, Lady Butterschloss and I—did not know if they were both in danger of further attack."

"Yes, I imagine you were quite worried," said Hall sympathetically, deciding to introduce his infectious charm into the strained conversation. "I only learned what young Caxton had done when he told me about it after the accident. I think he is mad with romantic notions of cloak-and-dagger heroics. I had a word with his father, who has agreed to send Caxton to work for Caxton's uncle. He owns a salmon fishing fleet and packing plant in Vancouver, British Columbia. Working there should give Caxton a bracing dose of reality." His face bore a sardonic expression, one very familiar to William.

"And get him well out of the way," said William, blandly, tapping the cold ash out of his pipe into the ashtray stand next to his chair. "It might prove more complicated than that. Foxy is giving a deposition about Caxton to the Provost Marshall, probably as we speak." He pursed his lips and waited for Hall's reaction.

Hall went quiet for a moment. The only things moving were his blinking eyes. "I think we will be able to manage to take care of that," he said, with the steely tone he had so often used in William's presence. "I must congratulate you and Foxy on your investigations. Not that I would doubt your abilities for a moment," he said, dryly.

He feels humiliated, thought William. *Best follow Foxy's advice. Slowly, slowly, catches monkey.* "We both learned from the best," said William, forcing a smile. "You must think this election is terribly important, to have gone to all these lengths, I mean."

Hall's eyes glittered. "As a matter of fact, I do. As I warned the War Staff when I retired as head of Naval Intelligence at the end of the war, I think we are heading for another war, or more precisely, we are in one now. Hard and bitter as the war was, we now have to face a far, far more ruthless foe, a foe that is hydra-headed, and whose evil power will spread over the whole world, and that foe is Russia."

"Is that why you ran for Parliament in '19?" asked William.

"That, and because I wanted to protect the interests of the Navy and Merchant Marine against the cuts, treaty restrictions, and the loss of our air arm to the RAF. I didn't think my duty ended with my retirement," he said, with an unmistakable note of pride in his voice, along with the usual steel.

I need to keep him talking about his achievements and political mastery, thought William. *Appeal to his vanity.* "And the PM made you the Principal Agent for the Conservatives in '23," said William, "which meant you oversaw public relations and recruiting new members. Did that bring back memories of being in charge at Naval Intelligence?" asked William, trying to look interested.

"Not at all," said Hall. "It was the most frustrating job I've ever taken on. Too many restrictions for me. I missed the old free-wheeling days of the war," he said, smiling.

William chuckled, too, keeping up the act. "And, of course, it was your genius that brought America into the war," he said.

"Yes, indeed," said Hall. "We led Wilson to believe the Zimmerman message had been intercepted and decrypted by one of our agents in Mexico. Otherwise, the Americans would have learned we could decipher not only the German cables, but the American cables as well." He chuckled again, looking like a mischievous little boy. "We would have lost the war without America coming in. We thought the sinking of the *Lusitania* would do it." He stopped himself suddenly. "But the less said about that, the better."

Was Hall on the brink of confessing they deliberately decided not to protect the Lusitania, hoping a U-20 would cross her path? William thought with outrage and disgust. "I understand your motivations now. We are in a non-shooting war with Russia, and that is why the Labour government has to be defeated before the Anglo-Soviet treaty is signed."

Hall leaned forward. "Exactly," he said with enthusiasm. "You understand me perfectly." He slammed a fist into his palm. "And now you can see why I was so keen on getting Churchill elected into the Conservatives next week."

William took on a conspiratorial tone. "And the Zinoviev Letter? I take it that is part of the plan, too. Releasing it to the press, I mean."

Hall scarcely missed a beat. What did it matter now if William had found out about the Zinoviev Letter? His face filled with boyish delight. "Yes, yes! It will appear tomorrow. Labour won't have much of a chance to reply and defend themselves before the General Election on Tuesday. It is sure to tip the election our way."

William pretended to agree with Hall. "And is that why Arensdorf had to be killed?" He dropped it like a bomb from a Zeppelin on a country manor.

Hall sat back in his chair, brushing the air with the back of his hand as if there were a fly annoying him. "Arensdorf. I had nothing to do with that. That was all down to Ball. Arensdorf went over to the Soviets after the war." Ball's face registered his disgust. "He was useful, up to a point. MI5 kept a close watch on him. When it seemed he was too dangerous, Ball had him killed. A bit heavy-handed, in my opinion, but we've managed to cover it up," he said, brusquely.

William's face became expressionless. "Was he dangerous because he knew the Zinoviev letter was a fake?" he asked, flatly.

Hall became rigid, all the boyish camaraderie gone. "I couldn't possibly say."

"Did Ball pay Gruter off, or did he have him killed, too?" asked William as if he were discussing a shopping list.

"He paid him off," said Hall, his voice like steel. "Gruter is in Buenos Aires by now, and quite comfortable there, I imagine."

"You didn't think that Ball was going a bit too far?" asked William. "He was acting from purely political reasons, and he is an officer in MI5."

"This is war," said Hall, a note of anger in his voice. "I would work with the Devil if he was proficient."

"Naturally, I understand," said William. He paused, then gave a half smile. "And how about you? Are you planning to stand for Parliament again? You've been out of office since '23."

Hall's face relaxed into a self-satisfied smile. "As a matter of fact, I do. I am planning to stand at the next opportunity."

"I wish you luck," said William. "By the way, I also have a point-of-view about the future, and it is that I intend to protect those closest to me."

"I told you," said Hall. "What Caxton did was a mistake."

William's voice turned cold. "And to Addie, the young girl who was with him, and if I am not wrong, will soon be engaged to him."

"Yes, of course. I am sorry about that, too," said Hall. "Wasn't meant to happen, as I said," he mumbled.

William gritted his teeth, then said briskly, "Nonetheless, you did make sure Claxton was put into position to cause Dinny no end of trouble, including a possible court-martial. And the scandal could have ruined Addie's career at GCCS." William stood up, indicating he intended to leave. Hall stood, too. "Just to make sure there are no more mistakes or accidents that can affect anyone close to me, I want you to know that I have a little book.

"You have a little book?" said Hall, testily. "What about?"

"It is a little book of my own writing. It is a journal, rather like Teague's. You know, the one you took from the LSE," said William, looking straight into Hall's blinking eyes.

Hall registered a very slight surprise, "You know about that, too?"

"Yes, and it could go badly for you if you don't return it. Those fines can pile up," said William, relishing the surprise. "But, as for my journal—journals, to be precise. They contain quite a bit of information about what went on at NID during the war. And of course, I've started a new journal while investigating what you have been up to, trying to get Churchill elected. It contains copies of the submarine decrypts, too. I would hate for it to fall into the wrong hands," said William, steadily.

"You wouldn't dare," said Hall, angrily. "For one thing, it would violate your oath of secrecy."

William's eyes glinted with an adamant resolve. "Don't think I would hesitate for one minute. When I sup with the Devil, I sup with a long-handled spoon. And I have taken precautions, as you can well imagine, in case anything unfortunate should happen to me. There will be no way you could possibly prevent my journals from coming to light. But there really is nothing for you to worry about, is there? Because you are never going to meddle in my affairs, or the affairs of anyone close to me, again, are you?" He paused for effect. "Oh, and you will see to it that Lt. Dashwood is returned to duty at Admiralty within the next twenty-four hours, am I correct?"

Hall's face was flushed with anger, his eyes blinked furiously. Without another word, William turned and left the room. As he opened the door, he heard what he assumed was the ashtray stand being knocked over and landing with a loud crash. William closed the door without looking back, with a smile of deep satisfaction.

Chapter Thirty-Two

Friday, October 24, 1924

Foxy was flat on her back on a cold, dank floor. She opened her eyes. *Someone hit me, hard, on the head.* She was in total darkness. Her hands and feet were not bound. There was no gag in her mouth. Her head was filled with pain. These few facts registered immediately. She rolled onto her side to try and get up. She vomited, groaned, rolled onto her back again, and passed out. She opened her eyes again. She had no idea how much time had passed. Her head swam, and she was nauseated. *In through the nose, out through the mouth. In through the nose, out through the mouth. How they told me to breathe when I was in labor. In through the nose, out through the mouth.* The nausea abated, the pain did not. She swooned again. When she opened her eyes, she felt tears coursing down her cheeks. She had been dreaming of Timmy, her little brown-eyed boy, laughing, his short, chubby legs running after a red ball she had rolled to him. *This won't do. This won't do. But what can I do?* Her head pounded, but she felt much less dizzy. She lay very still, listening, trying to work out where she was. *I must still be in the Admiralty Building. A blow like that would have knocked me out for a very short time. There are no windows. I am not bound or gagged. I must be in the sub-basement, where no one would hear me if I screamed my head off. I rather wish it would come off. Anything is better than this pain.* She closed her eyes and drifted off again. She woke up to a loud, repeated, percussive sound, like a jackhammer, followed by rattling. She listened. *Water pipes. There are water pipes on what must be the wall. If I could only...* She sat up slowly. Her head swam. The dizziness was almost intolerable. Her head throbbed. She groaned and sat very, very still. *Breathe. In through the nose, out through the mouth. In through the nose, out through the mouth. Think about where it doesn't hurt. Take my mind off where it does hurt.* She considered her toes with intense concentration. *They don't hurt, not one little bit.* She checked her knees, elbows, arms. *They do not hurt. They do not hurt.* She gritted her teeth against the pain in her head. The slow breathing had alleviated the dizziness. *Now what? I have to get over to those pipes.* She laughed a silent laugh. *How am I going to do that? I must protect Dinny and Addie. That's how I wound up here. Trying to protect them. Trying to find out who wanted to harm them.*

She rolled over very slowly onto her hands and knees. She tried to hold her head up but could not. With her head drooping and the dizziness returning, she stayed where she was, frozen, except for her slow breathing. *Crawl three and stop. Slowly, slowly catches the pipes.* Her knees trapped her skirt against the floor. She couldn't go forward. She stopped. *Now breathe, breathe. Count to ten.* She reached behind her with one hand and then the other, lifting her knees, and gently pulled her skirt up. Her knees hurt against the cold, hard floor. She moved forward to the count of three. She stopped to breathe slowly. At ten, she crawled forward again to the count of three. After stopping and going five excruciating times, she felt her head bump gently against a wall. Stars exploded in front of her eyes. She rolled over, her back and head braced by the wall, and blacked out. She opened her eyes again. Her throat was dry. She was thirsty, so thirsty. The pain in her head had settled into a dull throb. *I have to get out of here. No one knows I am here. The Porter will notice when I do not pick up my rain things by 5:00. William will notice when I do not arrive in time for lunch. But what time is it now? Pipes. Where are those pipes?* She reached her arms up over her head. She felt a rough wall. Then, her fingers felt a pipe, a big, round pipe, a water pipe. *Now, I need that gun. Thank God I wore a skirt with my hidden pocket. Wouldn't McCreedy be surprised?*

Without moving her head, she pulled her skirt up further and reached into the pocket tied around her waist. She pulled out the revolver. *Now, all I have to do is reach that pipe with this.* The throbbing in her head made it difficult to think. Her body was not interested in responding to any orders. She felt very weak. And thirsty. And still a little dizzy. She tried to figure out how to move her body to get the gun close to the pipes. She roused herself. She put the gun back in her pocket. She rolled over with her face a few inches from the wall, her knees folded under her. She reached up. *Yes!* Her hand wrapped around a pipe, a smaller pipe, she thought, than the larger one, which must be above it. Holding on, with what little strength she had, she managed to get one foot under her and push up. Then the other foot. She rested her body against the wall, drained of all energy. Her head throbbed; the dizziness was worse. She gripped the pipe and let the wall hold her up. She breathed slowly, closed her eyes, and dreamed while not being quite asleep, of playing tennis, hitting the ball, and then walking over to a small table with a large, cool glass of lemonade, and drinking it down. She roused herself again. She reached slowly into her pocket, pulled out the gun, and holding it by the barrel, tapped out with the butt of the gun on the larger pipe the universal Morse code for help S.O.S. ...- - -...... ...- - - ... ...- - -... *I am in the Admiralty. Everyone will know what this means.* She kept it up until her arm was too tired. She slipped the gun into her pocket. *Mustn't let it drop.* She leaned her head against the wall. It was cool and helped ease the pain. She dozed, standing up. She woke, suddenly, as her hands started to slip. She gripped the pipe tightly in one hand, reached into her pocket with the other, pulled out the gun, and began tapping again, keeping it up until her arm tired, then resting, and tapping again. She knew her strength would fail her eventually, but she had to keep it up as long as she could. Over and over again, she tapped out ...- - -... ...- - -... ...- - -.... Then rested, half-conscious. Finally, her body said *No more.* She blacked out, her hands loosened, she slid to her knees, her body leaning against the wall.

She dreamed she was standing in a silver-blue meadow. Robby was there in his uniform. Everything about him was golden—his hair, his face, his hands, his uniform. He glowed with a golden nimbus surrounding him. He held a large, silver-blue, evanescent ball. He smiled and tossed it to

Foxy, who was a vision of shimmering silver from head to toe and wearing a shimmering silver-blue gown. She caught the ball and tossed it back to Robby, laughing. He caught it and threw it to William, who was also a vision of shimmering silver—his hair, face, hands, and uniform. Then, Robby smiled, waved to Foxy, and slowly disappeared into golden dust. William caught the ball and turned to Foxy. He threw it high into the air toward her. She looked up and could see the ball, a tiny silver speck high in a dark velvet sky. It was falling toward her. It was growing larger and larger. What if she didn't catch it? What if it broke?

Her own cries awoke her. She was calling out for help. But it was not for Robby, her beloved husband, killed in the war. She was calling for William. *William, my dear, dear William. My Oberon.* She lost the struggle and passed out.

When Foxy did not return in time for lunch, William was uneasy. His confrontation had made it clear to him that the zeal of Blinker Hall meant he would stop at little or nothing to make sure the election was successfully manipulated. That went double for Major Ball, who had gone so far as to order a murder to assure the Zinoviev letter was accepted as authentic by whatever Conservative newspaper editor received the copy. On the other hand, Foxy may simply have been delayed. But it was unlike Foxy to tell Mrs. Flowerdew she would be back for lunch and then not come without calling to say so in advance. By 2:30, he was worried enough to call the Porter. He said Lady Butterschloss had not signed out, and that her raincoat, hat, and umbrella were still there. He called the office of the Provost Marshall and was told by an acerbic clerk that Lady Butterschloss failed to keep her appointment that morning. He called McCreedy's office and learned he was at a meeting in Bristol.

William told Dinny he was going to find Foxy. The threatened storm broke. He had to drive slowly through a blinding downpour. He asked the Porter if he had seen Lady Butterschloss yet, and was told no. He checked in his dripping raincoat. *Where to start?* He went to McCreedy's office and asked Seaman Ridley for the keys to the ARO. Foxy had taken them and not returned them. Deeply alarmed, William rushed to the ARO. The door was locked. He pushed against it with his shoulder. It didn't give.

"Can I be of assistance?" It was Seaman Field.

"I order you to help me break down this door. A life may be at stake," said William, who was still in his uniform.

"Aye, aye," said Field, who relished the idea of doing something other than carrying messages around, especially if it involved a rescue operation, and especially if it involved breaking something.

Field smashed the glass case holding the axe, kept ready in case of fire. William stared at him in astonishment. In his panic, William had not even noticed it. Field soon had the door in smithereens. The two men stepped into the ARO. It was deathly still.

"Lady Butterschloss may be in here, injured," he said to Field. "You search that side, and I'll search over there."

As he looked down each aisle of books, William thought he heard the unmistakable signal for help coming from the far wall: ... - - -.... ...- - -....
"Field," he called, "can you hear that?"

"Aye, Sir," said Fields, furrowing his brow. "It sounds like an SOS. But..."

The SOS stopped. The room fell silent. "Where does this pipe come from? Do you know?"

"No, Sir," said Fields. "But I can tell you one thing. There is a loud hammer in that pipe. I hear it often when I come in here. My uncle is a plumber, and he says when you hear that sound, it means there is air in the pipe."

"Yes, yes," said William, impatiently. "Get to the point."

"I was just coming to it, Sir," said Field. "That hammer can be caused when the water is being forced upward, like from a basement."

William stared at him for a split second. They were in the basement. Then, his face lit with a flash of insight. "The sub-basement," he said excitedly. "Come with me. And bring that axe. We may need it."

The sub-basement was pitch dark. William felt against the wall next to the bottom of the stairs. His hand found the switch. Hanging lights lit up one after the other with a dull light down a long hall. There were doors on either side as far as he could see.

"You take the doors on the right. I'll take the doors on the left. Listen carefully for any sound," he said.

Field went to the first door and turned the knob. "It isn't locked," he said. "It is just an empty storage room."

The two made their way down the hallway, opening unlocked doors. On his third try, William came to a locked door. He banged on it, "Foxy! Foxy! Are you in there!" He listened. No response. "Smith, use your axe to break down this door."

Field grinned. This was the best day so far at the Admiralty. He applied himself vigorously to the oak, and soon smashed it open. William stepped into the room. In the dim light, he saw Foxy leaning against the far wall, unconscious. He rushed to her and took her in his arms.

She opened her eyes, blinked, and gave a slight smile.

His great dam of reticence, which had held in check his decades-long love for Foxy, gave way. William was overwhelmed with joy and relief. There came unbidden the silliest words he had ever uttered. "Oh! Let us be married! Too long we have tarried!

"But what shall we do for a ring?" she replied, softly

William followed the ambulance to the hospital. Foxy was diagnosed with a severe concussion and admitted to the hospital. The doctor found no sign of skull fracture but warned William that Foxy might need emergency surgery and never fully recover.

William kept vigil throughout the night in a chair next to her bed, dozing off from time to time. Foxy woke occasionally to ask for a drink of water and quickly drifted off to sleep again.

A Sister came in just as dawn was breaking to check on Foxy's vitals. William left to find himself a quick breakfast and a morning paper.

It was Saturday, October 24. At the first newsstand he found, he saw the headline in the *Daily Mail:* Civil War Plot By Socialists' Masters. He found a seat in a teashop that opened early, ordered breakfast, and read the "deck," or multiple, stacked subheadings:

MOSCOW ORDERS TO

OUR REDS

GREAT PLOT DISCLOSED YESTERDAY

"PARALYSE THE ARMY AND NAVY"
AND MR. MACDONALD
WOULD LEND RUSSIA
OUR MONEY!
DOCUMENT ISSUED BY
FOREIGN OFFICE
AFTER 'DAILY MAIL' HAD
SPREAD THE NEWS

The article included what was intended to be the damning information that the letter had been in the hands of the Foreign Office, the Prime Minister, and the Home Office since mid-September. The official copy had been circulated to top Army and Navy officials on Wednesday. "A copy of the document came into the possession of *The Daily Mail,* and we felt it our duty to make it public. We circulated printed copies to other London morning newspapers yesterday afternoon. Later on, the Foreign Office decided to issue it, together with a protest dated yesterday, which the British government has sent to M. Rakovsky, the Bolshevik Chargé d' Affaires in London."

The copy of the letter included a drawing, purporting to represent Zinoviev. His features were coarse and crude, with a large nose, oversized ears, curly, dark hair, half-closed eyes, a downturned mouth. He looked sinister and degenerate. The caption made the anti-Semitic point clear: "Zinoviev, whose real name is Apfelbaum."

William shook his head in disgust. When he returned to Foxy's bedside, he found Addie there.

"You need a break," she said. "I'll sit with her. Why don't you come back later this afternoon?"

"You'll call me if there is any change?" It was less a question than a statement.

"Of course," said Addie.

William looked at Foxy's pale face against the white pillow and left.

Addie took Foxy's hand. She opened her eyes, smiled, and said, "Hello, Addie. I've got a helluva headache."

"I'd be surprised if you didn't. Do you remember what happened?" she asked.

Foxy spoke softly but clearly. "Bits and pieces, like a jigsaw puzzle, I cannot quite fit together. I remember I found the stolen *Lusitania* file and the Zinoviev letter. It is a fake. Gruter wrote it. Be sure to tell William. It is in my courier bag."

Addie did not want to upset Foxy. She did not say that the courier bag was not found with her. Nor did she tell her that the Zinoviev letter had been published that morning in all the major London papers. She watched as Foxy drifted off. She awoke fifteen minutes later.

"Still here? How long was I asleep?"

"Not long. Dinny sent along three books for you. Shall I read to you?" she asked.

"What are my choices?" asked Foxy.

"Wind in the Willows, The Inimitable Jeeves, and *The Secret Adversary,"* answered Addie.

Foxy said, "I haven't read that Christie yet. It isn't one with Poirot, is it?"

Addie smiled. "No. She introduces the duo of Tommy and Tuppence, who are short of money and opportunity just after the war. They become partners in seeking adventure, willing to take on any assignment, regardless of the danger. I have to warn you, though. It opens with the sinking of the *Lusitania.*"

Foxy's brows rose. "Does it? What a coincidence. I think you should read it to me. It might jog my memory."

Addie laughed. "That is exactly what Dinny said."

Foxy settled into her pillows as Addie began to read: "It was two p.m. on the afternoon of May 7, 1915. The *Lusitania* had been struck by two torpedoes…"

"No, it hadn't," murmured Foxy. "Only one. But Agatha wasn't to know that, was she?"

She exchanged a glance with Addie. They both smiled.

"…in succession," Addie went on, "and was sinking rapidly…"

The days passed quietly for Foxy, her world narrowed to the confines of her private room, the shades drawn because she was sensitive to the light. Her room was filled with bouquets of flowers. Doctor Foale came by twice a day. The nurses took her vitals regularly day and night. William and Addie made regular visits. Josie came by each evening after work. Addie brought Foxy her silk pajamas, robe, and favorite slippers with the turned-up toes. Mrs. Flowerdew sent dishes intended to delight the senses and raise the spirits: neat squares of pineapple upside-down cake, Chelsea buns—"not laced with anything but cinnamon," she wrote in a note—chocolate mousse, apple tarts, and pear custard pie. Gradually, Foxy regained her strength. At first, she could not sit up because of the vertigo. After several days, she could stand and walk short distances with the support of a nurse. Her appetite returned, and she looked forward to Mrs. Flowerdew's treats. For the most part, she slept, listened to Addie or William read chapters from Christie's novel, and recounted what bits and pieces she could remember of her ordeal.

She remembered finding the *Lusitania* file and reading the Zinoviev Letter. She remembered going to Room 229 to see if that was where Gruter had hidden the marlin spike he used to knock out Arensdorf. She remembered the door opening suddenly. Then, she drew a blank. She could not remember the name of her assailant, but she knew that she had known him. She remembered in shards her effort to get to the pipe, and how she tapped out S.O.S. until she could not stand. She remembered William taking her in his arms as she lay on the cold, hard floor, and that he proposed to her and she accepted, but that it might have been only a vivid dream. She did not mention it to William.

Outside, political turmoil reigned. The Foreign Office protest to the Russians, published along with the Zinoviev letter, came too late, as if the Prime Minister had been forced to disown the letter only because it was leaked to the Press. Prime Minister MacDonald made things worse for himself. On Monday, October 27, at Cardiff, he called "the whole thing a political plot" by the Conservative party and Press. The accusation was irreconcilable with his earlier published protest—which assumed the Letter was authentic—to the Russians. MacDonald seemed to be accusing his own Foreign Service of an unforgivable error in certifying the letter as authentic. The political magazine, *Punch*, published a cartoon of a scruffy, dangerous, hulking "Russian" figure, stalking the streets of London, wearing a signboard that read, "Vote for Macdonald and Me."

On Tuesday, Election Day, Doctor Foale came to see Foxy. "I've just been looking over your latest X-rays," he said.

"Oh, yes," said Foxy, sitting up a bit straighter. "And what do they tell you?"

"You are a very lucky woman, Lady Butterschloss," he said, solemnly.

"An interesting turn of phrase," said Foxy. "Not one that would have sprung immediately to mind, all things considered."

"Yes, I can well understand why," said the Doctor. "But the good news is the subdural hematoma that was putting pressure on your brain has drained away by itself. There will be no need for surgery."

"That is good news," said Foxy. "Does that mean I can go home?"

Dr. Foale nodded. "I understand there is already a Sister in attendance who can look after you," said the Doctor. "I will give orders for your treatment. You can go home today if you like. But you will have to take it easy. Otherwise, you will take longer to recover properly. Lots of rest and quiet."

That night, she was tucked into crisp, white sheets in her familiar room at the Chelsea house. Sister Parker quickly took her in hand, making sure there was not too much "excitement."

She thanked William, again, for rescuing her, and found herself still tongue-tied. Words were inadequate. He took her hand in his, "You made it easy," he said, "by tapping out SOS."

"With the gun you insisted I take," she said, quietly.

She fell asleep as William read her the concluding chapter of *The Secret Adversary*. During her days in hospital, she had drifted in and out of sleep, each time dreaming again the dreams she had during her ordeal. Timmy's chubby little legs running after a ball she had thrown, laughing his wild, toddler's laugh. She herself, in a long white skirt and blouse, slender and youthful, returning a tennis ball with a forearm shot to an unseen opponent, then going to a table and taking a long drink of lemonade. Robby, in gold, tossing a large, silver-blue ball to a silver-blue William, then waving to her and disappearing into gold dust. William, tossing the ball high into the air, and it falling toward her. Each time, she awoke before she caught it. This time, she caught it. Her eyes flew open. "Ball," she said.

"What?" said William.

Foxy looked at him excitedly. "It was Ball. I just remembered. It was Joseph Ball. That's who assaulted me and left me in that room. I was never introduced to him, but I knew who he was. I often saw him when I delivered papers to MI5 from Room 229." She shuddered as she remembered his big, meaty hand covering her mouth. "He hit me with a marlin spike. Gruter used it as a paperweight. I thought it might be what he had used on Arensdorf. Gruter must have been hurrying to escape by using the fire escape and stopped at Room 229 long enough to hide the spike."

Foxy had been talking rapidly, the words tumbling over each other. "Foxy, slow down," said William. "You will overexcite yourself." Foxy took a few deep breaths.

"Why would Ball have been in Room 229?" William asked. He had not yet told her what he learned from Blinker Hall because he was concentrating on her recovery.

"Ball must have been behind killing Arensdorf, then spirited Gruter out of the country. Once he was paid off, Gruter told Ball where he could find the files and the marlin spike."

"That is what Blinker Hall told me," said William. "I didn't tell you about my meeting with him because I didn't want to agitate you. He said that Ball told Gruter to kill Arensdorf because he knew about the Zinoviev letter. I think Caxton saw Arensdorf eavesdropping on Blinker and Ball when they met with Gruter. Caxton would have been eager to tell his hero, Blinker.

Foxy thought for a moment about the day Caxton confessed to her. "I think that is probably right. He was so overwhelmed with revulsion at seeing Arensdorf killed—and Gruter thanking him for helping—he could not bring himself to face how involved he was. I thought Gruter was thanking Caxton for having shoved Arensdorf, but I think now he put the blame squarely on Caxton for causing Arensdorf's death by revealing Arensdorf was eavesdropping."

William nodded and thought for a moment. "According to Blinker, Ball gave Gruter a ticket to Buenos Aires and a substantial sum of money. But why didn't Gruter take the evidence with him?

Foxy smiled. "The last thing Gruter wanted was to be found with the government files, the draft of the Zinoviev letter, and a bloody spike in his possession. He was probably whisked directly to the waiting ship. He might even have been worried that MI5 would betray him if he had the evidence on him." She sighed. "So, Gruter gets away." Then a thought struck her. "I didn't file the deposition about Caxton with the Provost Marshall," she said.

William looked at her and shook his head. "I wouldn't worry about that," he said. "Blinker told me the family agrees Caxton is unstable. The plan is to send Caxton to work for his uncle at a salmon processing plant in Vancouver."

Foxy's jaw dropped. "You don't say. I thought that kind of fix would have ended with the war, but I can see now that the war hasn't ended for the likes of Blinker Hall and George Ball."

"You are quite right," said William. "Blinker thinks we are in a non-shooting war with the Russians and their spread of Communism. I imagine that is what is motivating Ball as well."

Foxy looked at William. "It hasn't escaped my attention that neither you nor Addie have said a word about the proof the Zinoviev letter is a fake. It is in my courier bag, along with the missing *Lusitania* file."

"As I said, we did not want to upset you." He paused, "Ball evidently took your courier bag," said William.

Foxy rolled her eyes in frustration. "You don't mean to tell me the Zinoviev letter appeared in the Press."

"With all the alarm bells ringing," said William. "It has done great damage to MacDonald and to the Liberal Party as well. We will know how much when all the ballots are counted."

Foxy sighed. "We really turned out to be rubbish as detectives."

"I wouldn't say that," said William. He gave Foxy a reassuring smile. "We found out who was behind the effort to get Dinny court-martialed, which is where all of this began. I have convinced Blinker to stay well away from me and anyone close to me. And he has agreed to see to it that Tris is released from Invergordon."

Foxy laughed. "How did you manage that?"

"Tomorrow, I'll reveal all," said William, gently. "You need to get your rest."

The next morning, William dressed in his uniform and drove to the War Office in Whitehall. He had no trouble gaining admission to the office of Major George Joseph Ball, Head of B Branch. *Whatever the B means. Bastards? Baboons?*

Ball rose from behind his polished mahogany desk. He was large, beginning to go to fat, with a pasty, flabby face, thinning black hair pasted against his head with Brilliantine, and large, round glasses. "Good to see you, Ainsworth. We haven't seen each other since…when was it? 1919?" His office walls were bare. A tiny half window cast a weak, gray light. He gestured to one of two seats in front of his desk. He took his seat behind the desk.

"Cigarette?" He proffered a silver case. "They are Turkish."

William shook his head. He recognized Ball's false bonhomie for what it was. Ball was nervous, on the defensive.

"I thought you might be coming by," said Ball.

"I assume that means Blinker called you after our visit," said William, his voice expressionless, his face blank.

"Yes, yes, he did. You were understandably upset. About the whole *Lusitania* business, I mean. Terrible shame about that Caxton boy. Went too far, obviously."

"I am here because of the Zinoviev letter and Arensdorf's murder," said William.

There was a brief silence. "I don't see how that has anything to do with you or anyone close to you," said Ball. "It was something that needed to be done, don't you see? We are in an undeclared war, but it's a real war, nevertheless. We have got to defeat those Bolshie bastards." As he warmed to his subject, Ball's voice rose in pitch, his eyes seemed to gleam, and he pounded a fist on his desk. "And we have won this time, by God. Have you seen the election returns? It seems the Conservatives will be back in power again. There will be no Anglo-Russian Trade Treaty. We've beaten them at their own game!"

"How do you mean?" said William, still expressing no emotion.

"Propaganda, my dear boy, propaganda. Or what the Bolshies call agitprop," said Ball, positively beaming with delight.

"As it happens, Old Boy," said William, in clipped tones, "it does have something to do with those close to me."

Ball became very quiet. "Go on," he said.

"Last Friday," said William, "I have it on very good authority that on the second floor of the Admiralty, you struck Lady Butterschloss unconscious with the marlin spike Gruter used to bash Arensdorf over the head before breaking his neck. Then, you took her down to the subbasement and locked her into a windowless room."

Blood drained from Ball's face. A twitch developed under his right eye. His body was tense, but he kept a calm, friendly voice. "That was an unfortunate accident, don't you see? She took me by surprise. It was just an automatic reaction. I had the marlin spike in my hand—I was there to retrieve it and used it without thinking." He began to bluster. "I was going to leave her there and make my escape. I figured she would come to in a few minutes. But when I looked in her bag and saw she had Gruter's draft of the Zinoviev letter, I knew I had to act fast. Get her out of the way just long enough…until the letter appeared in the newspapers the next day. I went back, you know, after the first press run that night, to open the door so she could escape. But I saw the door had been broken in, and she wasn't there. Naturally, I assumed she was rescued and that she was all right." He looked at William. "So you see, it was all an unfortunate accident. No hard feelings, I trust?"

He rose and held out his hand as he came around his desk to William's chair. William rose and struck without thinking, unaware of what he was doing. The blow landed squarely on Ball's jaw. Ball went down like a sack of sand dropped into the ocean. Or a tiny corpse wrapped in a weighted shroud. "That was just an accident," said William, rubbing his knuckles. "No hard feelings, I trust."

Ball levered himself up on one elbow and touched his jaw. He spat out a tooth. "I think you may have broken my jaw," he yelled. "I'll get you for this, Ainsworth."

"I doubt that," said William, coolly.

"What makes you so sure, you bastard?" shouted Ball.

"Ask Blinker. He'll tell you why," said William. "I'll see myself out."

Epilogue

The Conservatives were swept into power with a majority of two hundred and nine seats. Labour lost forty seats, and the Liberal Party, one hundred and eighteen. Stanley Baldwin became Prime Minister. Grigory Zinoviev and the Russian government strenuously denied the authenticity of the Zinoviev letter. Baldwin appointed a Cabinet committee to investigate. It concluded the Letter was genuine. Winston Churchill was elected to Parliament and became Chancellor of the Exchequer.

By December, Foxy was fully recovered and preparing for the annual Christmas festivities at the Butterschloss estate, including the Christmas Eve Open House. Addie, Dinny—his ribs completely healed—Tris, and Josie stayed with her. Clive Edgerton, who had resigned from MI5 in disgust, stayed with William on his estate. Cordelia Parker and Hosea Wilkinson were engaged and preparing their new home on Badger Hill Farm, one of the properties Dinny had inherited. He gave them a rent-free tenancy to grow varieties of cannabis for medicinal purposes and loaned them the money to build a large greenhouse and fully equipped chemistry lab. They planned to employ locals, especially veterans and widows, to help the local economy. Wilkinson was initially unwilling to abandon the exotic plants in the Chelsea Conservatory until, with William's consent, he hired an apprentice, his niece Allene Jephcots, to take over under his supervision.

Dinny resigned his commission with the RNRV. He wanted less danger and intrigue in his life. He accepted a position with the fledgling Imperial Airways, subsidized by the British government to develop international, commercial routes to the far-flung corners of the British Empire. His job was to develop long-wave wireless communication. Addie continued working at the GCCS. They planned an engagement party for early January.

Josie spent considerable time with Foxy. They had the idea of starting a collective factory making wool felt linings for winter boots. The high level of unemployment meant that many people could not afford new boots to replace old ones. The wool liners would extend the life of boots, and the factory would help the local wool industry, as well as employing those living in the villages on the estate.

Dinny, Addie, Josie, and Tris devoted many hours to working on a spectacle for Christmas Eve. Josie and Addie were often heard laughing with their heads together, working out the geometry for the stunt. Dinny and Tris were in charge of the practical logistics. They sent to London for electric colored light strings used by the very wealthy for their Christmas trees, wired them to the backs of a herd of sheep loaned for the project, and attached each string of lights to purpose-built battery cases carried in a small pack around the neck of each sheep. They enlisted local shepherds, giving each color-coded graph paper indicating where the sheep were to be on the night of the spectacle. The shepherds taught their brilliantly trained dogs to run the sheep through their paces in a rehearsal fraught with maverick sheep, whistling shepherds, barking dogs, and shouted directions from the four masterminds, who collapsed several times into paralytic laughter.

At last, Christmas Eve arrived. The local townspeople, farmers, and their children gathered after sunset. They wore heavy coats, and hand-knitted wool mufflers, hats, gloves, or mittens. Their breath created silvery clouds in the crisp air. Silence fell as the first sheep poured down from the crest of a hill and streamed into the sloping pasture, the little colored lights shining from their thick coats. Then, everyone applauded as wave after wave of lit-up sheep followed. At first, the scene was a chaotic tangle of shimmering red, green, and blue lights. This drew gasps of surprised delight from the crowd. The sheepdogs ran to the commands of their owners, and the sheep gradually obeyed the persistent dashes and barking of the dogs. The lit-up sheep at last formed the word EWEL in a dazzling display.

Silence fell over the crowd. "Ewel. Wassat supposed to mean?

Then came a wave of laughter. "John, ye great fool. It is how a sheep would spell Yule! Get it?"

The cheers and applause reached a crescendo that echoed off the hills. The crowd wanted to see it all again, but unfortunately, the lights tended to singe the wool. So, the guests crowded into the large barn where cakes, cider, and ale were laid out for the annual Christmas Barn Dance. As the string band struck up a tune, the dancing began and continued far into the night, the younger children bundled under knitted blankets, asleep in the hay. The story of the Christmas Sheep was retold in the local pubs in the winter evenings for months after. Foxy could not remember ever having been so bedazzled and convulsed with laughter at the same time and was grateful for the way the ingenious stunt had brought together a community—still shattered by the loss and sorrow of war—with gaiety and laughter.

"A triumph," said William, who was standing next to Foxy in the doorway of the barn as the small band struck up a waltz.

The images that led her to recognize Major Ball were thrown up by her subconscious as symbols tied to her memories—Little Timmy chasing a ball; herself playing tennis. But the evanescent vision of Robby surrounded by a golden nimbus, tossing the silver ball first to her and then to William, that was something different. It was not a memory. It was a vision, a fantasy, perhaps, or a message—Robby giving her permission? No, it was her unconscious giving her permission to join the unpredictable game of life with William, to shed the shell she built around her out of her desire to cling to Robby and never let anyone else in, as if that would be a betrayal of her lost love and open her heart to possible pain again.

"Before we join in, I have something for you," said Foxy to William. She led him just outside, where the stars sparkled in a clear, dark sky, and there was a silver sliver of a waning moon. She handed him a small, rectangular package wrapped in brown paper and string. "I special ordered this. It is a first edition."

William looked at her quizzically. He pulled off the string and wrapping.

Inside was a book in brown binding. The cover was a large oval of yellow and white bearing the name of the author and title: *Nonsense Songs, Stories, Botany and Alphabets* by Edward Lear. He looked at her in surprise, hardly daring to hope.

"Open it at the bookmark," she said, feeling giddy.

The cardstock bookmark opened onto the poem "The Owl and the Pussycat."

"Read the bookmark," said Foxy, grinning from ear to ear.

William held the bookmark up to the light pouring from the barn. Foxy had written, "But what shall we do for a ring?"

William looked at her. "You mean?"

Foxy had a wide, silly grin on her face, "Yes!" she said.

William did something he had never done in his life. He whooped. Not just a quiet, subdued whoop, either. A loud, throaty, unreserved WHOOP! He grabbed Foxy around her waist. They kissed a long, lingering kiss. Then, hand in hand, to the sound of the band, they danced by the light of the moon. The moon. The moon. They danced by the light of the moon.

Historical Note

The Lusitania Code closely follows primary and secondary sources about the naval battles of World War I, Winston Churchill's account of the sinking of the *Lusitania*, the record of the hearing held after its sinking, conversations with Colonel House just prior to the sinking, Commodore Bill Turner's life, and the controversy surrounding the Zinoviev Memo.

Anyone familiar with the accounts of the sinking of the *Lusitania* will know there is disagreement about the cause of the second explosion. There is no doubt that there were munitions in the hold, but whether they would have exploded remains a matter of debate. I choose to accept the argument that it was caused by exploding munitions.

There remains disagreement about the authenticity and origins of the Zinoviev memo. I am persuaded that it was a fake, but I invented the account of its origin.

The depiction of Admiral Sir Reginald Hall, KCMG, CB closely follows the historical record.

Major Sir George Joseph Ball was highly placed in MI5. Both he and Hall were involved in getting the Zinoviev memo into the Conservative papers just prior to the election of 1924. Whether their involvement went beyond using the memo for political purposes and included composing it is not known. Major Ball would have participated in the entrapment of the Wheeldon Family.

His involvement with the Arensdorf and Gruter is entirely fictional, as are all of the events and characters in that plot line. My description of Major Ball's physical characteristics is entirely fictional because no photography or painting of him exists.

The names of the women who worked in Room 229 on the hatted codes are accurate. They deserve more recognition for their contributions to the war effort, but little information is available.

The maps can be found at the following online sites:

W&A K Johnston's war map of the Dardanelles and Bosporus, 1915. National Library of Wales, 1915. Public Domain. https://commons.wikimedia.org/wiki/File:W_%26_A_K_Johnston's_war_map_of_the_Dardanelles_%26_Bosporus_(5008041).jpg

Français : Julian Corbett (1854-1922) Première Guerre mondiale. Attaque alliée (Angleterre et France) contre la Turquie pour forcer le détroit des Dardanelles en 1915. Évolution des cuirassés anglais lors de l'attaque. (NB : les cuirassés français sont à peine mentionnés). Public domain. 1922. Source: https://www.naval-history.net/WW1Battle1503Dardanelles1.htm

Order of battle at Jutland. (2024, May 11).

In *Wikipedia*. https://en.wikipedia.org/wiki/Order_of_battle_at_Jutland. Creative Commons license.

A Note from the Author

The seed for this mystery was planted when I first learned about the women who worked with the famous codebreakers of Room 40 in the British Admiralty during World War I. They have been diminished to invisibility with the designation "typists." They were highly educated and intelligent, and utilized the first mechanized decoding machines. Their contributions deserve to be studied.

Since ancient times, storytellers have described their characters as seeming to come to them fully formed. That was the case with Lady Emmeline "Foxy" Butterschloss. She insisted that I demonstrate how remarkable a detective a female cryptologist can be.

She has been my guide in bringing to life the history I explored as a media scholar of war propaganda and other fantasies, such as orthodox economic theory. Throughout my academic career, I was grimly fascinated with how the manipulation of public perception creates a truth—or what Stephen Colbert calls "truthiness"—that profoundly shapes lives and determines the fates of millions.

In the UK, 1924 was a critical election year. Falsifying the history of the Great War, smearing politicians and union organizers as Communists, and planting fake news were integral to the campaign that brought the Conservatives, including Winston Churchill, to power.

In Foxy, I found an indomitable and entertaining spirit who often leaps before checking if there is water in the pool, who will defend those she loves like a great brown mother bear, and who learns that much as she would like to be left alone to nurse her sorrows and her losses, the broken world is too much with her late and soon and needs her talents, wit, and spirit.

Another way of saying this is that I wish I were Foxy.

I hope you feel the same.

Acknowledgments

Nancy Holzner has been an invaluable guide and mentor. She has generously shared the knowledge she gleaned from writing the Deadtown books, and I cannot thank her enough.

The archivists at the Churchill Archives Centre, Cambridge University, were supportive and generous in providing access to the archives of Winston Churchill and obtaining permission to quote from the unpublished autobiography of Admiral Sir William Reginald Hall. As anyone with experience in utilizing historical archives will attest, they are an exceptional group.

Special thanks to Miriam Leo, an early beta reader who offered beneficial advice about Foxy's character.

About the Author

Linda Robertson's headstrong and intelligent character, Lady Emmeline "Foxy" Butterschloss, is an inevitable result of her interest in how politics, propaganda, and power are reflected in popular culture. Linda founded the Media and Society Program at Hobart and William Smith Colleges in 1996, making it the oldest program at a liberal arts college in the United States devoted to examining the influence of the mass media on society. She has co-hosted a weekly, very popular local public radio program, featuring lively banter and serious analysis of the press and politics. Linda has produced several historical documentaries about the role of abolitionists in upstate New York and a feature-length documentary recounting the collaboration between Harriet Tubman and her biographer, Sarah Bradford: *Daughters of the New Republic: Sarah Bradford and Harriet Tubman* (2016).

Along with Professor Bill Waller, she can be heard on the weekly podcast *Plato's Cave: Economic and Media Analysis in Dark Times.* It is available on Apple Podcasts, YouTube, and Spotify.

The Lusitania Code is Robertson's first venture into fiction, bringing to life the turbulent period after World War I, when British politicians, spies, intelligence officers, and newspaper magnates sought control over the forces shaping the broken post-war world. If it wasn't the first time political cover-ups and "fake news" were used to distort history and influence elections, it was the time when these techniques were polished and refined.

Robertson not only brings these forces to light in a dramatic and often amusing narrative, but she also honors the forgotten women who were codebreakers for the British Royal Navy during World War I. Dismissed by history as "typists," these were highly educated women who used the first mechanized decoding machines to help the Admiralty decipher both the German military and diplomatic codes during World War I.

Linda is retired and lives in a small village in upstate New York with her amazing Maine Coon cat, Nokia. She relaxes by painting with watercolor, enjoys the company of fellow writers who meet virtually each week, and enjoys leisurely walks along the many trails in her part of upstate New York.

Also by Linda Robertson

The Dream of Civilized Warfare: World War I Flying Aces and the American Imagination (2005)

Daughters of the New Republic: Sarah Bradford and Harriet Tubman. Documentary (2016)

www.ingramcontent.com/pod-product-compliance
Lightning Source LLC
Chambersburg PA
CBHW060519160726
47991CB00001B/102